GLIMMER TRAIN
STORIES

EDITORS
Susan Burmeister-Brown   Linda B. Swanson-Davies

COPY EDITOR
Scott Stuart Allie

DESIGN
Paul Morris

SOCIAL MEDIA EDITOR
Carmiel Banasky

COVER ART
Above and Below by Jane Zwinger

ESTABLISHED IN 1990

PUBLISHED TRIANNUALLY
in April, August, and November by Glimmer Train Press, Inc.
P.O. Box 80430, Portland, Oregon 97280-1430
Telephone: 503/221-0836   Facsimile: 503/221-0837
www.glimmertrain.org

PRINTED IN U.S.A.
Indexed in *Humanities International Complete*

Glimmer Train (ISSN #1055-7520), registered in U.S. Patent and Trademark Office, is published triannually, $38 per
year in the U.S., by Glimmer Train Press, Inc., P.O. Box 80430, Portland, OR 97280. POSTMASTER: Send address
changes to Glimmer Train Press, P.O. Box 3000, Denville, NJ 07834-9929.

ISSN # 1055-7520, CPDA BIPAD # 79021
DISTRIBUTION: Bookstores can purchase *Glimmer Train Stories* through these distributors:
            DEMCO, Inc., 4810 Forest Run Road, Madison, WI 53707 ph: 800/356-1200
            Peribo PTY Ltd., 58 Beaumont Rd., Mt. Kuring-Gai, NSW 2080, AUSTRALIA
            Small Changes, P.O. Box 70740, Seattle, WA 98127 ph: 206/382-1980
            Ubiquity, 607 Degraw St., Brooklyn, NY 11217 ph: 718/875-5491
      SUBSCRIPTION SVCS: EBSCO, Divine, Subscription Services of America, Harrassowitz, Swets, WT Cox, Blackwell's UK.

Subscription rates: Order online at www.glimmertrain.org
or by mail—one year, $38 within the U.S. (Visa/MC/check).
Airmail to Canada, $48; outside North America, $62.
Payable by Visa/MC.

WRITERS ASK
USE OF
LANGUAGE

"I have learned more from
this issue of *Writers Ask* than
from any article read or writing
group attended." —Gail Zaranek

Glimmer Train Press also offers *Writers Ask*, a quarterly
newsletter filled with accomplished creative-writing teachers'
and authors' practical and thought-provoking insights into
creating substantial fiction. Topics in Issue 73:

Research • Taboos and Secrets • The Writing Life

One year, four issues, $22 within the U.S. ($24 Canada, $28
elsewhere), Visa, MC, or check to Glimmer Train Press, Inc.,
or order online at www.glimmertrain.org.

In this issue are many stories of people cornered by the impossibility of their situations and taking desperate measures to try to do the right thing and find their way forward. Harrowing at times, but in the end, the human push to persevere and to extend a hand is breathtaking.

We wish all of you a healthy and heartening winter.

Warm regards,

Susan : Lind

Submitting Work to Glimmer Train

Your short story manuscripts are welcome all year. To make submissions at our site, go to www.glimmertrain.org and click on *Submit Your Stories*. Complete writing guidelines are on the site, too.

SUBMISSION CALENDAR

Jan/Feb............**Short Story Award for New Writers**. Open only to writers whose fiction has not appeared in any print publication with a circulation over 5,000. Most stories run from 1,500 to 5,000 words, but any lengths up to 12,000 are welcome. Prizes: 1st place – $2,500, publication, and 10 copies; 2nd/3rd places – $500/$300 and possible publication. Deadline: February 29.

March/April....**Fiction Open**. Open to all writers. Most stories run from 3,000 to 6,000 words, but any lengths from 3,000 to 24,000 are welcome. Prizes: 1st place – $3,000, publication, and 10 copies; 2nd/3rd places – $1,000/$600 and possible publication. Deadline: April 30.

March/April....**Very Short Fiction Award**. Open to all writers for stories from 300 to 3,000 words. Prizes: 1st place – $2,000, publication, and 10 copies; 2nd/3rd places – $500/$300 and possible publication. Deadline: April 30.

May................**Standard** submissions. Open to all writers. Any lengths up to 12,000 words are fine. Payment for accepted stories: $700. Deadline: May 31.

May/June ....**Short Story Award for New Writers**. Deadline: June 30.

July/August .....**Fiction Open** and **Very Short Fiction Award**. Deadline: August 31.

Sept/Oct ....**Short Story Award for New Writers**. Deadline: October 31.

November ....**Standard** submissions. Deadline: November 30.

Nov/Dec.........**Family Matters**. Open to all writers. Most stories run from 1,500 to 5,000 words, but any lengths up to 12,000 are welcome. Prizes: 1st place – $2,500, publication, and 10 copies; 2nd/3rd places – $500/$300 and possible publication. Deadline: January 2.

One of the most respected short story journals in print, *Glimmer Train* is represented in recent editions of the *Pushcart Prize: Best of the Small Presses, New Stories from the Midwest, The O. Henry Prize Stories, New Stories from the South, Best of the West, New Stories from the Southwest, Best American Short Stories,* and *The Best American Nonrequired Reading.*

We love being the first to publish a great story by an emerging voice. Let us read yours. Stories accepted for publication are presented in *Glimmer Train,* where literary fiction persists in the real world.

Your subscription helps make this possible. Thank you!

CONTENTS

I remember those socks, easy to put on and perfect on cold Maine mornings.

David Mizner is the author of the novels *Political Animal* and *Hartsburg, USA*. He's written about U.S. foreign policy for a number of publications, including the *Nation*, *Jacobin*, and his blog *Rogue Nation*. Somewhat strangely, he's also an associate producer of the movie *Spotlight*. Twitter: @DavidMizner.

YOUR SWIM

David Mizner

I stand up from the towel and walk toward the ocean, and although in middle age I've mostly shed the desire to be, seem, rugged, I like to cut a semi-tough figure for my daughter and my son, and anyway I want to go in, or to have gone in, so I run and dive into a wave—cold!—and when I surface I think of Bob Marley, who, I once heard, would swim out till he was spent, forcing himself to struggle back. No grand test for me today. There are sharks here.

When I stop swimming I can stand, sort of. I can bounce between waves. On the beach lunch is happening. Daisy's eating with Jonathan's two girls, using the cooler as a table, and even Sammy joins in. Jo laughs at something Frances said. Our families are falling in love.

Check me out, cherishing the moment. For most people, I suspect, to feel present is to seem to stop thinking, to unplug the analytic buzz saw, and for them awareness that they have felt present comes only in retrospect. But my in-the-moment moments are a collaboration of my feeling self and my thinking self, there's no distinction, because for me there's no greater feeling than thinking, and, at any rate, it all happens in the brain, there is only the brain.

Bah-rain, Jonathan and I call it, as in: There's trouble brewing in Bahrain. The "joke" was born before I knew where Bahrain was; I now know it's a tiny island country in the Middle East where the monarchy is waging a bloody crackdown on pro-democracy protestors, and I'm aware of the gross irony of white westerners using the country's name for a pun in their self-analyzing sessions. Aware, for what *that's* worth.

On the beach Jonathan hands out a second round of turkey-and-avocado sandwich halves. He and I used to assume that we wouldn't "take" vacation as adults because our *lives* would be vacation. There would be no conventional jobs to vacate. The arrogance! No, our lives are not as radical as we hoped. They're not radical at all. But expectations adjust, compensate. This Cape Cod vacation is a success and here, today, now, I'm euphoric.

I remember pulling off Jo's bathing suit last night. And I pull off my own so that my erection can float free. I can complain about marriage with the best of them, can play the harangued husband to a T, but the truth is, I feel much freer inside the marriage than I did on the outside. You're one of the lucky ones, asshole.

On the beach there's a dispute between Sammy and Abbie. Tug-o-war with the Tupperware of watermelon chunks is my guess. Daisy, who at eight is ready to be a CEO, intervenes, but her efforts will probably make Sam's crying worse. I can hear, or imagine I can hear, his wails, which always seem genuine, emissions of soul-pain, not bids for attention. Sammy's sadness might be heavy enough to sink the whole vacation.

Jo takes him onto her lap and he stops crying, I think, but he stands up and walks down near to the water and flops into the sand. He's a flopper. His legs go limp. He leans on you, hooks his hand on your belt. I usually resist the urge to push him off.

Jo doesn't go to him. Our latest strategy. Just stick with something, Dr. Baum tells us. Sammy's sorrow wrecks me. Scares me. Where'd it come from? Where'd *he* come from? Daisy makes sense; she has Jo's poise, my nose, our sarcasm. Sammy, though, with his earnestness and sensitivity—did Jo have secret sex with one of the folk singers she used to go see? But Jonathan claims I was like that as a kid. Maybe so. Maybe that's why Sammy's sorrow scares me. I don't know. Sammy reminds me a little of my father, actually, but he had to survive the Holocaust to get that kind of world weariness. Sammy is six.

He's up on his knees now, looking for me. I don't raise my hand because he would wave me in, but he sees me anyway and waves me in. I look away, pretend not to see. Sticking with the strategy. Do I get a prize, Dr. Baum? Is my boy all better now?

Sammy and his struggles, sometimes it seems Jo and I talk about nothing else. On our rare nights out we make a no-talking-about-Sammy rule and break it a hundred times. We worry about his life, his ability to cope, our ability to help him cope.

Sammy is with me thirty-seven years later when I decide to kill myself. I have pills. The right time will reveal itself, I hope. A moment after the right time is too late. Or, the right time—once your brain goes—is too late. The right time is just before the right time.

Sammy moved back here when Jo got sick. He's lived in his childhood home for thirty-five of his forty-three years. He's set up a living area—bed, recliner, lamp—in the corner of my bedroom, the bedroom where I will die, where Jo had planned to die before complications—and confusion about what she, we, wanted—sent her to the hospital. I let her die three years and a hundred procedures later.

Always needed by Sammy, I now need him. The other night he held me and rubbed my back when I woke up screaming. The cancer was drilling into the nerves in my spine. So Sammy got heavier pain meds, which deaden my brain and make me want to cry but I can't cry because of the antidepressants. The heavier pain meds constipate me so I'm nauseous so I'm not eating. Or the cancer makes me nauseous so I'm not eating so I'm constipated. Anyway, I want to shit as much as I want to live. All this I can bear, it won't kill me, harharhar. But the encroaching boredom, my declining ability to think interesting thoughts, or to find my thoughts interesting, if that's not the same thing—no, I might be able to bear that too.

What frightens me most is losing control, ceding it to doctors or, even worse, to Sammy. My death alone will be hell on him. I'm determined not to make him have to choose when and how I die. I could give the decision to Daisy, citing her seniority, but she'd keep me alive forever, hook my heart up to a nuclear computer or inject my spine with baboon semen or whatever the latest thing is. If I tell anyone about my suicide plan, it'll be Jonathan.

I'm going to kill myself: now *there's* an interesting thought

Sam, reclined in his recliner, sees me looking at him. "Want me to read to you?" he asks.

"What are you reading?"

"*Jude the Obscure.*"

"Again? Jesus."

"What? I like it. I can read something else."

"No, no, that's fine."

Sam's voice is a lovely instrument, deep and rich, authoritative, with a slight rasp from cigarettes, a voice that could make money if not for the trembles and tics that come when he feels anxiety, which is almost all the time. Listening to him read is the closest thing to a pleasure in my dying life. But he's read only a sentence—*Whatever his wetness, his brains were dry enough*—when the phone rings, and then my three granddaughters are on screen waving from the backseat. I feel nothing at the sight of them, nothing but the deepest weariness, as if my blood were drying cement. I think about the three pills, white, red, and black, the Exit Packet, in the drawer beside my bed.

Now Daisy is on screen driving and talking. My baby, my girl, so hard to reach. "So we worked it out," she says. "We're coming the weekend of July 16."

"That's six weeks away," Sam says.

"Good counting!" Daisy says, and the girls echo her minus the mockery. "Girls are still in school next week and then camp. You know how our summers are."

Sam twitches as Daisy speaks, her words jabbing him.

"Why don't you do self-drive?" Sam says.

"What's it matter? Okay. Whatever, fine." She crosses her arms, looks at the camera. Smiles. Her face is tanned and bony. She doesn't seem happy in her life but claims to be. Jo and I probably failed her too. "You look better today, Dad," she says. "More color."

"Darker gray?" I say.

"Come on, Dad," she says. "Positive thinking, okay?"

• • •

In the hospital, eight years earlier, Jo looks up at me with cancer-bulged eyes and tells me to be a better father after she dies. "I'm a good father," I say, pathetically.

She grimaces and I watch her urine rise. I don't know why the pee tank is out in the open or why her pee is orange. "Sam will need even more from you," she says. "Be there for him, okay? We've always been back and forth—you know, are we doing too much for him, helping him too much? And yeah, yeah, we want him to be more self-sufficient, but after I die…Just, just *be* with him, love him, honor him, okay?"

"I will. I promise."

She shakes her fists, a machine beeping because she pulled a wire loose. "I don't want to die," she says. "I just fucking don't want to die."

I'm awake now in the night and thinking of that exchange, the closest thing Jo and I had to a goodbye conversation. Sammy, a bad sleeper since the womb, is also awake, reading, and it occurs to me to have such a conversation with him right now. But it doesn't come easy, real talk, despite the years we've spent grieving side by side. I was that new kind of father, affectionate and sensitive, yet as if following a classic script, we tightened up around each other. Even for "male" things, wet dreams, masturbation, girls, he went to Jo.

"Still reading *Jude*?" I say.

"He's my boy."

"I want to talk to you." He closes his book around his feather. My son, like Jude, is from the nineteenth century. "We need to talk about, about when I'm gone."

"We don't have to do this now."

"My three-months-to-live was a month ago."

"So I guess you're saying no to the clinical trial?"

"I'm dying, Sammy. I want to talk about your life after I'm gone."

"I'll be okay."

"Yeah?"

"No. I'll be me. But hey, at least I'm not in Italy, right? I've got my walks, my birds…"

"And the house, money, enough if you're careful. And Jonathan and Frances will be here for you."

"And what's it matter anyway because sooner or later I'll be where you are."

Maybe it's because I'm dying, but I find his attitude healthy. Is it possible that in his warped way, Sammy has found peace? No, not peace, but—

A pain spears my lower back. Somebody somewhere is sticking pins in a voodoo doll of me. The pain forces me up onto my elbows, which shake and give way, and my head falls back onto my pillow. "What's the matter, Dad?" Sammy has come over and placed his hand on my shoulder. It amazes me, crushes me, my son who never used to touch me touching me so easily. "What can I do?" he says.

"Nothing. Stay just like that. Don't move."

Now Sammy's shaking me, because apparently I was asleep. "I'm not Jo," he says. "It's me. You were having a bad dream." He's wearing a Sox cap, which makes me see it's Jonathan, not Sammy. "You're okay," he says. He picks up a clump of sweaty hair and moves it off my forehead like turning a page. "I was thinking we'd go for a ride to the Cape," he says.

Jonathan seems an absurd old man at the moment, with his cap and the hair sprouting from his ears and his thinking he'd take me on a fucking outing. In fairness, though, he doesn't know I've taken a major Turn for the Worse, I'm only just realizing it myself. My throat is so constricted—with un-shat shit, I imagine—that I'm not certain I can talk.

"The Cape?" I say. "Nothing left."

"No beaches, but there are views. Eh. You're right. Probably be depressing."

We decide to go out to the balcony, but when I stand I can't stay standing. Jonathan lowers me into the chair, which I drive through the door and down the ramp that we installed for Jo's dying days. Even though it's June and sunny I'm shivering, so Jonathan puts a blanket around my shoulders and another across my legs. I didn't think dying would be like this, didn't expect to be so conscious of my deterioration. In a dream one night I was on a platter and people around the table were taking bloody, stringy scoops.

Through slats I see overgrown lawn, a corroded Adirondack on its side. From the Kellers' Victorian comes the sound of engine-revving. After sitting vacant for a year, the house is now a survivalist commune of some sort, or maybe just a flophouse. The town's succumbing. Last month there was a murder, the first in sixty years, and two more this month.

"I spent my life in a suburb," I say.

"Haute-meal bourgeoisie," Jonathan says, unearthing a pun from when everyone in our circle was mad about steel-cut. "How bad are you feeling?"

"Awful. Worse. I'm just so sick."

Jonathan, whom I met in nursery school, rubs the back of my neck. Starts to say something, stops. I don't mind. Not everything needs to be said. Nothing needs to be said, not between us. When the time comes I'll say something like I love you, thank you.

"How are *you*?" I think to ask.

"I've got the bladder thing and the back thing, but I'm okay."

"And dans le Bah-rain?"

"Ah, *that*…Well. My best friend is dying."

"Right."

"Did you know Bahrain's not a country anymore? It's part of Iran."

"It's amazing science still can't make sure someone shits."

"Toward the end my dad said only his family and his bowels were on his mind."

"I'm one for two."

"Liar."

"Yeah."

"Listen. Sam hasn't told you…a few months ago I introduced him to a woman over the phone. She edited for me a while ago. They've been in touch and tonight they're going to meet. They're going on a date."

"Really? Oh, man. Shit. He's going to be so nervous. Who is she?"

"Her name's Caroline, mid-fifties, divorced, smart, kind. Might just work."

"Mid-fifties? Not a potential mother really."
"Jay, this is their first date."
"I know but…"
"Tessa's daughter-in-law just gave birth and she's fifty-nine."
"It's fine," I say, because Sammy probably shouldn't be a father, and in any case bringing a baby into this wrecked world would be an act of cruelty. Jonathan and I, our generation, failed humanity, of course. "It's just sad he'll never have a child."

He looks at me and his shoulders drop in seeming disappointment. But it's sadness, I realize, because I'm crying. Tears stream as if there's a backlog, the need as much physical as emotional. The tears are cool on my chest. I'm raining on myself.

By my bed Sam has presented himself before his date. "Do I look okay?" he says, chewing on a finger already blackish with blood along the cuticle. Oh, Sammy. As if to accentuate his paunch, he's tucked into his black jeans a faded black T-shirt featuring the yellow N-line logo, a memento from Manhattan, which he fled after the Times Square attack. He's wetted down the upper portion of his hair but his waves hang dry and curl up around his ears like peyes. He's still attractive, with those marbly green eyes that used to turn heads, and he's smart and sweet and principled and I still believe there are more than a few people, maybe including Caroline the film editor, who would be able to love and live with him.

"This is so stupid," Sammy says. "I don't go on a date for years and now with you here like this…"
"I want you to go."
"I don't want to go."
"Do it. Do it for me. Please."

Loud beeping. The fire alarm. Jo frying hamburgers. Maybe just once you could remember to open a window. Maybe just once you could cook, she says, and I end up yelling at her because I'm angry at myself. The beeping, though, isn't the alarm but the phone and with a vicious punch to my chest from within I remember that Jo is dead and I almost am. A message on screen but I can't read it. "What's that say? Jonny, read that, it's probably from Sam. Jonny, where are you? What's that say? Help me. Please, please. Jonathan, are you here?"

A stirring, a wet cough, and then that schnoz in silhouette. "It's from Sam. It says, 'Having nice time. I like her and I think she might even like me.'"

At Jo's prodding, Jonathan, who'd often said he'd never leave Boston, and Frances have moved into a house less than a mile away, and now, on their second evening as our neighbors, they're sitting in Adirondacks in our back yard. A middle school photography club has helped Sammy, given him an outlet, and his relative peace is also mine. The feeling of having docked in a safe harbor cuts my apprehension about smoking pot, which since my late twenties has sometimes made me panicky. I take my first-ever hit off a vaporizer, Jonathan's new purchase, part of his effort to pretend he hasn't gone suburban, although what could be more suburban than ex-radical-wannabes getting high behind an $800,000 Dutch Colonial?

We all vaporize. Jo surprises me by taking part. She laughs as Jonathan retells the story about the junket in Bermuda during his advertising days when he found himself dancing with Paula Abdul in front of three hundred execs. He does an approximation of his approximation of breakdance moves and now he's belly-down on the lawn because bodyguards flattened him when he grinded up against Paula Abdul. We're all laughing now and the evening is golden and I remember to try to remember, try to file the moment away.

During dinner—grilled ribeye, zucchini, roasted potatoes—Jonathan says he's glad he moved and here's to the beginning of a good part of our lives. "The best part," I say.

Now the kids have come home and gone to bed and the vaporizer reappears and Jo as a joke puts on Paula Abdul and we all dance and I find my face too close to Frances's. Whoa, what the? We wanted our version of the sixties—did we get the seventies instead?

Of course not. A half hour later they've gone and Jo and I are in bed. I can't sleep, my mind firing from the pot, so I go out to the balcony.

There is the yard and the Adirondacks. The grill and the table, its umbrella fluttering in the warm breeze. I feel love for my life, I love the shit out of it, but then my brain does what it does on weed, calls bullshit, probes deeper and of course sees the coward's safety of my suburban life. I've had too much to drink to take a pill so I'll curl up next to Jo. That's how I want to die, lying next to her.

Inside I startle at the sight of Sammy in the doorway. "I can't sleep," he says.

His bed is a hint damp from his night-heat. I've been ushering him to sleep his whole life. He was such a serious baby, his disposition already set. You'd try to make him laugh and he'd look at you as if to say, That's not vaguely amusing. The thought of Sammy as a baby creates in my gut a bubble of longing that I try to absorb by flexing my arms and my legs.

I tell him to lie on his stomach so that I can rub his back, which is warm and bare. I can feel his pulse there. "I don't want to do photo club anymore," he says.

"I thought you loved it."

"Mark Mallek said my photos are creepy."

Good thing Mark Mallek's not here. I'd tear his face off. "Your photos are great. Creepy? Creepy's a compliment. Some of the best art in the world is creepy."

"You think my photos are creepy?"

"No. No! I think they're powerful. My point"—I'm always caught between denying his weirdness and praising it—"is you moved him. He had a strong reaction. That's good."

"I don't *want* to go to photo club again. Please don't make me go."

"I won't *make* you go, but…but I want you to go. Please think about it some more because it's been really good for you. Let's talk about it with Mom in the morning."

When I wake up Sam and I are lying on our backs and holding hands. It's light out. I kiss his forehead and intentionally breathe in his stale breath.

I go back to my room and get under the comforter. I tell myself that this, the burn of sadness, is part of the deal, it's what life is, it's what it should be, it means I'm alive, and when the brain-trick fails to do the trick, I hug Jo from behind. I cross my arms over her breasts and push my erection against her ass.

I awake to a smell. Meat. Sausage. Italian sausage. In Sammy's corner, he and Jonathan are eating pizza. The smell turns from disgusting to delicious and back to disgusting. Jonathan laughs. I should be pleased to see them enjoying each other. And I am, but I'm jealous too. Disappearing even before I die.

Now Caroline the film editor has manifested at my bedside. I understand why Sam wanted us to meet but it's not fair, it's just not fair, a strange person touching my arm when I've taken another Turn for the Worse. Just a few more turns and I'll be there. I need to vomit but can't get movement in my throat so I'm in a permanent state of gag.

With her mustache of wrinkles, Caroline looks too old for Sam, but I'm not in a position to be choosy and neither is Sam. What's she like? No way to know. I put my hand on hers and try to convey meaning as in *Take care of my boy*, but I probably look like a dumb dying guy.

"You're going to look at birds?" Jonathan asks.

"Yeah," Sam says. "Share my geeky passion with her."

There's self-deprecation but no self-hatred in his words and again I wonder if my boy has forged a kind of peace. Self-acceptance, maybe. But I'm not sure it's new. It could be years old and I've only just noticed. It could be that near death, free from hope and expectation, I've finally stopped wanting my son to be someone he's not.

Or maybe I'm telling myself he seems stronger to try to justify leaving him.

I stopped being sure about things when Jo died. I'll take few certainties with me to…to the crematorium. Sammy will go there, pick up the ashes of me.

Once Sam and Caroline have left, I tell Jonathan that I'm going to kill myself. I have to look away because I can't bear his eyes. "Okay," he says. "If this is what you need—"

"It is."

"Have you told Sam?"

"I can't."

He looks at me.

"What?" I say.

"I just think—you might not be able to see this, but taking care of you has been good for him. This would be part of that."

I lose what I'm about to say, the thought scrambling on its way to words. "And what...," I say. "What if he doesn't support?"

"Oh, I think he would—wouldn't he?"

"He's still hoping I trial, clinical."

"Hmm."

"My," I try to yell. "It's my decision."

Now he's come over to try to calm me because I'm thrashing. In eighty years, this is the first time I've wanted to hit him. "Hey, hey, hey, hey, hey," he says.

Now he's in the chair by my bed. He rubs his face. Scratches his head with both hands. Age spots in his bald spot. "Of course it's your decision," he says. "And I'm going to help you. But I just want to make sure..."

He's talking too much for me to listen. I feared Jo was fighting for time because of me. I told her this, and she didn't say no. She said, "My death isn't just mine." But my death is just mine. Jonathan isn't my wife. Neither is Sam. If Jo were here... If Jo were here...

"I think I could eat a croissant," I lie, knowing he'll go to the bakery.

"Really? Okay. I'll make a run."

"Thank you. I love you."

He turns and looks at me from the hallway, too far away for me to see his face, so I don't know if he understands. I suspect he does. "I love you too," he says.

When I hear the front door close, I remove the Exit Packet from the drawer. I have a problem, though. I made a code for the lock on the pill case, which is synched to my phone, but I can't remember it. Jo's birthday backward, my usual one, doesn't work. I search myself, my life, for clues. Who am I? Husband of Jo, father of Daisy and Sam.

Son of Fred, who survived the Nazis, and Marcia, who survived Fred. A family joke, masking so much pain. I used to be a lawyer. Why was I a lawyer? To pay for my life. It was a good life. I played squash. Read spy novels. Red Sox—loved the Sox, and there it is maybe? Jim Rice's 1978 stats: 315-46-1939. I punch in the numbers and the case pops open. Yay, now I can kill myself.

I have water but don't think I can swallow the pills whole so I grind the white one between my teeth, and its bitterness stirs up saliva that helps me get down the bits. Lucky man till the end. Pretty sure this one is a sedative and I hope so because I'm sweating and my chest is getting battered from the inside. Red even bitterer, like berry morning in Vermont the time Sam fell, his temple on the rock, all that blood and screaming. I still have brain to think. Of what? Jo, her legs, her ass ass ass, her smiling face in the backyard beach of my life that I tried to love. I did. Love. Not enough never enough like now I'm suiciding while in the woods Sam walks with the woman showing her birds waiting to hear what I think wanting to speak to his father his only one I was his father that's what I did, what I've done.

I spit out the pill, what's left of it, and it creams my chin.

Sammy keeps waving me in and starts shouting so I act as though I've just noticed him. I put my trunks back on and head for shore. Watching me ride a wave, Sammy bounces with excitement but when I've arrived he flops down into the sand. The wind feels cold blowing me dry. I sit down and lift up his head so that his cheek is on my calf. "What's the matter, kiddo?" I say.

"Abbie said I was weird."

"Don't listen to her. You're not weird."

"I feel weird."

"Yes, you do!" I rub his belly. "You feel like, like chicken pot pie."

He looks up at me: not funny.

"Weird isn't even an insult. It's good to be weird. Who wants to be *normal*?"

"Me."

"Eh. Normal is boring."

Jo's shadow arrives before she does. "What's happening over here?"

"Dad said I'm not weird; then he said it's good to be weird."

Jo gives me a mock double thumbs-up—good job, idiot—and kneels. The parenting cavalry has arrived, the emotional intelligence unit. "You know what I think, Sam-Bam?" she says, stroking his hair. "I think those words don't really mean anything, normal, weird, because they're based on the idea that there's a norm. There isn't. So-called normal people are weird to so-called weird people. I think Dad's weird but a lot of people don't."

Sam half-smiles, presses his cheek against my calf.

"It's silly to put a label like that on people," Jo says. "Here's what I know, Sammy: You're an amazing, awesome, smart, sweet boy, and your father and I love you so much, and we always will, no matter what. Okay?"

Sam nods.

Jonathan is walking to the water with Abbie, his budding Mean Girl. I'm expecting him to have her apologize, but they keep their distance. I'll bring it up with him later, do my best not to turn it into a big deal. Protect the communal good feeling. There are still four nights left, half the vacation. An hour or so till gin-and-tonic time, then to PJ's for fried clams.

Jo sits down behind me and wraps her arms around me. I feel her breasts on my back. "Ooh, cold," she says. "How was your swim?"

INTERVIEW WITH MIRANDA JULY

by David Naimon

*Performance artist, actor,
filmmaker, and writer
Miranda July has had
her work presented at the
Museum of Modern Art,
the Guggenheim, and the
Whitney Biennial. She
is the writer, director, and
star of two feature films,*
The Future *and* Me
and You and Everyone
We Know, *which won*

Miranda July

Photo: Mike Mills

*a special jury prize at Sundance and four prizes at Cannes. Miranda
July's short stories have appeared in the* Paris Review, Harper's, *and
the* New Yorker, *and her 2007 debut collection* No One Belongs Here
More Than You *won the Frank O'Connor International Short Story
Award. In 2009 July designed* Eleven Heavy Things, *an interactive
sculpture garden for the Venice Biennial; in 2011 she wrote the nonfic-*

tion book It Chooses You *for McSweeney's; in 2013, 100,000 people from 170 countries subscribed to her email-based art project* We Think Alone; *and in 2014 she launched* Somebody, *a phone app that doubles as social experiment. And now, to show us once and for all that she can do anything she puts her mind to, Miranda July discusses her debut novel,* The First Bad Man.

Let's start with the novel as a form. If I'm imagining that I'm you, I'm thinking part of the attraction is, "I haven't done a novel before." How is writing a novel different than imagining writing one?

Yes, that was the attraction. I wish it were something deeper or more profound but a dare is pretty much the level that I operate at. In a way, I thought it would be the hardest thing I'd ever done, because everyone says that and people are always not finishing their novels. It *is* hard, but it's a certain kind of hard that is comfortable for me. It's *all* on me. It's all an internal, private process. Whereas the hardness of making a movie is much more fundamentally uncomfortable. You're hiring. You're firing. You're accidentally losing other people's money. So that was a surprise. I was like, "Oh, if I were the kind of person who did just one thing this seems like something I'm suited to." However, I'm not. I definitely don't want to write a novel again as my next thing. But my husband commented that I seemed pretty happy during those three years.

I read that when you moved to Portland in the nineties and were developing your performance art, that you intentionally avoided seeking out internships, that you wanted to keep far away from ideas on how you should do things, so you could figure it out on your own. Is that also true now, decades later, as you wrote your first novel? Did you want to feel your way forward with it on your own terms, or did you seek out others, editors and readers, as you might with a film project?

I'm still that same kind of person who won't look at a book and think, "I want to do something like that," just out of my own weird DIY pride. I come at it thinking, "Luckily I'm the first person to ever write a novel so it's wide open." Obviously I know that's not true and I'm a massive reader, but I do isolate my brain a little. And yet I do have a really high tolerance for notes and feedback at this point because that is such an integral and unavoidable part of making movies. So I relied a lot on friends and feedback. Some friends read many, many drafts, and that was invaluable.

Did you start with a conception of the type of novel you wanted to write, or did you start instead with an image or a scene or an emotion and then build your way forward?

I did actually start with an idea that I sold to Scribner and wrote about sixty pages of. And then I made my last movie, *The Future*, and I realized through that process that this idea that I had come up with wasn't going to work. It was too personal. In the movie I was playing someone like me or someone you could imagine was something like me. And there is nothing like that experience to make clear all the pitfalls of that. I felt really free in the parts of the movie that were more surreal or just not so much about me. And this original novel idea was drawn from my true life. I then had a very clear idea of the type of novel I wanted, the type of story in which I could never play any of the parts. And that it should have some surreal elements…I literally had a list like you might have for your future life partner, on your dream board. And then I waited, and it came all at once. I say "all at once," but after years.

Let's talk about Cheryl Glickman, the protagonist of The First Bad Man. *Can you introduce us to her? Who is she? What is she about?*

She is forty-three. She lives alone, has always lived alone. Has she ever had a relationship? Doesn't seem like it. She has all the systems that you accrue when you live alone. The ways of doing things. She has a lot of pride about that. She may seem pathetic to her co-workers but she actually has a fair amount of righteousness about the brilliance of her own methods. I should add that she is not a *knowing* character. She is not the type of person who would use the word *gender*. Despite the self-defense nonprofit she seems to have missed sexual politics entirely.

Tell us more about her systems. She works for a self-defense nonprofit and yet she also seems very defended. As you say, righteous but also alone. Her life takes on a kind of baroque ritualistic quality.

Her systems I relate to a lot. The idea of keeping the house clean all the time by essentially not living in it. Like having one set of dishes so they can never build up. And ideally not even using them but eating out of the pan. [*Lowers voice.*] *Which I do when I'm working in my office.* "Carpooling" is a term that I coined, that will maybe catch on, as applied to if you need to bring something to another place in the house, you wait until you have a lot of other things that need to go in the same direction, you know, just for efficiency.

What really rattles Cheryl's world is when she gets cajoled into accepting her boss's daughter, Clee, as a roommate, a twenty-something feral sort of character. What I found really fascinating about their relationship is that I expected this to go the route of an "odd couple" roommate scenario, but instead they end up finding love, almost accidentally, by reenacting the self-defense scenarios in the DVDs Cheryl brings home from work. I literally could not imagine Cheryl and Clee finding a connection through words. They physically wrestle their way toward love instead. Tell us about role-playing as a way of connection, of approaching another obliquely. Is that a philosophy for you, or a methodology in your art?

I think I was unconsciously interested in exactly what you were saying. I remember the point in the book where I wrote the word *surrogate* (which I eventually took out because it was too knowing of a word for Cheryl). I realized this idea of standing in for something else, or role-playing as a way of being more honest and more present than you could be if you were "being yourself" is really powerful. I wanted to somehow get at that, have people using it who were not part of a community of people who were into playing roles, who were doing it in a self-invented way and for mundane reasons. Cheryl gets into it to cure a health problem she has. It's definitely not sexual for her. She is not aware of that, anyway. We also haven't mentioned that Clee is her physical opposite. She is like the kind of blond, busty bombshell that stops traffic, which is a weird thing to contend with for any other kind of woman.

It definitely feels like role-playing is a recurring theme in your work. For instance, I think of your story "Mon Plaisir," where a couple on-the-rocks accept roles as extras in a film and through performing their parts are able to find each other again. And similarly your new app, Somebody, is a strange way to use technology to have real people in real time play-act your text messages to people they don't know.

Once I was done with the novel and working on Somebody, I realized this was a really good example of me being interested in one thing and approaching it in two completely different mediums. I didn't know if anyone would pick up on that. It's often said that my work is about connection, and that to me feels a little wrong. That implies that people are *really* connecting, *really* knowing each other. I'm not sure that's even really possible. It certainly doesn't happen in my work. But sometimes it can happen through the strange ways people go about it, by playing a role that is different than them. It can be so revealing that it has a tenderness to it that is more present or open than what we think of as the proper way to aim for intimacy. That is so interesting to me. It's like art itself, the way that each person comes up with their very misguided path to connection and then that connection is usually very fleeting. Even in that story "Mon Plaisir," it seems like their whole romance might be able to restart, but it's really just there when they are doing that scene and not again.

Do you use role-playing or specific constraints when you are doing your writing?

This gets at this very subtle definition of role-playing that I've been trying to figure out how to articulate. It could just be a way of saying, "How do you get somewhere without going straight toward it?" I certainly do that in writing. If I know I need to make a character have more pride, if I've overhumiliated them, I don't go straight toward pride and think, "What is it about pride and how can I capture that?" I take a left turn toward something that happens to be interesting to me, and then I find a way to get there through that wrong thing—that wrong thing that nonetheless has a beating heart or else wouldn't be interesting to me. Okay, it's a stretch to call that role-playing, but I think in general we get stuck so often because we think the right path is the straight one, and that we are being really good if we keep on trying to do our work by sitting at our computer and looking at the screen. I think there's a sort of tyranny of A to B. So in this book I was often trying to show, "Look, a baby was made in this book," but it is almost impossible to trace the path of how it was made, even though that is one of the most fundamental processes. There is no other way to make a baby, ultimately, than the sperm and the egg, but I really tried to believe in this book that it could come about through one woman's fantasies.

When we think about the weird paradox that sometimes fiction feels more true than nonfiction, that it gets at a deeper truth through being fiction, and about what you were saying about role-playing—that assuming a role, delivering the lines that aren't your lines from a script that someone else is giving you, as a way to liberate yourself toward yourself—it points at how our own self-narratives are also scripts.

Right, basically anything that allows you to be present. And a script might do that more. Because with the script you are like, "Oh my gosh, here I am. I feel nervous. My heart is beating." It might allow you to be more there with everyone than the script you are always following.

I have a question about avant-garde art and gender. Of course there are men who, like you, are doing innovative, cross-genre, imaginative work, but when I think of where the vitality is these days, I often think of women— artists like Sophie Calle, Marina Abramovic, Miranda July, Shelia Heti, Chris Kraus, etc. Do you think that that just speaks to where my focus is as an individual, or do you think this is a particularly vital time for women of the avant-garde?

I'm with you on that. I feel like I'm so enmeshed, that it would, of course, seem that way to me, because Sheila Heti is one of my best friends, and those are the people I'm looking up. But I will say there is a lot more support happening among women in power now. We're supporting each other in a way that wasn't happening for me even through Riot Grrrl, and for a long time after that I felt very alone. It's a little bit because of the internet, because it is easy to do; but it's funny, I noticed with this book that all these women rushed in. Powerful women tweeted and retweeted. They seemed really determined, like, "We're going to help Miranda on this one." And I know this feeling so well. There will be some obscure book of poetry and I'll think, "I can really help this woman." I know a lot of men, and they are all nice people. But none of them did that. They just didn't. I don't think they are thinking about it. I just think the women know how meaningful it is. It's not just a co-marketing thing. It's really a political standing-by-each-other thing. Because everyone is also getting a little bit knocked down too.

In preparing for our conversation, I read lots of interviews and reviews of your work, and almost without fail these articles mention how polarizing you are as a figure, how people either utterly adore you or find your work deeply exasperating, with no in-between. The ubiquity of these comments, their repetition, made me wonder if part of this is a gender double standard, a way of knocking women down. I liked Lauren Groff's review of The First Bad Man *in the* New York Times Book Review, *which looked at the origins of the word "whimsical," and suggested that this was indeed a way that serious work by women is dismissed. It made me wonder if male artists with similar aesthetics, say Michel Gondry or Wes Anderson, get the same treatment of their work, are polarizing in quite the same way.*

Sure, those guys are called "twee" and "whimsical," even Dave Eggers is, for all the hard work he does in the world. But "annoying," I think, is specific to women in power who aren't playing up their sexuality, who are somehow not fitting the exact mold, whether it is an energetic thing or a physical one, and who are unapologetic about it.

That makes me think of Lena Dunham.

She changed the landscape quite a bit. Since the last time I had something out, things have changed, and frankly it's so much for the better. You can't get away with diminutizing a woman in the same way anymore. Not just her—there are waves of culture.

It does seem like one of the upsides of new technology is that women can create narratives in social media before the narratives of the larger culture get set, and these new-technology narratives affect the larger cultural ones.

Exactly. It's almost like you can surround something and proclaim it safe or hands-off and carry it into the world. Yeah, I have to say it is shifting a little bit. I also think the "polarizing" thing is a story that was picked up by the press. For example, there was a *New York Times Magazine* cover about me. The interviewer was lovely and we had a great time together. But then the piece was completely slanted to, "She's loved, she's hated." It quoted some barely existing blog called "I Hate Miranda July." I remember talking to her later and saying, "Wow, I was sort of surprised that that was the through-line." And she said, "You know, that was one tiny part of what I wrote, and my editor pointed at it and said, 'There, that's the story.'"

So it is possible we think of this as half-half—half hate, half love—but really it is a media-generated phenomenon that is self-perpetuating, that I'm participating in unwittingly.

Yeah, the truth is I always feel like saying, "I feel pretty lucky. I'm making a living doing exactly what I want." You'd have to give people who hate something a lot of airtime and mental space for that to be equal to people who are passionate about something, because frankly you just don't care as much about the things you hate. It feels different to me now. I remember my husband saying, "You were right, you said this is going to pass and it seems like it is passing."

In the last several years you became a mother, and motherhood is one of the themes in The First Bad Man. *Can you talk about how the experience of becoming a mother informed the book?*

The original idea for the book had a baby in it. I didn't have a baby yet. But I thought I would probably have one in the course of writing the book, so it was a little gift for myself—"I know nothing about babies now but I assume this is a topic I'll be interested in over this time." And it was true. I was writing in the hospital, taking little notes. I think partly because my whole life had changed, and the only thing that made it through the divide was the book. "I can at least carry this book into this new land where everything else is just screwed." That's how it seemed initially. And so I wrote tons of stuff for the book and thought, "Oh my god, now this book is going to become very very personal." And then I moved out of that phase and ultimately what stayed were a few sentences and the beating heart of a writer who actually knows what she is talking about when she writes fiction about motherhood. I got farther and farther away from my story and it came back to being Cheryl's.

Your work is sometimes described as "social practice art," and you've collaborated with Harrel Fletcher, a professor of Art & Social Practice here at

Portland State University. I'm sure many people aren't familiar with that term. What does it mean to you?

God, Harrel could do a really good job of this. I often just say that I do this whole catalogue of work in a few different mediums that is participatory. Because for me, "social practice" is often work that is within a community but is no less "fine art." It's like deciding you could take a guided walk with a group of people and that would be the piece. It doesn't have to be a picture on the wall. It can be a living engagement with people. That is object enough.

Do you feel like the online store that is connected to the novel is a nod toward social practice and community engagement? It feels as though what happens within the narrative, between Cheryl and Clee, is a strange form of social practice art, even though that is not what they are doing explicitly, but the store feels like another mode from which one could approach living in the world of the novel.

This idea of a store as a piece of art, I've been thinking about that for a while. I love that it is participatory and that it is using real money and real objects, and that only one person is ever going to own each object. It is a kind of intimacy that doesn't relate at all to fiction. With fiction, we all read the same book, own the same book, so the idea that one person might own the cup that's in the book is just *wrong*. I enjoy that the writer part of myself is aghast— "What?!? There doesn't need to be the cup. I just need to write the cup." I like messing with that. "Really, why? Why is it so precious?" I'm curious. Maybe it is precious, maybe I've messed it up. I enjoy even those fears.

There is something you said in an interview with Rachel Kushner in Bomb *magazine: "The whole time I've been building my audience I've also been trying to unbuild the walls that come with having an audience, with having power." I wonder if part of the reason people always say your work has to do with connection is because of this dynamic, this desire for the person receiving the art to not just be receiving but participating. So in a sense the theme of permeability, of reciprocity seems more apt.*

Exactly. I do try to do that with my books and movies too. I'm really thinking about the audience. I don't know how it comes through. It probably doesn't, which is why I end up doing these actually participatory works. The feeling of being in an audience is so uncomfortable for me. I associate it with listening to my parents, who are monologuers. That feeling of being trapped, stuck, unseen. It's not like it was some sort of torture, but everything I do runs the risk of being something like that. I am asking people to listen. So I think that's why it feels so necessary to me. I don't want to put people in that position where they are supposed to lose sight of themselves and get lost in my world and then feel bereft.

Who are some of the artists who were touchstones for you or people you are particularly jazzed about now?

I'll go with right now. I'm reading a book, a brand new little book by the playwright and director Richard Maxwell. It's called *Theater for Beginners*. It is that, a book for actors, but it is also one of those soon-to-be classic books that you could replace *actor* in every sentence with *person*. I've been finding it strangely moving. And it's pocket-sized, so I can keep it in my purse. Dovetailing with that I've been using the meditation app Headspace a lot. It's probably the most popular meditation app, but I would never have thought that that was even a good idea. It seems like a bad idea, but in fact it has helped me keep it up in a way that I hadn't. It has been profound for me this year.

I just finished Ben Lerner's book *10:04*. Super interesting. And his previous book, *Leaving the Atocha Station*, is incredible. I also just discovered that the Swedish filmmaker Roy Andersson has a website. He's in his late sixties and I love his work. You can look him up and there's a lot to look at online that is really interesting.

Is there a next unfamiliar form that you are attracted to, something you've never done that has a charge around it somewhere on the horizon?

I kind of think from now on it's all going to be permutations of other things. But new things get invented. Apps didn't exist, you know? But I am doing a few things. I'm working on a big public art project that will happen in London next year through an organization called Art Angel. And I have a new performance called "New Society" that's a very audience-participatory performance that I will be doing over the course of the year in a few cities. And I'm working on my next screenplay. *Or so I say.* [*Laughs.*]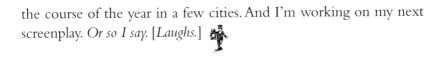

David Naimon is a writer and host of the literary radio show and podcast *Between the Covers* in Portland, Oregon. His work has appeared or is forthcoming in *Tin House, AGNI, Fourth Genre, StoryQuarterly, ZYZZYVA,* and elsewhere. His writing has been reprinted in *The Best Small Fictions 2016* and cited in the 2016 Pushcart Prize volume, *The Best American Essays 2015,* and *The Best American Travel Writing 2015.* His podcast and writing can be found at davidnaimon.com.

Little victories: celebrating new pants.

Zain Saeed was born and raised in Pakistan, and is currently working on his first novel as an MFA candidate at the University of Texas at Austin.

THE EARTH IS A STINGY BASTARD

Zain Saeed

The first and only Memon in my life was walking around this deserted beachside park in circles trying to prove some sort of point. "Come back, Memon!" I shouted, flinching slightly, expecting clenched brown fists. I used to walk around school calling people "Memons," because I was a grown-up boy and could swear, till I ran into an actual Memon who introduced me to a right hook and some proper swear words, like "bhainchod" and others that involved my gaand and lund and so on. There were apparently a lot of them walking around. The term referred to a community of frugal peoples, not an insult; who would've thought it?

As I watched him walk I thought of things that rhymed with Memon and found "gay bun," "daemon," "Cayman," and "hey son." Then I shouted these at him.

He shouted something back about him having a name, bitch, and about this not being funny, gaandu, and other things I did not understand because he switched to Memoni as he had a tendency to do when he was properly mad, like, bad mad.

The sky was perfectly black and littered with the kinds of stars you were sure would fall down if someone so much as poked at them, although I failed in trying to make them do so at that point in time.

There was a sea breeze that made sand stick to your arm, and the occasional whiff of rotten fish from a truck passing by. A couple of car horns seemed to be arguing over something.

I said okay, jaani, what are you doing, jaani, come back and sit with me, jaani, so we can talk about things.

He told me to stop calling him jaani, because he wasn't my jaani, that I wished he was my jaani, and so on. There were times when I thought all Memons were part of one big theater group and kept spontaneously using lines from plays they'd done in real life.

"Okay, Hass, okay, I'm sorry, come back. I'm rolling another from the Peshawari stuff."

Pieces of hashish from Peshawar—the charas—used to come in two sizes: small boulder and big boulder. It was dry by the time it got to us in the south. We'd heat it up till it felt like play dough, pinch some off the boulder, and keep the rest in a cold, dark place for other happy times.

I caressed two Gold Leaf cigarettes between my thumb and middle finger and got all the tobacco out, beautiful.

"What's the scene, bro?" Hass said as he came and sat down next to me on the bench.

"Scene is on, bro. Could you cook that up for me?"

He took out his keys, stuck the piece of charas to the end of a key he said he never used, and heated the hash up with the fire from his lighter. Then I put it in the paper and so on.

Once the joint was lit we sat back and gazed out over the sea, which looked its best when there was no sun around shining light on various objects that floated on the surface and the brownness of it all. The charas smelled of dead things that used to have souls which reeked of heaven.

"Jaani, that is fucking beautiful," he said.

We were Karachi born and raised, never going anywhere, no sir, never.

"You know I saved two hundred rupees on the Peshawari? And you call me a Memon!"

"I call you a Memon *because* you save two hundred rupees on things."

"I want to stay here forever and ever."

"On this bench?"

"No, bro, in the zone."

"Yeah, I want to stay in the zone too."

We worked in two different office buildings now, doing things for people we hadn't even met, buying things we didn't need, and then living like shit. He'd been brought up to do all these things except living like shit, but I'd studied philosophy in college, and working in a bank was, like, number three on my list of preferences, bhainchod! The zone was cool.

"Tell me something," Hass—M. Hassan Masood, as he was formally known—exclaimed suddenly in the middle of a great almighty puff.

"Yeah?"

"What's the scene with that donkey?"

There was a random donkey about fifty meters away loitering in a two meter radius, because she was, first, tied to a tree, and then, tied to a cart, in what must have been a really confusing series of events for her. It seemed like she didn't really get the point anymore.

"Animals, bro."

"Yeah, jaani, animals."

"Do you remember the thing, did your Ammi Abu do that with you, where if you talked while eating your food they said it would go into a donkey's stomach? Why a donkey?"

"They told me it was Satan's stomach."

"That is some heavy shit, jaani. I'd give this donkey some of my food, though."

"I'm sure Edhi has a package for donkey care."

He looked at me as if I'd lost my mind.

"He's not real."

"Who?"

"Edhi isn't a person."

"Bhainchod, what are you saying?"

"He's a CIA conspiracy."

Hass had a knack for this sort of thing, even when no Peshawari shit was involved. It had taken us six months to convince him that Sylvester Stallone was really not a fictional character. It was very hard to do because that Memon brain of his was fucking logical, like, completely.

"How do you get that idea?"

"Have you ever seen Edhi?"

"Yeah. Everybody has. He's always on TV."

"Without the beard, I mean."

"Well, no…"

"Exactly. Ever paid attention to his eyes?"

"What? No, not really."

"Exactly."

"What exactly?"

"Think *dictator*."

"What? Musharraf?"

"No, jaani, how can Edhi be Musharraf?"

"How can Edhi be anything when he's already Edhi?"

"Zia-ul-Haq, bro."

It was times like these that I'd wish human skulls were transparent, so I could see what was happening in that head of his, and whether I should worry about something similar happening to me unless I cut down on the hashish.

"Bhainchod, he died in a plane crash years ago!"

"Did they find him?"

"Well…"

"Exactly."

"What the fuck are you talking about?"

"Jaani, it was all a conspiracy. He knew he'd fucked the country up, so, like, he faked his death and grew a beard and is now saving people and shit. It's pretty obvious."

He said everything so nonchalantly that all I could do was sit up straight on the bench and squint at him, which I did for a good five minutes while the donkey made strange noises that I'd never heard coming from a donkey.

"Are you sure that's not a horse, Hass?"

"Na, it's a donkey, I'm good with figuring out disguises."

"A Memon thing?"

"You know it."

The joint was now on its last few grains of squishy happiness. The number of cars on the streets had thinned as it usually did on Monday night at eleven thirty p.m. The stars were still fucking huge. The only thing missing was a moon, which was in hiding.

"Speaking of disguises, do you know a tulla will never stop you for running a red light if you're wearing sunglasses while you drive?"

At that very moment the donkey, which was only minutes ago pretending to be a horse, decided that the circumstances it found itself in were perfect for, amongst other things like pawing the ground and whining, giving birth. Hass didn't seem to have noticed.

"No, I did not know that. Why?"

"Jaani, it makes them think you're rich and shit and probably know people that will get you out of paying the fine in no time, so they, like, don't see the point."

"Whatever you say, bro."

He took one long pull, threw the joint on the floor, stepped on it, and jumped off the bench.

"Let's go then. I'll prove it to you."

"It's nighttime, bhainchod."

"So what? It doesn't matter. It should work at night too."

It was getting late anyway and the donkey was now in full push mode, and I didn't think I could stomach the birth of a baby donkey, cute as it may be. Actually, hmm, no, not with the amount of charas I'd already consumed. So I said yes, bhainchod, fine, let's go, you can drive the fucking car.

I owned what Hass called "the philosopher's car," a white Suzuki Mehran 1995, because all it was good for really was a roof to have a conversation under. It had a tough time doing that thing of getting from point A to B without catching fire, or shedding plastic at random intervals. You had to drive it a special way, stoned, and remain extremely philosophical about all that happened around you.

Hass got into the driver's seat and asked me to hand him my sunglasses, which I did. He gave me a disapproving look on discovering that they were indeed yellower than most things we'd ever seen. I shrugged and told him to drive, bhainchod, they were really cheap, what's your problem? He told me about getting ripped off, etc.

Nargis—that's what she was really called—made her way slowly out of the parking lot with Hass at the wheel. She had a persistently rumbly stomach, so we had to more or less shout over her.

"Can you even see where you're going?"

"Of course, bro! I'm following the stars!"

We drove for a while along the beach, watching the waves foam, smelling things we couldn't explain, and getting our faces all oily. Sometimes the oil dripped off in little droplets when it was very hot. When I was in college we used to drive on this street every day, jaani, every day after classes, laughing at all the people wasting their time applying to jobs and stuff, pretending they'd figured shit out. We had big dreams, man, big dreams. I was going to be a professor, he was going to run his father's company. There would be lots of women involved. Nargis would be a thing of the past. We'd live like kings in a city that couldn't produce the amount of hashish we were going to consume or afford to house the mansions we were going to live in.

The only thing we managed to achieve was a switch from a small boulder of hashish a month to a big boulder of hashish a month, while the city began to fall apart around us. Hass's uncles fought like mad over his father's business when the latter was shot somewhere over something. They took each other to court, etc. They completely ignored Hass, who one day just packed his bags and moved to an apartment in another part of the city, which was so bloody huge it was like moving to another city, because he had no one left to stay for. I had no such bad luck. I did everything that I wanted to do, but fell victim to people telling me philosophy majors go hungry, and let the whole dream drop without exploring it any further. I was only just beginning to realize that there was no possible way they could have known anything about the things I couldn't have done, when I myself had no fucking clue.

We'd moved away from the sea and were now coming close to the first set of lights.

"Just you watch, jaani, I'm gonna run this red like a boss," he said as he put his foot down.

"There's no tullas around, jaani."

"Ah shit, what's the fun?" We stopped at the red, or, rather, Nargis did, because she didn't take kindly to unplanned bursts of acceleration. Hass started her up again. She groaned, but gave in.

"Have they all gone to sleep or something?" he shouted as we moved on.

I told him I didn't know, can anyone really sleep in this city?

We carried on past tall apartment buildings that might have been gray at some point, but were now brown, residential areas with huge houses doused in darkness because it was load-shedding hour, and passed a Caltex petrol pump from where we could see that we were approaching another set of lights.

"Okay, jaani, I got a good feeling about this one," he said as he pushed the glasses a bit lower down the bridge of his nose to be able to see the road.

As we approached the lights both of us went, "Oh, bhainchod," at the same time when we spotted the little crowd gathered up ahead, complete with tulla machinery, like black Toyota Hiluxes, and a random assortment of their things that said "Police" on them. Hass slowed Nargis down as we crept past the crowd, necks craned to the right, trying to get a peek through the people assembled in a surprisingly perfect circle.

He said, "Let's check this out, bro," and parked Nargis on the side. I did not object because it did seem quite intriguing, and it wasn't like I had somewhere to be. Then we walked toward the crowd.

The whole scene was illuminated by the one yellow street light hovering on top, which made Hass say things about the lighting seeming too good to be an accident, and I smell conspiracy, and so on.

We couldn't see what was going on from the outside of the circle, so we asked a small bearded man, who was having the time of his life bobbing up and down on his feet to catch a better view, what was going on.

"Uncle jee, what's the scene?" I asked.

"Someone got hit by a goli." It was the first time in my life anyone had ever answered a question of mine while on tiptoe.

Both Hass and I started to snicker uncontrollably, because yesterday, just yesterday, jaani, we'd been discussing how the word "goli" meant both a bullet and a pharmaceutical tablet.

While both of us comprehensively lost our shit imagining someone having been hit on the head by a tablet of Paracetamol and their
resulting confusion, four men, three of them fat and one of them a
reporter, turned around and gave us a look that pretty much told us
that this goli had nothing to do with a pharmacy, not that we didn't
know that already. Our heads did strange things at times.

That was when we stopped giggling, stood up straight, and slowly
swam out of the zone. We pushed and shoved our way through the
crowd and finally emerged about a foot away from a hand—we don't
have police tape here, you can get right up close and personal, enough
to breathe the air leaving the bodies. Three tullas dressed in their usual
black shirts and khaki trousers were sharing a joke on the opposite side.
The ambulance driver, who as we later found out had pronounced
the man on the ground dead ten minutes ago, was having a cigarette
sitting on the hood of the police car, waiting for someone to come
claim the body. The people around us had their arms crossed and were
chatting animatedly amongst themselves: What political party? Who?
AK-47 or something smaller, do you think? There was lots of nodding
and smiles of understanding and a buzz of life.

The man on the ground had been shot through the head. His pants
were miraculously devoid of any traces of blood.

"What do you think this was?" Hass asked with his arms crossed.

"Don't know, jaani, one of those target killings, I suppose. Hello,
uncle jee, do you know what happened?"

"They're saying he was standing here waiting to cross the street
when two men came on a motorcycle and shot him and ran," said a
man selling peanuts.

"Yeah, Hass. The same."

"Ah, God save this city. How much are the peanuts, uncle jee?"

"Fifteen rupees."

"I'll take them if you give them to me for ten."

I looked the other way.

"I'm not making any money on these."

"Oh, uncle jee, I know all about these things you say."

"I'm not lying!"

"Fine. Twelve rupees then. That's all I'm willing to give."

We stood in the circle for another fifteen minutes, Hass munching on his peanuts, having made his ancestors proud, and me smoking a Gold Leaf, having lit one in the midst of all the haggling. We talked to the people standing around and exchanged our views on what could have happened, and what did happen, and what this man's hopes must have been, and which political party he represented, and whose conspiracy this was, and where his kids and wife were if he had any, and whether he owed money or lives or anything at all.

Having waited long enough for someone to show up and identify or maybe take away the body, the tullas and the ambulance driver, cigarettes in mouths, put a cloth over the dead man, and while calling him a motherfucking fat fuck, lifted him up from either side and carried him over to the back of the ambulance. They then threw him inside with an almighty heave and shut the door.

The crowd had slowly begun to disband by that time. We were one of the last people there. Even the reporters had left.

"So, jaani, that's what happens when you get involved with this shit, huh?" Hass said.

"Yeah, but why?"

"It's logic. You take something from the city, it takes something from you."

"Yeah, bro, but what did he take?"

"We'll never know, jaani, we'll never know." He scrunched his now empty packet of peanuts and threw it away over his shoulder as we walked back to Nargis, who seemed to have given up on trying to calm herself down, and was now smoking unashamedly by the sidewalk.

"She does not look like she wants to be bothered," I said as we began walking toward nowhere in particular, waiting till Nargis was calm enough to flip open the hood and have her radiator bathed in water.

The road was almost deserted except for the people dispersing from the crime scene and a few cars whooshing by us at random. The palm trees, brown from having been planted in completely the wrong city, looked slightly stoned, if I'm honest, moved occasionally with the breeze from the sea, towered over us as we walked along the sidewalk of what had now become a dual carriageway. All streets in the city became dual carriageways after midnight by the mere whim of us, the citizens. There was no light because we were still in the middle of load-shedding hour, and there was an undertone of generator-buzz in the air. I tried to move the stars along with my finger one more time, then gave up.

"So who do you think he was?" Hass asked, now completely out of the zone, probably extremely hungry with the munchies in spite of the peanuts.

"Some political worker, I guess." My vocabulary had now become unworthy of Nargis.

We kept stepping on each other's feet trying to avoid straying too far toward the middle of the road. A water tanker drove by.

"Maybe he was born to the wrong people," he said, looking somewhere far away, the dead man and conspiracy the last thing on his mind.

"It'd be fun if you had a choice, wouldn't it? Like, who do you want for a family?"

"I'd sure as fuck not pick mine, save me half the hurt in life. Memon this, Memon that. Funny thing is it sounds like they've met my uncles."

I wasn't sure of my preferences or anything else at that moment, so I kept silent and walked. People were just alive till they weren't. Philosophize that, brain.

"It's just population control, jaani, someone's gotta do it," Hass said after a long pause.

"But what about the people who die?"

"I don't know, but the Earth recycles, it doesn't waste things. Quite a Memon thing to do, if I may say so myself."

"Yeah, but there must be a reason why it chose Karachi for most of its recycling."

"The city's sick, jaani, when it dies people won't notice."

"That is deep shit, bro. He's a subtle devil, this God character, isn't he?"

Suddenly, in the midst of all our reflection and dramatic walking, the world lit up. Both of us went, "Ooooohhhh," at the same time like children did in school when the electricity got turned off or came back on. It annoyed every teacher I knew, but for us it was a reflex, and we never stopped. Fluorescent tube lights outside houses flickered back to life, lamps ignited, ceiling fans and air conditioners and refrigerators inside houses were infused with new life. People who were still awake wiped the sweat off their bodies and stood underneath fans and turned on the TV. They would soon flip to a channel talking about the man we'd just seen, stay on it for twenty seconds if they lived in the area, five if they didn't, then lean back on the sofa and put on the cricket. The ones that had already gone to sleep would feel a gust of wind from the ceiling fans and turn onto their backs so the sweat on their faces could catch the wind and feel like cold water. Those who had generators, poor souls, would need to get up, walk to wherever it was, turn it off, then try to get back to sleep, praying this was the only time they'd have to do it that night, but knowing it probably wouldn't be.

Nobody left, though, even those that had somewhere to go. You don't leave places that lose their sanity for you.

"Let's see if Nargis is ready," I said as I turned on my heels and began to walk back in her direction. A fish truck like the one we'd smelled in the park drove slowly by, adding to the rottenness of it all, but you got used to it.

Nargis had stopped smoking. I took a bottle of water out of the back while Hass sat on the passenger seat and began rolling another joint. I prized open Nargis's front, propped it up with a stick, and poured water all over her engine and inside the radiator, which bubbled.

By the time I sat back in, Hass had already lit up.

"I wonder if that donkey's okay," he exclaimed suddenly.

"She'll get by, they always do."

I put the key in the ignition, turned it, heard Nargis begin to rumble, and smiled. Hass shouted over her.

"By the way, did you see? The tullas didn't stop us for running the red! Sunglasses, jaani, sunglasses!"

These are the little victories we stayed for, that made life beautiful.

*Fishing with Dad in Wisconsin, my favorite sweatshirt,
those bellbottoms, and miles and miles of water.*

Stefanie Freele is the author of two short story collections, *Feeding Strays* (Lost Horse Press) and *Surrounded by Water* (Press 53). (The title story was first published in *Glimmer Train*.) Stefanie's published and forthcoming work can be found in *Witness, Sou'wester, Mid-American Review, Western Humanities Review, Quarterly West, Chatta-hoochee Review*, the *Florida Review, American Literary Review, Night Train, Wigleaf,* and *Five Points*. stefaniefreele.com

EVERYTHING BUT WHAT WE NEED

Stefanie Freele [signature]

Stefanie Freele

For some neighbors, it happened while taking a shower, the shampoo suds crowning their heads like lightweight cauliflower; for others, it happened while doing laundry, their machines groaned, protested and quit. For us, it was when we were watering the mint. Mint doesn't need a lot of water, and we'd just finished giving the rest of the garden a good eighteen-minute soak, and were spending the last minute or two giving the mint a little drink. We were Tuesday-Thursday-Saturday people, and our scheduled watering timer hadn't yet gone off when the pressure lessened and the stream receded. Had we known what we know now, we would have let it trickle till the end, filling up the tub. But you've heard what they say about hindsight. Since we were on minute eighteen, we adjusted the time and decided to give the pressure a moment to build up again.

Except it never did.

Of course there was the river. If it was in say, Michigan, that slow-moving ribbon would be called a creek, but here in California, a land of few lakes and minimal fresh-water resources, the dismal algae-filled just-a-hair-over-stagnant ditch earned the majestic title of River. Of course, in the winter, given just two or three days of steady rain, it would rise to its name and jump the banks, causing havoc and disarray along its riparian travels.

Glimmer Train Stories, Issue 98, Winter 2017
©2016 Stefanie Freele

45

For us, luckily it was only a mile walk. We use the term *walk* because the road was blocked off to cars, to water thieves, and we had to walk through the empty vineyard at night, usually around three a.m., to fill our buckets. We saw other bucket fillers, but no one told on each other or made a stink. We did this in the dark, sharing the river bank with deer and coyotes. We all knew we had to drink, we all knew certain small sections of our gardens could not be neglected. Certainly you can't blame anyone for needing water.

It wasn't till much later that we discovered how Ernest Schmingelheffen had pressed his energy-saving dishwasher button on his way out to the airport, toward North Lanarkshire, England, to be exact. He had a comforting plan: stay with his aging aunt and enjoy the moisture of another country. It might be their last stay together, and she had been kind to him as a child. They shared a fascination with Rachmaninoff, admiration of good tea—not that ruddy English stuff—and art museums. They'd have a fine time of it, plenty of liquids and no restrictions.

Even though there were only a few dishes in the washer, Schmingelheffen wouldn't be back for a few months, and he didn't want the food particles lingering and growing. He figured the excess of doing a load for only four plates—a lasagna pan, a spatula, several forks, and a teacup—was fair; after all, he'd be gone three months and using zero precious California water whatsoever. He left with a clear conscience and a strong desire for a window seat on the plane.

While Schmingelheffen squirmed impatiently in the taxi to the airport, the mechanism washed his dishes, saving water all the way, beginning to dry with the air-dry energy-saver option. The cycle interrupted itself, began, and washed his dishes again. And again, and again, and again, and again, and again. For approximately seven weeks, the now-broken dishwasher washed that same blue-glass lasagna pan over and over. Who knows when the leak started? By the time someone noticed the long patch of green grass on the slope below Schmingelheffen's house, it was too late.

We were dry. The entire town's water supply was dry.

Except for the aforementioned river. And that is what brought us to the real dilemma.

Of course, the vineyards, being the last to get the water rationing, were doing fine on their own; most of them don't need as much water as they'd been watering with anyway. It was greed that drove that overwatering. More production, more cases, more money. Oh yes, it is always about money, isn't it.

A lot of people moved. Found jobs in wet places like Bellingham, Washington, and Green Bay, Wisconsin. Visited relatives in balmy cities with names such as Lihue and Pensacola. Those of us who stayed were thirsty, dusty, and desperate.

Thus, the bucketing.

The city posted notices that spoke of strong encouragement to vacate temporarily, hopeful messages that the issue was being worked on, and, finally, stern evacuation mandates.

There are always some who refuse to leave in every disaster, right? As you can guess, we weren't about to abandon our six kinds of sage, our seventeen versions of mint including lime, chocolate, orange, and citrus. We had grafted our apple trees, coaxed our lemon, and babied our single orange. We weren't going anywhere.

We surveyed our resources: plenty of our canned herbed tomatoes, shelves of jarred pears, blackberry, and pickles. More than enough deer meat and wild pig sausage. Tons of corn for the chickens, and the goat always found something to eat.

The answer lay in hiding and taking stealthy trips to the river. We had a generator, plenty of books, and movies about oceans. We had propane, but the closest version of water was a two-hour drive to a little gas station that couldn't keep enough bottled in stock for all the tiny towns around it.

And ours was a tiny town. Three hundred seventy-seven residents. After the water cutoff, maybe fifteen or sixteen residents. Four of them lived in our house.

We spent enormous amounts of time watching sea specials and reading books about shipping, fishing, and coastal issues. We did plenty of rain dances, prayed endless prayers toward the cloudless blue sky, burnt sage, conjured water spirits, and, every night around three a.m., walked the mile to the river, two buckets each, quickly dipping in and walking silently back, in four separate vineyard rows. Half our buckets went to the garden, half went to us: bathing, drinking, or just sticking your hand in it deeply and watching it waver around.

Although maybe not too many people walked for their water in the United States by this era, we knew our ancestors survived doing this, so we could too. We took turns with the lone pair of night-vision goggles. Twice we arrived to lower our buckets while, across the wilted river, a raccoon family washed their hands.

You could call us crazy. After all, there was an entire country immersed in regular deluges of water, snowstorms till June in Maine, thunderstorms every week in Minnesota. Why would we want to stay where dehydration threatened us daily? With no perceptible moisture in the air, the remorseless climate sucked us dry. Our skin, our lips, our hair, all parched. You'd be a fool to go anywhere without carrying something to drink.

We'll tell you straight. It was the garden. We could leave the oregano—we had plenty dried and jarred—but not the peppers, certainly not the cucumber plants, which took a bucket each every other night. We settled on letting go of the silver thyme, but not the basil. You have never tasted a better lemon cucumber than one freshly sliced during a historic drought, in an evacuated town, where occasionally all that is seen in the streets is a fire truck patrolling the area. As we said, it was dry.

Our garden was hidden behind the house and the set-back garage blocked it from one side. We hurried up shelves around the fences, put up boards, a tarp. For all appearances, our property was just one of the many empty evacuated homes, waiting. The only way you'd see our illegal green would be via helicopter, which is what flew above on September 13, on a day when it tipped 105 and we could smell smoke. We already knew there was no water to put out a fire in the area, one of the many reasons for evacuation.

Oddly enough, it was Schmingelheffen's ill-grown grass that set fire. Tall grasses, oily chemise brush: the land was only doing what the land would do in the absence of humans, the occasional brush fire cleansing.

The smoke thickened, the helicopters swarmed. We studied our precious half-filled buckets. Two, we dumped on the cherry tomatoes.

Two, we tightened the lids. The rest we dumped into each other and set in the rarely used car in case we needed to take off. In case the fire got close to us and the mint.

You would definitely say we stayed too long. We were coughing nonstop in that thick air. The helicopters were buzzing, sirens shrieking somewhere. It was already so hot out, who could tell if it was getting any hotter.

But, somehow, we made it through. The wind changed and the fire headed west. Go ahead and head west, we said. Ash covered our driveway, it had been that close. Our hair was temporarily grayed, even though we had closed up every window and toweled underneath the doors. The air reeked of burnt plastic, camping, and the general sick-scent of something melting that shouldn't be.

We didn't sleep that night and took turns in twos to go to the river, instead of the entire group at once. We filled up.

It was preposterous, truly. We can say that, now that February has brought twelve straight days of rain, one evening of thunder, most of the town back and the need for sandbags. That summer was preposterous. That is clear to us now. How none of us got giardia is a miracle.

The asparagus, long chopped, cooked, and eaten, is resting below in the soil somewhere, waiting for its triumph next May. Everyone predicts it will be a cooler year, one of morning fog and spring showers.

Nonetheless, eight filled buckets are stored in the garage, stacked two rows tall in the corner from floor to almost ceiling, like Roman columns in front of a temple. Despite the rain, the flooded front yard, and the calf-deep puddle on the street corner, stored water is a welcome and common sight around here.

As far as everyone knows, Ernest Schmingelheffen is still in England listening to dark and difficult piano music. All that remains of his house is a blackened chimney, rubble, and an important-looking For Sale sign. Either Schmingelheffen planted daffodils that are coming up again, or someone took the time to put those yellow flowers in the ground along the darkened walkway, giving the abandoned property a rather homey appearance, or, at the very least, a touch of innocence.

Portrait of the artist as a young prince, dressed by his mother.

Ezekiel N. Finkelstein was born in Brooklyn, New York, grew up in Rockaway Beach, Queens, studied philosophy and English at Skidmore College, and returned to NYC to "hang loose upon the city," eventually gathering an MFA from CCNY. After teaching writing and literature classes at CUNY colleges for many years, he is now living part of the time in rural Maine, working and writing.

CLAYTON AND THE APOCALYPSE: SCENES FROM AN EARLIER LIFE

Ezekiel N. Finkelstein

In the opening shot of the movie of his life, he's screaming, on his way down; in his voice, as he falls, is the suggestion of regret (as someone had said they'd heard): everything follows in flashback. Suicides, like traitors, and heroes and geniuses, force you to read their entire lives back through their defining acts.

I found his voice—twice—on my answering machine many months later. I'd been away when he'd called, so his messages were way back on the tape and had never been erased. It was eerie, of course. He was asking me for the number of a cousin of mine who ran a rehab clinic. I'd given him the number once, but he hadn't called. I'd never called him back this time.

Not long after this I had a dream in which I was driving up 6th Avenue and I saw a crowd and this guy, a cabdriver, was trapped, drowning, underneath the little square drain in the middle of Father Demo Square off Carmine and Bleecker Streets, by the pizzeria. You could see his upturned face enjailed beneath the perforations of the drain cover, like he was almost entirely underwater. I stopped, though not right away, and tried, lamely, to use a straw to suck him out or to bail out the water. Then his face went under. I drove and found a phone booth on what still looked like 6th Avenue and called 911.

Ezekiel N. Finkelstein

But the voice I got was my own answering machine, my own voice. I called again, but I knew the whole time it was too late. First I'd hesitated to do anything because I'd already thought it was too late; then I'd tried more desperately. But it was always too late. Or I was too paralyzed.

1. Prelude to a small story about Clay, death, cabdriving, New York City, and the apocalypse

For about ten years, from my mid-twenties to mid-thirties, I drove a taxi cab in New York City. Typically I'd drive two really long—usually sixteen-hour—shifts on Saturday and Sunday, sleeping some in-between and finishing around two a.m. Sunday night. This gave an epic cast to my weekends. Sometimes, if I needed the money (I never, just about without exception, drove when I didn't need the money), I'd drive Friday night as well. Sunday nights whenever I got home I would take a long shower, in winter a bath, and then collapse onto clean sheets into exquisite beyond-dream sleeps that lasted well into Monday afternoon. When I'd awaken, cleansed and rested and my fat money-wad within arm's reach, I'd consult my nice stash for a ten-spot and any stray singles I hadn't handed in and head off with my books and notebooks for my local café of choice for breakfast and the newspaper, and after that I would write and read. I lived like this for years. My weekdays were mine in which to write and read and loaf; my weekends belonged to dollar bills and pot holes and the people of the city who could afford me. Have you ever handled money for a living? It's dirty. My hands were filthy at the end of a shift. Washing them felt like a religious act.

Arguably the main character of this story is NYC as it was when it was still an urban center of certain magical (in effect) synchronicities, sequences, idiosyncrasies, moods, and dark and desperate strivings. It still might be such, I suppose, if you're young enough or have nothing to compare it to; it's possible. It's hard to tell what's "out there" and what's a function of your perception, your age, your time. (At forty your balance seems to shift, it seems to me: what you've lived begins

52

Glimmer Train Stories

to outweigh what you will live.) I usually think, though, that a few years ago NYC (that is, at least Manhattan and parts of Brooklyn) passed a certain critical point in its attempt to resist its assassins; in its recent spiritual artistic intellectual political decline; in its twenty-year "progression" toward tameness, safeness, and standardization; but maybe it's just me who's passed that point.

The dives and streets and avenues of the city aside, however, this is mainly a memory-tale of my friend Clayton and some experiences and visions our young manhoods assumed in common. It features some strands and strains of our friendship, and our assorted consort-ings and strivings in and against the times we lived in. At our best I felt that we were working and helping each other to converge on a common integrity, coming from opposite poles of experience and strength. (At our worst I felt we were trying to survive, if necessary at each other's expense.)

2. First meetings

The first time I met Clay must have been when I was working at a brief-lived bookstore on 8th Avenue between 42nd and 43rd Streets, about two doors uptown from ShowWorld or whatever that place was called. The bookstore wasn't a porno store at all; in fact it had a lot of good books, all of which were remaindered or discounted. The owner had a warehouse and wholesale business, and he opened up this place just to get rid of and I guess store some of his books. I worked there for about nine or ten months before I started driving—hacking—and then for a few months I worked both jobs, keeping my bookstore hours and driving twice a week. That was when I met Clay. He came in the store and we must have vaguely greeted each other, or I must have told him that I'd seen him at the garage. He had started a few months before me and since, at the very beginning, even a few months can impart to a fellow driver the aura of a veteran—at least from the perspective of a complete novice—he had that air of a slightly more experienced "salt" for me, though that we were similarly new drivers was also part of our understanding. It took him about fourteen sec-onds to start referring, although in his peculiarly factual, shy way, to

Ezekiel N. Finkelstein

how much money he made per shift ($150), adding that most drivers didn't make that much, he thought. That was Clay.

The next time was when we were waiting to be dispatched, sitting outside. In those days the garage was on a side street on the lower west side of Manhattan. Now you can't even turn around in that neighborhood without bumping into a tourist or shopping stadium or Thai restaurant or something, but in those days it was pretty deserted. There was practically nothing on this street other than the taxi garage and parking lot and an old Portugese-Jewish cemetery. The cabs were parked all up and down the block and in the parking lot that the fleet owner owned, and we were dispatched from the first floor of an old brownstone. I can't remember whether anyone lived upstairs then, but there was a jazz studio, either in that building or the one right next to it—I said hello to Max Roach in the parking lot next to it, once, at the end of a shift. Anyway, you walked into this dilapidated brownstone where all the dark green paint was shedding and curling and the doorways and floors were crooked and the walls were sagging, and it was filled with putrid cigarette smoke while you threaded your way through all the drivers standing around smoking and talking, and you slid your "picture" (your hack card, license)—and underneath that, probably, a few dollars—under the leftmost of two glass windows like in a toll or token booth, but actually built into the wall, behind which, elevated slightly, stood one of two dispatchers. Marty, the chief crazy bastard, was the one who'd take your money and your card and, if you were new, basically tell you to get the fuck out of his face until he called you. He was such a notorious Ahab—he even had a big waddly limp—that for years, even after he'd retired, cabbies would pull up next to me at red lights, see our garage's insignia on my door, and ask whether "Marty the fuck" was still working. Drivers throughout the city had passed through our garage; it was kind of the Ellis Island of taxi drivers—mostly because they let you drive before you got your permanent license from the TLC, and the "management" helped and sped up this process. (This was why you put up with being treated like shit for a while but, if you were serious about driving a lot and regularly and being treated half-decently, soon moved to another garage.) But it was

54   *Glimmer Train Stories*

CLAYTON AND THE APOCALYPSE

also just a convenient place for impatient rookies and non-regulars, because it was in downtown Manhattan (which meant you didn't have to spend a half-hour crossing a bridge before you got your first fare), because the day drivers had to be in by four rather than five so night drivers could get out "early," and, most of all, because you could drive whenever you wanted. You just had to show up and wait.

The waiting period was, is, called "shaping up" or "shape up." If you wanted the freedom of driving whenever you felt like and showing up whatever day you wanted, when you wanted to drive a night shift you were expected to "hand in your picture" around three p.m. and then, depending on your seniority, how often you drove, your reliability, how much money you "tipped," Marty the prick's mood, or how he liked you, and the availability of cabs as the day drivers pulled in and gassed up, they called your name and you picked up your license and trip sheet and car keys at the window. There was usually a long call of names between three forty-five and four, and if you didn't get called then, you were often kind of screwed, not getting out until four thirty or five or later, or not getting out at all, if they had more drivers than cars that night. Anyway, we used to wait draped all over this brownstone, inside and outside, standing and sitting, alone or in twos or groups—in the small room where the dispatchers' windows were; in the main room around the insanely etched-in and knifed-out old table or by the lockers; in the hallway, on the old wooden inside staircase, or on the front porch or stoop. Some guys just sat around reading or smoking and staring. Some talked quietly, some loudly and stupidly, some joked in clumps. The drivers were a diverse crew—regulars, artists of all kinds, students, drug fiends, ex- and future businessmen on the lam from the IRS, hapless retards and bums, fairly dire tough guys, leathered queers it wouldn't occur to anyone to fuck with, recluses, all-around weirdos, old guys who'd been doing it for thirty years, recent immigrants who'd just arrived in the city.

Clay must have been one of the first guys I spoke much to. We were sitting on the front stoop, and I was probably reading something or writing in my notebook, and we talked. He had a New England accent but a working class kid's cut words and phrases. I don't think he was writing plays yet, then, and I don't remember whether he said that he acted, but he had the tough sexy good looks of a street kid (we were both in our mid-to-late twenties) turned actor. I bought him completely, thinking that he reminded me of a movie character, that I'd never met anyone like him, but that of course I had always known that such people actually existed (because I'd seen them in the movies), and of course this must be what such people were like. It was exciting. He was six feet tall, dark haired, movie-star handsome but in an interesting way, with close, fairly deepset, quick, darty, playful eyes and a charming, completely open laugh and smile. His manner was disarmingly direct and humble. He told me that he wrote, that he was working on a novel, and that his favorite writers were Dostoyevsky and Mario Puzo. When he said "Puzo," my reflex college kid's judgment was condescending, but then he said that he thought the highest, noblest thing a person could do was create something, and I felt, How lovely! What a simple, beautiful, wholly intelligent sentiment, the kind of clear—naïve?—unhedged thought of which I was already not quite capable.

3. Chi?

When the slew of names was called between three forty-five and four it was very dramatic, because for a long time they'd called no one at all, and then for a while they'd dribbled a few guys' names out, one or two every five minutes or so, but then there was a long roll-call of fifteen or twenty names coming pretty intensively, gathering momentum, and I always thought of us as fliers, bombardiers breaking formation and soaring out over the city for our private missions in service of an obscure romantic collective. If you were one of the newer or part-time guys like we were, you'd get right in your car without bothering to check anything and tear right out down 7th Avenue, and if it was busy you'd pick up a fare before you got to 14th Street, and you figured you were going to have a good night. Everything was momentum, grace, fate, electricity, magnetism—being part of an invisible current in space and/or time in which, if you were the right combination of spontaneous and wise, you could keep inside the city's magic. Everything was sex, desire: if you and the car were one and in the flow of the city, your desire, in tune to a sufficiently disinterested love and tempered by a decent respect for justice, would always give you the right move to make, the right thing to say. If the driver of the car to your right called you a lousy piece of shit who didn't know how to drive, but you were "in synch," there was always something honest to say or do that would properly deflate or enlighten him, connect you or sever you cleanly from one another.

In some spiritualities, this flow, I believe, is called "chi" or "the Way." I thought of it as kind of an electric grace that got turned on or that you tapped into (I could never decide which). When it was on, or you were "in it," you were cooly astride your world, in gear: nothing detractive could touch you; every move you made was right. You'd have ten fares in a row who were fascinating or cool or beautiful or bright or just nice—or good money.

Of course it helped if it was late at night, and there was a good run of music on the radio, and if you were a little high.

You never had this for a whole shift, of course. You were lucky if you got it for a couple of hours. Most of the time, driving was quite monotonous. I'll discuss hookers and violence another time.

4. Reservations for the apocalypse

I felt that with Clayton, more than with any other friend—or even lover—of this period, I shared a vision, which was, for lack of a better word (but this was the word we preferred), *apocalyptic*—spiritually, poetically, and politically. We had absolutely no interest in the preservation of uncivil society as we found it. We felt that the human world was increasingly closing down on us and that this gradual, mechanical lid needed exploding. Later, toward the end, I worried that Clay's apocalypticism got crazy and stupid, out of control, too obsessive, too literal, even silly. But when we first confided our apocalyptic hankerings to one another, things were quite different. I remember our first mention of it as almost shy, confessional. I may be imagining that, but I don't think so. We didn't know anyone else who embraced political radicalism and spiritual revolution as seriously—and humorously—as we did. We thought that the system of organized repression, oppression, low-grade chronic war (capitalism), and occasional acute war (capitalism with an overt vengeance and other fundamentalisms) was due to be politically and cosmically detonated. It was 1987. 2000 was close enough to *see* but far enough away—and we young enough, I guess—for it to retain its mythological aureole.

That year I had been away for four months—something I managed about once every eight years—and I returned to the city on a sickeningly hot, sticky July 4th night. The following night I drove, and after I'd pulled the car in for the night, Clay had stopped to talk to me on the street before we headed our opposite ways home. We didn't know each other well at all yet; I don't know how specific his impulse was to tell me about the book he'd just found. I don't know whether he told eighteen other people that night or just me. The book was about the freeing of the "will," which in this book meant—though it's a little more complicated than that—desire. I can't remember how he recommended it. The next day—or the afternoon before, I can't any longer remember which—another friend I was having lunch with mentioned the same book. Let me just say for now that it was presented in its introduction by the author as a "channeled" book from the "highest" source, and that its ostensive aim, as Clay and I understood it, was consistent with that of Blake's or the early Freud's or of any other of our great liberators: to release you into living an unrepressed life, and thereby ultimately to free the social sphere.

The book was profound but poorly written; rather, it was awkwardly written. A little later I came to think that however awkward, arduous, its syntax, the book was written in the most effective language in which it could have been written. (Now I don't know what I would think.) At first, though, I thought it curious, if also encouraging, that a book supposedly dictated by God could be written so badly. The next time I saw C we were rushing past each other on foot on 8th Street, but we stopped to talk for a minute about the book. "I'm a better writer than God!" I joked. He laughed, which he did wildly and readily. When we saw each other after this, our conversations grew more intense and detailed, focused on the book, the teachings of which, we both felt, were psychologically the most advanced and potentially freeing and radical that we had come across. We were searching and still believed that it was possible to get something resembling answers to decent, honest questions.

Much, much later he was to say to me, "Didn't you always know that a book would change your life?"

O Christ, will you not save us!?

5. *Miscellania and elegy of sorts,*
after the formula of Joe Brainard's I Remember
I remember telling him I thought all people were basically bisexual, and his first response being a mixture of discomfort, if not horror, and probably wanting to punch the shit out of me, but his being obliged to respect me for my honesty and, later, his admitting it (if one can "admit" something on behalf of "all people").

I remember asking him why he, and other tough kids and guys, never looked other guys in the eye, and his saying it was because of their fear of feeling queer—and this was why they, and he, fought.

I remember his tiresome showcase monologues on all his sexual conquests, delivered around the table in the shape-up room in the new building from which we got dispatched after the brownstone got "renovated."

I remember feeling love and attraction for him, but always being too chicken to act on it, and I remember his only being able to go for it or act gently and honestly (except on the phone) when he was high on coke, and I remember the time he wanted to, but he was coked out, and I didn't want to, and besides we were older.

I remember Michael G at the memorial for Clay at Keith's apartment on Bleecker Street, saying that he was scared of Clay—how honest of him to have admitted this, especially as it was often such an important part of C's presentation (it was also Michael who had flattered Clay after seeing one of his plays, saying that he was so talented that it was scary).

I remember being at a party with him on Dean Street in Brooklyn and his being pissed at me because I had told him that his poetry sucked and he should try reading some real poetry, like Yeats's instead of Bukowski's, and his kind of pressing his palm hard against my head and telling me he could crush my skull like an eggshell, it would be so easy. Thanks, Clay.

I remember his saying to me once, as an aside after a joke of mine, when he'd been telling me about some truly murderous friend of his, that I was "intellectually dangerous," granting that this was different from, but not "less than," being physically dangerous. I was pleased. (Thanks, Clay.)

I remember how at a certain point the balance between love and support vs. competition in our relationship felt like it must have shifted in favor of competition or psyched-outness (at least for me), because at a certain point I felt like it was destructive for me to be around him (even though we probably rarely saw each other anyway after he quit driving and started dealing weed), and I had to distance myself from him,

and I remember how after seeing him once at his apartment on 10th Avenue and possibly scoring slightly, I was riding my bicycle down 11th Avenue feeling diminished under the shadow of his influence and powercuts, and my bike lock got caught in the spokes of my wheel and I flipped and dug a ridge in my chin and was bleeding all down my pants legs, and I locked my bent bike on 23rd Street and took a cab across town to Cabrini, where the doctor did a not particularly brilliant job of stitching me up.

I remember how at thirty-five I realized that if I did not change the way I lived I would not live past forty,

and I remember that around this time I began to distance myself from C (because his image of me, or my image of myself, was insufficient?), and I decided to get off the train headed for, or the platform waiting for the train headed for, the apocalypse or The Apocalypse, and this was not that difficult, really, because it was taking so long to come and now everybody was talking about it, and who cared, anyway, I still had my own life to live, whether it came or not,

and I remember C would watch the L.A. riots or spreading fires or earthquakes on CNN and call me (and a hundred other people, probably) up saying the "Apawcalypse" was coming,

60

and I remember he would joke (this was earlier, when I myself was as enthusiastic as he) that I was spending the apocalypse (for sometimes it was an event and sometimes it was the long road and process leading to the event) drinking coffees in cafés in the east village,

and I remember that he would "jailsurf," as I thought of it, and go to protests and sit-ins, and get crazy limp, and get arrested and be carted off to jail,

and he was physically and politically brave, and he knew how to box and would sometimes punch people who maybe needed to be punched, though usually he seemed to feel guilty about it afterward and end up getting hit or somehow fucked up or undermined himself,

and I remember, as he told me the story after we'd become estranged (or was it to my answering machine?), the time his girlfriend called the cops because he'd said he had a gun and was going to shoot himself, and forty cops came to his apartment and he wouldn't let them in (I think because of all the pot in his apartment, because he was dealing), and when they got in he was struggling against them all (like Samson), and it took dozens of them or something finally to subdue him,

and I remember, when he told me (or my answering machine) this story, I felt sick and jealous and intimidated, sick because who wanted to hear any more about his macho braggadocio boasting superhero exploits, and jealous and intimidated because they were so physically heroic, or brave, or at least strong,

and I remember my friend who met Clay saying that C made him or tried to make him feel like a woman, and he wasn't used to this species of machodom any more, no longer being in high school in Queens.

I remember Clay telling me the first time he did dope, and I remember his telling me, proudly, I thought, that he had a habit, and I remember thinking that he didn't and he was just playing, and as always having to be everything more or bigger or further or better or worse than me or someone else, and I remember thinking his survival center was too strong for him ever to be in any real danger, and I remember finally seeing that or when he was hooked on dope and had a real habit but by then it was too late.

I remember how lovely and funny and brilliantly creative and unspiteful and sensitive and hopeful he was before he destroyed himself with dope and cocaine.

6. *I wish I could*

I wish I could remember some of our epic philosophical and emotional afternoon phone calls better. Once I had asked him what he thought about something that was written about "Heart" in the book we read (which I always referred to as "the blue book," because its cover was blue and the subsequent books had different, supposedly chakra-colored covers; though sometimes when I presented it to someone I'd introduce it as an "emotional survival manual for the end of times"), and he gave a pretty explanation: he thought of Heart as a kind of lake or solution in which all the other facets or aspects of the godhead would bathe or dissolve or swim. Or something like that.

7. *Biographical musings*

At some point I found out that he really hadn't grown up as a poor street kid, but that his parents had actually been kind of educated hippies, his father a preacher of some sort who had been to Harvard on the GI bill, and they had lived on, or as, a kind of commune in Boston when he was young.

But he'd always been a troublemaker and gravitated to the bad kids, though he himself was a skinny wimp and not tough at all until well into high school. Eventually he managed to hook up with the toughest Irish gangs and mafia fringes (he never told everything about this stuff—maybe there was some dark singular mystery he never gave up: there was one badass Australian guy at the garage who was convinced that C had killed someone once; I'm 99.9% sure not): all his friends from his teenage years were dead, he'd say. Before moving to New York to try to make it as an actor and writer, he'd worked for a few years in Las Vegas, running some kind of scam with a card calculator in his shoe.

I haven't said what a good writer he was. Everything he did, at least before he was drug-addled and lost between sentimentality and striving to make it commercially with a big screenplay, was the work of an artist, grounded, naturally graceful (he reminds me of Stephen Crane in ways, but I can't go into this now). He made lyrical, crafted work with its own sophisticated wit and direct intelligence, and the same outrageous (often quietly hilarious) honesty that his best conversation had. His plays were very good—smart, funny, absurd, political, wild. His short stories were surreal, little gems of wry heart and pathos: like the one where there was live jazz at the Munson Diner, which was only funny if you knew the city in general, but particularly this old dive diner on 11th Avenue where people were so beat they could barely lift their coffee mugs to their mouths. (They probably *do* have live music there now, and serve café lattes.) His poems I liked less, and I told him they were "lines, not poems" (which is probably when he wanted to puncture my skull), but before he destroyed himself with dope these were okay too, probably, or maybe even much better than that, since his voice then was inevitably direct and deep and couldn't help being somewhat disarming.

8. Estrangement: dangerous amateurs

There were undoubtedly many incidents, some of which I've mentioned, which caused me to withdraw—or us to diverge—in the last years, but we weren't officially estranged until late December of 1994. My girlfriend at the time, Maria, had filled out all the necessary paperwork for me, so I, amid my usual ambivalences, had gone back to school that year in September. Meanwhile by the autumn she and I had broken up, all but finally, or at least she had moved into her own apartment (I had told her that she could keep living with me if she wanted to, but that my brain would explode). Still, when I felt sentimental I felt like we could get back together. Neither of us was any good at detaching. She more than once said that was why she did it.

So it happened to be the morning after my first night with another woman that C called me and said that he and my ex-gf had been having an affair for three weeks. I yelled at him that she was his problem now and he better fuckin take care of her (for such was the kind of relationship she and I had come to enjoy over the years, that I could hate her and wish to be done with her and be hurt by her and feel protective of her at the same time), and I slammed the phone-head down on the hardwood floor a bunch of times before hanging up. This was what triggered our more official estrangement. I would have tried to reconcile with him, I think, eventually, but he really made no attempt at all. Actually it had already been months since we'd seen each other or even spoken much: what I didn't know was that his drug problem was completely out of control by this time; he'd been using heavily, shooting up and doing all kinds of other shit. Maybe that was afterward, I don't know. At some point he also shaved his fucking eyebrows, I heard, and got a mohawk, but I never saw him like this.

Clay always had to take everything as far as he could. While my approach was to try everything at least once—or ten or twelve times, at the most—Clay's motto was *Excess and Conquest*: he would try what you'd tried and take it as far as he could. So if you'd snorted dope a few times, he had to pick up a slight habit. If you were subversively depressed, he would be more depressed. If you fucked prostitutes occasionally, he would fuck them more—he would be more whoring, more pansexual, more politically radical, more adventurous, more brave, more crazy, more stupid, more anything you were (if he loved you and/or respected you). He had to consume you and who you were, because he didn't know who he was, exactly. I don't say that he didn't also emulate or compete with good parts of his friends, but the habit was dangerous: the parts of you that he competed with and consumed were sometimes toxic (with friends like me, yes, but his other friends were a lot worse).

My pose was defensive: I'd protect myself from you and take what I wanted, kind of on the sly. I did not compete directly: I'd make secret raids into enemy territory on occasion, and otherwise defend my ground. I was never promiscuous, exactly; just selectively reckless.

And at a certain point I figured out that I needed balance rather than excess, derangement, and disintegration—all Blakes, Burroughs, and Rimbauds aside.

So this was why I never went back for Clay—I mean that it was Maria, technically. Perhaps it would have been impossible anyway, but I would have tried. I would have tried to save him. I think. I would've. I'm not excusing or justifying my behavior. I'm not; I'm guilty. I banished him from my Light; I felt that this was my only self-preservational move, though undoubtedly this was my injured ego talking. If Maria was the mothergod and C was the bodygod—sexual, physical Poseidon—then I was the mindgod-skygod, Jehovah-Zeus-Apollo: a little nasty, vengeful. I had to banish him from my Light. He was too draining; he was taking me down. I took Maria back into my love, though. If I had been stronger, more advanced, I would've gone back for C as well. I mean I would have had the desire and wherewithal to. But he made no attempt, really, either, as I said. He called me I think four times that year. I think we actually spoke on the phone twice. He told me about his first suicide story in the summer with the cops and all. I told you. I didn't take him seriously because there was still all the dumb alienating braggadocio, like he not only wanted you to hear his story but to feel like shit at the same time. Was I madly distortive in my own chronic competitiveness? In my great generosity I told him not to try to kill himself any more. He left two messages on my answering machine, that summer and in September. I never called him back. He jumped from the fortieth floor of the Marriot Marquis in December of 1995. Apocalypse be damned: I loved this man. He was my brother.

9. *Last scene: Christmas season, NYC, 1995*
Before he even opened his eyes, he knew that he would do it today. It made him a little sad, but not as sad as living.

He'd show them. He was ready.

The sorrow was so tremendous. Chances lost, lost dreams, ideals. Mercy had no visible agent. Justice was pissed on. Government and courts run on scum and fraud, words were pure shit, faith a screen for executioners run rampant like hillbillies on steroids, love a fraud or hunted con.

Since he'd gone back on the stuff again, his desire was dead. He knew this was the last time. They'd know, they'd finally know. He pictured his hawknosed father finding out—the deciding knife: the final shame, the blot the old pecker would never outlive.

He walked into the kitchen, needles and stash all over the table. Constipated. Poor body: it'll soon be over. Tie up. Tie up, my drearies, Death is Lord of all. Take my time. He drove the needle in. Dreamfluid cleaning the system. Pure poison. Today was the day. In a while, wash it down with coke, mix with death.

An hour later—it was noon—he was out on 10th Avenue, freezing, gray, the city a giant sewage system bringing shit to shits for shits to shit out. But now it was strict polished muscle shit, fascist shit with swastikas and stripes. Nothing left. He'd practiced this all summer. He'd been arrested once for climbing out onto the ledge, but they'd let him go after an hour or two when his girlfriend had shown up. Now it was different. That was rehearsal. He was always methodical, a perfectionist.

Walking across 43rd Street, wobbling slightly, he passed DaBella. Would he see?

—Ey Chass, you look like shit. What're you doin?

—I'm doin it today, Frank. I'm on my way.

—Doin *what*, becoming a streetcleaner? What're you gonna do lookin like that?

—I'm jumping. You'll see.

—Yeh sure, you been saying that since I knew you. You're too chickenshit.

—You'll see.

He walked on. DaBella snorted, confused, watching him as he staggered off.

Today's the day, mothafuckers, he muttered to himself, taking a left up 9th Avenue, almost bumping into a parking meter. You'll see. You'll all see. You're all full of shit.

When he jumped—it felt like forever, at the same time like no time—immediately he was the soberest he had ever been—he was surprised. He realized he'd made a mistake: he was falling. He'd always thought of it as *jumping*, but really the jumping part almost didn't exist, it was all just gravity, free fall, dive at best. Oh Christ, what have I done?!

His heart stopped and he saw in numb time the frozen faces of the tourists below at their tables, his own passing faces at various ages, his mom when he was an infant staring and staring at her face like the sun: all that love, balls of love…he saw his angel—he recognized her—and the others waiting for him, sorrow stricken but dutiful, loving. He'd always known they were there—how many times had they saved him? like the time with the truck on 6th Avenue…it was cruel of him to have done this to them…his guardian must've called her friends in…O Christ—

In his screams on the brief way down, the tourists thought they heard a kind of remorse, though no one could make any words out. Remorse is said to be the emotional acknowledgement of objective error.

The Ethereals bore his spirit away, while the tourists and waiters in the courtyard scrambled away from the bones and flesh lying in gruesome collage. The ambulance attendants arrived to cover the crashed bloody body and drive it to the morgue.

10. Perhaps

Perhaps, if you are young, or old, or weird or deluded or unhappy enough, you're still wondering whatever became of The Apocalypse, that swoon, siren of our self-destructive youths? I'm not sure. I think it happened. And will it be followed by a reign of love? This, of course, is beyond my cognition, and perhaps entirely open in fact. Doesn't it depend? I have seen this, though, or thought it, and I think it is something like what Clay was trying to explain to me that time: the cosmos is first of all love. Love is the matrix, the cradle of the universe, and it is this circumambient amniotic love that you avail yourself of when you pray, if you pray, when you pray.

Me, my mother, my sister in Palm Springs in the early nineties.
We had recently moved from Chicago to California. I guess
we were missing the snow. Photo credit: my stepfather.

Taiyaba Husain was born in India and raised in California. She has an MFA in fiction from University of Michigan and a BA from UC Berkeley. She is a former Fulbright scholar to Mumbai, where she went to begin writing and researching her first novel. She currently lives in Los Angeles and teaches in the Writing Program at USC. "How You Respond to an Emergency" will be her first published story. You can connect with her on Twitter @TaiyabaHusain.

HOW YOU RESPOND TO AN EMERGENCY

Taiyaba Husain (signature)

Taiyaba Husain

Your mother comes into your room at dawn on a chilly fall morning. She wakes you up by roughly shaking your shoulder, which has only recently begun to heal after you'd dislocated it during a summer of swimming frustrated laps in your parents' backyard pool. You sit up in bed and wince. Then her face comes into focus, and you know that something is terribly wrong. Her eyes are great bowls of dust when she tells you the news that will change the shape of things forever.

You follow her out into the hallway, down the winding carpeted staircase and into the family room where, on your parents' big screen TV, you see the Footage. The Footage that your six-year-old niece at that very moment is also watching across the country, in Jersey City, where your sister, the ethnic studies professor, is running late to teach her morning class.

"Darling," your mother says. The word itself is a sentence. It is what she has always called you, and in her accent it sounds more like *dahling*. "Do you understand the significance of what is happening?"

And you don't understand. At all. "It's awful," you say somberly, because at least you understand that somberness is expected of you.

You move into the kitchen and fill the coffee pot. You reach for the newspaper, which your father has already read because he is up this early every morning. The front page is full of non-news, the most use-less stories ever written. Your gaze drifts outdoors, to the wisteria that is climbing up a trellis, to an errant star-shaped leaf that is falling into the pool, to the cargo train in the distance that moves day and night, back and forth, carrying things that you have catalogued in your imagi-nation since you were a child (heads of cabbage, bales of hay, lumber).

"Is now a good time to get on the freeway?" you wonder out loud.

"Darling, do you still want to go to this interview? With all that's happening, I'd like you home with me."

You've been home with her all summer, and what you want more than anything is to leave this house and start your adult life. True, the internship is unpaid and you'd need a loan from your parents to be able to move to the city. Still, you are young and hopeful enough to imagine that it would be hardly any time before your position as a gofer at Paramount Pictures morphed into an assistant director job. (And you would be lying if you said you hadn't already been practic-ing your Oscar speech.) "Yes," you tell her, as you run up the stairs to shower. "I want to go to my interview."

When you are ready, your mother walks you out to your car and packs the passenger seat with a picnic of fried egg and cheese sand-wich, a peeled tangerine, and a travel mug full of coffee. She slips a letter into your purse, and based on the smear of lipstick across her mouth, you know it's something she expects you to read before you go in for your interview. (You are familiar with such epistles, as they have appeared in your lunch box on the first day of school every year since you were old enough to read). After you have fastened your seat belt, your mother puts her hand on her head and rapidly murmurs the travel prayer, finishing by blowing into your face, as if spraying you with the breath of God Himself. As you drive up the hill, you see her receding figure framed against the palm trees, which sway in the Santa Ana winds.

Your sister, the ethnic studies professor, calls a week after the Event and asks to be put on speaker phone. You roll your eyes because she has always been this melodramatic, this hungry for attention. She tells you and your parents that earlier that morning, four men from the government had shown up at her door and taken away her husband. She cannot locate him, she does not understand what is happening. Her sentences are barely coherent. Your heart lurches because you can hear your niece crying in the background. You and your mother board a flight to Newark that night, and as you look out at the yellow patterned dots of the city that is so close, yet so out of your reach, you feel angry at your father. Why isn't *he* traveling to New Jersey? Why is it always your mother who has to handle the difficult things?

In Jersey City, your mother and sister are busy from morning to night. For the two weeks you are there, you pretend you are your niece's mother. You slice apples into crescents and carrots into sticks. You take her to her playgroup and go for long walks in the neighborhood, gaping at the autumnal landscape. Your niece is full of annoying questions, which you do your best to answer. You notice that she does not ask about her father. At home, you park her in front of the television and expect her to entertain herself while you try to work on a screenplay. You are still laboring over the first scene heading when she comes to you with her jack-o'-lantern smile. "Look," she says triumphantly. She has drawn an image of two gray buildings on fire, with stick-figure men and women tumbling out of burning windows. You gasp. You turn off the TV. You pull her close and tell her: "Don't draw that. Draw something else." Your niece frowns. She returns to the coffee table and you to your screenplay. When she comes back, you are contemplating your first line of dialogue. Your niece gives you a skeptical look, no tiny teeth in sight. She has drawn your name in red block letters. The bottoms of the letters are melting, dripping blood-like into a blue puddle in which red stick-figure bodies appear to be floating. You pat your niece on the head and ask if you can keep her drawings (whether for posterity or for psychological analysis, you will decide later). When you go to bed that night, you hear your sister's crying, your mother's familiar placating sounds. You shut your eyes. You are grateful that you are not anyone's mother.

Yet you are sufficiently impressed that even this far from home, your mother is so well organized. She is the one to call lawyers, to get in touch with congressmen. She is the one to wield the term "held incommunicado" in front of news reporters. She rouses so much rabble that you believe she is the reason your brother-in-law is eventually released from the city jail where he has been detained. When your sister brings him home, he is all in one piece, but he moves with the numbness of the bereaved. There are others, he tells you. Other similarly bearded, unfortunately named men still being held in windowless rooms. Your sister is no longer a quivering puddle. She calls for blood.

You leave the distressed family and return home to complete your own triad. After breakfast the next day, you agree to help your mother run some errands. She goes upstairs to get ready, and when she comes back down, she is wearing a hijab. You are aghast. Her dark sheets of hair, like black rain. Her one beauty. You tell her this, and she snorts. It's her face, she tells you, reminding you of all the marriage proposals that trickled in for her even after she had agreed to marry your father. You go looking for your father, who you hope will have an opinion on this. You find him outside, talking to his tomatoes. He takes the news with a shrug of his shoulders. He prefers husbandry to husbanding.

You disapprove of your mother's decision, yet you are undeniably curious, so you go with her to the bank, the drugstore, the gas station, Costco. You have never been so aware of yourself in public spaces. People turn their heads to stare at you. The bank teller moves robotically, as if your mother is a robber who has instructed him to fill a canvas bag full of money. At the drugstore, an elderly woman standing near you at the check-out snatches her Metamucil and chocolate chip cookies and shuffles away to wait in another line. In the parking lot at Costco, you see an open spot near the entrance, and you floor your accelerator. You almost bump noses with a champagne-colored Volvo. You and the other driver stare each other down, and then you see her eyes dart to your passenger seat. Your mother is waving the car in with generous movements of her arms. You move your hand to the gear shift and are about to acquiesce, but with a shriek of tires, the Volvo reverses and crashes into the car behind it.

The world is upended, you think. You were born just a few miles from this suburb and have lived here your entire life, yet in one after-noon, you have become a stranger in a strange land. On the way home, you pass by your mother's gym, which she contemplates with a twist of her mouth. "I won't wear hijab there," she says. "Can you imagine how ridiculous I'd look on a treadmill?"

As the days pass, your mother's resolve to wear her identity like a badge grows, much like her wardrobe, to which she adds scarves of all colors. She has always prayed five times a day but has never required this of you. But now she pops her head into your room at intermit-tent hours and prods you to join her. She quotes scripture on Taco Tuesdays. You overhear her on the phone, talking to aunts and cousins, and the conversation always turns to the Event, to its ramifications. The only way forward, your mother tells everyone, is to stay steadfast and true, to kill them with kindness. You have to explain to her that that probably isn't the best metaphor to use right now.

About a month after the Event, you go to a concert in the city with your best friend, a stoner who has been working as a bag clerk at the neighborhood grocery store since the summer. All you want is to get your mother's voice, her proselytizing, out of your head. But the hip-hop duo from Brooklyn who you have worshipped since you were seventeen years old has recently converted to Islam, and their lyrics are now rife with allusions to the Qur'an. You cringe because you totally get the allusions and because the duo takes so many breaks to talk about the Event. You feel bad for them because of what is hap-pening to their city, and also bad for yourself because even now, after everything you have seen, you still can't grasp its full significance.

On the ride home, your best friend lights a joint. He rolls down his window because although he is bold enough to light up anywhere, he is conscientious about your upholstery. The smell of weed mingles with a faint smell of manure that drifts over from the farmlands east of Orange County. You are listening to a famous deejay on the radio simulate the sounds of bombs dropping. He is fuming, calling for the heads of all those responsible for the Attacks. You are introduced for the first time to epithets like towelhead and sand nigger. Your best friend

Taiyaba Husain

reaches over and shuts off the radio. You glance at him, and even in
the dark, you can see that his eyes are glistening with tears. Your brow
furrows. You think back to your gofer interview, which had begun
with questions like: *What's it like to have such a famous last name? Were
you born here? Where does your family live?* You feel uneasy when you
think about how you answered those questions.

You don't get the internship. Your mother does not appear to be disappointed on your behalf. She asks if you would like to enroll in an
LSAT prep class. You tell her no. A few days later she asks if maybe
you'd like to do your PhD. Your scowl, for now, is enough to send her
away. You join your stoner friend bagging groceries that fall, dislocating
your shoulder two more times by the time Christmas rolls around. It
is weed that saves you from matricide.

As the world famous beaches light up with winter bonfires and the
shopping malls are filled with crazed mobs, you settle into a different
kind of season. You and your best friend sneak into the movies during the days and lie in the back of his pickup after your work shifts.
You gossip about your high school friends, who you are both still in
touch with. His finger lingers, sometimes, when he passes you a joint,
or he playfully taps his boot against yours. When this happens, you
pull away from him, curling your body into the shape of a question
mark, your expression to the sky of who you are, of what you know,
at that particular moment in time.

One day you hear your father's laugh. This is such a rarity that you
leave your bedroom and go downstairs to see what's happening. You
find him in the kitchen, pouring store-bought eggnog into glasses for
your gardener and his daughter. Come, he tells you. This is a celebration.
The gardener's daughter has just gotten early admission into Caltech.
Your father is as proud of this girl as he had been proud three years
earlier—when the gardener's older daughter had gotten into UCLA.
These girls, your father tells you now, are exceptionally gifted. He has
not seen this level of mathematical skill in any of the young people
he has met in this country. The girl beams. What your father is also

74   *Glimmer Train Stories*

celebrating, you know, is his decade-plus of tutoring the sisters. You are still not sure whether they have such great math prowess or whether they simply had the patience to sit through your father's lessons. In any case, you raise your glass and fake-smile at them. You sip your eggnog.

You go back to your room and climb into bed. You pull your knees into your chest and burrow under your comforter. It is still daytime, so patches of sunlight peek in, intruding on your mood. You shut your eyes stubbornly and wait for the sun to go down. When you were little, your father tried to teach you things, too. He took you to a water conservation exhibition that was held a few miles outside of the city, in a warehouse near an orange grove. There, you learned about your state's history. About the farmers and immigrants who worked the land, about its fault lines and water reservoirs. Your father taught you conservation in other ways, too. While other fathers probably stood in their children's doorways and said things like: "I'm not Thomas Edison, you know," yours said: "You're lucky. We didn't have electricity when I was growing up. When the sun went down, I took my books outside and did my homework underneath the street lamps."

That story—every time he told it—made you cry. And it drove you further from him. When you think back on it now, you wonder if it was intentional. If he somehow knew that sharing sad snippets of his third-world childhood would create a rift between you. You find it unfair that he worked hard to give you privileges and then resented you for having them. But as a child, you responded in the only way that made sense to you. You became the Light Bulb Nazi. You marched from room to room, shutting off unused lights, giving disapproving looks to perpetrators of conservation crimes. You spent your evenings under a comforter with a flashlight, reading. Your father didn't have much to say about this. And why would he? It's not like you were good at math or anything.

In the early spring, there is so much pollen in the air that your face swells up like an angry balloon. Your allergies are so bad that you take a day off work and drug yourself on antihistamines. The doorbell rings in the mid-afternoon, and you go downstairs to open the door. Your

Taiyaba Husain

sister is standing there, her hair pulled into a severe bun, dark glasses
hiding her eyes. Your niece is beside her, and when she sees you, her
eyes widen with delight. "There's luggage in the rental car," your sister
says as she brushes past you.

You fetch the bags, which are numerous, and go into the family
room. Your niece has wandered into the backyard to look for her
grandfather, and your mother and sister are standing in the kitchen.
Your sister removes her glasses, and in unison you and your mother gasp.
Your sister's left eye is swollen into the shape and color of a chocolate
donut. Below that, her lips are curled into a snarl.

Your father comes in carrying your niece. When he sees your sister,
he stops mid-stride, his jaw goes slack. Your niece is smiling, and you
think it's because she is unaware of the tension in the room. But then
she says: "Nana, we're going to live in your house now, okay?"

Your father remembers urgent work that needs to be done and dis-
appears into his office. You stick around, pretending to play with your
niece in the family room so that you can eavesdrop on your mother
and sister's conversation. "I always sensed that something wasn't quite
right about him," you hear your mother say. "You introduced us," your
sister replies incredulously. "Still," your mother says. She clucks her
tongue. Your sister is quiet for some time, and then she counters with
a whimper: "He says he's so sorry…" You know this tone of voice.
This is what your sister sounded like when you were children, when
she was pleading for permission to go to concerts and sleepovers and
overnight school trips. Back when she was breaking down barriers so
that you would have an easier go at adolescence. In those days, your
mother always gave in, but today, she is steadfast in her position. "You
need to leave him," she says.

The ambivalence in your sister's expression is heart wrenching. There
is a tragic elegance to a woman otherwise fiery and resolute who finds
herself at a crossroads. And you discover that you are not immune to
this brand of pathos. What does *not* surprise you, however, is that even
on a day like this, you have found a reason to be jealous of her. (You
are, after all, a younger sister. It's practically your duty to wade in a
bath of sibling rivalry.) But it is not your sister's dilemma that you envy.

76

It is the sense you have always had of her as being equal parts your mother's and your father's daughter. Like now, she is marching up to her old room without a moment's hesitation, without an ounce of shame. She is like a shoelace being expertly woven in and out of the holes on both sides of a shoe. You pick up a suitcase and follow her up the stairs. For now you say nothing. You will wait for that chocolate-doughnut bruise to heal.

Later, you manage to work into a conversation with her the expression about fish and visitors stinking after three days. You instantly regret it. You adore your niece, and, as your best friend reminds you, there is pleasure to be taken in not being the only fucked-up daughter still living at home. You have been spending a lot of time with him. He helps babysit your niece, so your sister likes him. Your mother even invites him to the Fourth of July barbecue she hosts every year. He shows up carrying a bouquet of flowers, and soon he is doing cannonballs in the pool and eating halal hot dogs. He does not complain once about celebrating a national holiday without alcohol. In the evening, you drive with your entire extended family in a caravan out to Huntington Beach to watch the fireworks. The kids swarm on the pier. The adults don sweaters and walk arm-in-arm. Your best friend brings his camera, and your mother asks if he will take a picture of your family. You pat down your windblown hair, and your sister licks her thumb to wipe a stain from your niece's cheek. Your mother fastidiously arranges all of you around her.

The photograph comes out better than a studio portrait. Each of you is smiling, each of you looks content. Your mother's turquoise-colored hijab stands out against the black sky, and a firecracker explodes above her head, making it look like she has donned one of those fantastic hats that Southern women wear to church. Your best friend buys a frame for the picture and presents it to your mother. She makes room for it on the fireplace mantel, and when he is gone, she says to you: "He loves you. You could do worse." How can you explain to her that it is not familiarity that you crave? That what you really want is a meet cute. Or, maybe ten or fifteen meet cutes.

Taiyaba Husain

You have known your best friend since elementary school, and instinct tells you that you both will survive this crush, as you have crushed on each other intermittently throughout your lives. He will always be there for you, you think one day at work, as you watch him load a watermelon and a toddler into a mini-van. When your shift ends, he tells you he has something he wants to show you. He drives you in his car across the parking lot. He shuts off the ignition and lights a cigarette. And as if you are at the movies, you sit and stare for a long time at the side exit to the gym.

Eventually your mother comes out. She is wearing black leggings and a mini-tee. Her hair is tied in a high ponytail, and her face is flushed from her workout. She stands for a full minute, looking into the distance toward the hills, as if she can spot your house from where she is. A man exits the gym and comes and stands behind your mother. He has blond hair, cropped corporate-like, and is wearing the signature purple polo shirt of the gym employees. He is holding a water bottle. He inches closer to your mother. You see the moment when she realizes he is there. Her body curves ever so subtly into him, and they stand there, like a vertical big spoon and little spoon. The man then reaches over your mother's shoulder, muscles moving like fault lines along his arms as he brings his water bottle to her mouth. You watch in bewilderment as your mother slurps from the bottle.

A few minutes later, he walks her to her car, and the way he pats the rear bumper as she drives away gives you the impression that this man has just smacked your mother's ass. You stare at the empty parking space as if there is a chalking of a dead man on the asphalt. Your best friend is smoking noisily. He clears his throat but says nothing. It is not his reaction to have, he seems to know.

"She's so *old*," is all you can think to say.

Your best friend snorts. "I got news for you, kid. Your mom's hot. She always has been."

The most obvious explanation is that the man is your mother's trainer. This is confirmed the next day when you casually inquire about the muscles that have begun to pop up in her upper arms like little sand crabs. For how long? About six months. The next day, you park your car behind some bushes that cordon off the gym from the crafts store adjacent to it. You see them together again. This time they are laughing, bringing their heads in close together. You hold your breath, waiting for them to touch. You wonder if your world will explode if they do. Soon, you are on regular stake-outs, jotting down notes like a police detective, measuring the distance between your mother's body and the man's. When you start going through her phone, your best friend tells you that you've crossed a line. It all seems fairly innocent, he says with a shrug. You narrow your eyes. What if it was your mother, you ask him. At this he starts to laugh. He laughs so hard that you begin to feel offended on his mother's behalf.

One day the man sends your mother a text message, and you finally learn his name. You roll the blunt syllables around in your mouth but cannot bring yourself to speak them out loud. The message includes a photo of a sweating, over-sized Frappuccino, and the accompanying note says: "On our next cheat day?" That entire evening your mother floats around the house like a delirious balloon. She responds to the text with a smiley face.

You look at the message again and again. You recognize the coffee shop in the photo. It is miles from your home, miles from the gym. The idea of your mother driving that far to get a cup of coffee is more distressing to you than anything in recent memory. By the next morning, you have made a plan. You own no workout clothes, so you swipe a pair of your mother's leggings. Slipping into them, you feel like you are dressing for a play. If you donned a black scarf, you would basically look like a cat burglar.

You can count on one hand the times you have been inside a gym, so you are surprised that the smell—of salt and sports merchandise—is familiar to you. The place is capacious and so brightly lit that you have to fight the urge to use your hand as a visor. You walk up to the counter and get the attention of a woman wearing a name tag imprinted with the words Relationship Manager. The woman has arms like thighs, and while she talks to you, you get the sense that she has skipped a meal and needs a fix. She says she would like to give you a tour of the weight rooms, the cardio machines, the swimming pool, the basketball court, and the locker rooms before asking you to sign anything. You point to a blond head that rests on purple-shirted shoulders. "I want him to show me," you say. The woman calls the man over and gives him a knowing look. He grins. He looks like a Ken doll—he is probably used to such requests.

The tour begins, oddly, with a stop at the manual weight scales just outside the locker rooms. You hoist yourself onto the scale, and the man fidgets with the numbers and asks you about your weight loss goals. It has not occurred to you that you should have such a goal. You tell him a number that you think would make an anorexic orgasm, and the man's eyes pop in his head. He clears his throat and changes the subject. As you move about the expanse of the gym, you ask him detailed questions. You think that by getting him to talk, you will be able to gauge just how much of a shallow meathead he really is. To your disappointment, he is knowledgeable and fairly articulate. He is working on a bachelor's degree in nutrition and kinesiology, he tells you. He hopes when he is done to work as a nutritionist for the federal government. He stops for a moment to say hello to an elderly woman on an elliptical machine who is drenched in sweat. "Remember to hydrate!" he calls out cheerily. The man sees you frowning and takes this to mean that you are intimidated by the Skynet-like machines that populate the gym. They also offer aerobics classes, he tells you. The membership even comes with a complimentary session with a trainer. Ahh, you think. This is how they get you.

You agree to the terms of the contract and begin to fill out the paperwork. When you are done, he asks you to stand against a white wall so that he can take a picture of you for your membership I.D. At this, you inhale deeply so that the effort straightens your spine. You are terribly un-photogenic, you tell him. The man laughs. "It's okay," he says. "Think of it as a driver's license photo. No one's really going to interrogate it unless you do something wrong." You shake your head no. You've taken maybe one photo in your life that you think you look good in, you tell him. You reach into your purse for an envelope and hand it to him. You watch him closely as he extracts and then examines your family portrait from the Fourth of July. The amused smile falters. Disbelief skitters across the man's face, and, for just a moment, you feel a stab of guilt about what you are doing. "Can you crop me out of this one?" you ask him.

His lips form a thin line. He processes your paperwork in silence. When he asks how you would like to pay the fee, you hand him your mother's credit card. As you walk away, you feel your knees begin to quiver. Outside, you reach out your hand and collapse against a wall. You lean and breathe, waiting for your heart rate to calm. You look out at the hills, toward your house, where your sister is probably in the bathroom, crying into a hand towel, where your father is probably looking for new places to hide. Before you get in your car and return home, you toss your membership card into a trash can.

Fifteen years after 9/11, you are with your sister and niece at a costume shop on Hollywood Boulevard—blocks from the shitty studio where you lived in your mid-twenties—trying on wigs. Your mother, who has long since given up her hijab, has said just yesterday, after a particularly fitful vomiting session, that perhaps it's time for her to start wearing a wig. Your niece is twenty-one now and funny and willowy. She dons an ear-length sandy brown wig, which rests on her head like a corn husk. She wiggles her fingers in the air and prances. "Who am I, Mom? Who am I, Khala? I'll give you a hint. I'm *very* well educated, I'm *really* rich, and I have a *gigantic* penis."

The salesman smiles. You laugh out loud. Your sister lunges forward and snatches the wig off your niece's head. "Is this funny to you, darling? Do you have any respect? Do you have a clue as to what's happening right now?"

You see tension enter your niece's shoulders like an arrow. And you panic because what you want more than anything is for her to feel at ease with herself, to master her improv-ready body. You are afraid of all the things that could happen to take away her self-confidence. Your niece does not talk back to her mother. She leaves the store and for a few moments paces on the sidewalk. Then, in full view of you both, she lights a cigarette. You watch her with an inevitable mixture of tenderness and dread. You wish for her jack-o'-lantern smile, but you know that is just a memory from long ago.

Life is different now. The Diaz sisters have graduated from UCLA and Caltech; they have children of their own. Their father has expanded his business into construction. You and your husband live in the suburbs of Los Angeles. You write for a show on Nick Jr. that is always on the verge of being cancelled, and he works for an insurance company. He still smokes weed, but now he gets it from a medical dispensary. "Ohh, my aching back," he says to you with a wink whenever he lights up. Your sister left Jersey City long ago. She now teaches at the university from which your niece has just graduated. Your sibling rivalry has been in remission since the news of your mother's illness. Neither of you has been able to adjust. You are constantly rushing home, not to help but to seek comfort. It comes as a surprise to you both when your father steps in to parent you. He is late but not too late.

The world is different, too. Well, same same but different. Your country is still at war—but now with more nations, with more abstract nouns. Your politicians are in a boxing ring, taking cheap, below-the-belt shots at one other. They argue about women's bodies, about assimilating refugees. There is even talk of deporting people like you. Your state faces an increasingly brutal natural emergency, yet it pretends all is well by borrowing water from a neighbor. This manner of living does not seem sustainable to you, so you do your part. You go to another water conservation seminar with your father, and the next day he calls Mr. Diaz to make plans to have his pool demolished. You take a similar measure at your house, wincing as you watch men rip grass from the earth and convert your backyard into a concrete patio.

Your mother worries about the waste, too. She recycles dishwater and lets vomit simmer in the toilet bowl. You worry about the moments you have wasted, about how long it takes you to make sense of things. Mostly, you worry about how much time you have left with her. You know that you should be focusing on the present, but the past has become precious, and you mine it each day for meaning. You are looking for something substantial to hold on to when she is gone.

82

If you fail to find it, it is because you reach beyond your capacity, far back, into a time before you were born. You try to recall your mother's entire life. You see her as a child in another country, you envision her as a young bride newly arrived in America. You wonder about the things in life that have made her happy.

It occurs to you that in all these years you have never spoken to her about the gym trainer. Though you have thought about him. He resides in that part of your mind that holds the memories you try to forget. But lately, the man has become more present than past. One day when you are visiting your mother and it is just the two of you, you bring him up. You say his name to see if you can recapture that light in her eyes that you wrote about in your notebook. It is still there, you see. She has not forgotten, and you are afraid that she has not forgiven. You want to say something. But you are not sure if the past can be adjudicated. And even if it can, can it be done with the words that come to you now—these words that seem too small, too feeble to bear the weight of all that you have to say?

The author sometimes thinks he should have stuck to tempera paint and spools.

Jeffrey Rotter is the author of two novels, *The Unknown Knowns* (Scribner) and *The Only Words That Are Worth Remembering* (Metropolitan). His fiction and nonfiction have appeared in the *Boston Review*, *Oxford American*, *New York Times*, and elsewhere. He teaches fiction at Manhattanville College.

IN A LAKE HOUSE

Jeffrey Rotter

1.

The other night I drove too fast. I pushed the Buick LeSabre through scrub-pine blackness toward my father's lake house, racing, and I thought of them. White men like me, in basements like mine, listening. I thought of what they heard. A low complaint from the hollows of the earth. I drove faster and thought of Nora lying alone in Newberry Memorial. Dying again. I drove faster.

When they question me about why I had to inflict so much damage to set things right, I will not offer a very sensible explanation. Only that a home is so easy to take down.

2.

My father died in prison and left me his lake house, which was a net positive. But he also left me a boat and several thousand in debt, which meant my half-sister had to get a paying job. After she went into remission and before it came back, Nora worked at the Gruber's Lawn &Nursery on Route 391, not the original location in Lexington.

Two hours before Nora woke up, I would rise to brew coffee and boil oatmeal in Daddy's Revere Ware saucepan. Her diet required that she eat sixteen ounces (uncooked) daily. She turned vegetarian after the scare. I joined her when I hit a deer with the LeSabre. The long face screaming through my windshield, the grip of a stranger's hands around its tawny throat, the pinched-off scream and the soy-based burgers thereafter: it is one thing to strike a living thing intentionally with your car, another to do so in error.

After breakfast I would drive Nora to Gruber's so that I might enjoy the use of the Buick for the remainder of the day. All the way down 391 she listened to cassettes. I listened to her voice softly repeating. She was learning Spanish because a number of her colleagues originated in Mexico. These were good people who did not ask too much from our country, only to work and shelter themselves, only to provide for their children, or so Nora told me.

On Thursdays they laid out a potluck lunch for which there is a specialized Mexican term. Brown women arranged paper plates and pitchers of bright native drinks. Their men lit Sternos under chafing dishes, sent prayers to Jesu Cristo. My sister assured me that many of the offerings were meatless, though Gail of Gail's Whole World Grocery in Columbia cautions against the widespread use of lard in foreign cooking.

Nora is skillful with azaleas and with people, and there was never enough time in the day to admire her, even on weekends. She started out perfect. If she had a flaw it was the brown mark just above her pelvic bone, left side. Some mistook it for a tattoo of a candle, never mind the fact that a brown candle would be a pretty uninspired idea for a tattoo. It is in fact a birthmark, not her fault nor her choice. At night I would slip into her room and peel back her camisole to study the candle. At times it seemed I could light its wick with my eyes, burn it nightly down to nothing so that my Nora would be perfect at last. When we were kids a boy across the cove made a joke out of it, until Nora got shy and started wearing a one-piece. Then came the surgery and its two long scars and now she won't wear a swimsuit at all.

3.

Every Friday after I dropped Nora at Gruber's I drove down to Columbia to buy groceries at Gail's, oats mostly. One day about six months back I hung around the store to chat with the owner. She had so many interesting things to say about plumbing and celery fiber, subjects about which I know next to nothing. New ideas energize me.

Gail complained about the wings place next door. Their food waste was clogging up the sewer main. When the pipes backed up her basement stank of poultry, of blue cheese dressing. As a business owner she was paying for her neighbors' insoluble diet. In a perfect world, she said, there would be separate plumbing systems for good people and jerks. "Check it out for yourself," she said.

I had no pressing matters to attend to that afternoon, so I agreed. Alonzo kept an eye on the register while we walked downstairs. Gail was right: a distinct odor of dressing haunted the basement. Also hot sauce. Celery.

"Come back at Happy Hour," she said. "You'd think the rotting corpse of Texas Pete himself was buried in my wall! Makes a godawful racket." Gail urged me to press an ear against the wall. "Hear that?"

A voice swam through the masonry like moisture, a baritone belch. "That's water," she explained, "pushing its way through the celery fiber."

I had never felt sorry for water before, or not as intensely as I did at that moment. It groaned, supplicated, begged for passage like a peasant at an armed checkpoint. The water only wanted what was rightfully hers, the right to flow. I listened, anger flaring in my chest, until my ear went numb from the cold cement.

Gail perched on a tofu bucket. She rubbed her teeth with a finger until they squeaked. Despite her advanced age I found Gail to be sexually beautiful. Before opening the grocery she was a lawyer for Housing and Urban Development. On the register she kept a photo of Prior Gail: furtive in power suit and heels, sculpted hair like a catamaran, a woman of action. She retired into a natural lifestyle, adopting a hands-off approach to everything: teeth, bosom, finance. She wore her hair in a careless braid, silver and brittle as old rope. Even store hours were determined by the I Ching. Everything seemed to work out for the best and she regretted so much time spent "channeling chance."

"It's like that water," she said. "Gotta let it flow."

In addition to the Whole World Grocery, she ran a Libertarian book club and taught classes in Arbitrary Yoga and Mindful Neglect. Her sexual partner was a senior at Dreher High School. His name was Rob and his parents were said to be cool with it.

I told Gail it didn't sound much like plumbing to me; it sounded like a complaint. The natural rights of water contravened by inferior matter. Gail narrowed her eyes as if I'd blown smoke into her face. "Tectonic Sonorities," she said.

I shrugged.

"Don't tell me you never heard of the Tectonic Sonorities!"

I hadn't heard of much and was compelled to admit my ignorance. She said read Blavatsky, read Guénon. D'Avola. Old-sounding names. She fished a one-hitter from a carton of felt tampons, packed the bowl, and lit up.

"In," she said. "Tense shit. The Earth produces audible frequencies, a seven-tone scale that repeats itself on a ten-thousand-year cycle. Vedic scriptures acknowledge this. Geologists have no plausible explanation. Theologians are divided." She offered me a hit but I prefer to remain clearheaded in the presence of the esoteric.

I asked Gail if it might just be volcanoes.

She smiled. Volcanoes.

"If you want to learn more," she said, "ask Tony."

4.

That afternoon Nora caught a ride home from the nursery. When she walked in I had been in the basement for two hours, listening to the floor.

"Hobie, for the last time: if you can't remember to pick me up, you can't use the LeSabre!" She was hollering from the half-bath at the top of the stairs: "And how come the damn toilet won't flush?" I heard the impotent clink of the handle, a soft curse. "Did you space on the water bill again?"

I found her in the kitchen, rooting through a pile of circulars and unopened bills. "I left a twenty right here on the counter. Tell me you didn't spend it on boat magazines." Nora is the opposite of Gail; she worries.

"I had to turn off the water," I said, pausing to give the lie a buffer of credibility: "Leak under the sink."

"Told you this dump was falling apart. Your dad never lifted a finger around here, did he?" She sounded angry and I wondered if something had happened at work with the Mexicans.

"Speaking of lifting fingers," she said without hope. "Alan's hiring at the nursery."

"Is that right?" I said without interest.

"Felipe had to go back to Guatemala. His mother died."

Through the screen door I saw my bass boat straining against its tarp. A trailered boat is a jailed man. It wanted bass, yearned to be on the water idling over a largemouth. But fishing would have to wait. Over the winter a hairline crack had developed in its hull. Lubricant leaked down the side of the gear housing. I would have to replace the seals and buy some fresh epoxy.

"You might just be filling in for a few months," Nora said.

I'm sorry to say there was an air of resentment in my reply. I said I was not some replacement for an illegal. I knew that Alan Gruber spoke harshly to his Latin Americans, and I could not imagine how I might respond if he took a tone with me.

"The nursery doesn't really suit my temperament."

Nora knows I am perfectly capable of work, but I refuse to grovel. Revenue is generated by an imbalance of power, by the tension therein, by stooping and wearing coveralls so that you reduce yourself to a brown parcel with hands, a delivery of service. I am no parcel.

She tossed the circulars in the air and left the kitchen before they hit the floor.

5.

It was the following Friday, at Gail's Whole World Grocery, when I worked up the nerve to ask about Tectonic Sonorities. Tony was pouring cracked wheat into a bulk bin. Dust hung thick in the air, and inside it, like Peter O'Toole braving a sandstorm, stood Tony Matterhorn. He's thrillingly tall and broad in the chest such that an apron hangs on him like a necktie. His brushcut hair is blond and dense. The tattoo on his leathered neck is real yet so blurred with age that it resembles a hickey.

Tony was the first to speak: "You look at me and think *heart-attack survivor*, right?" he asked without looking up.

Jeffrey Rotter

I said no, I don't go by appearances. I knew he'd come from Munich, Germany, in the 1950s to join a nudist colony by Myrtle Beach, but it was difficult to picture him naked. He patted the bottom of the bag and rolled it into a tight log. I watched him swing a fifty-pound bag of brown rice onto one shoulder like it was a pillow.

"I bench two forty," he said.

Tony was no joke. I once saw him get out of his truck with a .45 and chase a fry cook into the wings place. From inside I heard pots, pans, shouting, and out walked Tony carrying a tub of frozen chicken wings. He stood in the middle of the dirt parking lot crying. From this anecdote I learned two things about Tony: he owns a firearm and he cares.

"I've been talking to Gail," I said.

He dropped the rice. "You from immigration?"

I had to laugh. I'm not *from* anywhere. "She said I ought to ask you about the Tectonic Sonorities."

Tony clapped a hand on my arm. The next day a bruise would show every joint on his five fingers. "Don't talk that hippy shit in my presence." His voice had the menace of engineering, of railway clocks.

I said I only talked what people told me to talk.

"Gail," he whispered fiercely, "knows *nothing* about these matters. With her Jewish books and her…New Age music! Nothing!"

With that he strode to the produce area and stared at the ceiling. A full minute passed before he returned. "Okay," he said. "Okay." His lips worked like he was making a calculation. Then: "What you mean to say is *Anleitung*. The voice from inside the earth is the Anleitung. The Instructions from Thule."

All this time he'd been looking me squarely in the penis, which I found unsettling.

"Have you ever slapped a woman for eating beans?" I asked, just to keep the conversation going.

He shook his head once, almost like a twitch: "No!"

"Or just held her in an uncomfortable position for a few minutes until she admitted she'd done wrong?"

I told him a story:

Certain beans fall within a spectrum of tolerance; these are gener-

IN A LAKE HOUSE

ally your limas, navy, field peas. One evening Nora came home from Gruber's smelling distinctly of pinto beans. She said here is how you say *cable bill* in Spanish, here is how you say *vacuum cleaner*, here is how you say *disability check*. I decided I would go out and run over a dog with my car.

It is one thing to hit a dog by accident, but to drive through the county looking for one is not easy. After two hours I had seen only one Rottweiler mix and a Welsh corgi that would not be lured from its yard by any amount of whistling. Eventually I had to gas up. As soon as I dipped the squeegee in its box of blue cleaner I knew it was time to go home and apologize.

"For what?" Nora was in bed reading a novel about gaijin, white shoguns, black vice presidents, Asian quarterbacks.

I said never mind, it was nothing, and retired to my own bedroom.

When I told Tony this story he smiled like I'd just gotten off a plane, like he had been waiting at the terminal to greet me. "You are okay," he decided.

I decided to find him okay, too. Even if he was German.

He sifted a handful of tabbouleh through his fingers. When his hand was empty he scooped again, and then repeatedly, as if the act had meaning. As if I were the tabbouleh or time was the tabbouleh or a white shogun was eating tabbouleh with Asian quarterbacks. I wondered if Gail knew he handled the dry goods like this.

"I think I heard it," I said. "That sound. Down in my basement. I turned off the water main and everything."

Tony stopped sifting.

"Sure you have," he replied. "You can hear it. I can hear it." He slapped his chest. "Because we are pure."

Alonzo came through with a push broom. I started to speak, but Tony raised the hand of silence. We watched Alonzo maneuver a ridge of sesame seeds into the produce area. Tony pulled me closer and whispered:

"*Because we are white and we are pure.*"

"When I press my ear to the floor," I said (now I was whispering as well), "I hear a moaning sound, like if you slowed down a porno."

"The Anleitung resonates below thirty hertz," said Tony. "A frequency

91

designed for Hyperborean ears, organs that are attuned to Vedic verse, to the Indo-German tongue."

I said that made a lot of sense.

He wasn't finished: "The Anleitung sends instructions from the leaders of Thule, lost city of the Aryan race, how we are to bring about an end to the Lemurian Age." Tony glanced around as if Lemurians might be lurking nearby.

"What's a Lemurian?" I asked.

He nodded toward produce. Alonzo squatted with a dustpan. He shot me the "you got it" finger. I shot it back. Now we both had it. I liked Alonzo except for his being a Lemurian, which I hadn't known until just then.

"The story of Man is more complex than your historians would have you believe," said Tony. I wondered if they had a different history where he came from.

I had so many questions, so Tony loaned me a book. The title was *Clarion Call of Thule*. I brought it home to read in the basement. I learned that the North Pole used to be near Delaware. When it shifted, a White Arctic Race called Hyperboreans headed down to India where they came up with Hindu and computers before moving to Germany. Some remained behind in a subterranean city called Thule, reachable by a global cave system. Tony's book had so much documentation that it is surprising more people don't know about this stuff.

I was at that time a first-year Christian Business major at Newberry College in Newberry. *Clarion Call of Thule* was a real eye opener. My geology professor (science elective) had taken great pains to show how fossils couldn't be more than six thousand years old, but here were whole cities ten times that.

When we were kids Nora started staying at the lake house on summer weekends while our mother worked at the hospital. I showed her how to dive for bottles, how to tell the ones that had been pitched in from boats from the ones that floated up from the flooded towns beneath the lake. Leaphart, Boyleston, Lorick's Ferry. One year Nora made a boyfriend across the cove. She was the one who missed out because that summer I found the best bottles ever.

6.

Tony drove out from Columbia to help me set up. He had taken a Wednesday off from work so I knew this was important. Another man followed in a Datsun pickup with a drilling rig hitched to the back. "Clayton Dowly," Tony whispered, as if his name belonged to a saint. "He is in possession of sensitivities that are beyond belief."

Clayton did not strike me as the sensitive type. Although he was slight of build, he appeared to have stolen the head and hands from a much larger and harder man. The tires on his sport truck were big enough for a tractor trailer. I watched with interest as he slipped off his boots. His socks, neatly folded, were stashed in his glove box. He rubbed a white ointment on the bottoms of his feet, and only then did he step out of the truck.

He clicked on a fanny pack stuffed with little orange flags on stiff wire. Without asking permission Clayton paced my yard. The noises he made were froggy and dissatisfied. Tony shifted uneasily. I began to worry. It had been a lot of trouble driving up here, taking a whole day off work. What if the sounds had all been my imagination? Then I remembered: I have no imagination. Tony nudged me, jerked his head in Clayton's direction. Beside the half-submerged window that let into my basement, he had paused. I watched him close his eyes, grind the balls of his feet in the dirt, and plant a flag.

"Right, then," said Clayton, after he had planted two flags between my azaleas and the basement wall. "That's that."

I walked over and stuck out my hand: "Hobie."

He removed about a dozen silver rings and slipped them in the pockets of his jeans. "Only two holes?"

Tony nodded. He was anxious to see the basement so I showed him downstairs. We moved a cooler aside to make room and he lay down on the floor. For several minutes I watched him inch-worm around the room, ear pressed to the floor. The act was borderline obscene, long buttocks rising and falling as he scoured the floor. Suddenly he stopped and, removing a carpenter's pencil from his pocket, made a swift X on the concrete. When he stood to survey his work, his yellow coveralls were dusted white. Four X's indicated key points across the floor, the locations for piezoelectric contact microphones.

"Strong signal," Tony said with German enthusiasm.

I felt as if I'd gotten an A without even doing my homework. "Thanks!" From outside we heard the squeal of a diesel generator and the hydraulic pulse of Clayton's driller. Again, I worried; the guys were putting forth a great deal of effort. This had better pan out.

"While Clayton gets started, I will help you assemble the gear." It was too late to call things off now. I couldn't exactly tell Tony not to bother. I have always held that eventual disappointment is better than an immediate letdown.

The geology department at Newberry College kept an array of mics and cables in a storeroom that wasn't entirely locked at all hours. A few days earlier, before unenrolling myself from the institution, I'd checked out four piezo crystal transducers, a pair of hydrophones, and two hundred meters of cable. To this array I contributed my own Bogen six-channel mixer and a Pioneer dual seven-band equalizer. The TEAC reel-to-reel officially belonged to Nora's ex-boyfriend, but he wasn't coming back, not after she got sick. My sister tells me that indigenous Mexicans developed their own musical systems. Tony agreed: strong evidence for links between Hyperborea and the Aztecs. But the ones Nora worked with weren't that kind of Mexican.

Before they left, Tony made a speech, the most consecutive words I had heard him speak, and apparently scripted in advance. He thanked me on behalf of Hyperborea, our fallen nation. On behalf of Thule, its vanished capital. He assured me that I was not alone: white men like me lay in basements and cellars all across the piedmont and coastal plain, each with his own quarter-inch rig to take dictation from deep in the Earth.

"Yours is a brotherhood that labors while others sleep or take business classes or draw a paycheck. You lie on bare subflooring, slabs that coolly sweat despite the heat, to drop hydrophones into boreholes, to reconfigure breadboards, to thread tape around a capstan!

"You escape the world's notice," he said. "The notice of wives and of children, because you are of little consequence and do not complain. Several of you are unmarried. The Anleitung will not be heard by a single set of ears, but by many companionable sets listening in concert!"

He wanted me to know that the work would be lonely, long, that sacrifices may be asked of me that seem strange or excessive. (I had no idea.) Our reward, he said, would be the gratitude of an oppressed race. "Hobie, when transmission is confirmed by the Council of Munich and the Fourth Degree Intimates interpret its Hyperborean counsel—" He gripped my shoulders. "—a New Cycle will begin! The Lemurian Ascendancy will be *no more!*"

Clayton said damn right.

I was deeply moved. I felt that I was a part of something. Or that I had always been a part of something and was just now being called on to save it.

By the time Nora returned from Gruber's, Daddy's old workbench groaned with hi-fi gear. I was in the driveway spraying out mixing tubs with a hose. My jeans were soaked up to the knees. I was sunburned and splotched with cement. "What the hell did you get into?" she asked.

Lying to family is never easy, but it's even harder when lying runs in the family. My old man never spoke a valid word to his wife or my mother, who overlapped chronologically.

"You tell her it was the County come out here." That was Clayton's advice. "Nobody questions the County."

I asked if this came up a lot. Were people often compelled to lie about his boreholes? Clayton replaced his rings, then, spitting across his hand, he polished them against his pants. He did one hand, then the other, watching me while I watched him.

Nora didn't appear to be buying it. I had to think fast. "They do these mineral surveys every five years," I said. "For assessment purposes and radon." I offered a variety of explanations, but the more reasons I gave the less she seemed to believe me. I followed her into her bedroom where she started changing out of her work clothes.

"Oh, come on!" she shouted, pushing the door closed.

"I am definitely telling you the truth, Nora." I wedged a foot in the door. "You should have seen the drill rig the guy used. His head was like…" I showed her the size of Clayton's head with my hands.

"No, I mean come on: get the heck out of my room so I can get changed!"

"He capped off the holes so you won't even notice once the mon-key grass comes back."

"Oh, for shit's sake!" I saw what she was looking at: my foot. The one wedged painfully between door and frame. "Really, Hobie. Wipe your damn feet before you come traipsing through the house."

My tube socks were stiff with clay. Behind me an orderly set of red prints led from the garage door to Nora's bedroom. I'd never known that I took such mincing steps and was ashamed to see them.

A man ought to stride. Daddy had shown me that. "Stride, you pug, you poodle, stride!" Only once, when a man from the dealership paid a visit, did I see my father walk in a manner unbecoming of a man. Don was his name and he toured our rooms like he owned the lake house. Daddy kept pace in little doggie steps saying it isn't here, Don; I left it back in the sales office. I'm telling you, Don, I turned this place upside down and it sure ain't here.

Don stood at the window. He looked out on our driveway where the crape myrtles bloomed and honeybees paid their respects. He turned and, planting hands on hips, stretched his yellow knit shirt tight across his stomach. I was only a child, thrilled by the capacity of Don's belly button, by the small blue ink stain at the bottom of one front pants pocket as he undid his fly and pissed a circle on the carpet.

Daddy followed Don to the door through marshy shag carpet.

"Think you're Lee Iacocca!"

"Think you're Henry Ford!"

"Thinks he's some Arab sheik can walk into my house, piss on the rug, and drive a man's Lincoln right out of his own driveway."

Early the next morning my father drove his old beater up to New-berry and ran over a man at the Shell station. He would have gotten out of jail after three years if he hadn't died in two.

Nora closed her bedroom door. I stripped off my socks, climbed in the LeSabre, and took a drive.

7.

From eight a.m. to five p.m. Monday through Thursday, while Nora worked at Gruber's, I used the Pioneer equalizer to sweep the spectrum for peaks until the most resonant frequencies emerged from each of my six contact points. The Anleitung hovers around 30 hertz, scraping the lower threshold of human hearing. Even when I sped up the tape to raise the mean frequency to 140 hertz, the voice was mournfully low. Desperate and low. Imagine an opera baritone waking up in a sealed coffin. Sometimes I thought it was saying *Aowumm* or maybe *Allo-oun*. At other times I heard *Oooowauwaumn* or *Waaoo-oamum*. It was a complaint, a plea for preservation that to my ears pleaded for my own survival, a complaint that was my complaint.

First thing every Friday, after I dropped her at the nursery, I would drive to Gail's to deliver Tony a fresh reel of recordings. This routine continued for three weeks during which he greeted me with growing zeal. I was doing good work, he assured me. Good excellent work. The mixes were outstanding. My tape labeling system very helpful.

On Friday he pulled me into the bulk aisle. "The Gessellschaft has been monitoring transmissions across the piedmont with curious results," he said, covering his voice with the sound of pouring yeast flakes. "There appears to be a change in the syntax, slight but significant." With my permission he hoped to send the reels to Munich for a proper translation from Sanskrit.

"Please, Tony," I said, pitching in with a sack of red lentils. "I would be honored."

"I want you to know something." Tony laid a hand on my chest. Our bodies were touching. "If these recordings meet with approval in Munich—and I feel confident that they will—Munich is certain to ask for a more substantive commitment from you. Will you be ready?"

"Sure," I said. "Is there anything more I can do now?"

Actually, there was.

8.

All weekend I was nervous about how Munich would judge my tapes. And then I decided that my anxiety was only a form of energy. This was serious business and what felt like terror might simply be the polar flow of confidence through my system, a cellular counterpart to the Anleitung itself. By Wednesday I was back to being nervous. I burned

Nora's oatmeal and by the time a second batch was ready she had to carry it to work in an empty peanut butter jar.

"Nora," I said, screwing on the lid, carefully wiping the outside clean with a damp paper towel. "Do you mind if some friends come out on Friday?"

"Oh, Hobie! You met somebody?"

"Nora." She knew how to hurt me, especially when she had no intention of doing so.

"I'm sorry. It's only that you never mention anybody."

"It's just a guy from Whole World Grocery."

She squeezed my shoulder. "I think that would be so fun for you to make a new friend! I can make you boys dinner!"

She smiled all the way to the car. I could tell she was about to overdo it.

"Say." Nora sat back heavily and looked at me. An unwelcome idea percolated behind her lips. "How about you join us this Thursday for potluck?" A guy my age named Sonny was looking for a fishing partner. Nora had told him about my bass boat. As long as I wore a clean shirt I'd do fine. I wouldn't even have to say much.

She touched the cassette player and a voice said pueblo, ciudad, país. Was Sonny a Mexican name? All the way to Gruber's I thought of Leaphart, of Boyleston and Lorick's Ferry: good white towns. Had they made the ultimate sacrifice so that foreign nationals could fish for crappie, shell crackers, and cats?

On Thursday I dropped Nora at Gruber's and continued on to the Pig to buy dessert, a carton of Swiss Rolls and paper plates. I will not be outdone at a potluck by resident aliens. When I pulled up in the nursery parking lot, the ladies were laying out a picnic table in the shade of the crape myrtle section. Oscillating sprinklers ticked out their measure of water and the air smelled brightly of peat. They looked up when my tires scrubbed the gravel, three ladies, brown and broadly grinning. One woman drew her clapped hands to her chest as if to say her heart had been warmed by my presence.

A flowered plastic sheet covered the table. On top of that stood a crock pot and two or three foil chafing dishes. There was one pitcher of something red, another of something milky. One lady arranged a pink bowl in the center, just so, then grinned as if she'd tied a bonnet on a baby. The paper sack from the Pig occupied the passenger seat. I regarded the Swiss Rolls with disdain, a father to his ungainly son on the first day of Pop Warner football.

Nora emerged from the shrubs with a man who must have been Sonny. He was dressed in coveralls, wore a white tennis visor, and picked at a spot on his chest. I thought he might be touched in the head—Gruber's is known for employing special cases—but when he looked up I could see he wasn't touched, he was cool. Too cool. Or so he thought. One word was printed on the crown of his visor: Rock.

Nora gently turned Sonny to face the Buick. She pointed at the top of Sonny's head and then mime-cast an invisible fishing rod toward me. Because she neglected to press her elbow firmly to rib cage she completely botched the release. Worse yet, her follow-through lacked conviction.

Sonny appeared satisfied. He followed her imaginary lure over the roof of the car and into the ornamental grasses. He moved in behind my half-sister to walk her through a second cast, gently immobilized her arm so that the movement flowed through her wrist. Although Sonny's technique was sound it meant his own arm was pressed to my sister's bosom. The LeSabre was still running, so I put it in drive. I spun the wheel to line up my hood ornament with a chafing dish.

Tony had said if I ever needed help with the Mexican situation at Gruber's, he and Clayton were at my disposal. I couldn't tell if this was a situation where I would need backup, I just knew Sonny and Nora were walking toward the car and I was upset. He draped an arm on the roof and slipped one hand through my window. I took it but did not say my name.

"Nora tells me you have a nice boat, man," said Sonny, looking all around the interior of my car like the boat might be in my back seat. I suppose he must have been high on grass. I thought about how Clayton would have acted, had he been in the car. He would step out with his knife and walk barefoot around the picnic table, planting little orange flags in the chafing dishes. Tony owned a .45 and had already used it to shame a fry cook. He would emerge from the ornamental grasses holding the pistol loosely at his side. Sonny would back away from my car, palms up: "Hey, man, take it easy. I didn't touch his sister, it's el verdadio." Then it would be my turn. "Who wants an English lesson?" I'd ask, calm and polite, as I strode toward the picnic table. The ladies would stop grinning, set down their Sterno cans, and listen up.

"When a group of three or more shares the responsibility of a lunch or dinner, we in America call it a *potluck*."

"Or occasionally *smorgasbord*," Tony would say, and I'd have to allow him that for being from Germany.

I told Sonny my boat was a Bass Cat XL. I said I was about to replace the seals. Probably get her out on the water this weekend, weather permitting. My eyes were fixed on the Buick hood ornament, on those three shields framing a distant Mexican casserole.

He whistled low and sweet. "Sweet boat, man! Same one Basil Bacon uses!"

That did it. Basil Bacon! I touched the gas and the Buick heaved forward, spitting gravel and sending Sonny running for the crape myrtles. My heart raced. There was ice in the sockets of my eyes. The ladies scattered, all but one who dashed back for her pitcher. "They don't have much," I remembered Nora telling me, "but what these people have they share." That pitcher was probably all this woman had in the world, an object worth laying down her life before a charging LeSabre. Second thoughts were creeping in, but by then it was too late to stop the car. Instead I swerved hard to the right, exploding a barrel of pink pampas grass. I kept driving, didn't stop, not until I had reached Gail's Whole World Grocery in Columbia.

"My sister says it's okay for you to come up to the lake house this weekend." What had happened at Gruber's was not yet entirely clear to me. I remembered people running from a fireworks display of rosy plumes. Nora's face. I was breathing hard, my face twisted hard to stanch the tears. Tony didn't seem to notice.

"And Clayton?" he said. "He can join us as well?"

"I forgot to ask about Clayton." Tony set down a crate of dandelion greens. He looked me in the penis. "But yeah, I don't suppose one more would be any trouble."

"Good," said Tony, turning his back to me. "I will remind him to bring a sleeping bag."

When I returned home, Nora was already there. I knocked on her bedroom door but she said she was tired. "Can we talk about it at breakfast?" I asked.

"I'll be tired at breakfast, too."

The light went out under her door.

The next morning she was not especially talkative. The ride to Gruber's felt longer than usual. I had to fill in the silent patches with questions and comments about the potluck—had it gone okay after I left? What was in that big pink bowl? "Sure smelled good!"

"Right here." We were about a half mile from the nursery. "Stop the car." She climbed out and started walking toward Gruber's.

"Nora?"

When she turned back all I saw was sorrow. Her anger had abated, had washed off like cheap paint to reveal a raw surface underneath, deeply grained with disappointment. "I have an appointment up in Newberry this afternoon," she said. "Dr. Meyer wants to run a couple tests."

"So I'll come back and get you early?"

"Don't bother. Sonny offered to drive."

When he dropped Nora at the house that afternoon the scene was complicated. Tony wanted me to walk him through my technique. In the basement I showed him how to use the equalizer to sweep the spectrum. I explained my principle of the "dynamic mix." As the day progressed the voice traveled from the basement subflooring to the yard. For the first three hours I increased the signal from the piezos and attenuated the hydrophones; at noon the mix was reversed; at three p.m. I balanced all six mics, bringing them up just shy of distortion.

A truck rumbled into the drive. Tony froze. "Who is that?"

"My half sister," I said. "A guy from work gave her a ride."

"What guy from work?"

Clayton stood on the porch smoking. Sonny got out of the truck and walked around to the passenger side. "Hey, man, can you give me a hand with her?" he said, smiling.

Tony drew up beside Clayton and whispered something in his ear. Clayton stepped on his cigarette and stared. I bounded down the steps toward the truck as Sonny opened the door and took Nora's arm.

"Hey!" shouted Clayton. "You need to let her brother handle that, slick."

My sister leaned against Sonny as if an unbearable weight pressed down upon her. I saw how thin her legs had become, how they buckled at an unorthodox angle. Sonny bore her up as if she were a sapling, a pricey ornamental lime tree like they sold at Gruber's.

Nora's eyes were half closed, and I wasn't sure if she'd acknowledged our house guests. I told Sonny I could take her from here. Nora looked up at me: "Don't you mean to say thank you?" Clayton sucked his teeth.

Sonny handed me a bottle of pills and told me it was for the pain. "She ought to get right to bed."

"Rock?" said Clayton, reading Sonny's visor. It was an unfriendly sort of question. "Rock."

Ignoring him, Sonny raised his chin at my boat. "You ever replace the seals?" he asked.

"You will have to leave," said Tony. "This is a restricted area." To me: "I told you, Hobie. No mixed blood on the property. It can compromise the recordings."

I felt crummy. Crummy that Tony might question my commitment. Crummy about the situation at Gruber's. About Nora.

"Not yet," I said to Sonny. "Hopefully next weekend. Thanks for… you know."

"It's no problem, man. You take good care of her, okay?"

9.

Grass grew in around the cement caps so you couldn't see the boreholes. The black cables that ran through a window well into the basement I concealed under pine straw. There was a momentary panic when Nora brought home four black plastic pots of azaleas and announced a plan to replace the old ones alongside the house.

"You do plants nine to five," I said. We were headed to Gruber's. The beige LeSabre was yellow with pollen, spermy with spring. She had forgiven me for the potluck incident, but still had me leave her on 391 a polite distance from the nursery. "Let me do the gardening around the house."

I didn't. The azaleas turned brown in their plastic pots, but by then

Nora was too sick to notice.

While I waited for news from Munich the recordings continued. I kept my weekly meetings with Tony, but more and more I found him distracted or unavailable. I asked Gail if anything was up. Had I done something to offend him?

"Who can tell? He's German."

This made sense. Hyperborea makes a virtue of detachment, of self-possession. I am paraphrasing from *Clarion Call of Thule* when I say, Each Man a City. Still, I couldn't help but think that Tony was mad about Sonny. Had his mixed blood corrupted the transmissions?

Finally I confronted him. "What's up?"

We were in the dairy cooler sliding cartons of goat's milk into the windowed case. He wore a heavy parka and gloves. I wore cutoff shorts and flip-flops.

"I fail to understand your question."

"I mean, am I doing a decent job? I don't know anymore."

Tony removed his gloves and flexed his fingers. As his eyes found my crotch I worried that he might hit me. "You are performing... fine."

"I'm bringing in new tapes every week. I fixed the hum in Hydrophone A. I had to lie to my half-sister, which I don't like to do."

"Hobie, listen to me: you have done all that can be expected of a person such as you."

I took offense. "A lot can be expected of me," I said, putting down a carton more firmly than I had intended. "I'm a person from whom people expect more than can be expected."

Tony lifted a milk crate and used it to butt open the cooler door. The warm air of the bulk aisle grabbed my legs like breading. It felt good to come out of the cold.

He smiled. "Okay," he said. "Then we will have to expect more of you in the future."

Nora's cancer came back. Tony and Clayton moved in to the lake house. I reacted poorly.

Word arrived from Munich. Mine were, indeed, genuine transmissions from Thule, certified and clear. I understood when Tony told me I would not be privy to their content—Fourth Degree Intimates only—but he gave me the message in broad strokes:

"Set the stage," they said. "Cleanse. Arm. Enlist. The Hyperborean infantry is driving south."

This was big news for sure. We were in Gail's basement when he told me, and we were whispering.

"The time has arrived for you to show us the true measure of your commitment," he said.

"Do you want me to kill somebody?"

"Munich has asked Clayton and I to take over the recordings."

"My recordings?" I worried. Those mics had been borrowed from Newberry College. I would be held responsible for them. "In my basement?"

"Hobie, I trust you," he said. "Clayton trusts you. But the Gessellschaft, they do not know you as we do." Munich had decided the transmissions were too sensitive for uninitiated ears. "The noblest way you can serve Thule, my friend, is to cede control of the lake house to us."

I agreed in principle but voiced a few concerns:

"It's my house," for example. And: "Where will I live? What about Nora?"

Tony said there were no easy answers. He reminded me that it was time to pick up Nora from work. "We will be in touch soon."

When I reached our rendezvous point on Route 391, she wasn't there. Sonny stood on the side of the road. I pulled over and rolled down the passenger window. "What the heck are you doing here?"

He removed his Rock visor, and held it to his heart. "Nora got dizzy this afternoon," he said, drawing a circle in the pollen on my hood. "They took her to Newberry Memorial."

He made as if to get in the car, but I punched the gas. I tore through Prosperity and up 76, leaving the Buick in the visitors' lot. I sprinted to oncology, where a nurse said room six, and when I rounded the corner her door hung open. A doctor stood over her, Meyer; I knew him from before. Nora's head was back. She took short hollow breaths. Her lids were blue. The arm that stuck out from the top sheet was too thin to belong to my sister. It was not Nora's arm. I turned and walked back to the car.

Clayton's truck was parked in the lake house driveway. I walked around the side yard and stuck my head in the window well. Through the cobwebs I could see his outsized head bob over Daddy's workbench, headphones stretched over his ears. Inside the front door I found two army issue duffel bags and a hunting rifle. I tiptoed to Nora's room but stopped when I heard the skitter of paws. A small white dog burrowed under the bed.

"Tony will be here in an hour." Clayton stood behind me.

"Okay," I said.

"You met Himmler?"

"Is Himmler a dog?"

Clayton laughed like he was on an instructional VHS: *How to Laugh.* He scared me, and I wanted Tony there as soon as possible. I wanted Tony to never come, and I wanted Clayton out of my damn house.

At the kitchen table he hunched over a sack of sandwich bread. He offered me a slice but I couldn't eat. My tongue was dry. The idea of water made a pinch in my stomach. All I could think of was Nora's open mouth, the clean death smell of oncology poured inside her. She had been so good, ate nothing but whole grains. Nora was good; she had envied no one for the assurances life no longer gave her. Meyer said if it ever came back we would have a serious talk.

"Did you pick out a bedroom?" I asked Clayton.

He said, "I can sleep any old place."

I said, "My sister is going to die." Clayton stopped chewing and started chewing again.

10.

When I phoned the hospital a nurse told me they were keeping Nora for at least a week. She suggested I make an appointment with Dr. Meyer. "He can tell you about the next steps." I didn't need to hear it from Meyer; I knew all the steps there were. Nora would either come home with a nurse or not come home at all. And she no longer had a home.

Regarding that, Tony said I could stay a few more days, until I found new accommodations. "You could," he said, "but wouldn't it be harder if we dragged it out?"

My first homeless night was spent in the back seat of the LeSabre.

Jeffrey Rotter

The hospital parking lot was so glaringly lit, crushed by sirens, that sleep didn't come. When a rent-a-cop tapped on my window at two a.m. I told him about my Nora. I said I had come from out of town and could not afford a motel. I had made an appointment with Dr. Meyer at ten thirty the following morning. Perhaps he could let me stay the rest of the night. The man took pity, but when morning came I was nowhere near Meyer's office. I sat in a drive-through putting together enough change for a steak biscuit and coffee. I had no need for a serious conversation.

The nursery was less hospitable than Newberry County Memorial. After the sun went down I concealed the Buick behind a greenhouse and leaned the seat back. From a distance the man looked like Sonny, but when he drew closer I saw it was one of the Gruber boys, Alan. He recognized me, I guess.

"Go home, Hobie."

I told him that option was no longer in play. Alan Gruber did not ask why. He knew me by reputation, and my reputation was that I was complicated.

"How is Nora holding up?" he asked, helping himself to the passenger seat. I said her thing was still in remission; whatever had happened to her at work was probably heat related. I enjoyed scaring Alan Gruber. You take your pleasure where you can.

He addressed me like a litigant, the spoiled shit: "We take good care of our employees, Hobie. I'll be sure to send someone over to see her in the morning." He got out of the car. "Meanwhile, I have to ask you to vacate the property." Mixed blood.

Back in the visitors' lot I signaled to the security guard. Various gestures and facial expressions gave me to believe he would not arrest me for staying the night. The lights shone brighter that night, the sirens called more frequently. A sense of rising alarm was pervasive. The armies of Thule, marching south, death striding through the oncology wing. I wedged my face into the vinyl upholstery until crumbs tickled my nose. Wadded up facial tissue shielded my upturned ear from the noise. I drifted off.

It was a familiar sound that brought me back around: it rose through the asphalt, the undercarriage, the padded springs of the LeSabre back

106   *Glimmer Train Stories*

seat: haunted low moaning: cleanse, arm, enlist. I climbed over the seat and started the car. Nora was dying inside that building, dying with her mouth open and without saying a word. Alan Gruber would win; he had the lawyers and cash flow. Meyer would win; he'd have his serious talk. The guard shouted about my headlights but I didn't listen. I gunned it, dark, onto 76 and knew Gail would be in bed with her teenage boyfriend, asleep with his parents' consent. Sonny would save up and buy his own bass boat, superior to mine, no leaky gear box. Alonzo would receive his associate's degree in business administration. There was a danger, however remote, if you were a bird, of getting so far above this horror show that you saw the pattern and chose never to come down again. What if Nora were to return home? Not die and return home? We were almost out of oatmeal. We had no home. She would want to know why. Who were these men and why did they have possession of our house? My thoughts were disordered and hot. Route 391 came to me empty, swift. Even the deer knew better than to cross my path. I saw their spectral heads hang in the scrub pine and then I smelled the lake through the trees, chalky water and sunken towns, and all the old bottles. No matter how many you recovered there were always more waiting under the mud. I had collected as many as I could but it did not matter because nothing was as precious as it seemed. Through the trees I saw Daddy's lake house, neglected azaleas, shitty roof, a truck in his driveway that did not belong to him. That man Don, he had urinated on my father's carpet. Had stolen his Lincoln. I edged onto our dirt lane and here where I usually slowed down, compelled to choose left or right around a big black oak in which I had carved two names, mine and Nora's, I sped up. When I saw a light glow in the casement window I pumped the gas and was doing about forty-five when the LeSabre struck the wall of Daddy's lake house, pushed through so that my bumper upset the credenza. I heard Clayton shout, saw him run out the back door in his briefs and surge into the water. I threw the Buick in reverse and though the hood had buckled up, though the windshield lay across my lap, though I bled from several openings on my face and one of my arms felt numb, I shifted into drive and I goddamn floored it.

*My grandfather, me, and my father. The first tree I
ever helped transplant. I'm sure I was a huge help.*

Gabe Herron lives outside a small town near Portland, Oregon, with his wife,
son, and daughter. His stories have appeared in *[PANK]*, *Portland Review*, and *Prairie
Schooner*. He has worked at Powell's Books for thirteen years.

SUZETTE

Gabe Herron

The rifle traveled to Oregon with my family. It was in poor con-
dition; one of 720,000, but worth more money than the walrus-
head man slid across the glass display case toward me. I didn't want to
touch it. I picked it up. There was a cigar-shaped fish mounted as a
trophy behind him. It must have been five foot long.

"What kinda fish is that?" I asked.

"Barracuda."

"How much did you loan out on that barracuda?"

"Didn't. I caught that down in Cozumel."

"Give you a good fight?"

He nodded, took a drink of his coffee, but wouldn't say more.

I walked away remembering the first time my father took that rifle
off the bedroom wall, handing it down with the stories he could
remember. I sat in the cab of my truck, laying the one hundred dollar
bills out across my knee. It felt like I'd been tricked somehow, which
I had; grief is a slick son-of-a-bitch that way. If you'd been there to
ask me what I was doing, I'd have told you in all honesty, "I have no
idea." But that wouldn't have been the truth either, at least not the
whole truth.

I'd already started buying Suzette without even knowing it.

• • •

Suzette is a descendent of Pauline Wayne, the presidential cow of William Howard Taft. Pauline grazed on the White House grounds, and produced milk for President Taft and his family. She was the family pet. I spent all I could afford on Suzette, which turned out to be $8,900. Truthfully, it was more than I could afford. I had a family with medical expenses I couldn't take care of, which meant I shouldn't have bought her at all. That's why I sold the Winchester at a reduced price. A family heirloom, but without heir, there'd be no sense in holding on to such a thing, which should have made it hurt less.

It did not.

Amy couldn't believe what I'd done either. She watched me unload Suzette from the living room window, her arms folded over herself. I led Suzette down the ramp and into the empty barn, empty because we'd sold off the other stock, knowing we couldn't take care of them, our son, and both work jobs in town without burdening good neighbors who'd done too much already. I felt bad about it too; herd animals don't like to be alone. That goes double for a calf. Suzette bawled as I walked away to explain myself to Amy—already knowing I could not.

"I know. I know," I said to her.

Obviously, I didn't know.

"I swear to God." She was tamping down hard on anger and fear. "I do not understand you sometimes."

"It just happened."

"Buying a show cow don't just happen." She rolled her hand the same way I do when bidding at auction. She did it several more times, eyes wider with each roll.

"I wa—"

"Well, heaven help us now." She shook her head and took a drink of sweet tea, eyes narrowing at me over the rim.

I took a deep breath. "I know it." I scratched my neck for no reason.

"And how the hell are we gonna afford this one, when we couldn't afford the ones we had?" Her lips thinned down to nothing. "How much?"

I rubbed my eye with my palm—as if having trouble recalling the exact numbers burnt in there. I told her. She couldn't find a thing to say to it. I offered: "She's descendant of President Taft's cow. I have it on good paper. She's a presidential cow…some of those high priced Holstein can bring down a million." I thought the concept of a million-dollar cow might take her mind off the nine-thousand-dollar calf bawling out in our barn.

"That's what you think you've got out there? A million-dollar cow?"

"No." I couldn't explain. I hadn't used the part of my mind that follow directions on a road map, or calculates feed costs when I bought Suzette; I hadn't used my mind at all. I should have told her that. Instead, I shrugged, "You don't know it's not a million-dollar cow, either."

"Well, if it is, Seth's gonna be real proud…if he's around to see it." It was a hurt on us both. I could see how badly she wanted to pull it back inside herself after it had leapt out. I forgave her quick as a quail. She grabbed the remote control for our AC, and threw it at my head. I turned my face and it bounced off my shoulder. She rushed off, embarrassed, "Presidential cow!"

Amy always does a thing all the way, even if she doesn't want to, and sometimes because she doesn't want to. She blasted out the back door, gone off to walk the creek alone, which is where she takes her troubles, and mine too, when I can't take them on my own.

Her father once told me: "You'll regret ever getting her backed in a corner." I was standing on his front porch one Saturday evening. It was late July. He was still wearing coveralls, but was finished with his work for the day—setting out drinking his beer. I was up there to take Amy out to the drive-in. Our second date. He'd known me most my life, and it wasn't meant as a threat—just fair warning. He'd known Amy most her life, too. I suspect he could see much further into our future than he let on, could see us hurting each other accidentally and often.

And he was right, of course.

We saw *Forrest Gump* three times that summer.

I've heard it's a good movie.

•   •   •

I spent the rest of that afternoon getting Suzette settled in. She wasn't near perfect. She was perfect. I mixed her milk replacement, and because she'd never seen a bottle, I had to back her into a corner and show her how it worked. She gave me a good hard kick to the ankle. It peeled back a flap of skin that bled through my sock and into my shoe. I squish-squashed around the barn. It felt like I'd stepped into a mud puddle the exact same temperature as myself. I should have had on my boots. After she finished the bottle, I let her suckle my finger to soothe herself down. I liked feeling the rough ridges on the roof of her mouth. I wiped her slobber off on my pants. I think it soothed me as much as it soothed her.

I went to the hospital to sit with Seth.

We watched the Beavers play football but they didn't win.

When he noticed my fussing with the homemade bandage I'd bled through, one of the night nurses cleaned up my ankle and laid a couple Steri-Strips down to hold the skin flap in place.

"Thank you," I said.

"It's nothing," he said.

"Not to the guy who's bleeding through his sock, it's not."

He smiled. "Keep it clean and dry for a couple days—would you."

He patted my back on his way out.

I wanted to say something to him, about how at that moment in time, with how my head was behaving, that small kindness might have saved something inside me from myself. But I never saw him again. And I wouldn't have said something like that to a stranger anyhow. I'd just have to repay his kindness to another when I got the chance.

It was late when I got back home. I followed my headlights up the gravel road to our place—not wanting to go back there much either. I found Amy out in the barn with Suzette, running the firm comb through her tail gently. I'd thought of a thousand words to say, but all that came out was, "I'm so sorry."

I could tell her eyes had been crying—dried now. She shook her head. "I'm sorry about throwing the remote."

"It's my fault," I said. "I had no right."

"What's her name?"

"Suzette."

Amy ran her hand down the length of her. "Suzette, you're about the most beautiful calf I've ever seen." A sob leapt out. She caught it and folded her arms across it. I walked over and hugged her from behind, wrapped my arms around her slender shoulders—there was less of her by the month it seemed. We rocked in the slow darkness of the barn. We stood like that for a long long time, listening to the crickets speaking to the darkness in their own night language.

That evening we saved each other in the bedroom as we often had—only the stakes had never seemed so high. We were both hesitant at first, afraid of where we'd be dropped off if this final salvation failed us, but it did not. And so we led each other away to safety once again—if only for the night.

In March, our son got better. We brought him home. We'd had him home before, a full two months, but this time his illness came back stronger. He backslid. I got out my chainsaw after we got back from the children's hospital—checked the lubrication hole in the bar to be sure it wasn't clogged—filled the oiler, filed the chain, every single cutter, and felled the giant maple in the middle of our wheat field.

It had been left there by the wisdom of generations. It wasn't overlooked, but preserved, and that takes more will than trying to bend something to fit your own curve. It wouldn't have come easy to the restless and pragmatic hands that built up this place. Its value calculated in future shade, and the sound it might make when the breeze moved through it—a high perch for hawks to hunt field mice, maybe even for its beauty, but it staggers the mind to imagine another that could see so far out beyond its self, and to never take a full benefit, but to cut your furrows around it for the whole of your life instead, a sort of wink at your son's son's son.

A wink at me.

Yes, sir, Son. I saw all the way out to you.

It was a risky thing I was doing alone, because an old tree like that can be rotten in its center, so that when you're back cutting, it might slab out and come apart high above you, or just simply explode due to the invisible pressures held within, shatter into so many pieces you won't know which way to turn before being smashed flat into the earth—heavy as the hand of God. That's what took my cousin, and you are literally flat after it's happened, about six inches thick, so I know how quickly all this can take place, so fast you don't have time to repent for the sin you just committed. But that old tree was solid through.

I don't know what its lumber might've been worth. The thought never occurred to me to think. That's how I get once I point myself in a direction.

I needed seasoned hardwood, a goddamned bunch of it.

It's what had been left to me for when it was needed.

It was now needed.

I'd have to say that by then, I knew what it was I was doing.

I thought about all the time I'd spent under its shade with Seth. *I pump the fuel bulb with my thumb.* The questions asked and the answers given. I remembered all the hours spent under it as a child with my own father. *I move the choke forward.* I could recall the hours I spent under it with my grandfather, beyond that too, for he told me of his father, and his father's father. *I pull the starter cord.* Those were good hours spent between us all—how unknown generations speak between themselves, so that they aren't lost to each other, not at all.

The saw crackled and coughed—blue smoke blooming out from behind.

There's some kind of magic that happens in places like that, where fathers and sons take their rests together after the work. Their arms made heavy and dumb by it, but their minds made clear and calm. There is something held in that spot that cannot be destroyed. It might be that the sweat and talk has seeped into the ground and made the taproot grow deeper. It's a foolish way of thinking. I know that. I'm a fool. And I'm not too embarrassed by it, but I do keep it mostly to myself. I can tell you this, a tree like that don't ever hardly fall over on its own.

That's the truth.

I'm the man that made that stump.

That's my part in this.

And there was no more shade left to take my ease in after that work. It was just another hard thing done in an ever-growing list of hard things done, so that I was becoming annealed toward my own life. And I didn't like the unfeelingness of it. No one wants to feel like a stone, but we'll become what's required to go on, to get to the other side of trouble—to see others through too…if we can. I assumed that was all part of how it's supposed to be, but with no previous experience to go on, what the hell did I know?

I went inside for my lunch to keep my eyes off what I'd just done. I brushed the wood chips out of my hair and raised the sawdust off my shoulders before coming in through the back door. Amy was rasping carrots for split pea soup. She put down the grater and raised her hands above her shoulders. I was preparing my defense, and getting ready to duck, if that's what was necessary.

It wasn't.

"I don't want to know," she said, "so don't even bother explaining it to me."

It was a relief, not to have to expound upon myself, or my doings.

I ate warm bread and drank cold milk while standing at the kitchen counter. The silence puddling up around our feet. I thought about things my father told me. It wasn't much. He wasn't a talker, but I know now what few words he did talk were backed up by many thousands of other words he'd spoken only to himself.

I was doing my best.

And all I could think to do was make ready for the worst.

I felt my father had been there with me as I felled that tree. It hit the ground so hard it moved the earth under my heels. It sent a jolt right through my feet up into my knees and spine. It was then, right after that impact, that I felt him standing behind me, the weight of his hand resting on my neck. How he used to do when I'd done something that pleased him as a boy. I couldn't shake the feeling off.

His hand.

It was that strong.

I snapped around, and when I did, the pressure vanished—just like that.

I looked up into the blue sky and clouds through the empty space I'd just created; never having seen the sky from this place before, it didn't look real. Two hawks circled each other over my neighbor's place. I wondered if they'd give up on my fields now, wondered too if I'd be overrun by field mice. Then I heard my father's voice, saying words that didn't seem like my own: *I guess it's been a good day for field mice then.*

I'd forgotten the sound of his laughter.

It made me smile.

I wondered if my mind was going.

Fuck.

Amy was worrying about me in that way, too. I didn't want to add to her troubles, but here I was, furiously moving beads about our abacus, trying to calculate the inscrutable. I would catch her looking at me every so often, and it was as if she didn't recognize the person she was seeing. It was unsettling, and I was getting that look more and more often. She was right to give it to me. I could feel things moving around deep inside.

I was changing.

I was changed.

It was a fright to us both.

Suzette had a black face with a white mark on her forehead like an ice cream cone had plopped there and drifted down to the center of her pink nose. Her long lashes set off full-dark eyes that could hold the entire world at once. I borrowed an old nanny goat from my uncle to keep her company; some of the sorrow went out of her eyes then.

There's a reason cows are revered in other cultures, and turned to hamburgers in our own. Those reasons get all tangled up on you if you aren't careful and look a calf too long in its eyes. I should have bought an ugly calf, is what I should have done. But it wouldn't have made any difference. We'd have fallen in love with her even if she'd had two heads and five spindly legs. It's this way when you have a sick child. You'll hunt down about anything to prop your heart up against its own weight.

I told myself that's why I'd bought Suzette.

I let myself believe that's what I'd done—give us something we could hold onto together. A thing to put work into and have some good come out of it. A place for our hearts to go and be softened toward life again. I thought myself wise for having done such a thing, but that wasn't what I'd done—that's not what I'd done at all. Those opposing aims revolved themselves inside me for so long they wore grooves for my bad dreams to turn circles in.

I finally awoke one day to realize what it was the doctors were telling us, what it was Seth had been telling us in his quiet way for the past week. What words no parent can hear because they can't bear up to listen: the darkest times weren't coming…they were here.

I begged for mercy.

I cried without making sounds.

I let the tears soak my pillow.

I whispered my supplications.

You can only do that for so long until you're a husk. You want to be strong, to hold things together at the center, so that others might let them go apart. I don't know why that is, it just is, but you're fooling only yourself. All centers come apart, otherwise, there'd be no center to begin with, and your pillow is still wet, whether you've soaked it in silence or not.

I made the deals every parent makes, and then more deals, offered trades: my life for his, etc. So many deals I couldn't keep track of them all, or keep them, even if I could remember. In the end, if it's nothing but silent words you've offered, it's nothing but silent words that are returned.

I had grown tired of the fucking silence.

A man who'd been at the auction house called me up that same week, asking around about Suzette. How was she progressing? Would it be okay if he came and looked in on her sometime? He owned one of her siblings. Did I know about her brother? He'd sold at auction for a good price down in Austin. Would I be interested in talking price on Suzette? "Nope. No, sir," I said. "No, thank you."

That afternoon Amy was up to the hospital providing what comfort she could—mostly just waiting. Suzette came to me without call. She was always happy for some company. I spent a couple gentle hours with her that way. She was truly a flawless creature—simple and perfect. The finest animal I've ever seen. The finest animal I was ever going to own. I led her out through the barn and into the field. She followed me as I went. It was in her nature—all the trust in the world. She stopped to eat her fill of new grass as she went along.

She ruminated in the early spring afternoon.

A day as full and beautiful as any day in May can be.

A light breeze moving just enough air to keep the bugs off. After a time, we meandered toward the pile of fallen maple, which I'd sectioned to length the summer before. The heat of August had seasoned the wood—drawn out the moisture, sending cracks of lightning breaking across the grain on the end cuts.

I unsheathed my knife, wrapped my arm around her neck, felt for and found her jugular, reached around with the blade, pushed it down, and drew it through to the other side in one smooth stroke.

Quickly as I could.

A sharp knife.

A blessing and curse.

The grass caught her blood before it could make the sound of spilling against the earth, no sounds at all but for her rattled breathing, which became harried as her blood came out. My own blood filled my ears, just as hot, so that each beat of my own heart was audible, and there was a moment in time when my heart synchronized with her heart, and we shared the same pulse for a moment, both our breathing harried now. I would not turn my eyes from hers, but held her gaze, so she would know I was there—not alone—and how very very sorry I was for this.

I believe she could see that.

She went over then—swiftly.

I went over with her too, and so, a part in me died with her forever. I held her body still as her legs worked circles against what was coming next; my pant knees soaked through in the warm-wet freshet. I shook my head—forced myself to be there—everything in me wanted to turn away and be elsewhere. I'd cared for her a great deal more than I'd been able to imagine. And I'd imagined it would be awful, and it was awful, God-awful, and a great deal more so.

I placed the knife out of view behind a tuft of grass with red sticky fingers.

I would never use it again—not for anything.

I arranged the wood next to her body, building small at first, with limbs and then trunks. I rolled her upon the small pyre and piled more and more wood atop her. I heaped it as high as I could manage. The last pieces I had to throw using all the back I had left to me. My arms shook with the effort, hung off my shoulders as if they held twin suitcases full of gold. The breeze stopped blowing, so that the flies were upon me, collected by the scent of fresh loss.

I was damp with death, covered with death, and bark dust, and blood, and sweat, and more death; death like a moving blanket.

I had to rest before I turned the soil around the pyre, cutting a sod ring to stop the grass from burning. I went around twice to be sure. I set the fire with stove gas and stepped outside the circle. I stood there, the heat building until I had to move back, and then back again, and then again—the heat growing so great. Eventually, the smoke turned black, until the air was strong with it.

Hair.

Hide.

Flesh.

Soul.

I watched as it carried her away through the sky in a straight dark line. I knew then with certainty. And I could feel myself being answered.

This would be enough.

Me, reading.

Lara Markstein is a South African-born New Zealander, who currently lives in Oakland, California. She graduated with a Bachelor of Arts in English from Harvard University, and received her Master's in Fine Arts from the MFA Program for Writers at Warren Wilson College. Her work has appeared in *Agni*, the *Greensboro Review*, *Necessary Fiction*, and the *Four Way Review*. Lara currently serves as the Program Officer at the UC Berkeley Center for New Media.

THE AMERICAN

Lara

Lara Markstein

1.

When I was eighteen, I lived in a small shared flat with an American and a German on an alley off Nguyen Thi Minh Khai in Saigon. That was the year I practiced waiting—for the monsoons to end, my money to run out, the coffee at cafés to muddy the sweetened condensed milk I drank by the glass between English classes I pretended to teach. Kirsten—the American—called herself a Communications Director for a nearby law firm. Her job consisted of poaching articles for the company newsletter, and I imagined her boiling paragraphs until the words toughened in white rubber strips. Hans was involved with elevators—the exact nature of his work too difficult to understand. He had wanted to fly airplanes once, but after failing to certify four times, had packed a single army duffel and headed east, still weightless, as he would be for the rest of his life.

We would not have been friends elsewhere, but in Vietnam we lost ourselves in each other's pockets, like the worthless five-hundred-dong coins we accrued, and later tossed in ashtrays.

"Do you smoke?" Kirsten asked when I moved in. I said no and she handed me a cigarette. "Neither." She and Hans had perfected the art of waiting by the time I arrived.

2.

We streaked through red lights on patched tires and oil-can exhaust, spat out sticks of gum we'd barely chewed in case the taste began to fade, emptied crates of Taittinger on Sundays when the grand hotels held brunch. We drew attention to ourselves.

We did not know what we were waiting for, but we were certain it would not be found in the cramped flat, with its clanky fan and thin walls through which we heard the neighbors hawk. You had to hunt what you were after. I saw my shapeless target gliding cut-tailed nearby, like a fat fish beneath the surface of the Saigon River, which carved through town. This pursuit, it was why we'd collected here: to offer every opportunity for something miraculous to occur that would change the course of our lives forever. Knit tight the loose ends, sand the rough edges, fire us into a form you could hang a coat on.

Kirsten coordinated most of these stunts. Our fearless leader, our Caesar, our five-foot-flat Napoleon Bonaparte. She was good at organizing; she'd slept with eighty per cent of the expat men in under two years, which took some arranging. I figured she was searching for love in her spare time. "Eternity isn't forever," Kirsten said. She was only twenty-five, but already had hair the color of eggshells that she dyed a plain gold. She believed this gave her special insight into mortality.

"I'll die of pills," she'd say, matter-of-fact. "Hans of complications related to AIDS." I spluttered a little and she smiled as if to say, "You didn't know?" Which I didn't, because it was the type of thing she made up.

When I asked her how I would go, she said my heart would stop. "In your dotage, dear. You won't fucking know." A dull death; it was the worst insult she could think of for someone of my youth.

If Kirsten was the cynical one, Hans was our Pangloss, our Pollyanna, the ice in our warm beer. He was well liked for this reason and invited everywhere, though Kirsten claimed it was because he was rich and too dumb to argue over the check. Streets might reek of durian, guards might blow their noses until a bribe's involved, but

Hans would notice only the fruit trees blooming on the roofs, and how the thin, silk blouses of the women on their scooters breathed in and out.

I thought sometimes he was waiting for Vietnam to turn into the country he'd dreamed.

And why shouldn't he? The world spun faster there. Buildings sprouted in tight, lightless cavities. Baby stores swelled, popping open on each block. Women clustered on the street side juiced oranges with an abandon I'd only ever experienced once in my life, in a converted garage where I convinced myself for a time I enjoyed sex, or at least that I did not hate my boyfriend, which was the same thing.

"Vietnam's one of the fastest growing nations," Kirsten liked to say. "Growth rate of seven percent. Oil reserves. They're building a space program." She had a head for statistics. The point was, anything could happen there and you had to be prepared.

So we dashed across the city, sometimes buying trinkets, sometimes clothes we haggled fiercely over, squabbling with the cut, the price, the bias, cotton, lace, organza, tulle. And still, raw silk scarves burst from my drawers, smothering the closet like a fine fungus, because I only ever wore one wool cardigan, not wanting to ruin the freshness of my purchases.

Mostly we found ourselves at the same three businesses: an expat bar, a Japantown club, and a pho place with plastic chairs and cheap beer where Binh, an old man who watched soccer on TV and would lose his life savings betting on Brazil in the World Cup, scowled when we ordered and shortchanged us consistently. Kirsten argued once about the bill. But he just picked his teeth and scratched his balls until she left.

3.

The Japantown club was also a brothel, like most late-night establishments in Saigon. With its wiped-down leather seats and dark lighting that hid the age of the faux marble, you might have been in any other of the high-rent drinking lounges that skewered the city.

We went because Kirsten's co-workers Davy and Quan had half-drunk liquor bottles they'd bought leftover behind the bar. The complimentary fruit plates were also better there, and the prostitutes were nice. They taught us drinking games. Most often we played a version of rock-paper-scissors that involved shooting imaginary guns. The women in their tight dresses twisted their shoulders from our barreled fingers carefully. When we tired of games, they drank, their mouths slackening a little so you could see the coming years thicken in their faces, their doughy beauty turning like milk. We paid them twenty-five dollars at the end of the night.

"Exploitation," Kirsten said once in the cab home. "Growing nations all struggle with this." The sky a closed purse between the office buildings, jangled with stars we couldn't see through the smog. "It's a ripoff, though."

"That's just because you like Davy," Hans said.

"If you were American you'd understand." She turned to me. "Right?" Though I was not American.

Davy, like most of the expat men, had a Vietnamese girlfriend who was beautiful. More beautiful, anyway, than Kirsten, who was thick and lumbering. "God knows what they talk about," Kirsten said.

Hans said, "Maybe they don't talk." Only he didn't seem to realize why that pissed her off more.

Hans spoke from experience. He bedded many of the women we met. I believe it was because he was twenty-eight, and could feel the weight of thirty in his bones. Kirsten and I laughed at the diseases we assumed he'd contracted, and he smiled on us benevolently.

Was it worth it? I might ask. "Of course," Hans would say, looking at me as though I had sunken skin where my eyes should be, like the men we walked past faster on the street.

4.

Some evenings I drank alone. I'd finish teaching at the English language institute and find a hotel bar where I knew no one. I liked how the businessmen took comfort in the familiarity of loosening their ties, how the staff creased their clothes in perfect lines. You could almost smell the starch. You *could* imagine you were in a novel from years ago if it weren't for the red-faced tourists wearing shorts that exposed their dimpled legs—the soft, sticky flesh like steamed dumplings, quivering.

The tourists came from Moscow, Beijing, Paris, Memphis. The Americans wore flag pins and fanny packs. They were returning vets, mostly. I got to where I could spot one across the room before he opened his mouth just by the pained look of wonder on his face, as if he'd fished up something he did not expect. Ammunition, a land mine, the boot he'd lost forty years ago, the body of a Mekong dolphin, long since extinct. These men all found their way to the empty stool at my side, eventually. They wanted to talk. I listened because they bought me drinks.

"I was here thirty years ago," was how most of them began. "Forty," Kirsten would have said. I held my tongue until after the third round, when I thought being blunt was charming, or at least excusable.

One night, I met Richie—a lucky one. I'd talked to privates swallowed by the jungle before, spat out mildewy, their flesh corrupted, scaled like fish; tunnel rats, dropped into tight holes with just a rope tied about their waists and a gun they couldn't swing. Richie had been a pilot and flown above the fray, sousing the forests in chemicals and flames, watching the sun set from the cockpit of the B-52 as he skirted the inland ranges before spinning back toward the coast, with its rubbery clouds, over the city of Hue.

"I was shot down," Richie said. He was defensive; he must have noticed my indifference. "I was shot down over a rice paddy. Not a clean one either. Filled with shit. Christ, it stank. I fell right beside a water buffalo. This was up north, near Nam Dinh."

Even there fortune had followed him. The locals carried him to their village, where they reset his mangled leg and laid cold compresses on his head from rags soaked in swamp water. The next day, they fed him rice cakes though their own ribs poked through their shirts, and led him into the forest, because it was too dangerous for him to stay.

These stories from survivors, they were all the same.

5.

After drinking with Richie, I'd wanted to visit Cu Chi.

"I don't do tourist shit," Kirsten had said. She didn't want to be lumped together with a bunch of ignorant foreigners. "All on some fucking find-yourself-in-an-ashram quest." We were at our usual riverfront American bar and she was struggling to light her cigarette with a match in the wind. None of us offered our lighters or pointed out that there were no ashrams in Vietnam.

"I'll go," Hans said. He liked to have a destination. He also liked the idea of sinking even further into the earth, growing heavy with the pressure of bedrock and clay. Davy and Quan didn't have other plans. We amassed like that, haphazardly. Although Kirsten deciphered grand designs.

"Davy gets bored if he has to spend all weekend with his girl," she said, triumphant.

Cu Chi was a dusty village north of the city in a sea of spindly mango trees that had never fully regrown after bombing campaigns. We crouched on our haunches in what little shade we found, while our guide spoke excitedly of the traps they'd made to kill Americans. Steel jaws, spikes carved from unexploded ordnance, bamboo stakes. Or was it steel stakes and bamboo jaws, roots for hands, a bud mouth, pollen prayers? The litany confused me. I wondered what one did in a tunnel with a tummy ache.

We were sick of the heat, sick of the guide's lame jokes, sick of the poorness of the whole exhibit when we arrived at the gun range, where you could shoot arms from the American War for a price. Our guide told us this with pride. "AK-47, M60 machine gun, M1 carbine, Russian SKS," he ticked them from his fingers.

Twenty dollars bought only six rounds of ammunition, but everyone leapt forward to join a long shadeless line that accepted credit cards. I did not have the money, and besides, the pounding of the artillery made my head ache. I purchased a Pepsi and sat on a tin bench that burnt the backs of my thighs instead.

The guns aimed at an empty field, blasted bare even of flies. The metal barrels twisted in the sun. If you squinted you could imagine they were organ pipes. I watched the backs of my friends' calves tighten. The muscles in their necks tugged the ligaments of their shoulders into hard, new forms. I couldn't see where their bullets fell and wasn't interested. I turned to Hans, scrunched over the rifle scope, but quickly looked away. A foreign, rigid expression had seized his features and his mouth worked around strange words. He spat out each syllable in a gob of saliva that stuck to his fleshy lips.

I did not understand their love of shooting things.

"We're American," Kirsten said, her body loose and recognizable once more. "Guns are in our blood." I was not American. I was not made of pistons and hammers but number eight wire and possum wool socks.

"In the Killing Fields in Cambodia the guns aren't bolted down," Quan said. "You can pick them up and shoot anything you like." Everyone agreed it was better there.

The rubbish bin overflowed and I had to carry my sticky can on the bus the whole way home.

6.

"I'm going to find the village," Richie told me one evening around my second daiquiri. He also told me his life history: married back in Michigan, a General Motors welder, two daughters—college educated. He'd done good. Of course, neither daughter talked to him, on account of his moving out of the family home into a motel room on the edge of town that he let by the week though it stank of damp cheese. "I wouldn't be alive if it wasn't for that man saving me. I'm going to thank him."

"I'll have another one," I told the waiter.

He watched a group of women beneath the snaking power lines outside. The cables, curling around each other, sagged beneath their own weight, and snarled tightly to a slanted pole. "I might have a son here, you know."

"Grandsons, too," I said.

7.

Quan was Viet Kieu. His family had managed to escape the country as

Saigon fell to the Communists because his father worked for the CIA, teaching VC how to fly out of helicopters. "They were poor learners," Quan said—a joke that held the weight of used-up laughter from years of practice, first in his south San Francisco elementary school and later at dinner with the Republican family of his girlfriend. The same girlfriend would leave him at the Barristers Ball for a friend with a New York job offer, causing him to purchase the one-way ticket that landed him in Vietnam. He was paid a piddling sum, but it was better than not being paid at all.

"Does your card-carrying fiancée know this?" Kirsten asked once. She was practical like that. I was still imagining what it would be like to have a body fall from the sky at your feet like a divine delivery. I wondered who cleaned the mess a human body made. Perhaps it hardened on the asphalt like an ancient, inky map. A sign: Here lies the human heart.

"*I* haven't told her," Quan said. We pictured the wedding endlessly. Not hoping for disaster precisely, but.

The wedding was in the marshland of District Two. Weeds sprouted in mud tracks. Storks swooped over a clay riverbed, which in the last rags of a breeze smelled of rotting fish.

Trucked in on air-conditioned buses, we trooped single file to congratulate the bride and groom. Then we stuffed as much food in our faces as possible over the hour-long lunch. Quan's was wedding three of five for the venue; the staff hovered to turn the tables around.

When the other guests returned to the coach, bloated and gaseous, we followed the families to a private waterfront room, where special label liquor lined a long table. Toasts were made, which we did not understand, but we swallowed the alcohol poured for us.

While I focused on keeping the glass from clinking against my teeth, the man beside me spoke of the United States.

"I love America. Plastic-wrapped cheese. What convenience!"

I tried to tell him I was not American, but Hans appeared with a chicken head from lunch that he'd stuffed between two plates. He shook the china by his ear with a twist and a clang and whoever the beak pointed to drank. The party members giggled wildly.

I sank into my seat. I wanted to ask Hans if he'd learned this game from our prostitutes, but he was already disappearing from view behind a man with a heavy silver watch, a suit sewn from thread of gold. I tried to reach out, but it struck me that Hans did not need my help. He would always be safe. He had an unfinished face; he could mold to any cast.

I was not surprised Hans was picked. I was a little disappointed no one had chosen me. The world crawled sideways, the river creeping upward, and I felt as if I might drown.

Kirsten and Davy must have thrown me in the back of a cab, because when I raised my head, I was no longer at the riverside pagoda, but in an apartment pool. I spluttered chlorinated water, which I washed from my mouth with Veuve Cliquot. Davy rooted in my handbag for more champagne, which I'd stolen from the ceremony. "Aha!" he cried, rising with the fresh bottle and smashing his forehead against a hanging potted plant. The terra cotta shattered, and blood dripped along his hairline into his ear. For some reason we thought this hilarious. We took turns pulling down the planters and throwing them up toward the sky like little bombs.

8.

I left alone that night.

"Kirsten wanted business experience in China—the emerging markets of the East," Hans said the next morning, handing me an iced coffee and manioc cake from the corner bakery. "But she couldn't figure out Chinese characters, so her father found her this instead."

When Kirsten returned, she did not acknowledge us, popping a Xanax and curling up in a lump on her bed. She bought Xanax by the box. For headaches, heartache, period pain. To make it through the day.

9.

The last time I saw Richie, he didn't want to talk. His eyes stuck on four Vietnamese women drinking martinis. Their laughter, like their hair, seemed shellacked to their perfect bodies. I stuffed my mouth with bar snacks, the nuts cracking between my loosening teeth. Eventually, I asked how his visit went.

"It was…" He couldn't find the words.

"Moving, enthralling, spiritual," I supplied a few I'd already heard.

"A woman remembered me. It was her brother I wanted to thank. I'd forgotten there'd been a girl. She's so much older now," he said, almost in pain, his tears like bricks that had lodged in his throat. Grief was like that: a building that had to be constructed piece by piece.

"You thanked her then." It was remarkable how vets expected you to tell their story for them.

"I told her how I had nightmares of everything that happened here. I told her how I almost turned my car engine on and covered the exhaust. I don't know how much she understood…," he trailed off. The women crossed their long legs slowly.

Lately I noticed this languor in the city. Shirtless men crouched on steps, smoking cigarettes, their eyes following me as I walked. Women wore loose clothing that could be bought at the market ten a pack. I once waited half an hour for my left hand to be manicured because the girl with the nail file stared over my head at her television soap.

"Troops arrived after I left. They burned the village. Shot every person in the house I'd stayed. She was out and they killed her whole family. I cried. We cried and cried." His face folded in on itself like sodden papier mâché.

"What did you expect?" I said. "A ticker tape parade?"

Half an hour later, Richie left with one of the ladies. Headlights cut the rain outside to stars, suspended between the cars; the sky empty as a pavement.

I charged the alcohol to his room.

10.

I'd come to Vietnam because it was not Auckland.

I was bored of my friends by the end of high school; their laughter irritated me. I didn't know how to break up with the boyfriend I'd been avoiding for weeks. Seeing men cry still makes me uncomfortable.

So when my grandmother died and left me some money, I bought a ticket to Ho Chi Minh City and cancelled my enrollment in university. I was going through a Graham Greene stage, and it was just luck I ended up in Vietnam. I could easily have landed in Mexico or Cuba. Or the Philippines—I was also a fan of W. Somerset Maugham back then.

I'd said I wanted adventure. I wanted out of my suburban life—the empty cul-de-sacs, the fenced-in yards, the choke of streets, feeding arterials to town. I couldn't breathe anymore on our island. If I stretched my arms wide, I could touch both coasts. The point was then to travel, to escape, to find what lay across the Pacific, which rammed our shores, eating at the earth we balanced on. Seabirds flew north, for days.

I guess what I really wanted was something strange, so unknowable I'd see only myself in its shape. I figured I'd find a purpose for my life if I could only recognize it. Phrased this way, the whole exercise seemed banal. A selfish endeavor no different from a housewife's affair.

11.

When Hans had business in Hanoi, I visited the north of the country myself. I was not a good English teacher and my classes weren't full so I had a fair amount of vacation, yet somehow I'd never traveled farther than Da Nang.

I started in Sapa, a town that hung off a mountainside sliced through with liver-shaped fields of rice. The guidebooks claimed locals dug the terraces with just their fingernails, but bulldozers lay fallow in the mud, rusting with rain. I couldn't afford one of the recommended tours, so I haggled on the side of a stone street with a gap-toothed woman, who insisted on carrying what looked like a heavy basket strapped to her back on our hike—I thought, uncharitably, to guilt me into raising the price.

The woman talked a lot at first. About her people, the Hmong, who were mistreated by the government, the struggle to provide for her son since her husband died, the intricacy of hand-made scarves—which I could watch being weaved and were, in fact, for sale. Americans usually liked them.

"New Zealand!" she said when I corrected her. "Kia ora. Good ice cream." And I thought of the Tip Top ice blocks that ruined our school uniforms, though I knew she was referring to the New Zealand Natural stalls in all the malls.

I wished she'd shut up. She was only three years older than me but her skin was scaled like bark, and I kept three paces back as if the passage of time were catching.

Eventually we walked through the villages in resentful silence, barely noticing the women who emerged from their huts as if—embarrassed of their poverty—they had to guard their sleeping mats from sight. A child pooing on the side of the road covered his eyes.

Later, in a bar where you could buy two cocktails for two dollars, a man spoke loudly about the authenticity of the people. How they'd not bought into the myth of the American dream, had preserved their culture, were *happy* here. "They're more real than the rest of us."

I wondered what it was about Americans that made them think everything was about them in the first place.

"Bullshit," a woman said. "I saw TVs. They had televisions in their huts." She sounded betrayed.

"They're so colorful," another backpacker said, wistfully.

"They're not goddamn parakeets." Her partner drank a weak beer. "Clearly. *They're* not allowed to leave. This place disgusts me."

But what was disgusting about the mountains, blanketed in emerald green fields of rice that shivered like water in the wind, and pinned the stretched daylight to the ceiling of the sky so that the blue ached? The entire valley screamed with life.

I waded through the mist on the way back to my hotel, a little drunk, my pants pressed wet against my thighs. I felt like one of Hans' elevators, suspended between two floors, and I stared at the sesame seed sky, and did not see the woman begging at my feet. Then I rinsed the grime off my body in a tub with no stop for the drain, a draft from the skew windows building clouds of steam above the water.

12.

I waited for the night train to Hanoi and Hans on the crowded tiles of the station, as the sun leaked over the flat-topped buildings. The roofs fell apart, quietly, stuck together with a paste of stone and lime and the ghosts of eggs.

I shared a sleeper cart with a family that trip, three chickens, a ripe bag of mangos. One of those chickens fretted all night as the train pitched through the countryside, and I slept fitfully. Around one in the morning, I leaned down and plucked the largest of the yellow mangoes from its bag. The chicken watched me with its marble eye, but I ate the fruit, biting straight through the bitter skin, forcing myself to chew the rind until I swallowed and gulped it all down. I slept well afterwards, my sheets sticky with juice.

It was five when we arrived in the city. Outside the station, men diced, drinking colorless liquor in their headlights. As the train whistled to the stop, they thronged along the tracks, pouncing on dry-eyed tourists who needed a ride. *Taxi?* they asked. *Moto?*

I did not want to pay double for the car, so I followed a motorbike man with a long cable of hair growing from the mole on his cheek. I'd heard somewhere this was good luck. The helmet he handed me hung from my neck by the strap as we swung through the empty streets, half green in the lamplight and the smog, the wind scraping the hair from my face.

I saw the red light a block away, felt the engine between my legs continue to hum. I wanted to open my mouth and call out, to warn him that we ought to stop. But it occurred to me that he knew. He saw the stop sign, too, and the headlights of oncoming traffic from the right. Perhaps, he even opened the throttle some.

We tore into the intersection and a cab skidded to a stop, metal screeching against metal, rubber burning, as I slammed onto the bonnet, smashing my head against the windscreen, before being thrown to the road.

I lay for a moment on the concrete quite still, feeling my heart batter at my chest. Then I tried to move my legs and when the right wouldn't budge, I moaned. It wasn't pain I felt, not yet, but fear. Men and women who'd been walking before the sun scorched the streets stopped and stared at me, curious, and I knew then none of the words I spoke made sense. *Hospital. Ambulance. Help.* Of what use were they here?

I twisted around, searching for something—I did not know what— a miracle of translation, maybe, a familiar face. But all I found was the motorbike driver, cradling his bloodied foot in his hands, and I choked on my tears. He watched me, his mouth contorted, disfigured by a loathing that seemed to rise from somewhere deeper, older than himself, somewhere lodged within the very tissue of his being, and I wanted to say:

I am not American. I am not Caesar crossing the Rubicon. I am not money. I am not guns. I am not a two-car garage in a single-family home with a flatscreen TV. I am not your individually packaged single-serve slice of cheese. I am not the health warning on your cigarette pack. I do not contain multitudes.

But I was silent.

13.

"Now you can say this was where you were hit by a car," Hans said when I arrived on crutches at his hotel. For the first time since meeting him, he sounded jealous.

"You'll be leaving then?" Kirsten said. I had no intention of going anywhere, but two months later I packed my bags and boarded a plane home. My money was almost spent and everyone was sick of having to discuss my lame leg, which to me was endlessly fascinating. I played the accident over and over again in my mind, repositioning each frame in the sequence beginning from my birth in a south Auckland concrete hospital.

I wrote to Hans and Kirsten after I left. For a time we kept in touch. But Kirsten moved back to the States to begin a law degree, and I never heard from her again. Hans, for all I know, still lives on 18A Nguyen Thi Minh Khai. He was the type of man who was destined to wait all his life, his deliberate innocence turning with age to a foolishness that begs to be misused. He will die with the same face he was born with.

When their photos appear on my computer screen now, they surprise me. My friends are made flat and foreign with the years. But I do not see them often. Mostly, I took pictures of the buildings, which all stand still.

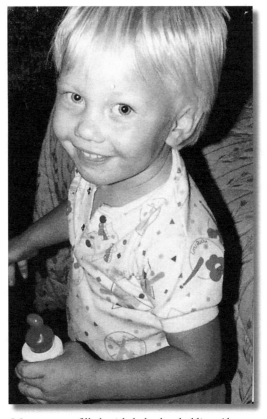

Me: age two, filled with baby bottle bliss. Always passionately curious. Always ready for adventure and naps.

Anthony DeCasper is a graduate of Chico State's English master's program. He lives and writes in Chico, growing up in the almond and olive orchards of Northern California. This is his first story accepted for publication.

REDSHIFT

Anthony DeCasper

The best part of having cancer is the cannabis. And the ice cream. All the ice cream I can fit into my white hairless body. I'm not really supposed to have either, but leukemia induces sympathy, so people make exceptions. And I always take advantage of exceptions. I'm a cop turned lawyer turned mailman. And I like to think I'm clever.

"How's that working out?" the doctor asks.

"What? The ice cream or being clever?"

"Matt, this isn't a joke. No more sweets. *Enjoy* the months you have left."

I'm American and I've lived a life of naive seriousness. So why not reverse it for death? Nothing else is working. The quack tells me, "If there is ever a time to be serious…"

"This wouldn't be it. Look, Doc, I need this. I'll cut cannabis but not the ice cream."

The Doc won't let me leave until I promise to slice my simple carbs. Not because of cancer, but because of the diabetes. Before I leave the hospital I ring Anita to tell her I've cut ice cream but not cannabis. And she doesn't say anything back.

Anita is breathing heavy through the phone and our television is blaring in the background. And she's slurping air, as if through a stirring straw. She gets like this after her third vodka tonic. Our son had called from overseas when I was at the doctor's, my wife tells me. Now I'm pissed I missed my boy's call because I haven't heard his voice in months. I can hear *Wheel of Fortune* through the phone noise. The puzzle is a Before and After category and I'm really good at those; it's the one category my wife struggles with and I always have to help her. We don't have dinner plans, so I suggest picking something up. I try and end the conversation by telling my wife I love her, because we all need to say that more often, but she interrupts me:

"Act Your Age of Innocence!"

"What? I said: I love you, hon."

"I just solved the Before and After puzzle: Act Your Age of Innocence."

I stop by the grocery to grab one of those ready-made dinner meals they usually have in the deli with the margarine mashed potatoes that liquefy into soup in the microwave, and broiled chicken with the white gravy that congeals diseased brown in the store coolers. The doctor told me to avoid ice cream, so instead I grab a bottle of Coppola cab. He did say to enjoy the months I have left.

But standing in the novelty aisle I have a small existential dilemma: how do I enjoy the *time* I have left without enjoying the *things* I have left? So I rationalize getting a pint of ice cream anyway. The months I have left, I say aloud to my reflection in the just-opened foggy freezer doors as they fade back into clarity. I'm good at justifying, but I think when we aren't willing to let something go, we are all great at justifying bullshit to ourselves.

I tell myself I'll finish my treat in the car before getting home and I'll toss the trash in a neighbor's can. I'm proud of myself. I usually get peanut butter chunk with caramel swirls and all the fun nostalgic stuff, but I concede to this boring burnt honey ice cream because I figure it has less sugar. And I think it's clever, too: burnt stuff in ice stuff, hot and cold—the best of both worlds. It was artisan and organic and expensive, so of course I buy it.

I park at the Sevillano Middle School parking lot in our neighborhood. The cloudless winter sky is stained glass and the cold air captures my breath in little white puffs of exhaust that evaporate into the cathedral of early night. I crack my windows and keep my heater humming. I roll on the radio hoping to catch mindless sport highlights, but every station is covering the fall of Baghdad and all the palace looting, so I turn it off.

I push back my seat. After reclining a little I dig into the sweet cream. It's no peanut butter chunk, but no real complaints either.

In the far corner of the large open school field is a dusty softball diamond with isolated patches of green crab grass surfacing in the out-field like lonely islands. Before it was a school field it was a strawberry field. Before it was a strawberry field it was a landlocked grassy plain where kids like me used to build dirt bike ramps and smoke stolen cigarettes from our farmer fathers. The field always looks magnificently yellow—golden like a little girl's Easter dress—in the oily dying light.

Two teenagers are sitting on home plate with their heads snapped up into the dusk, pointing. I lean my eyes against the window but I don't see anything special in the sky. The moon is round and red like a cartoon apple.

The red glow of the moon reminds me of the first time I learned the universe was expanding. As a youngster, the idea of universe expansion was exciting and optimistic and powerful and novel and hopeful, like teenage sex. But now, it bums me out thinking that everything is always moving away from everything else. What kind of *expansion* is that, anyway? A red glowing expansion of bummer, that's what. That's adult sex. It's not The Big Bang, it's The Big Bummer.

I love when the ice cream melts around the edges in that lovely space between the ice cream mass and the carton. It's dessert plasma. Star fuel that ignites my mind numb. I swirl my spoon in those delicious icy voids and let the gravity globs of cream on my spoon plop right down the blackness of my open throat.

I don't see the police officer parking behind me. The officer's shirt is too small or his biceps are too big. He asks me if he can help me with anything. He is sporting a flattop. I didn't even know you could still get that haircut. This guy is a stereotype and I'm not sure if I'm supposed to take him seriously.

"This is my ice cream," I say. "You can get your own."

I obnoxiously slurp the melting ice cream chowder off my plastic deli spoon. The officer walks back to my license plate. Above my *Vietnam Vet* decal is my round bumper sticker: *My Son's a U.S. Marine.*

The officer's voice is less stiff when he returns and he crouches next to my window, as if we are now frat buddies. He points to a sign posted next to the lot entrance stating no nighttime parking, and he tells me to be mindful of these signs in the future. I have no interest in playing along with him. I've played along all my life and look where it's gotten me. My burnt honey is melting.

"But officer, it's dusk," I say in my lawyer voice.

There is a large vein in the officer's neck, coiled like a rattlesnake, and it starts to twitch. The officer stands from his squat and asks me to step out of my car. He stares off into the dark distance, squinting. The red moon is lower in the sky and it buries itself into the blackwashed olive orchard fringing the horizon.

"My daughter is over there, too," he says. "She's Air Force."

But I don't want to reason with this fella. The teenagers are looking at us from across the baseball diamond, and I feel tough.

"Look, you've made a mistake," I say.

"Good, so we have an understanding?"

The teenagers are walking at us. Obviously the kiddies are interested, and this excites me.

"We do. I'll leave when you apologize," I say with a sharp tone.

"Excuse me?" the officer hisses. "When I apologize? *Excuse me?*"

"You're excused."

"All right, tough guy." The officer's voice lowers into a matter-of-fact tone, as he puts his hands on his hips. His feet are wide with his toes pointing out, douchey power-stance style. I almost burst out into laughter at this fella. He yells: "You think you're clever, tough guy?"

"Yep, this *tough guy* is clever as burnt honey ice cream. I'm the best of both worlds."

And saying this reminds me that my precious sweet cream is on the dashboard, dissolving. When I reach for the ice cream the officer uncoils and strikes.

Ice cream whips all over my seat, crashing onto the officer and me like a comet's tail. "Jesus, that's goddamn organic," I scream as my head slams the pavement.

The paramedics are hovering with blinding lights, probing me for signs of life. The air smells of iron and blood. Officer Flattop is next to his patrol car with his hands crossed around his body, and he's talking to my wife and another officer in a plaid blazer. Anita is in her pale bathrobe that covers her like a white elephant. Her mascara isn't streaking. She's not crying. She's not red in the face. Not even a frown.

She is tired. Her eyes are saggy and disappointed. She looks her age, but I would never tell her that. Even when she bleaches her hair blond and gets her nails filled she looks her age. Even when she puts on her face with the purple eyeliner and vibrant blush to cover the aged creases of contempt that splinter around her small-town eyes like cracked windowpanes, she *still* looks her age. She's no longer a young country hardbody from a NorCal orchard town, yet not old enough to be sweet and soft and wise. So she's stuck in a menopausal mushy flux that makes her attitude on life appear more bitter and bitchy than lost and uncertain. It breaks my heart seeing her like this.

And I know, somehow, she's already let me go.

I know, somehow, that the real disappointment is something we can't touch—it's not even drifting in my blood. I know that the real concern standing in my wife's mind is that our baby boy is drifting terrified in Baghdad, fighting a war none of us understand. I am helpless. She's helpless. And it breaks my damn heart.

An EMT is asking me my name, location, date. Name location date.

"My name is Odonata, California. The location is Easter. The date is Now."

"Matthew," the other EMT says. "What's your last name?"

"What's a Matthew?" I say with a heavy tongue.

I lick my lips and consider reciting a bible verse from the Book of Matthew, but that will be pushing it. The skin around my lips is crusty and sugary from burnt honey. I wonder how long I can pretend to not remember. I wonder how long I *want* to pretend to not remember. I want to hold my son.

I want to run my fingers through his warswept oil-slick hair, wiping away the sand and horror from his face. I want to pretend my son is on his way home right now, and he's stopping to pick up an orchid for his mother and a treat for just the two of us. My boy is a sucker for peanut butter chocolate treats. Our favorite late night ritual after Anita goes to bed is watching ESPN sport highlights on our shitty black and white TV in the garage, eating ice cream out of metal mixing bowls.

Now one of the EMTs is talking to my wife. They power walk toward my gurney. Anita still has her makeup on from her waitress gig at the Copper Kettle. She doesn't really need to work. We aren't that strapped for cash, but my wife likes cocktails, and my wife likes blackjack, and those are two activities you should never do while you're lonely. Her hoop earrings are discoing the patrol car lights in these beautiful self-transforming diamonds.

"Stop fucking around, Matt. Shame on you. Stop pretending."

My wife is resting her weight and frustration into her left hip, like she does when she's talking to rude customers who flag her down for more ranch dressing for their home fries. Twenty-one years of marriage and my wife's condescending hip-lock still digs into my manhood, and she knows it. I raise my hand up to her.

"Hi, I'm Baghdad. It's my pleasure."

In the hospital my doctor shuts the door and leans in, talking in a whisper.

"Now, this…this is clever."

And he winks at me. The small room is sharp like bleach. Pale blue sterile walls. The buzzing fluorescent lights that stick to the ceiling sound like flies hovering over shit. Hospital shit.

"I'm not sure what this…this means, but right back at you," I respond, winking.

The muted television is mounted high on the smooth wall, and the channel is a news program showing maps of Iraq with red and blue arrows pointing at Baghdad. Young college somethings in business suits who've never heard the whip of a gun crack the silent night, or who've never been to the Middle East, sit behind a desk analyzing and critiquing war plans and exit strategies. Doc smirks with half his face and I can see he's scheming.

"Since your memory is fuzzy, let me help you…"

He tells me that before I left his office and before the burnt honey and before the police officer ordeal and before the paramedics, I had promised him I was going to cut out the bullshit. I had promised I was going to tell my wife that the cancer had spread into my lymph nodes. I had promised to tell my wife I refused treatment because I just couldn't put her and the kids through that again. I had promised that I was going to eat only vegetables.

And I know he's lying about the only vegetables part, but I can't call him out. I'm supposed to have no memory of anything. Nice try, Doc.

"I promised all that?" I say with surprise. "Well, if I did say that then it's true."

I look directly into Doc's eyes and tell him I don't remember anything, but if I did remember something, it was that I always told the best version of the truth and I always meant well. I slip in that I will eat all veggies if I must but that doesn't sound natural, nor does it sound like something I would promise.

I almost crack, but I keep my composure.

I can hear my wife's high-pitched clucking in the hospital corridor. The same voice she always uses whenever she's talking on the phone. She's shouting, "Chocolate…chocolate with peanut butter…no, nothing with vanilla."

The doctor puts down his pen and clipboard. He forces all the air out of his lungs, as if blowing out birthday candles.

"Matthew, we're all here to help. You don't have to do this alone."

Turns out, the worst part of having cancer *is* the sympathy. And the sorrow. All the sorrow I can fit into the marrow of my shaking bones. A person isn't supposed to see their own sorrow in others, but cancer has a way of slowing things.

Terminal disease is traffic: where you spend most of the time angry at other people just living their own lives and being in your way, so you glare into passenger windows like you know everything about those people as they pass you by in their gas-guzzling SUVs.

I've gone from near death to cancer remission, to cancer with a re-mission of death twice before. I just don't have any fuel left in my reserves for this next battle. I'm the one with faulty blood pumping through my pipelines, but I have to watch everyone dry up and die around me first.

Sorrow and sympathy make people forget there is a whole universe out there separate from the self, but I can't blame them. Our universe is expanding: shifting apart—separating from itself. I used to be a lawyer and I used to think I was clever.

"How was that working out for you?" Doc asks.

"What? The perspective or the sympathy?"

"C'mon, Mattie, no more jokes. Are you ready?"

He stands, waiting for my response. And so am I. The door opens. A warm draft moves over my cold toes and up my legs and around my bony, sunken face. I'm holding my breath. I'm holding onto everything I can. My heart beats in my wooden red-veined ears, knocking like a solicitor.

And I'm waiting.

SILENCED VOICES:
FRANCISCO PACHECO BELTRÁN

by Cathal Sheerin

In the early hours of April 25, 2016, Mexican journalist Francisco Pacheco Beltrán documented on his website the extreme violence that had occurred a few hours earlier in his home state of Guerrero:

Francisco Pacheco Beltrán

A night of terror enveloped the tourist zone around the port of Acapulco when gunfights broke out at various spots along the Costera Miguel Alemán, closely followed by an organized assault carried out by an armed group on a hotel popular with the Federal Police. Social media users shared videos showing a heavy police presence on the streets. High caliber weapon fire could be heard coming from all directions. All this took place around ten p.m., when citizens were out for the night; many sought refuge in shopping centers for fear of being hit in the crossfire. For a short period of time, Acapulco became a virtual war zone, terrifying the citizens who have complained to the government over the lack of security and the violence into which Acapulco has descended: it is the most violent city in the country."

When the shooting had died down, news outlets reported that one gunman had been killed and a police officer injured. But the "night of terror" was not over. It had yet to claim its final victim: Pacheco.

It was not yet daybreak when Pacheco left his house in the city of Taxco in order to accompany one of his daughters to the bus station. Having safely seen her off, he headed home. The night had been long and, as he turned into the road where he lived, he was probably thinking of catching a few hours' sleep. That would have been around six thirty a.m., which is the time that his wife and another daughter heard what they described as the sound of firecrackers going off outside the house. Curious, and perhaps a bit annoyed, they went outside to see what was happening. What they saw was Pacheco lying in the road, soaked in blood, dead. He had been shot twice in the back of the head—executed. There were no witnesses.

Pacheco, fifty-five, had been a journalist for many years. He was editor of *El Foro de Taxco*, a reporter for *El Sol de Acapulco*, and a correspondent for the radio station Capital Máxima. Like many journalists, he also ran a personal blog where he posted reports online about the increasing violence and corruption in his state.

When Pacheco was murdered, he was—at that point—the fifth journalist to be killed in Mexico in 2016. January had seen Reinel Martínez Cerqueda and Marcos Hernández Bautista murdered; Moisés Dagdug Lutzow and Anabel Flores Salazar had been February's victims. And, as this is being written, two more—Elpidio Ramos Zárate and Manuel Torres—have been added to the list.

At this rate, 2016 will quickly surpass 2015 as the most lethal year for Mexican journalists since President Enrique Peña Nieto took office in 2012. Taking the most up-to-date statistics available regarding lethal and non-lethal violence, free-expression organization Article 19

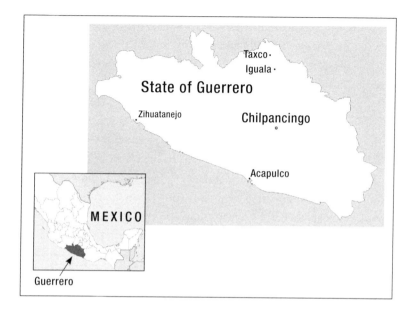

reports that there is an attack on journalists every twenty-two hours in Mexico.

According to Mexico's National Commission for Human Rights, 109 journalists were killed, mostly because of their work, between the year 2000 and the start of 2016. Though the geographic focus of the violence may change—at various times it has been Veracruz, Chihuahua, Guerrero, Tamaulipas, Oaxaca—the intensity never abates. In recent years, many journalists have fled Mexico; many more have chosen to remove their bylines from articles, preferring anonymity to death.

A few years ago I interviewed the Mexican journalist and poet Rolando Nájera. I asked him about what it was like to work and live in an environment where violence always seemed to be waiting just around the corner. This is what he told me:

> My job has become riskier, and this has forced crime reporters to change the way they work. Many of them now work in groups where they can protect each other. I lived in Ciudad Juárez during the years of the worst violence, when they used to kill up to eighteen people a

day, when they used to burn down businesses. The assaults, the extortion, the robberies, and kidnappings were everyday occurrences. The violence meant that people went out less frequently and locked themselves up in their houses. Juárez was converted into a ghost town, the streets were empty at night, and the people spoke of nothing except the violence. The daily question was, "How many did they kill today?" With every murder, the victim seemed to be closer to you. At first, it was the body of a stranger discovered in the outskirts of the city, then it was an acquaintance, then a neighbor, then a friend, and then came the moment when it was a member of your family.

Some years ago, when I was the editor of *Periódico PM*, I was a victim of death threats made by criminals. They phoned me at home to tell me that they were watching me. They said that I should go to the window, from where I would see a van parked in front of my house… I didn't sleep very well in those days. I used to receive emailed threats every day because of my work. During that period, the newspaper received a direct attack. The reporter Eugenia Cicero and the photojournalist Jaime Murrieta (may he rest in peace) were beaten up by hooded men while they were trying to report on an incident…

When you see that so many innocent people have died and that no one does anything about it, it's difficult to trust the authorities. When you see how investigations are manipulated, when you see that there are never concrete results, it's difficult to trust. And because of this, people don't report crimes. So it's a vicious circle where impunity is the protagonist.

Most journalists killed in Mexico die because they expose either the drug trafficking cartels or corrupt public officials, or the links between both. Those who carry out the killings enjoy almost 100% impunity, largely due to the corruption and inertia that are endemic throughout the Mexican states. Police and employees of local administrations are often implicated in attacks on journalists: Article 19 reports that 41.5% of attacks in 2015 were carried out by public officials.

And at state level there is little aptitude or willingness to protect journalists who are under threat: in 2012 a "hit list" containing the names of a number of journalists who were to be killed was circulated in Veracruz State; when the worried reporters went to the authorities, the only help they received was the advice, "Get out of town." In many cases, local officials would rather keep their heads down (and intact) than delve too deeply into the "who" and "why" of so many killings of journalists: murders are reported, details are taken, information is entered into databases, press statements are issued, and then the cases are let drift.

Pacheco's journalism criticized the Guerrero State administration generally, and the city administration in Taxco particularly, for their inability and, at times, seeming reluctance to tackle the worsening bloodshed on the streets. Guerrero's State governor, Héctor Astudillo Flores, had in fact asked journalists like Pacheco not to report on the violence in Guerrero. But Pacheco refused to be silenced, and then the violence silenced him.

Letters calling for a thorough investigation into the killing of Francisco Pacheco Beltrán may be sent to:

Héctor Astudillo Flores
Gobernador de Guerrero
Palacio de Gobierno
Boulevard René Juárez #62
Col. de los servicios
Chilpancingo
Guerrero
Mexico

Cathal Sheerin is a journalist and human rights campaigner. He is a consultant for the Writers in Prison Committee of PEN International.

*My grandmother has for years been insisting
I use this as my author photo.*

S.P. MacIntyre earned his MFA at the University of Illinois, Urbana–Champaign, and his work has appeared in *cream city review*; *Hobart* (web); *Cease, Cows*; *The Rattling Wall*; and, now, *Glimmer Train Stories*. He was born in Los Angeles but currently lives with his wife in South Florida, where he edits newsletters and writes about epistemology and finance.

PINCH

S.P. MacIntyre

My son was allergic to nearly everything. My girlfriend and I couldn't pick him up without wearing non-latex gloves, which we couldn't afford and couldn't always steal. Antihistamines were out—gelatin in the gelcaps. When he wasn't screaming, he'd breathe out this endless, droning whimper that sometimes pitched up into a whine. Day and night, the noise. When he did scream, usually for the few hours after we fed him his special formula, the force and friction sometimes caused his throat to swell shut. Left long enough—and I'm ashamed to admit we started leaving him alone a lot—sometimes his joints would lock up and he'd have a seizure and we'd have to take him to the county hospital up in Sylmar for some epinephrine, which we always ran out of because we either sold it or took it all ourselves.

My girlfriend's name was Sadie, but she wasn't sexy. Once she quit diet pills and uppers and had the kid she got a little fat around the ankles. And everywhere else. Her parents were Lebanese-Armenians who brought her over from France in the eighties, and I suppose when we started dating I liked the way her mouth moved, the way it shaped to pronounce words—a hint of nasally French mixed with the elongated Armenian vowels in *Poghosian* or *Inch*. I didn't know she was pregnant until around the seven-month mark. Late in the game. We had to make some serious life choices. And when I stopped chewing blotter like bubblegum I realized that Sadie's face had gotten that wide-pored burnt look you see in longtime meth users, like she had a mask-face that hung loose on her face-face.

So I guess I stayed with her for the kid.

Sadie named our son Abraham, after her great-great-grandfather who saved a village from a bunch of Kurds or Turks or something. I've always had a problem with the burden of so much history, and, besides, the name reminded me too much of rote memorization and itchy yarmulkes, so I started calling him Pinch. Because I couldn't. Pinch him, that is.

Those first few months after the birth didn't treat us well. We started using again in a serious way to stay awake, and then just because. We couldn't bring in much money after I got fired from my video editing job—I had to resort to selling for Crackhead Mike from time to time—and she couldn't leave the apartment, so we fought a lot. There was an afternoon, a couple weeks before my big decision, when I came home and she had gone at the walls with a claw hammer looking for a baby monitor she thought she'd lost, sending a bunch of gypsum dust into the air that made Pinch sick. A friend of hers had come by with a bunch of whippets. I'm not one to judge, but it didn't sit right with me, and I only bring it up because, in retrospect, I should have known something was going to happen.

So one night, I was prepping Pinch's special formula and Sadie was making mac and cheese on the hotplate we had put on top of the broken stove. Pinch cried in the other room, so I tried to hurry before his tears gave him a rash. Sadie had been sloshing the cream and cheese powder for a bit when she turned to me and said, "I think I might be a bad mom."

"You're not a bad mom," I said.

Sadie spooned out some of the macaroni gloop and let it spill back down into the pot in a wet-sounding cascade. "I think I want our son to die."

"What?" I said.

"I want to get rid of him. Our son."

"Oh. That's not what I thought you said."

"What did you think I said?"

I screwed the top onto the formula bottle. "I thought you said, 'I think I want some pie.' I was on board with you for a second." I looked up from the bottle and I met her narrow eyes pressed into a blank stare. "Not really so much anymore."

"Josh, this is serious."

I put the bottle down and put on my serious face. "Yeah, no. For sure. It's a problem. We should totally talk about it."

"We are talking about it," she said.

"We should probably talk about it some more, then," I said.

"Okay," she said.

"Okay," I said. I didn't really know how to continue, so I asked Sadie to give me a sec. I went into the laundry room where we kept the coke in one of the metal exhaust tubes—we had sold off the machines a while before. I tried to think hard about what Sadie said, since it worried me so much, so I smoked until my feet felt sweaty.

When I felt ready enough to deal I returned to the kitchen. Sadie had put Pinch in the oven; his screams seemed muffled and ragged.

I consider myself a pretty unflappable guy, but with my heart batting against the inside of my chest like a moth in a killing jar and the cocaine giving everything a furious urgency, I'm surprised that the only thing I could muster was, "What are you doing?"

Sadie looked weird. Her face was more loose than usual. Her eyes were always sunken with dark, veiny circles, but now they seemed recessed: tight, beady, focused on nothing. She folded her arms so tightly against her breasts I thought they would burst. Sadie didn't answer me. "What are you doing?" I asked.

Sadie responded in a too-loud voice, as though she were speaking to someone in another room, "This is better. We can go back to—it'll be like before." Then, after too long of a pause, she added, in a much quieter voice, "We'll just keep him there for now, until we can figure out what to do."

I sniffed a bit. My throat was raw and I was having trouble unclenching my jaw. At that moment, all I could think was that my mouth was dumb. Those exact words—*my mouth is dumb*—had earwormed their way into my head and kept repeating. I wish I had said, Sadie, think about what you're doing, you're hurting our son; listen to him, Sadie, he's hurting. What I actually said was, "The oven's broke." I even touched one of the knobs to illustrate the fact.

Sadie shrugged. It made me angry.

All at once words sluiced out of me that I can't remember exactly, but went something along the lines of, "I don't think you've stopped to properly consider what you're doing, nor do I believe you've taken a moment to mentally pore over the ramifications, the fundamentally super-awful consequences, of putting our child in an oven, broken or no—something that perturbs me and with which you can assuredly, if you take a moment, empathize." Something like that, but probably with more swearing and yelling. I have a bad habit of letting things build until they all release at once.

But regardless of what I said, I could see Sadie's face come back to life after that, the muscles working and her eyes meeting mine. Some essential part of Sadie started rattling around in her brain and twisted together a few ragged wires. In a calm, exhausted monotone, Sadie said, "Probably we should go to the hospital."

On the drive over to the county hospital Sadie stared at the freeway lamps and didn't say anything. All the lights thrummed with that pre-dawn halo and seemed to sync with Pinch's choked screams in the back. Dirt and red splotchy hives dotted his skin.

The ER waiting room was full of people covered in infected welts or burns or ulcers or cuts, sweating in the air conditioning, shielding their eyes from the dim fluorescent lights, and scratching at cellulitis or ringworm or nothing at all. Mexicans, Vietnamese, African-Americans, Persians, Indians, Salvadorans, Caucasians, Koreans, people I couldn't even begin to pin ethnically: everyone focused on their own little personal patch of misery. Aside from the addicts and poor, immigrants waited with their whole families—kids and parents and siblings and all that—and staring at them made me sort of miss my parents, but only a little. None of them acknowledged each other except to bum a cigarette or ask for change for the vending machine, and they all ignored me and my rasping infant.

There was a twenty-hour wait for most everyone, though the hospital usually expedited kids. By the time they called the fake name I had put down and Pinch and I were pulled back into triage, however, day had broken and I had lost track of Sadie, who went out for a cigarette with a guy and didn't come back. They took Pinch into the pediatric ICU and I went back to the waiting room, as usual.

I had plenty of time to sit and fidget. The itch was starting to come on and I knew I would get buggy any second. I jostled my knee and scratched until my skin turned flaky white and then bloody. My thoughts came on rapid-fire and inchoate, and I kept returning to the time leading up to Pinch's birth.

I used to think his sickness resulted from the drugs and drinking. I've seen on TV the way meth can mess up a kid: hearts on the outside, no brains, no bones, just cartilaginous muck holding them together for the few agonizing weeks they stayed alive.

Now, though, I started to think it was blind luck, a divine casting of lots or some celestial dreidel that came up *gimel*. What happened to my son could've happened to any kid in the world. Here he was, a sickly kid born to a pair of drug addicts. I had decided that, for the most part, stuff just happens and there isn't much I can do about it except accept it.

Though I suppose we didn't really "accept it" when we found out Sadie was pregnant. Because of the way her body was shaped—thick, with gangly, spider-like limbs—we just thought she was getting fatter as time went on. We used protection, and nausea goes hand in hand with what we do; I, at least, had no idea.

After some months Sadie started vaginally spotting in a serious way. The county hospital staff, to rule out an infection or parasites, made her take a piss test and discovered she was pregnant and absolutely twacked out of her mind. Because of that, the hospital 5150ed her. Standard procedure. By the time she was out of the hospital, she was already into her third trimester and we had to ask Sadie's parents for money to have it "taken care of." Even though they were religious, they understood that *drastic measures* were necessary. We drove to Glendale to meet with them; it was the first time they had met me. Sadie looked like the perfect fifty-fifty blend between her mother and father: her mother's full figure, her father's thin, angular face, both of their brown eyes and their blue veins that seemed to rest right under the surface of their skin. I couldn't help but stare at her father's white hair that came out in thin milky bristles like tarantula fuzz. They spoke with a calm eagerness, mostly in Armenian, and seemed very sure of what needed to happen. I kept my eyes on her father's temples. The skin was raised like a scar where his veins were, and through the whole conversation they refused to throb with any hint of inner turmoil. That didn't sit right with me. But within an hour they cut us a check for a few grand to go to Colorado for a late-term abortion.

We went to cash the check and then get a "pick me up" for the long drive we never ended up making. I guess I was relieved, but scared too. We decided to keep him, to get clean or try.

Then Pinch—baby Abraham—was born. Very prematurely. Since Sadie'd been 5150ed and tested positive for drugs during the pregnancy, the state assigned us a caseworker: a girl I'd actually gone to school with who ratted me out for "selling" her weed she had got caught with (though she actually stole it from my bag). How's that for happenstance?

But sitting there in that waiting room, feeling the creeping anxiousness crawl under my skin, the ramifications of all this ugly randomness began to dawn on me. What if Sadie never came back? What if they took Pinch away? If either of those things happened—well, my feelings would be complicated by a dreadful, conscience-rending stroke of profound relief. I would not have to return home to change the HEPA filters, clean the sheets and bottles in dye-and-scent-free detergent I'd need to lift from the market, or dust the apartment with the only implements I had: a size two acrylic paintbrush and the motivation from whatever grains of crystal I could recover from the rug. Hell, I became so resigned I messaged Crackhead Mike to arrange a meetup.

They finally called me back into Pinch's room and a nurse stood watching me from the corner. He had tubes coming out of his mouth to help him breathe, and each breath came with a small wheezing gust from a nearby machine. Except for this sound, Pinch was completely silent, his eyes closed, not struggling or seeming to be in any pain. Aside from all the tubes, his small pediatric bed had only a white hypoallergenic sheet and blanket—there were no clothes and no toys or stuffed animals to keep him company. Pinch had no toys or stuffed animals at home and I doubted he ever would, and, in that moment, this thought killed me. Red, scaly welts and receding hives covered his body. He was so underweight that I could make out his ribs and, even six months after his birth, I could still see his pulse against the soft spot on his head.

I thought: what the hell kind of life is this?

I thought: what if he would be better off dead?

I thought: I must be a bad dad, too.

I thought: he might not even be my son.

I thought: it's terrible to be in so much pain all the time and have nothing that can help relieve such a burden.

But he was my son: I couldn't abandon him the way my father had abandoned me. I had to do something about this. There had to be something I could do; things couldn't go on like this. Time to get serious and think. What could I do? What could I do? I said it out loud: "What can I do? Tell me what to do."

He didn't answer, nor did the nurse. Pinch kept on sleeping. Like a baby. It seemed so weird and miraculous I felt like I was about to cry. I wanted Pinch to have this peace every night.

But whatever peace that moment possessed got crushed by a four foot eleven terror: Ava Glück, the Glückster, Pinch's caseworker, the woman who'd originally 5150ed Sadie and who used to sneak out of class to smoke weed with me when we were kids.

"So you're going by," Glück looked down at her chart, "'Isaac Dickson' now?" Her lips twisted in some caricature of an *I got you now* grin, the kind of grin that appears on movie fighter pilot faces as they go in for the kill—more of a snarl than a smile, really, because part of her lower lip was permanently swollen, which did little to take attention away from the mirror-shattering device she called a face with its drooping nose and the awful, hairy mole right under her left nostril. I didn't hate Glück because she was ugly, or even because she had the power to take my kid away. I hated her because she, to me, embodied every young Jewish-American Princess my mom tried to set me up with in high school, with their BMWs and houses in the hills and horses, their smug entitlement and false sense of superiority and shallowness. I hated her because she reminded me of my mom.

With Glück in the room, the nurse left to give us privacy, though I wish she had stayed.

"Are you high, Josh?" asked Glück. "You look like you haven't slept in years."

I wiped my nose and sniffled—my nose always ran. "Having a rough day," I said.

"With such extensive...'suspicion' of abuse and neglect," she said, making air quotes with her fingers and moving over to the edge of Pinch's bed, "all I need to do is file a report with CPS." She smoothed an edge of the blanket so it covered Pinch's exposed foot. "Yup, one quick phone call and baby Abraham here becomes a ward of the state—probably end up with a foster family more messed up than—"

"I'll take him home now, then," I said, readjusting the blanket Glück had just touched.

"Not quite so easy, that. See that little pink band?" she pointed to the bracelet on Pinch's wrist surrounded by hives. "That'll trigger alarms all over the hospital if he goes one step out of the pediatric ward."

"What do you want, Ava?"

"Well, that's just the thing," Glück trailed off, placing her clipboard on the counter and cocking her hip before looking me in the eyes. "I've been having a bad run of luck myself. Some money trouble, student loans, stingy parents—I'm sure you can understand—and while social work gives me the warm fuzzies from helping people, it doesn't quite, you know, pay."

"You have my deepest sympathy."

She put her hand out and leaned against the countertop, which I think was meant to make her seem at ease and in power but instead looked weird because the counter was almost as tall as she was. "You know people, bad people. If you can…use those people to help me out a bit, maybe I'll look the other way again."

"Don't you think that I would get money if it was that easy?"

Glück shrugged.

This whole conversation mixed with a comedown was stressing me out more than I already was. I felt the bugs start to crawl under my skin—"formication" is the word I learned in college. I shifted my weight from one foot to the other and back because my entire body felt covered in raw nerves. "How much?"

Glück clacked her acrylic nails against the counter in thought. "Let's say ten grand?"

"I'll mail you a check."

"I want it by tomorrow."

"That's stupid. No. Fuck you."

Glück gave me some explanation about the hospital discharge process and the protocol for reporting to CPS being somehow tied to that—I don't remember all the details. "Besides," she continued, "this…*poor child* deserves better."

"What would I need to do to stop all this? Like, aside from hitting up loan sharks who'd probably take my kid as collateral anyway?"

"I suppose you could pass a drug test."

"Sign me up," I said. "Let's pencil it in for next month."

Glück pulled a plastic cup out of a nearby cabinet in dramatic fashion. "I'd have to watch you, of course." Her eyes darted down and back up my body in a way that made me want to tear off my dick and throw it across the room while I ran away screaming, arms flailing.

"So dollars it is."

"I figured as much." After Glück put the cup on the counter—it was like watching a growth-stunted child reach up to put a cup away at the behest of her parents—her demeanor changed and softened. She looked at Pinch, my small bundle of bones and breathing tubes, lying on the bed with a look of such high-minded benevolence and sympathy I wanted to rip her heart out. "You know, there are plenty of good Jewish parents out there; they want a son of their own, and they want one young enough that he won't remember his parents or going from foster house to foster house. And you can bet that who-ever he ends up with will have the means to deal with this whole—" she swiveled her wrist in the air at all the tubes and machines, "thing. You can just call it quits, dump the shiksa, get clean in jail, try to have another kid down the road."

I was getting more agitated and nauseous. When I spoke I spoke with every part of my body in some kind of motion. "Please stop talking about him as though he were a piece of meat. He's my child and he wants to be with his family."

Glück picked up her clipboard and made her sneering face again. "The little shit doesn't 'want' anything. Get me twenty grand by tomorrow and I'll make this all go away."

"You said—"

"Whatever," said Glück as she walked out, turning one last time to say, "I hurt you because I care, Josh." Her voice seethed with so much compassion and tenderness it hit me like a machete. I heard her in the hallway asking the nurse to come back.

I put both of my hands on the guardrail of Pinch's bed. He started to stir in discomfort, but he raised an arm and rested his hand, small as a thimble, against one of my knuckles. I'd like to think he was trying to say, "There, there. There, there. You'll figure something out."

After I called Crackhead Mike, I went out to the car. Sadie was lying down in the backseat, her head resting against the baby's seat. She held on to a crumpled ball of foil gummy with something black and a thick straw that had been torn in half—like one of those straws big enough to suck tapioca balls through. I originally thought she was asleep, but she kept using her fingernails to shave little white worms of plastic off the car seat. Her lips were chapped and split, and when she talked I could hear the suck of flesh as the dry parts of her mouth and throat came apart.

I told her about Pinch's predicament, about Glück, about the security and the breathing tubes and Child Protective Services and the money. She stared absently at a splotch on the floor of the footwell that could have been a dark sweat stain as easily as it could have been faded blood. I asked her if she could ask her parents for money. I would drive down to Glendale to pick it up so we could get Pinch out before he was *processed*.

"No," she said. "No parents." She made several smacking sounds with her mouth while working up the energy to speak more. "In Europe."

I grabbed the foil from her hand and uncrumpled it to see if there was enough black tar left for me. "What are we going to do about Pinch, then?" I asked, looking around for a lighter.

"Pinch," Sadie said, the word drawling out slow and desultory. "Pinch, Pinch, Pinch. I want my baby Abey baptized." Sadie scooped up her hair in her hands and let it fall over her face and into the car seat. She went on a long, detailed rant about having Abraham baptized in an Armenian church with ornate stained glass in arched windows depicting the annunciation superimposed over a Coptic cross, the air hot with pine incense shaken from simple gold—Sadie's voice quivered and stuttered—censers embossed with crosses as Abraham, offered in a shroud of Armenian silk so purple the Jacarandas would stoop in shame, was dipped once, twice, and again with such delicacy even St. Cyril would weep.

Sadie had studied theology in college; it had been a long time since she talked like this. It was as though she had been retaining it all, keeping it dammed and buried, carrying it around inside her, waiting for the occasion to cough out this burning effusion of language.

I finished freebasing and balled up the foil again. "So do you want to call your parents? About the money?"

She didn't respond.

"I don't think Pin—Abe'd do well in holy water," I said as I started the car. It took a few tries and the engine made a grinding noise.

She started picking at the plastic again. I left the hospital and headed to the freeway.

• • •

The drive to Santa Monica down the 405 took an hour because of construction, though with the heroin I felt like I was being carried in a sling: I leaned my seat way back and let life carry me forward—usually about three feet at a time, with the way traffic moved. The drive gave me plenty of time to replay events in my head and feel generally shitty. I had no idea how to get that money, and all I could think about was foster care and the awful, like, abuse stories I'd heard about it.

More than a mere pick-me-up, I needed to see Crackhead Mike for something else. After I lost my job, he had offered to introduce me to a friend-of-a-friend with work, something a little more time intensive and "strenuous"—is the way he put it—than delivering eight-balls to parties in Long Beach. Thinking that it involved taking a shot of canola oil and swallowing a hundred condom-wrapped pellets of coke, I had politely refused. Now, though, an advance on some mule money seemed like a decent option.

Doing drugs the way I used to, before Pinch got born, you develop a pretty good sense of timing. You learn how to feel the different parts of your body as though they each have their own itch, and when those need to be soothed with a specific balm. But this urgency begets a weird sort of opportunism, so you learn how to satisfy bodily need with what you're actually able to get. Noz will sit in for PCP, but that gets expensive if you can't steal it so it's good to keep some ketamine handy; Adderall or Ritalin will hold you over between meth binges; crack is cheaper but coke is easier to get, and you can always make crack if you have cocaine and baking soda handy; pretty much anything you can steal from the pharmacy will ease up an H withdrawal, though you can freebase Dilaudid the same as black-tar; meth and heroin combined work if you can't get MDMA; mescaline, mushrooms, and peyote are good to mix if you can't get acid; and since acrylic house paint is banned in California and department stores lock up their spray paint, it's better to huff computer dusters or propane. Keeping up with it all was exhausting, and Pinch's birth threw my whole system out of whack, which made it harder to "ease up" on some things. I had

162

started showing up to work late or not at all because I couldn't hit that pharmacological sweet spot that would allow me to work frame-by-frame on the Amiga for nine hours and then stay up all night. I had one friend in a bad way who got caught pulling a smash-and-grab at an electronics store. I hadn't yet resorted to that kind of stuff, but after some months of my kid screaming, my girlfriend copping all my shit, and always feeling like something's crawling under my skin that itches so bad I'd scratch to bleeding and then scratch more until I had my own fat under my fingernails, doing something disagreeable seemed more and more appealing. At any rate, things were a far cry from when Sadie and I'd just met and kept a propane tank by the bed so we could fire up and fuck all night.

"I have a joke for you," said Crackhead Mike when Sadie and I got to his place. I sat on his broken futon bed and Sadie fetally curled in one of his Ikea chairs. He continued, "What's worse than finding a worm in your apple?"

I lifted my hands, exasperated. "I don't know. Half a worm in—"

"The holocaust."

Nobody laughed, though Crackhead Mike had a big smile on his face. I normally didn't find him funny, but today I felt damn near deadened. I said, "Funny."

"Fucking asshole," Sadie said loudly from the chair, partly into a cushion. She and Crackhead Mike used to have some sort of arrangement that ended with her not liking him much, but she never talked about it and I never asked about the details.

Crackhead Mike chuckled at the outburst and used a credit card to chop the coke into thin white lines on a pewter hand mirror. He was a big guy who had, with an equal mix of discipline and negligence, matted and twisted his hair into long dreadlocks, though he had started to bald on top. His paunch had a sort of second under-paunch that his "חי Times" T-shirt didn't cover and which muffined over his Nike shorts. We'd also gone to Hebrew school together and stayed acquainted through college when he started dealing and I started dabbling more seriously. He got his nickname when, in high school, someone dared him to snort a white powder—probably gypsum—they'd found in a Starburst wrapper, which he did in the middle of AP History. He took his damn time dividing up the lines, sweeping them around in wormy squiggles before straightening them, which he knew drove me batshit. My legs each bounced to different time signatures while my eyes darted between the coke and *Raging Bull*, which played on his TV. "So how's your skank whore of a girlfriend?" he asked.

"Fuck yourself," said Sadie from the chair without opening her eyes.

"Good. Things are good," I said. "So how are things with y—are you going to finish with that or what?" He was still chopping and straightening the lines on the mirror.

"'Nigga, I ain't frontin',' " he rapped. Crackhead Mike knew the difference between "fronting" as in lying and "fronting" as in giving someone an advance in lieu of payment, but believed that doing the latter constituted lying to himself when it came to trusting people.

I unlocked myself from the couch and went over to rifle through Sadie's pockets—she had a couple fives and some singles. She didn't move or put up a fuss, just moaned a bit, and I wondered how much she had 'based before I got to the car. I gave the cash to Crackhead Mike, who raised the mirror benevolently, as though offering a sacrifice.

Crackhead Mike's apartment was full of knickknacks he had gotten from blanket-top sellers along the beach: a Nigerian flag he used as a cover for his couch; wooden grinning statues holding oversized tribal masks that, when removed, revealed large wooden penises; droopy, swooping psychedelic glass sculptures resulting from someone's failed attempts to make bongs or pipes. I leaned over the mirror and saw my reflection stuck between the lines and it put me ill at ease: my eyelids puffed so much they seemed about to burst, the scab I had at my hairline wept, the muscles of my jaw worked in swells and recessions. It might have been the movie playing in the background: it was the part where Jake LaMotta got jailed and started hitting his head against and punching the concrete wall of his cell, screaming at himself, "Dumb. Dumb. Dumb. Dummy. Why? Why? Why? Why?" over and over as his fists and elbows and head struck the wall with dull, meaty thwacks. I looked down at the coke again and saw framed between the white lines Pinch's bloodshot eyes set in my face. "Why'd you do it? You're so stupid. You're so fucking stupid." I straightened away from the mirror. "I'm not that bad. Why do you want to treat me like this? I'm not that bad. I'm not that guy."

I said, "Mikey, things aren't going great."

He brought the mirror toward his body protectively. "When are things not, like, for you, not great?" he asked.

"I'm actually really in a bind right now."

"I can't lend you any money, dude."

"Mike," I said, getting to my knees and resting my elbows on his neon surfboard coffee table, "I need you to hook me up with something, anything. I need some serious cash quick; they're going to take Pinch away." I explained the situation, during which he snorted the lines I'd bought and fed back some language to show me he was still listening.

When I mentioned Glück, he lifted his head and said, "The Glückster? Shit, I hate JAPs. Almost as bad as Persian and Armo girls, right, Sadie?"

She didn't respond. When I turned to look, her body, still in the same position, heaved with stifled sobs. Her whole face contorted around her silent crying.

Crackhead Mike started chopping a new line. All the unshavable little hairs surrounding his labret had brushed up a collection of fine white powder. "Armenian girls," he said, shaking his head.

"I need help," I said. "I need a lot of money fast."

"I heard you, man," he said, handing me the mirror, which I took without thinking. "Why doesn't she turn tricks or something?"

"Because I'd spend the whole time turning you down, you shit," Sadie yelled, surprising me, her voice ragged but clear of its earlier haze. She got up and stomped to the bathroom, slamming the door.

Crackhead Mike breathed a heavy sigh and leaned back on his couch but kept his butt on the edge, making his body recline at an uncomfortable-looking angle. His legs were splayed wide so that his belly fat could rest between them. "Dude," he said, pausing. "Dude, do you remember how the Glückster was in school? Way it sounds, she

S. P. MacIntyre

doesn't care if she gets the money or not. I think she wants to fuck with you before putting your kid in the system and getting you arrested."

"I'm trying to think," I said, snorting a line, "but I can't come up with anything else. I need to try to make the money thing work."

"Your 'rents?"

"Would prefer not."

"Hers?"

"Peaced out."

"Consider turning Glück in to the police?"

I leveled my gaze as I put the mirror down on the coffee table. "Think they'd take me seriously?"

Crackhead Mike took to playing with his dreadlocks, spinning one around between his thumb and index fingers. "Has it occurred to you," he started, "that maybe—and hear me out on this—everything would be better if Pinch, like, wasn't around?" Crackhead Mike's words, rattled off rapid fire, hung in the air for a second in a noticeable, heavy way. "I mean, you could get back to the good days, maybe move back to Panorama City, get a job, live it up again. Sadie'd be better off too, not having to stress and stuff. Now I love Pinchy-poo like a son or whatever, but wouldn't letting him go be in your best interest?"

I wish I could say I didn't entertain the idea, and I wish I could say that some long-deprived thing straining to bind me together didn't want to throw my hands up and say *Fuck it.* "I just need a number, Mikey," I implored. "A name, a number, and a reference from you."

Sadie began heaving and sputter-coughing in the bathroom.

Crackhead Mike pulled at the edge of the Nigerian flag until it partially draped over him like a blanket. "Yeah, okay, I know a guy," he said. "He's been buying a ton of leva from me, so I think he's moving some serious weight."

"Leva?"

"Levamisole. For cutting dope. But you're not going to like this guy, Josh."

"I don't need to like him; I just need to help him move some product."

"I think he's a skinhead," said Crackhead Mike, pulling a baggy

166   *Glimmer Train Stories*

from the couch cushions previously covered by the flag. "By the way, I'm out of rocks, so how much more powder do you want to buy?"

I sucked up some of the drip sliding down the back of my throat. Locust wings fluttered against the valves of my heart. "I think—just the number. I just want the number."

Crackhead Mike let his arms go limp beside him, flopping the baggy on the couch. "You're really fucking with my chi here, Señor Buzz Killington. My phone is all the way over there," he said, pointing to the shelf across the room where his pay-by-the-hour cellular brick sat next to a gem-encrusted pewter menorah wrapped in coiled, serpentine dragons.

"Thanks, Mike."

"Whatever," he said, replacing the baggy and unfurling the flag. "Make sure you clean up after Sadiekins when she's done in there. I worry about that girl."

"Thank you," I said, "I can't tell you how much I appreciate this."

Crackhead Mike started flipping through the channels now that *Raging Bull* was over. "Get your shit together, Josh," he said. "And don't hit me up again unless you intend to buy."

I hadn't seen my parents in three years, but I decided the time had come to drop by and see if they could help resolve my predicament, which they had been perfectly willing to do for the years leading up to them cutting me off and kicking me out.

I had gotten into a bad car accident—drove head-first into an Asian lady in my rinky-dink Paseo—and run off before the cops showed up. I went home, snuck in, and collapsed on my childhood bed under my Screaming Trees and *Requiem for a Dream* posters. The accident cracked three of my ribs; the airbag tore up my face. When my parents found me passed out they checked my pockets. I don't even remember what I carried, probably angel dust and microdots. The family lawyer got me out of jail by sending me to rehab: Mom and Dad agreed it would be the last time they'd "come to the rescue." I met Sadie in group and moved in with her after we got out. Everything that followed was a bit of a blur until things fell seriously apart.

S. P. MacIntyre

Crackhead Mike's hookup wouldn't be ready until early the next day, so after Sadie and I left Santa Monica we fought rush hour traffic on the 405–101 interchange. The cars clogged the arteries and thoroughfares as we crept all the way to Woodland Hills, where my parents had a house in the foothills of the Topanga Pass, on one of the many streets named after famous painters. Their house was typical for the San Fernando Valley, a poorly thought-through mix of stucco and clapboards, the result of too many cheap remodels, but with a well-tended lawn to distract from the sagging crossbeams that threatened to collapse like a lung in an exhaled gust of air. The clay shingles gave it that *ethnic flair*—a casual nod to the aesthetics of a region dotted with adobe Missions and Mission Burritos that many cathedral-roofed lower-upper-middle-class homes tried to shoehorn themselves into, whether they were the column-decorated "palaces" of Reseda or Calabasas McMansions.

My parents said they enjoyed the *character* of the house, that my mother didn't feel *comfortable* driving farther up the hill where the nicer houses perch or farther into the valley where traffic was awful, that with everybody talking about repealing Prop. 13 property taxes would—etc., etc. I didn't blame them for not wanting to move—my parents lived far enough away from shul that they could justify driving their car to a nearby strip mall on Saturday mornings and walk from there—but I hated growing up in that area. The trapped feeling bred resentment in me until I chose to expel it all in rebellion.

This came up in group therapy a lot, when I was in rehab, how I thought I was purging myself with the drugs but was actually just infecting myself with something else, but I don't know. I sometimes think I didn't have a choice in the matter, that my behavior was an accident of birth, and if I had grown up in poverty I might have gone in the opposite direction, kept on with my filmmaking degree, become a Hollywood mucky-muck like my parents wanted, like my dad was. It's like no matter what I had, I wanted the opposite, and if I had nothing to start with maybe I wouldn't have burned my life down.

We parked the car in the cul-de-sac while we waited for my dad to get home from work. Sadie reclined in the passenger seat while I tapped my fingers against the wheel. I was coming down pretty hard and getting impatient.

"So do you have any ideas?" I asked.

"Stop asking me that," said Sadie.

"Give me a straight answer."

"I feel sick."

A memory squirmed into my consciousness as I looked at the creamy white walls of my parents' house. I saw the faux-rustic cabinets and shelves of the living room—designed to be imperfect so as to make them seem authentic—and my father's Remington replicas. I recalled crawling around as a child and finding brown recluses hiding in the crevices and on the inside lips of the furniture, and, beneath those death machines, the dried, faded brown husks of ladybugs and black beetles and gangly crickets. There always seemed a lifeless or dangerous thing lurking out of sight, just behind some façade or some expensive-looking something-or-other.

"Josh," Sadie started, "Abey—I think we should—"

"Here he is," I said as my dad pulled into the driveway.

"I'm going to be sick again," said Sadie.

I watched my dad get out of his car, the bald back of his head reflecting white like an eye. The garage had always been crowded and I could still see the multicolored stacking bins full of sporting equipment and tools and plastic-coated linens and my old AYSO and USCF Junior trophies. I remembered my dad sitting on my bed after my accident. Breathing came hard then and his extra weight on the bed felt like extra weight on my chest.

"Dad," I had said. "I'm in a real bind, here."

"What do you want I should do, son?"

I didn't respond and he went on his whole spiel about everything he and Mom had done for me, every opportunity they had given for me to redeem myself, every broken promise I had made. He told me about their decision to send me to rehab and cut me off afterward, because, as he said, "We can't do anything else for you. You've tied our hands, Joshua."

Months after that, I popped open the garage door to grab a dusty old duffel bag to put my clothes in. My mom stopped me by the stacking bins.

"This is love, you know," she said. "We're doing this because we love you."

That morning I had stepped out of rehab and was then looking at spending the night on the street. *Cranky times a thousand* is how I answered the desk lady when she had asked me how I felt on my discharge. "If this is love," I said to my mom as I rummaged through the garage, "I think I'd rather you fucking hate me."

My mother pulled a bill out of her pocket and offered it.

"What's this?" I asked.

"It's one hundred dollars," she said, looking me straight in the eye. I held the bill in my hands.

"What the fuck am I going to do with one hundred fucking dollars?" I said, making a wide, flinging arm gesture as if to throw the bill away, but ended up putting it into my pocket.

"I never want to see you again," my mom said, the last thing she said to me before going back into the house.

"You're killing me," I yelled after her, over and over. "You're killing your son." I started knocking over all the orderly bins, sending those neat stacks to chaos on the garage floor, not looking for stuff to take and sell like I should have, but just to do it, just to disrupt my parents' bullshit sense of order one last time.

Sadie finished throwing up on the footwell floor and I snapped back to the present. She used her shoe to spread the yellow-brown bile around the mat so it would absorb faster. "You going to hit up your dad or what?" she asked.

My face felt flushed and I gritted my teeth. I tried to rock my body side to side to gain the momentum that would propel me out of the car, down the street. But shame weighed me down—that was it. I felt embarrassed, shameful, much the way I had when I crawled into my old bed with broken ribs, when Glück walked into the hospital room or when Sadie described her perfect baptism or when I begged at Crackhead Mike's table. My father closed the garage door behind him, and when he did I started the car.

• • •

"Josh? Josh?"

I didn't respond.

"I think maybe we should let Abraham go."

"You would say that."

"No, I mean, I've been thinking," Sadie started. "We can call my parents, negotiate rehab if—when we go to court. Maybe Abey will be better off—it's a burden off our shoulders."

I knuckled the steering wheel. "You were going to kill him," I said through gritted teeth. "'Burden.' He's our son."

"What the hell kind of life would he live?" she yelled, so loud it made me jump. "How long before he chokes or goes into shock? And how much more do we have to struggle? He's—with us, he's a parasite. He'll kill us; he's been killing us. With somebody else maybe he'd stand a chance at—I don't know."

"You're not big on the whole maternal instinct thing, are you? Our son deserves parents, Sadie," I said. "At least one parent."

She went quiet for a long time. Then, in a flurry of motion she unbuckled her seatbelt and opened the car door. One of her legs had already swung out and she hunched her body forward as though she were going to launch herself onto the pavement sliding fast by us. I hit the brakes and grabbed her arm, swerving in the street as she tried to loosen my grip. She couldn't hold the door open much because of the momentum, so it kept bouncing out and in as she pushed it.

"You're crazy," I yelled, coming to a stop on the side of the street. Once we stopped she stopped fidgeting, just sat sideways in the seat. "You're crazy," I said again, softer this time.

"I'm crazy?" she asked, turning her head to the left and looking at me over her shoulder. "You're calling me crazy?" She turned her head forward again so it faced out the window. "Let me out," she said, pointing to a KFC.

Like before, another phrase wriggled into my head that I couldn't shake, the echo of it rattling around as I tried to think. I looked at her back, at the tangled and frizzy mess of her black hair, and I thought, "I do not know her." Over and over again, this phrase played in my mind like a mantra.

"You're just going to go get high," I said.

"And you wouldn't? Get real, Josh. It's over. We fucked up and now it's over. Get it through that stupid brain of yours."

Night came to reflect the light of the San Fernando Valley back on its narcissistic self—so self-absorbed in its own glow that it left no room for stars in the sky. It was nearing four a.m., the time I had been told to go see Crackhead Mike's hookup, a guy named Glen Ott living in a townhouse in Chatsworth. Chatsworth—a small sprawl of porn warehouses and easy-to-rob office parks—the final point of my day's geography. It would be daylight soon and I couldn't think of any other way to solve my Pinch problem beyond going to the hospital and taking him out without checking him out—sure to draw attention the second I touched him and he started crying. Not to mention the standard contingent of LAPD officers that manned the metal detector by the ER's entrance. I imagined running down the halls with my screaming son, his blanket rubbing his skin raw, orderlies and cops chasing after me, and the thought was not appealing. I had no other ideas, so for inspiration I lifted a bottle of vodka and a two-liter of soda from a CVS. After that, there was nothing else to do but lean my head against the steering wheel and think until it was time to go up to the door.

The guy was scar-skin pale and answered the door with a cigarette in his mouth. He was cordial enough and invited me in to sit down on a metal folding chair next to a collapsible card table. His window blinds were drawn against the streetlamps and the only light came from a lampshade-less bulb set on the floor. The air was stuffy, even for the California heat. A faint fecal smell breathed through the air, like fertilizer or a long-untended lavatory or even soiled clothes.

Glen sat at the card table across from me and ashed his cigarette into an open In-N-Out cup. "So you're buddies with Cocknose McFatfuck," he said.

On acid one time I'd decided that there was no such thing as white people or black people or anything in between: there were only pink people. White skin, looked at hard enough, was pink skin. Brown skin was pink skin that had intensified into a deep, deep purple but was still pink. Everyone I had ever met fell somewhere along the pinkness spectrum until I met Glen Ott. His skin was so ghostly translucent I thought it was a thin rubberized film spread over the palest core of gristle and bone, a result of what I later learned to be severe anemia. His flesh was gaunt and sucked in tight to his body, making his cheeks hollow and his veins look affixed. His eyes were the darkest part of his body, beady and set deep in his skull. Taking in everything and making predatory jumps from place to place on my body or around the room. Every expression he made pulled his skin into a thousand creases and folds, though when he listened he stared expressionless with a face as smooth and white as soap.

He listened in this way as I explained that I was currently under a state of financial duress that needed immediate "monetary remediation" or whatever.

"What," said Glen, "don't get enough allowance from your parents?"

I stared at him until I realized he might consider me to be mad-dogging him, then I looked at the spit and whatever else beginning to seep through the wax ashtray cup. Really, I was just trying to control my breathing and blinking; my hands and feet felt sweaty from the come down, which the vodka had done little to soothe. I'd feel hot and begin to sweat and then switch to freezing. My pulse thrummed in my inner thighs, my temples, everywhere.

"You are Jewish, yeah?" he asked. "I thought you people had a sense of humor."

"I've always considered myself more Jew-*ish*." I wobbled my hand in the air on that last syllable—one of Crackhead Mike's jokes.

"Good. I like the Jews. You can *quid pro quo* with them. They have a simple prime directive—money—I find easy to work with." He lit a new cigarette with his old one. "Simple needs, simple desires: it makes you people reliable business partners."

"I plan on giving all my money to the needy."

"Like Hillel?"

"Look," I said, "this is a little time sensitive, all right? I need to know what I'm getting involved in right quick."

"You smoke?" he asked.

"What?"

"Cigarette?" he offered. The way Glen talked was similar to the way his eyes moved: frenetic, jumpy, threatening. Even this offer seemed a threat.

"Don't touch the stuff," I said.

"Ever drive by Sony Studios down in Culver City? On Washington, east of Tito's Tacos? Isn't it weird that it's pyramid shaped? Or a ziggurat, I guess you'd call it. Zigguraty. Why do you think the Hollywood Jews made it that way?"

"Dude," I said with a forceful tone.

"Helminthic therapy," he enunciated the syllables so carefully I could hear his dry tongue sticking to his palate. "Alternative healing. I sell a miracle cure to wacko actors, rich movie-exec types sick of colonics wanting to try some new quackery, stupid suburban housewives in Sherman Oaks with oodles of money and a general disdain for things like the whooping cough vaccine and steroidal nasal sprays." Every time he exhaled I got a whiff of rancid beef. "Lupus, alopecia, aquiferous uticaria, allergies. Anything autoimmune, I cure it. For a while."

I blinked a lot. "So you sell herbs or whatever?"

"Eh, close." He paused and stared down at the smoke coming off his cigarette in squirming wisps. "I think the pyramid thing is a statement—Sony Studios. A symbol of a reversal in fortune thousands of years in the making. From slave to state. Out of the desert and into the armchair."

"No evidence we were ever slaves in Egypt," I said. "Archeological digs are casting doubts and stuff on that."

"You go to college?"

"I dabbled."

"You a crackhead?"

"I dabble."

"Hmm," he said. "Hmm. Well, that means you're probably okay with doing some work in a sorta legal gray area. But that also means you probably want the money to buy more. And, judging by your eyes and the way you're jostling your leg and your fucked up lips, I'd say you're in a pretty bad way."

I stopped moving my leg and ran my tongue over my lower lip—it felt split and torn up, the scraps of skin sharp and poking. "I've recently been reconsidering my priorities," I said.

"College educated crackhead. Tsk tsk," he said. "You're a screaming, fiending baby. A little bundle of simple needs that only other people can provide, and it's never enough. A suckling, mewling parasite. Jewish crackhead. Money. Drugs. They're practically the same, you poor, needy thing." He was shaking his head with the cigarette in his mouth. "Poor, poor thing."

I leaned forward and placed my fists on the table. As I did so, Glen set his feet wide apart on the ground and for a moment his thin muscles tensed, his entire face flexing into folds in a manner that wasn't exactly a flinch. He looked prepared to strike. "Look, man," I said, "I'm starting to take some serious umbrage with the shit you're saying. I get that you have some issue with the random fact that my mom happened to be Jewish when I was born, and I get that your average recreational drug user is less than reliable, but if you asked for people through Mikey you must've known what you'd get, so stop dicking me around, you racist asshat."

Glen raised his hands, palms facing me. "Mea culpa. I don't mean to offend; I have nothing but respect: our lord and savior Jesus Herman Christ was a Jew, so I know you're not all bad. And the cocaine thing, well, that's just it: I need someone kinda desperate. No one else will do." He stood up and dropped his cigarette into the cup. "Follow me."

He led me up the townhouse's stairs and down a narrow hallway to a closed door glowing red beneath the crack. The fecal smell got stronger and, when he opened the door, a wave of stagnant, hot wet air struck me full on. Even though my septum was messed up, the smell still stung and sat heavy in my sinuses. It smelled like rich pasture soil, a mishmash of loam and dead leaves and clay with something septic rotting beneath the surface and barely covered up by a thin mist of Febreeze—the lemon kind—hanging in the air.

S. P. MacIntyre

The room was lit only by heat lamps arranged in rows upon all kinds of surfaces—an expensive-looking kitchen table, a rickety nightstand, a dresser with no drawers. The lamps stooped over Styrofoam takeout containers layered with blackish dirt, what I now know was a mix of vermiculite and human feces. The blurred silhouettes of shadows loomed in the red light. In the center of the room, an enormous wooden spool placed on its side served as a table; on top of it was a collection of mason jars, a dirty immersion blender, a stack of rags, a pile of surgical gauze and medical tape, and an aquarium net faintly stained and clotted with something muddy. I've seen a lot of messed up stuff, but this was totally new to me.

"What the fuck is this?" I asked.

Glen took a square of gossamer from the center table and placed it over the dirt in one of the takeout containers. "Joshua, I'll tell you what I'm going to do," he said as he gently prodded the corners with his index finger, smoothing out the wrinkles in the fabric over the surface of the dirt. "I'll pay you $300 now, up front, in cash as a sorta deposit—a down payment, an investment. In six months, depending upon your delivery of a workable sample—something I can use, proper burden and whatnot—I'll pay you another $10,000 in cash, for you to do with as you please, and you'll never have to see me again."

"Seriously. What the fuck is this?"

He turned and caught me again with those eyes, cast completely in shadow by the room's lighting. He looked at me through dark, eyeless holes. "Hookworms," he said. "*Necator Americanus*, if you're fancy. The most common parasite in the world—one-tenth of the world's population is infected. Why do you think there's no allergies or bullshit, milquetoast ailments in Africa? These little things keep their host healthy so they can stay that way, too."

I imagined, in that moment, Pinch crawling on my parents' floor, the way I used to—healthy in a way. Full of worms but free of allergies. What? No. What a disgusting thought. And yet I imagined him laughing; I've never heard him laugh. "Have to be honest," I said. "I have some scruples. Worms and bugs give me the heebie-jeebies. I

176   *Glimmer Train Stories*

don't know if I like where this is going. And can you turn on a light?"

He flipped a switch near the doorway and uncovered fluorescent lights came on above. In this light his pale, waxy skin had a greasy sheen. His shoulders were rolled forward and his movements only came with visible strain. He coughed without covering his mouth. Glen no longer looked sinister: he looked ill.

"Look, Josh, it's simple," he said. "I infect you, you do nothing about it for six months, you come back and reinfect me so I can go on leading the glamorous life of a reservoir donor." He explained that he had been doing it for too long and was now taking horse dewormers to clear up the parasites until he was no longer anemic. "Six months," he continued. "I call you and the few other guys I'm dealing with. Everyone able to give me a good stool sample when I ask with enough larvae to restart my operation gets the ten grand."

"Could this cause, like, health concerns?"

"Do you have malaria or AIDS?"

"No."

"Then no," he said. "And if you want to keep all those worms alive, that means no deworming agents, no aspirin or anything containing aspirin like Pepto Bismol or Alka Seltzer, no pumpkin seeds, no cocaine that's been cut, no tonic water, no manuka honey, no chicken or beef livers, no nitrous oxide, no blood thinners, no alcohol, no anxiety pills, sleeping pills, or pain pills, no antibiotics, no albendozole, no Viagra, and no nicotine."

"Damn. Organ meats. What a loss," I said. Ten grand. I hadn't had that much money since I took a student loan and dropped out my last semester of uni without paying any of it back. That much filthy lucre could support a lot of filthy habits. Sadie and I would be able to put it to good use, maybe go back to the good times, the way things were before—before Pinch. Pinch. Pinch laughing. Pinch laughing because he's a survivor, a fighter. Pinch laughing because he's home, because he's loved, because he has a family who'll always be there for him. Pinch laughing and me, Sadie, my parents, Sadie's parents, Crackhead Mike, even the Glückster laughing too. No, I thought, Glen's arrangement wouldn't do. "I need more money up front if I'm going to do this. I need at least twenty grand."

"No," said Glen. "I'll give you $300. If I gave you any more, what incentive would you have to come back?"

"Dude, I totally get that, but I need the money today. I swear on my word that I'll be able to get you what you need six months from now."

Glen's eyes darkened again, but this time it wasn't the lighting. "No, you needy son-of-a-bitch. I'm not going to give you money so you can buy drugs or pay off some loan shark who's threatening whatever you gave him as collateral. Tough shit. You can take the offer I gave or get out."

"You don't understand—"

"No, *you* don't understand." Glen spread his arms out wide, all his veins sticking out at attention. "This is how I make a living. In two months all of these worms will be sold or dead. I've got alimony payments to make. If I give you all my money now, I got nothing to hold me over and my kids, wherever the hell my whore of an ex-girlfriend moves them next, don't get their Flintstones vitamins. Every single guy I hired out asked for more money, and every single one is a dirty Scot or a filthy Jew. God, you're all such presumptuous, greedy dirtbags. Take, take, take. Mine, mine, mine. Always desperate for more, more, more."

I let his words sink in to me. The room went quiet except for the electric buzz of the heat lamps and the fluorescent lights, but even that sound seemed to get sucked out of the air. His words burrowed down and down until they hit something electrical and raw. I threw a punch at him.

Faster than I could react, he grabbed the arm I launched and used my momentum to pull me forward, landing my neck in the crook of his elbow. He placed his other forearm behind my neck and straddled me from behind. I tried to pull his arm away, but my fingers could find no purchase. The pressure built behind my eyes and in my temples; my diaphragm spasmed as it tried to suck in air.

I fell. It felt like I was falling in the dark for so long I no longer knew which way was up. Everything was washed in noise, a dense humming that resolved into pulses. I was nearing something round and bright.

The sound became a baby's cry. I had landed against the floor, on a carpet grainy with soil and cigarette ash.

One of the red coils of the heat lamps had fallen to the edge of the table above my head. The baby's cry I had heard was me sucking in air, which came back out of me in sobbing bursts. I cried. I cried so hard that every muscle in my body contracted. And when I realized it was me crying, I cried even harder until my face hurt, until my body went entirely rigid, and even then the crying would not stop.

Of all the things that had happened the day I was told that I would lose my son, of all the things I had said and things that were spoken to me, of all the feelings and memories and sensations that had rushed in and out of me, this is the thing I recall with a halo of absolute, crystalline clarity and which still baffles me more than anything else: Glen, genuflecting beside me, leaning over me, his face a fold of concern and paternal tenderness, saying, "Hey, hey, hey," cradling my head in his hands, brushing the hair from my face, pulling my arms gently apart, "Hey, hey, hey," bringing my body close to his, hugging me until my muscles loosened, wiping my tears with his finger, "Hey, hey, hey."

"It's okay," he said. "It's okay."

I told him everything. Between sobs, my voice strained from the tight swallowing sensations in my throat, I told him about my son Abraham and his allergies, about Sadie and the oven, about the sleep and the silence of the hospital bed, about Sadie's perfect baptism, about Glück and the foster homes full of loving, sober people, about my parents and the spiders beneath their furniture, about Michael and the labret and the drugs I couldn't say no to. I spit all of these things into Glen's shirt. It all spewed out of me in a gush. I felt purged and clean. I felt awful. I had never felt better. I pulled away and a trail of mucus ran from my nose to his shirt.

"I'm sorry," I said.

"No, I understand," he said. He placed my head back down on the ground and shifted his weight. "I went through hell to keep my kids; I'm going through hell now trying to get them back." He stood up and pinched the corner of the gossamer he had placed in the container, offering it up as a final, gentle benediction. "But I can't give you any more than what I've promised. Your problems are your problems, not mine. Wipe off your face. Are you doing this or what?"

Frost had settled on my windshield while I slept in the hospital parking lot. The sky was cloudless and the sun was climbing over the hills, promising to make up for the early morning coolness. On my arm where Glen had taped the piece of gossamer, little red lesions had appeared. They looked like bug bites, but were flat and scabby. If I looked closely enough, I could see a red tunnel emerging from each lesion, arcing and coiling under the surface of my skin with a monstrous, surreal randomness, the so-called *creeping eruption* that would spread up my arm and toward my chest. When visiting hours arrived, I took the mason jar with the gossamer I had stowed into the hospital. Without the lid, I was able to get it past the metal detectors no problem. Many of the same people I had seen the previous night were still waiting in the ER lobby. I wish I could say I didn't end up using the $300 to buy more cocaine. I wish I could say that I've quit and haven't relapsed in the six years since that day. I got my visitor's pass and found my way to Pinch's room. When the worms find their way through the gossamer to the skin it feels exactly like that: a pinch. Followed by an itch. My baby son still slept on the hypoallergenic sheets; this room had been unaffected by the turmoil of the previous day. But I knew his life was about to get difficult—foster care, adoption. Almost as difficult as it would have been if I had scooped him up and carried him out of the hospital and drove off with him. I wish I could say that I've made an effort to get my son back in the past six years. I wish I could say that Sadie had stuck around to help me instead of running off with some guy. But in the moment I wasn't thinking about all that, about all the things that might have been or could happen. In the moment I was only thinking about my son, with his pink skin against the white, white bed, the mason jar in my pocket, my hands smoothing the gossamer fabric against his skin that had just been against mine. A gift, or what I hoped would be one. He began to stir.

I said: things are hard and they won't ever get easier for us.
I said: I'm sorry.
I said: this is the best I can do.

*Portrait of Writer with Duck: posing with
aquatic friend in spotless home.*

Theodora Ziolkowski's fiction and poetry have appeared in *Short Fiction* (England) and *Prairie Schooner*, among other journals, anthologies, and exhibits. She is the author of the poetry chapbook *A Place Made Red* (Finishing Line Press) and is originally from Easton, Pennsylvania.

WE THANK YOU FOR
YOUR CLEANLINESS

Theodora Ziolkowski

Theodora Ziolkowski

O ur landline is broken, I think. That's what I keep telling my
fourteen-year-old son, anyway. Josh is lacing his skinny jeans
with chains now, and wearing a hoop over his left eyebrow that I told
him made me think of cattle or that line we love from some film we
can no longer name—*How now, brown cow?*—only he just rolls his eyes
at the allusion and arranges his face into a dull expression I find both
galling and endearing. He doesn't believe our landline is broken because
how can something be broken that's hardly ever in use? We have cell
phones, yes, and so it's true we usually forget about the rotary phone
that is the color of pumpkin pie. On the rare occasion that someone
does call the house, the connection always sounds crackled. Polter-
geisty. But I can't bear to throw the phone away when it belonged to
my husband Mike who liked those kinds of things.

I'm baking cookies for Josh and his friend Kyle when it starts ringing, and think it must be Aunt Louise or a telemarketer, because only
Aunt Louise and telemarketers have this number. But then when I
answer, all I hear on the other line is a kind of rasping noise—like
whoever is on the other line is choking on a Dorito or something.

Glimmer Train Stories, Issue 98, Winter 2017
©2016 Theodora Ziolkowski

Cradling the receiver shoulder to ear (I am wearing oven mitts; it is like I have marshmallows for hands) I get no answer to my "Hello?" but breath.

The gasping goes on for a while, until the timer for the cookies goes off, and I tell the line not to call again unless it's going to say something worth my time.

After I take the cookies out, I find the boys suckered into their beanbag chairs, their eyes fixed to the screen, video game controllers in hands. From the side, Josh and Kyle could be Siamese twins fused together by their skinny jeans. Sometimes I wonder about those chains teenage boys wear loop-de-loop around their pant legs nowadays—all that jangling.

I don't know why I let Josh get into his games the way he does, but he gets A's and B's in school and is an all-around good kid. My mother-in-law Alice used to complain about my allowing a game system in the house. Alice's words: The hours Josh spends monkeying around with a controller are hours of brain constipation.

"Who was that?" Josh asks without turning around. On the screen, there are tree stumps and men on horses. My son and his friend are far away from the patch of suburban Florida we occupy; on screen, my son and his friend travel through a village of moss.

"Don't know," I tell him.

"Some weirdo, huh?" Kyle says.

"Some weirdo," I say. "I think the landline is broken."

"It's not, Ma."

"But it sounds funny."

"Nah." Josh pauses. He sits forward in his beanbag. Kills a fire-breathing dragon with the sweep of his sword. "You sound funny."

I'm standing in line at Target, my basket filled with a box of frozen tilapia filets, a carton of Greek yogurt, and a rotisserie chicken (living with a teenager, there is always a shortage of protein), when my phone vibrates in my purse.

I move forward in the queue, rummage for my phone.

The sky is a dull purple today. Through the tinted Target windows, the wind shakes the stunted parking lot trees, and it is a true October morning: the pumpkin spice lattes are in such demand it's a predicament to mankind.

Even the customer in front of me is drinking one, the whipped cream stuck in his beard hairs. I can smell the warm, buttery pumpkinness of it.

When I find my phone and answer, the breathy noise on the other end commences.

"Hello?" I repeat, "Who's there?"

And then the voice goes sweet and kind of gritty, like peanut brittle is all I can compare it to, and what I think at that moment is: Target is so red. What a red, red store.

"We thank you for your canniness," the voice says.

"My what?"

"We thank you for your cleanliness," says the voice.

This time, I think I get it right.

"How did you get this number?"

I begin wringing the strap of my purse, a crinkled green faux-leather thing my husband rescued from a yard sale that I'm unable to rid myself of—despite the ink stains lining its interior, the compartments riddled with holes.

The customer enjoying the pumpkin spice beverage in front of me—he is probably in high school, not much older than Josh—is buying a tube of deodorant and a liter of ginger ale. Expressionlessly, the cashier swipes his soda so vigorously it will probably explode when the poor guy opens it.

On the phone, the voice says, "We thank you."

"I'm sorry?"

"We. Thank. You."

"Look, I think you have the wrong number, will you please—"

"Amy. Amy?"

"Yes, I'm Amy."

"It's me, Amy! Stasia. Your Stasia who comes to your house on Tuesday. Your new Martha Maid, Stasia. Such generosity you have, Amy. Such kind woman."

The cashier is scratching snow from her scalp as the young man carries away his goods and I unload my basket and flip my phone closed. The rotisserie chicken shines like a river rock.

"Good morning," I say.

One by one, the cashier—Crystal, her employee name tag says— shoots my purchases with her laser, as I wonder whether my cell phone is broken, too. Or maybe it's just my ears hearing these calls filled with breath, first on the rotary, and now on my cell—

In my head I want to go, "My ears are broken, the whole world is broken," even though clearly some voice is talking to me and it has the wrong number, the wrong person. And maybe this denial is because of my paranoia. Maybe this denial warrants attention.

I could consult Josh about this predicament. Maybe he could tinker with the phones. That, or flip me one of his sarcastic quips that make me feel like the smallest mother in the world.

I swipe my card as Crystal plops all the proteins—surf, turf, and Greece's live and active cultures—into a plastic bag.

That poor chicken, I think. It's sweating.

I'm watching reruns of *The Young and the Restless* and by God: Victor's come back to life—again!

It's kind of pathetic but wonderful, really: sitting alone in front of the TV with one of those popcorn tins painted with a Christmas village. I'm wearing long johns and my hair is in a scrunchie. It doesn't get much better than this, I tell myself. Really.

I haven't talked to Josh about the phone business yet because he's in one of his brooding moods again. It's the way he gets after he's played video games for hours and doesn't do as well as he hoped, which means there must be one less outlaw on the loose or another dragon left to impale. We had TV dinners for supper, which we didn't eat in front of the TV like you would think but instead outside on the patio, in the pinkish navy dark. Josh says everything tastes better when it's in a segmented tray, and watching how purposefully he eats his corn and peas and pizza from their little compartments makes me believe it. I worry about him.

When I asked Josh earlier about his video games—when I asked what is the point of them, why do you get so angry?—he said, "Why do you get angry when the chicken's still cold after it's been in the oven for hours?"

He was slumped across from me picking at the skin around his fingernails. He does this when he's concentrating, I think, or when he's bored—who knows? I'm only his mother.

"Why do you get angry when you see something that reminds you of Grandma Alice?" he went on. "And anyway, I don't always like being the good guy. In the game, I mean. It's cool to be mean for a change, it's freeing. But whatever. It isn't that I lost, it's that I could have done better. You get it, don't you? Getting angry when you could've done better?"

Even though it's late and my contacts are shriveled and I have the urge to burrow my face in the popcorn tin, I can't turn in and forget about everything just yet. Not when I get to thinking about those mysterious calls again. How this Martha Maid Stasia has access to me. How she's confused me for a presumably second Amy DeFacto and through this error has procured both my numbers.

I've never hired a maid in my life.

I snag my laptop from the back room, climb into bed with the comforter puffed out around me, and Google my name. And what pops up first is me! Me, Amy DeFacto, closely followed by a list of varying usages of "de facto." I click on my name, and—aha!—there's my profile page with the unspecified blue silhouette of a head as my default photo. When I signed up for the dating site, I'd been under the impression that when you simply searched someone's name, all of their personal information would be hidden. That's what my sister-in-law Linda told me when she suggested I stop being such a sad sack and give the site a test run, anyway. She said strangers wouldn't have access to my details; she said that I might as well try to get my life in line—which was easy for her to say. Like her brother had been, Linda was a pragmatic kind of a person. She appreciated life for all its intricacies. Sometimes just getting by is key, she'd told me.

In any case, I guess I mustn't have saved my profile settings right, because there it was: Amy DeFacto. Home phone. Cell phone. Address withheld.

Interests: *I'm in mourning and don't know exactly what it is I'm interested in.*

Maybe a hug.

Likes: *2*

Hobbies: *Isn't that the same thing as "interests"?*

Or should I not be interested in said hobbies?

The next call from Stasia comes when I'm in the shower.

After Josh went off to school, I made a pot of tea and sat down at my computer to work. When I couldn't think of anything interesting to say about the pineapple doormat I was supposed to be promoting (I kept typing "Pineapple" in a column), I decided to call it quits.

After Mike passed away, I took a temporary leave of absence before fully resigning from my teller's position. I couldn't stand dealing with so much paper anymore. So many checks and forms and documents to sign. Mike wouldn't be at all surprised by this, I suppose. Mike had always thought I would be a good reporter or in some profession that works with words. This, of course, was the highest compliment coming from Mike. Mike was all about the poetry of language. And because I didn't see myself ready to pull on my pantyhose every morning and stand behind that tall marble desk talking to people, I applied for a freelance copywriting job for a furniture company downtown. The elderly couple who run it specialize in quirky upholstery. Hence, the pineapples.

"You're so funny," Mrs. Brown told me the day I came in for the interview. She had me sit across from her, at a table covered in fabric swatches and Tupperware containers grimed with old lunches. "Your smell," she remarked, her face drawn in like the underside of a mushroom, "you're like an icebox filled with vegetables. You have such a *pulverized* smell to you."

Mrs. Brown reminded me of my late mother-in-law, only smaller. And with a voice that wasn't coarse and school marmy but high-

188

pitched. Mousy. Which is what I realized I should've said in reply: *Your voice, Mrs. Brown. It's like a lump of fur and whiskers.*

When I hear the ringing echo in the shower, my first thought is that I had left something on the stove and that what I am hearing is the smoke alarm. Towel flung around me, I go slipping and sliding from the bathroom, down the stairs and to the kitchen to answer.

The phone feels warm against my ear: a surprise, since the rotary had done nothing but sit in its cradle since the last time Stasia called.

"You are not fine today, Amy," says Stasia. "Amy is not doing good?"

Panting like a dog in heat — something Aunt Louise used to say— I wonder if any passerby can see me from the foyer window. I run my hand through my hair, still slimed in shampoo.

"You have got to stop calling me," I say into the receiver. "Unless you tell me who you are and why—"

"Stasia, Amy. I'm Stasia, from Martha Maids. You remember, no? Such shiny counters and floors you make for us even before we come. I want to thank you for the check, all that generosity. Your house is always clean already there is hardly time for dust to settle. Such kindness you have, Amy. Such security you give!"

I lean against the wall and press the heel of my hand to either temple, the way I learned to do from the psychiatrist I had for a few sessions and then ditched when I realized I was paying for a service that required me to get up and get dressed; to sit inside a drafty office listening to the sound of my shrink combing her Japanese sand garden while she asked me to try to determine why what I had for breakfast that morning had made me cry. I sigh into the phone.

"Stasia," I say. "I think there's been some mistake. I'm not who you think I am."

"No, Mrs. No. Your numbers I have."

"I have to go now, Stasia."

"Very good, Amy. Very good, you are busy, this I know. Such a good busy woman, it is a shame you are no mother. Always know that we thank you, Dolores and I who come to clean your home…"

"Stasia?"

"Yes?"

From the foyer window I can see the school bus pull up across the street. The a.m. kindergarteners pile from the door, swinging their lunches and dry noodle-covered art projects.

"Will you be calling again?" I ask. And for a moment I want to be the other Amy DeFacto. To climb out of my skin and into her clean house.

Stasia laughs so brightly my chest aches.

"It is Martha Maid policy to call new customers and see if a pleasing job has been done. They tell me here I don't need to call you every week, but I like to, you know?" says Stasia. "Like feathers is your voice when you are glad."

The idea to repaint the walls comes while I'm doing Josh's laundry. It's while checking all the pockets—so much black, so many zippers—that I resolve that the walls will be green: jade for the living room and foyer, mint for the bathroom, and a mossy, fairy-house green for my bedroom.

I'm patting some detergent into the machine when the phones ring again. First my cell, then the landline. After I last spoke with Stasia, I'd felt a glimmer of hope at the prospect of her calling again. And then pain. Pain for my loneliness and for hers.

I turn the washer on and don't answer either of the phones.

Painting the walls will give me a new project that maybe Josh and I can work on together. It will be another distraction to focus on. It will help me to not think about Mike, who's been gone for five years now; that, and the fact that I have a teenage son and don't know anything about boys or teenagers. Maybe I'll even stop counting Josh's pockets and zippers and baking so many cookies for the boys that their faces are getting puffy.

Later that night, Josh comes home with a bruise around his right eye. When I ask him what happened, he says, "Where were you? I tried calling and no one answered."

When he doesn't show for dinner even after telling him through his door that I've fixed pasta primavera, his favorite, I flip open my laptop and return to my online dating profile. I delete my account and eat pasta primavera standing over the stove.

Once, when Josh was a baby and my husband was still alive, the three of us—plus my mother-in-law, Alice—took an impromptu drive to the shore. Alice insisted I pack the pimiento cheese sandwiches and Snapple iced teas she brought in a cooler. She wore a flowery, bright bathing suit even though she claimed to hate the water. At one point, when Mike and I were relaxing in our beach chairs and gummy with sunblock, a seagull dive-bombed Alice who had been bent over, feeding pieces of sandwich to Josh.

What was terrible was that after I realized that Josh was okay, I'd laughed and kept laughing. Loud, revolting laughter. And it was impossible to control myself until, his hand on my wrist, Mike asked me to stop. I was upsetting his mother.

With the walls I've made a good deal of progress. Anywhere you go, you feel like you're in a forest or sea foam.

One Saturday morning, Josh and I are sitting in our new green kitchen when I suggest we go have an afternoon out in town.

"And do what?" Josh asks.

Since I began painting the walls, Josh has seemed even more distant from me. And while the bruise around his eye he refuses to speak about has nearly healed and his silence has melted, when he's in the room he's kind of like a gothic mannequin, only moving.

I suggest a matinee, bowling, the mall. I can't tell whether Josh hates all of these ideas or the eggs I've cooked him. He keeps shuffling them around on his plate.

"Well, do you have any ideas?" I press.

"Maybe we could just stay here."

"I think we should get you out of the house."

"Why?"

"You're inside all the time and it smells like paint here. You've been playing a lot of video games lately, and—"

Josh sets down his fork.

"And what?"

"And I don't think it's good for you."

"Oh yeah? And why's that?"

Josh's voice is hollow. It quavers in a way I haven't heard it do since he was in the first grade and Mike and I sat him down on the couch to prepare him for some of the changes that accompanied Mike's diagnosis. *What's going to happen to your daddy is this…*

The day my husband left this world our front lawn was covered in acorns. Josh was playing outside and Mike had felt well enough to sit out on the porch. He was draped in an afghan with a moose on it. My husband loved moose and he loved that afghan, even after it began to smell like a doctor's office and fruit pops, and he still insisted it was fine, don't put it in the wash. Please, Amy. Just leave it.

I'd left Mike and Josh just for a second. Josh was under the trees, pretending to be an airplane, his arms stretched out, making engine sounds. He was wearing a red sweatshirt, his light-up Skechers. He was nine and already a speed-reader like his father. Our floors were heaped in Josh's chapter books and Mike's secondhand historical novels, his paperback detective fiction, his poetry.

The phone was ringing and that is why I left Mike and Josh and went indoors. The sunlight pooled across the kitchen, rosied the countertops and floors.

When I returned to the porch, Josh had transformed from an airplane to an elevator and my husband was slouched to the side with his head down.

It was Alice who had called.

For a second as I stare at my teenage son in the house that has always been our home—the cookie batter crusted on the countertops, Josh's height ticking the entryway—it seems that Josh will say more, that he wants to keep talking, but stops himself. And he doesn't have to say anything, because his face says it all.

You're the one who needs help. You're the one who can't take a go at the world on your own. Not after Dad died. Not after you became not you.

I want to shake Josh. To beg him to talk, won't you please talk, won't you please just tell me what you're thinking?

"We can stay home," I say instead. I keep my mouth set. For a second, I hold my son's gaze, and then I see myself empty in his eyes.

The phone begins to ring and we let it. It isn't long before it goes to voicemail, and there is my recorded voice on the answering machine, telling the caller we're not in right now, but you can leave a message and we'll get back to you, and then Stasia's breathing filling in the space that follows mine. And then, "We thank you, Amy. Dolores and I. Dolores, she was in for me yesterday and said to me what a place, what pretty flowers in vases. What nice floors you can see your face in. We thank you, Amy. We thank you for your cleanliness."

And then comes the click of Stasia hanging up, the speakers shutting off. I imagine myself sprinting to the rotary phone, holding the receiver up to my mouth and screaming.

Josh folds his hands in front of him. Suddenly, out of nowhere, I am surprised by the length of his fingers and limbs, the set angle of his jaw. He is growing up. The face of his youth, the one that together my husband and I knew, has already transformed into something new. With his dark hoodie zipped to the top of his neck and the barbs of gel-teased hair, Josh is a stranger to me.

"I'm sorry," he says softly. His response surprises us both, I think.

I want to say, *Tell me what's going on with you. That bruise around your eye. Tell me who did it. Are you being bullied? Are you being hurt?* Only I push my plate aside and seize his hand from across the table instead.

And as if he's read my very thoughts, Josh stands and shakes his head. Suggests we go to Pizza Hut. He knows I like the breadsticks there. We both do. He apologizes again and again, but doesn't cry because he's Josh and he's my late husband's son, and because he's tougher than anyone I've ever known.

By the end of the weekend, Josh agrees to help me with the painting, and even asks Kyle to lend us a hand as well. Soon, the three of us get into a routine.

When they get home from school, I've got a plate of pizza rolls for them and some juice. Soon as they finish, we set to work. And I remind them to do their homework and hope to goodness they're keeping up with it, though how can I nag when together they're being such a crutch?

I continue to receive Stasia's calls, all about my cleanliness—or rather, I learn, Amy DeFacto of Bridgeport County's cleanliness. And since I've begun to pick up again since Josh is making progress—he's beginning to talk to me about dragons and sometimes Algebra II—I've gotten used to Stasia's calls. And as the weeks and then months pass, I've decided I neither mind nor fear the calls so much. If anything, I look forward to them. Because while Josh is at school, they're a break from writing about doormats, maybe. Or just because it's nice to listen to someone's voice on the other end and not worry about what I say since I know I'm invisible to my listener anyway.

Come Christmas, I send Stasia a gift through Amazon Prime. It's so easy to ship anything from Amazon Prime. And besides, I can't mail her anything directly myself, or she might notice where the package came from—or should I say, didn't come from—meaning the fiction would all be over, which at this point in time I'm afraid to give up.

The gift is a small broach in the shape of a wreath. It is the steeped seaweed green of our kitchen walls with a little red bow at its center. I hope when it reaches her, it is as pretty as it looked online. And according to Stasia, it is.

"I will wear it every day, Amy. Every day I will think of Christmas and of you and your giving. Such goodness!"

Josh doesn't mind my talking to Stasia so much, though at first when he noticed my jumping up to get the phone, he thought it was a little weird. I try to explain it to him, but still he can't understand what I get out of talking to a woman I don't know.

"It's whack, Ma," he says. "Why don't you let me talk to her? I'll tell her not to call."

And so I nod and change the subject, so relieved am I that he's talking to me again, and so happy to listen.

Early spring, I suggest Stasia and I meet. By now, I know it's time to tell her the truth. That I am not, in fact, the woman she cleans house for. Not the Amy DeFacto of Bridgeport County but the Amy DeFacto of Orange County. It could get weird for Amy DeFacto of Bridge-port if this keeps going on. Amy DeFacto who keeps a clean house.

On the day of our scheduled meeting, I set out early and stop at the depot for an everything bagel with cream cheese. Only going early means getting caught in the commuters' rush, which in turn means having to wait behind a man in a yellow poncho drenched in cologne.

My bagel is too hot to eat when I get it, the cream cheese is soupy, and it is not an everything like I'd ordered, but blueberry. And I can't help but feel like a hobbit or something, being given a hot blueberry bagel.

Turns out that the other Amy DeFacto Stasia has confused me for does not live as far away from us as I thought, but just a mere hour and a half drive up the coast. Halfway there, I get the worst case of allergies—probably because the spores are duking out all the paint fumes I've inhaled from my house, or because it takes a considerable amount of energy for me to leave the safety of its comfy walls, or because I've built up an intolerance to nature that is, paradoxically, intolerable—and arrive at the diner Stasia suggested with my throat full of phlegm.

After recognizing no one who bears the countenance of the Stasia I've composed in my head—though of course, I have no clue what Stasia really looks like; I just have this idea of a flame-red shag cut and a milky, near translucent complexion—I ask a worker if there is anyone he knows by the name of Stasia there, and he perks right up and hands me a paper bag. Tells me it was left for me by Stasia; are you Mrs. Amy DeFacto?

I order a Greek salad and a cup of coffee. Inside the paper bag is a piece of stationery bordered with bluebells and a pile of what looks like garlic, but I soon enough realize to be bulbs.

"Sorry no come, Mrs. DeFacto. Too much cleaning, you understand. Take this from me as a sign of my sorry. I wish I could see you in your clean house some day but I understand you are busy that is what Mr. DeFacto says when I ask so okay I get it no Stasia and Amy together yet but soon soon!"

•　•　•

I don't know much about Emily Dickinson beyond my American
literature class at Florida State, except how did Stasia know the perfect
gift! Tulip bulbs with a tag attached to a bundle of roots on which
Stasia has written, *Emily Dickinson Buds*. I will grow these tulips like
the lonesome poet whose poems I know my husband so loved. I will
fill the lawn of my green-filled house with color, which will contrast
with how I picture Emily Dickinson: white dress, lace cuffs. Hair
twisted low at her nape in a bun.

Somewhere in my house is a copy of her *Collected*—a dog-eared
version with a scratch-and-sniff sticker Josh must've put on its cover
when his father was still alive and the book belonged to him—which
I remember just before finishing my lunch at the diner, ordering
a jelly doughnut to go, and making the trip home with my bag of
bulbs.

When I locate the book, I discover that the banana sticker on the
cover is faded; it looks kind of awful, now. Like a cream-pie-scented
phallus plastered over the image of yellow and pink roses.

Lying on the bed and flipping through the volume, stuffing my
mouth with doughnut jam, I come across this poem:

> She slept beneath a tree
> Remembered but by me.
> I touched her cradle mute;
> She recognized the foot,
> Put on her carmine suit, —
> And see!

> (With a Tulip.)

Now, I'm not sure what this tulip parenthetical means, but I like it.
And I know that Mike would have something to say about it. It's like
tagging on an ermine or pearl earring to one of Vermeer's *Woman/
Girl With* portraits. Vermeer, whose uses of light I've continued to
consider, sometimes, and admire. Even after I lost my sex drive after

my husband died. Even when on vacation last summer at my sister-in-law Linda's lake house in upstate New York, Linda suggested aiming the hot water where I wanted to be touched, warning that I was in danger of becoming a virgin all over again. And even after I'd told Linda that was impossible, she'd said to me, "No. You're Amy and you're human and it is impossible not to want."

I dream that my husband and mother-in-law are still alive. Learn of their living together on some island of their own, where all of the staff has very white teeth and creased grouper faces that make me self-conscious and aware of the dampness of my clothes, as I wander through the speckled-pink corridors of the place they've made their home.

I find them eating red licorice from cardboard boxes painted with mermaids. They are wearing knit hats with baubles on them. Sunlight pours in through the windows. The floor is white and padded; it crumbles under my footfalls like talcum powder.

When I try to take Mike by the hand, a knot of those gray, wrinkly workers laugh at me. Mike looks up at me absently, his jaw slack and wiggling. He is trying to place me.

"He doesn't want to go," Alice says. She hits her chest with a gnarled fist and coughs up a fly. "What took you so long?"

I wake to Josh calling up from downstairs, asking when's dinner, and I'm half-asleep still and crying for my husband so much, whose Emily Dickinson book is trashed with a banana scratch-and-sniff sticker, when the mattress starts vibrating.

My first thought: the water pressure at my sister-in-law's lake house in Upstate New York. But then I realize that it's only my phone going off. And it's Stasia. Phoning to see if I received her gift.

"Oh Stasia," I say as the tears run over my lips. "You should've come. I was there. I drove all the way over to see you."

"Mrs.? Mrs.? Hello, Mrs.?"

"I'm here, Stasia—"

"Mrs.?"

"It's me, Amy."

"Mrs., I fear you're going away. Your voice is a fuzz. Where are you?"

"I'm here, Stasia!" I can hear a pair of footsteps coming up the stairs. And maybe it's my husband. Maybe it is Mike come back to me. Coming to help Josh and me fill in all the hard-to-reach spaces in the walls, I think, as I wonder if Emily Dickinson wanted to be touched. If Emily Dickinson, watching the sun rise and fall behind the privacy of her window, ever touched herself.

"Amy, I am going to go now. This is not a good time for you?"

"Ma?" Josh is calling. He is rapping on the door. I imagine him bringing Mike with him. Dragging him from his moose afghan. Pulling him up for air. "Ma? You okay, Ma?"

I thank Stasia for the bulbs, ask if her not showing at the diner was because of anything I did, and she says of course not. That she understands that I don't need her anymore. The agency had already called.

"You were good enough already," she says. "You were good to go and I thank you for all the bonus. It makes sense to discontinue with us, Amy. You always keep such a nice home."

I realize I have been clutching one of the tulip bulbs so hard that it is beginning to come apart in my hand. We have not yet painted the bedroom, and so the walls are still papered in snowdrops, the ones that had always been here, even before Mike and I were, and I am telling this to Stasia when the door swings open and in walks my son. He is carrying a bucket of paint in one hand and a roller in the other. Kyle is not with him, he must not have joined Josh after school, but of course I wouldn't know this because I have been tucked away upstairs in my bedroom, alone.

Stasia is saying something to me about how brave it was for me to keep going; how good of me it was to continue sharing my life—which was a life, she said, that already sparkled—while my Josh, ever determined and set on the future, is beginning to paint the walls.

I want to tell him to cover up the floors and the furniture with sheets so we don't get them dirty, but then I see how he is painting everything blue—bottomless, cerulean blue—and I go to join him,

holding the phone to my heart as Stasia thanks me again and again—
For your cleanliness, Mrs. DeFacto. For all you did to appreciate our work.
You flower, you gem.

This is a photo from the late 1950s, and I remember growing up with it—with my parents pointing to it and reminiscing about a part of their lives—and mine—which always seemed long ago, just the three of us in a New York apartment, my father in graduate school, writing his dissertation about the fieldwork he had done in Trinidad, where I was born.

Perri Klass is professor of Journalism and Pediatrics at New York University, where she is the Director of the Arthur L. Carter Journalism Institute, and practices pediatrics at Bellevue Hospital; she is the National Medical Director of Reach Out and Read, a program that works through pediatric primary care to promote parents reading aloud with young children. Her most recent novel is *The Mercy Rule* and her most recent nonfiction book is *Treatment Kind and Fair: Letters to a Young Doctor*.

HEART ATTACK ON A PLATE

Perri Klass
Perri Klass

Ever since their mother got sick, this is how their father is eating. I'll have the steak and eggs, with extra home fries, and a side order of bacon—and do you have some cream for the coffee? And what kind are those big crullers? And that's just breakfast, which Diane has been having with him some mornings at a diner near the hospital. To be fair, he was always the one on the high cholesterol side of the argument; it was their mother who quietly, over the years, moved the two of them to low-fat milk and egg-white omelets, though she never broke him of the habit, in upscale Italian restaurants, of doing a comic double take when olive oil was poured to accompany the bread. In tones faintly informed by Catskill shtick he liked to ask any elaborately Mediterranean waiter, You got a little bit of butter, maybe?

But now he's angry because their mother is the one who is sick, their mother who took her vitamins and ordered grilled fish when she could have been having pasta with sausages and cream, and this confirms all his suspicions that virtue is not rewarded and the evil prosper in this terrible world. So, sure, might as well go ahead and get the side of bacon, though they both know what it will taste like, what everything tastes like, right now. Diane watches him struggle to open the little foil packets of butter and jam to load up his white toast, and she can see as his slightly shaky fingers peel back the tiny triangle at the corner of the gold foil that he is angry and heartbroken. What he always knew was true is more than true, it is personal. It has come out of the depths like, yes, the monster of the lake, and breathed evil vapors over their plans for this summer—he was already reading the concise history of Scotland recommended by the elderhostel program, thinking probably that on the first day he would explain to the group that he has always felt some special connection to Scotland. He was planning to take along his boyhood copy of *Scottish Chiefs* by Jane Porter, and he has twice said furiously to Diane that Mom was planning to read it as well, did Diane realize that? Your mother doesn't think she read it when she was a girl, he said, she said maybe she just didn't remember, but she wouldn't have forgotten it, I told her that, and she was going to read my old copy. You never read it, did you, you or your brother, he added, somewhat accusingly.

But their mother would have read it gamely, as she was willingly signed up for Edinburgh and Glasgow and Mull and Skye and Iona—when she was first hospitalized, he had the brochure in his pocket, he showed it to her every day, telling her to hurry up and get better so they could take their trip. And she would have found the book fascinating and the scenery beautiful and the history all new and striking—there's so much to learn about the world, she would have said. And where does it get you? Where? A hospital bed and tubes and poison running through your veins and never the same doctors two days in a row and half of them so young it's embarrassing. That's where it gets you.

Diane is not good at running interference; that was her mother's job. In temperament, so go the family assignments, she is actually more like her father, the oldest, the one who knows what she thinks and does her share of the talking.

She has come out without earrings, very unlike her; more than thirty-five years of pierced ears since that twelfth birthday trip to the mall, with her mother. Even that road leads to grief and terror. But she came out this morning without earrings in her ears, and she sat through a university faculty facilities planning committee meeting without earrings, without noticing that she had no earrings, but now, leaving the meeting and hurrying along the street toward her office, she touches her ear and realizes, and immediately feels underdressed, unfinished, disheveled. Actually, getting dressed, she had chosen earrings in her mind; there is a string of amber beads around her neck, and she had planned to wear the little round silver-rimmed amber earrings (not the larger, still reasonably lightweight but much more obtrusive amber eggs that she perhaps mistakenly bought in Alaska two years ago), but somehow she came out without them.

So she ducks into a store: I pass this place every single day but I have never been inside. See, she thinks sourly, there is so much to learn about the world. There are shoes—mostly boots, some ankle high, some of them well up over the knee. A rack of slightly forlorn platform sandals now on sale, with the weather turning cold. And among the pocketbooks, which have way too many buckles and fasteners and chains, there is, yes, a rack of cheap earrings, hoops too big for any adult to wear, chrome clips and oversized glittering crystal studs. Diane finds a card of reasonably sedate small disks, each set with tiny crystals—two black, two silver, two bronze, two gold—and pays at the cash register, where the clerk has five metallic studs in each ear and a ring through his lip. This suggests to Diane that perhaps the idea behind the card of earrings is that they are all meant to be worn at once, multicolored sparkle for the multipierced ear. But never mind that; as she goes out of the store into the cold drizzle, she is already detaching one of the bronze crystal earrings, already pressing the clear plastic backing up against the back of her earlobe, feeling the sharp end of the post securely penetrating through, thinking at least in passing about the mysteries of scar tissue formation, about the way that the lining of that hole through her earlobe, raw and tender and sore and bloody on her twelfth birthday, has become a sealed and sturdy channel. Doesn't let herself veer any further toward the sores that have started to form near the surgically implanted I.V. port or, even worse, the one on what the nurses call her mother's left flank. Flank. As she is pulling the second earring off the card, a student falls into step beside her.

"Professor Block, I was just coming over to your office hours!"

Diane is embarrassed—isn't this kind of like being caught getting dressed, primping on the street—or maybe she is embarrassed because she has been found out as a shopper in stores that are not only too young for her but also cheap and tacky. This embarrassment actually prevents her from slipping the card and the earring into her jacket pocket; she has to own the earring and her sidewalk costume adjustments.

"Hello, Callista," she says, and her fingers find the familiar spot on her earlobe—after thirty-five years of daily practice, after all—and the second earring is on. "Why don't we talk as we walk, we're going to the same place," she continues. "Unless you find it too rainy and you want to hurry on ahead, of course."

"Oh, I'm from Seattle, rain doesn't bother me," says Callista, who is bareheaded, like Diane, and carrying no umbrella. Diane actually has one, buried in her bag, but it's only drizzle and she needed both hands to put the earrings in.

So the two of them, gradually getting damper, walk the last two blocks together, and Callista describes, at some length, her not very well thought-through idea for a multimedia project on New York City in the seventies and the punk rock scene and the grittiness of it all and the danger and the art. Oh, and the drugs. It must have been so great.

Diane and her brother Gary meet at the hospital at the end of the day. The rain is heavier, and now they are both carrying dripping umbrellas, wrapped up in the plastic bags that are dispensed in the hospital entrance lobby. They take the elevator up together, with a bunch of those young doctors, scrubs and white coats and laminated name badges on lanyards around their necks. The elevator stops at every floor, and the doctors all have their cell phones out, as does Gary. Diane, on principle, leaves her phone in her bag, but it's doubtful that anyone notes her gesture—or her lack of gesture. They swipe and read and text and swipe, and the elevator creeps slowly up the building; there must be some meaning to this, Diane thinks, that the messages and thoughts can travel so fast, so instantly, to any part of the hospital, of the city, of the world, while the technology of getting to the tenth floor is so agonizingly old-school slow. Are these moments in the elevator, which she has so self-righteously determined to wait out without email or chat or messages, are they actually an opportunity to notice the world, to connect with other human beings, callously closed out by reflex interactions with expensive handheld devices? Or is elevator waiting time really just a distillation of hospital boredom, of the ways that every request and every decision means hanging around, waiting, waiting to be called, to get a medication, to see a doctor, to have the nurse come when you press the call button. And then that underlying arrogance, that sense that you are waiting because somewhere someone else cannot wait, and emergencies are absorbing all the speed, all the immediate crack expert responses.

Sure enough, when they get to their mother's room, their father is in a frantic stew because he requested pain medication—well, according to him, *she* requested pain medication—and it's been twenty-one minutes and the nurse hasn't come back yet. Twenty-one minutes! But he's whispering all this, even though they have a private room, and there's no one to hear, and on the whole, the whispering is a good sign, Diane knows, because it's much easier to deal with her father when he's on the near side of open hostility, when he hasn't gotten to the point of demanding supervisors and ombudsmen and union representatives.

"What's the nurse's name, I'll go find her," Gary says. He goes over to the whiteboard on the wall. "Veronica?"

"Veronica was yesterday," their father hisses furiously, angry at Gary for not remembering, for not paying closer attention and keeping better track. "They don't update things, the new one didn't write her name, she hasn't been in here for five whole minutes since she arrived—it's because they know I'm keeping an eye on your mother, so goodbye Charley! I'm supposed to do their work for them—and then I do their work for them and quote unquote assess the patient and let them know she's in pain and no one shows up to give her the medicine. She needs a pain pill! Twenty-two minutes!"

"It looks like she's sleeping," Diane and Gary say, more or less in unison. And at that point, their mother's eyes blink open, and they can all three of them, Diane and Gary and their father, see that what she opens her eyes to is pain and confusion. She looks at them, the three of them, Diane and Gary and their father, and she doesn't even smile in recognition or appreciation, and that is, as always, what tells them how far she has gone away.

They take their father out for dinner, after the nurse has come with the pain pill and the night attendant has arrived. There's an old-school Italian place a few blocks away, but he makes a face, and they end up at a pricey burger restaurant that ostentatiously grinds its own blend of grass-fed beef, and hopes soon to franchise. Their father has a bacon blue cheeseburger, and asks that the fries be cooked well done.

"Not the burger," he tells the waiter. "That should be medium rare. You know what medium rare means?"

"Warm red center is what it means here." The waiter is extremely tall and extremely thin, and his entire neck is tattooed in what looks like a paisley pattern. Unexpectedly, he has not a single earring, and it occurs to Diane that perhaps the multiple stud look from the store this morning is already passé.

The well-done fries are very, very good; both Diane and Gary, who did not themselves order fries, can't stop dipping into their father's portion (served in a brown paper cone, carefully positioned in a spiral metal holder custom-built to hold brown paper cones of hand-cut french fries), and soon enough he repents his generosity and snaps at them to order their own, but of course they don't. And of course he repents his grouchiness and urges them to take more, and of course they refuse, and then they give way when they see that he's getting upset, and take more fries, which are kind of cold by then, but still absurdly good.

Gary has to go. Messages are piling up on his cell phone, which

he checks partly hidden, under the table, so as not to provoke a lecture from their father. His kids, his office, his wife. Diane nods, flaps
her right hand once in dismissal—fine, go—and stays to keep their
father company as he finishes his burger. It's kind of a mess—the
blue cheese is runny, the bacon makes the signature potato flour bun
slide a bit on the burger, and her father has spots on his white shirt
and grease all over his hands. Diane thinks how her mother would
have produced wipes from her handbag. She pulls extra napkins out
of the dispenser on the table, pours some water from her glass onto
the wadded paper, and tries to dab at her father's shirt. He knocks
her hand away.

Diane isn't asleep when her father calls her at two a.m. to say that
he called the night attendant's cell phone number twice and she
didn't answer, and so then he called the nursing station, and the clerk
refused to go check on the night attendant. Lazy, everyone is lazy,
everyone is so unbelievably lazy, the night attendant who is taking
how much an hour and is probably asleep in the chair, the nurse
who never goes near the room because the night attendant is there,
doing the job that a good nurse ought to do, the desk clerk, who
can't be bothered to move her fat behind. Diane says, Dad, I think
you ought to get some sleep. That's why we pay for the night attendant, after all, so you and I and Gary can get a break and get some
rest. You weren't asleep, were you, either, he says, and she lets it go,
and they are both thinking, of course, of that hospital room, where
he may well be right that all is not well and never will be, where
they are relying on the fifteen-dollar-an-hour kindness of Agnes or
Caroline or Ottile or María Concepción.

In the morning, the attendant—actually, it's Daphne from New
Zealand—assures them that it was a good night, no pain, a lovely sleep
she had. It's hard to stand in that room and believe that anything has
been lovely, looking at the untouched breakfast on the hospital tray,
each dish hidden by its pebbly pink plastic cover, a round cover for the
bowl of oatmeal, a larger one for the plate of scrambled eggs, a smaller
one for the cup of coffee. Her mother did one morning take a sip of
coffee through a crooked straw, but then she spat it out, pushed the

straw away so hard that the coffee splashed all over Diane's hand, and she could feel how thin it was, how tepid.

She sends her father to the coffee shop to get his own breakfast because she can tell he doesn't want them both to leave. He brings her back the world's largest cheese danish, and when she shakes her head, no, he takes a defiant bite. Gary thinks they ought to tell him they're worried about him; Gary thinks they should try the old, You can't take care of someone unless you take care of yourself song and dance. But her father does not take care of people, not even himself. That was her mother's job. And whatever they might say to him, he of course already knows. Looking down at the fresser sandwich, combined corn beef and pastrami, the day they walked a block farther and ate at the deli, her father said, It's a heart attack on a plate. Suicide by sandwich. Then he ate the first overstuffed half while Diane waited for her matzoh ball soup to cool to the point where she could take a sip without scalding her tongue, and Gary ostentatiously ate a salad. It's not so great, their father said, his mouth still full. It's not what I'd call the real stuff. The pastrami is dry. You mean it isn't fatty enough, don't you, Gary said, and their father picked up the second sandwich half. Nothing a little mustard won't cure.

Callista comes to Diane's office hours. There are dark circles around her eyes—or could that be makeup? She has a generally rumpled air, her brown hair somewhat stringy, her big blue sweater loose over a black sports bra. She's been working and working on New York City in the seventies—she's found these great photos? And this account of a club, the cocaine in the bathroom? And maybe if she could do something multimedia because the music is so amazing? Except, she says, the only thing. She's under a lot of stress right now. There's this other course. And the thing is, her roommate had this terrible experience—well, two terrible experiences. First she was in this really abusive relationship and now her father is dying. Can you imagine?

Wait, stop, says Diane. This is your roommate? Your roommate's abusive relationship, your roommate's father? As in, why am I hearing about this. Yes, says Callista. So it's been pretty stressful. I mean,

I'm trying to be her support system and all, but I might be in over my head here.

Yes, Diane says. I think you might.

Ordinarily, as a teacher, Diane prides herself on her sense of humor, her sense of irony: A student came to me for an extension on her project because—get this—her roommate is in an abusive relationship. But she doesn't have the energy today, she doesn't want to know where Callista is going. Doesn't want, to tell the truth, to have to come to grips with the multimedia project on fascinating evil dangerous graffiti-covered New York in the 1970s; she's been teaching this writing-and-reading-the-city course for a number of years, and she's already graded this project any number of times, and it's not usually very good.

Her parents lived in the city right through the bad times. Lived in the city and worked for the city, her father in labor relations, her mother in special ed. And for what, she imagines her father asking, angrily, thinking of her mother, as if yet another loyal service is being disregarded, punishment where there should be reward. All those years she taught those kids no one else could teach, and look at her now.

Diane herself remembers the graffiti days of the subway system well enough; she has plenty of friends who were mugged, though it would never occur to Callista, or to any other student, to ask. And to be fair, Diane wasn't hanging out in the filthy club bathrooms where her students imagine they would have been ingesting mind-altering substances with suspiciously skinny musicians, nor was she trolling the old unreconstructed 42nd Street with the hookers. She was getting good grades and going to college and coming home for vacation. She is staring at the surely unnecessarily stringy hair of this perfectly pretty college girl, and thinking about her parents, and how they hung in there when so many of their friends headed for Westchester and Long Island and Jersey, her parents and how they took care of one another and made it through, and for what—and if she doesn't get Callista out of her office quickly, she is going to be crying in front of a student, and a not very good student at that.

But there is no moving Callista. So instead she holds up a finger, as if she has just remembered an emergency reason to rush out in the hall and say a word to the departmental administrator—and then ducks into the women's bathroom, sobs silently in a stall for a minute or two, staring straight ahead at a poster about intimate partner violence, and then splashes some water on her face, rubs it dry with paper towels.

"Here, you might pass this on to your roommate," she says, handing over the poster, frayed at the corners where she yanked it away from the tape. Then, briskly, "So, given all this stress, Callista, would it help if you had an extra week to work on this?"

As easy as that, she has her office to herself again. Can look out the window, see that it has started to rain, imagine herself in an hour or so walking into the hospital lobby, taking a plastic bag out of the dispenser to hold her umbrella, and joining the crowd at the elevator bank. Out loud she says, "I do not think I can do this."

But there she is, of course, wet umbrella in its plastic bag, shoes slightly soggy on the ugly linoleum floor of the family room. There they all are, Diane and Gary and her father and the oncology fellow, Dr. Douglas Carrigan. That he seems about Callista's age is no longer a surprise; the male doctors feel even younger than the female doctors to Diane. They seem like nervous children doing their best in a high school play in white coats that someone's father arranged to borrow from the local clinic. But Dr. Douglas Carrigan is wearing his own white coat, with his name embroidered in red script above the vest pocket, and presumably his own stethoscope as well, presumably a real one. He has short, bushy, mouse-colored hair and beard and moustache, close trimmed around his slightly puffy face, and he holds his hands clasped together in front of him, leaning forward in the blue chair, moving his clasped hands up and down for emphasis whenever he speaks.

"We've discussed her at our conference," he tells them, enthusiastically, as if this is the best news that anyone could want to hear. "We presented her case to Dr. Neckendorf—he's the man who really wrote the book on aggressive adjuvant chemotherapy in these

210

situations—we were very fortunate to have him—to be able to present her."

"So tell us our options," Gary says. "Tell us what Dr. Neckendorf recommended."

"What he recommended when we were so fortunate to have him," their father mutters.

Gary can't stay to take their father out to dinner. Daphne is back again for the night—they cannot, any of them, figure out the mysteries of the night attendant agency and who gets sent when. Ottile and María Concepción, the two most frequent flyers, have both offered to take the case off the books, have both said they have friends who could help out, who could do it cheaper, without the agency. But Diane said no, and Gary agreed; it's probably silly to take any comfort at all in the idea of the agency, of someone screening and tracking the women who sit through the night with their mother, but it gives them a feeling that there is something professional going on as they leave in the evening. And their father, of course, would hate the idea of off-the-books. A kiss on the forehead—her eyes are staring up at them, or maybe past them, and the pain medicine, thank god, seems to be working, so with luck she has no idea where she is right now. Good night, they say, each in turn, and tonight she says back, each time, heartbreakingly obedient, Good night, good night, good night.

Take good care of her, please, Diane let herself murmur to Daphne, who said, No fear, we're going to have a wonderful sleep.

Gary gives Diane a harassed apologetic explanation—the children, the family dinner hour, his wife isn't well. Diane nods, and waves him off, and takes their father out herself. Or more accurately, takes him home, makes him take a cab with her, since it's still raining hard. And here, what luck, is a cab just pulling up to the hospital entrance, and they get in and go to a diner he likes, around the corner from her parents' apartment, a place where he's been eating for maybe thirty years. And probably ordering the Salisbury steak and the loaded baked potato with butter, sour cream, and cheddar. Certainly he is well known to the waiter, who wears bright red suspenders over his regulation black vest, and who actually looks older than Diane's father, as he shuffles from table to table like he might at any moment give up and sit down.

"You get a garden salad with that," he says, leaning heavily on a corner of their table, pouring more water.

"Blue cheese dressing." Diane's father is already buttering a dinner roll.

"You got it. How's she doing?" The waiter's name tag is on the side closer to Diane but her eyes seem to be watering; she blots them with a napkin and reads his name: Constantine.

"Not so good." Her father shakes his head. "Bunch of bastards." Constantine nods.

"They've got this one guy now—Neckendorf—the biggest bastard of them all," her father says. "Think he comes to see her? Think he stands up like a person and takes responsibility? Herr Doktor Big-Shot Neckendorf?" He shakes his head. "I hope their insides turn black and rot."

At home that night, Diane suddenly finds herself wondering, is it time to call her ex-husband and let him know. He liked her mother, both her parents. He sends them a holiday card every year—a photo of his twins, who are now four years old. A somewhat tactless move, perhaps, since if he had stayed married to Diane—if things had worked out—if he had gotten tenure and stayed in the city and in academics—if all those things, then the twins or their equivalents would be grandchildren. Still, Diane's mother sends a card back—one of the ones she gets for donating to the summer camp foundation; the cards are drawn by the special ed children themselves and are not usually very attractive. But then, to tell the truth, the photos of the twins are not so very attractive either; other people nowadays go for casually dressed children in action outdoors, but Diane's ex-husband, or, more likely his wife, is still living in the era of a velvet holiday dress for the girl and a matching blazer for the boy, side by side on the sofa. Everyone somehow overstuffed.

She doesn't call him. She should probably call him, she should probably call a bunch of people. All the people who will be hurt later that she didn't call. That they didn't know what was going on. But call them to say what? Things aren't going so well, no visitors please, Dr. Neckendorf is gravely concerned? How can we have slipped so suddenly, all of us, right out of our lives and into this?

She gets to the hospital the next afternoon, after teaching a class in which none of the students are willing to talk at all, and she finds her father talking to the oncology fellow, Dr. Douglas Carrigan, the guy with the mousy beard. They are standing together just inside the door of her mother's room.

"Have you been to Scotland?" her father asks as Diane comes in, braced to hear whatever the bad news may be.

"No, I haven't. But I hear it's a beautiful country."

"Douglas is a Scottish name, is why I ask," says her father.

"My dad's family is Irish, originally. Carrigan." He looks over at Diane, probably hoping to be rescued, but as far as she is concerned, he's on his own.

Diane puts her coat and her bag down on a chair, walks to the bed. Her mother's eyes are open, and she's staring at the ceiling. Diane bends over, kisses her, then turns her head so that her own cheek is against her mother's.

"But *Douglas* is a Scottish name. Did you ever read a book called *Scottish Chiefs*? A classic?"

"No, I can't say I have."

"Cold!" Her mother's voice is louder than Diane has heard it for a couple of weeks, and both men turn to look. "Your face is so cold!"

"Yes," Diane says. "It's freezing out. At least they keep it nice and warm in here."

Her father and Dr. Carrigan have both come over to the bed.

"Nice to see you wide awake," the doctor says. "How are you feeling?"

But her father's head is in the way, he is bending over, his face as close as Diane's was a minute ago. "Gloria!" he says. "Glory, honey! Glory, baby!"

He waits, then straightens up. He looks bewildered, frightened, abandoned. "She's gone again," he says, accusingly, to the doctor. "She was back with us for a minute, but she's gone again."

"It's probably the medication," the doctor says. "As we've discussed, in elderly people, this much pain medicine can have major side effects."

"But she was just here! You heard her!"

"And it can come and go like that. At least we seem to have good pain control." The doctor is edging away, heading for the doorway. "We're going to discuss the case with Dr. Neckendorf again—he'll probably want us to get another scan tomorrow—I'm going to try and get her on the schedule—I'll let you know as soon as we've made a definite plan—"

And he's done it, he's at the door, he's out; he nods to Diane, to her father, from the safe outside of the threshold. "Have a nice evening," he says.

Callista has turned in—a week late—her list of sources, scenes, major topics. Yada yada, Studio 54, yada yada, cocaine, yada yada, the Ramones. Diane wants to write on it, Oh, grow up. But she doesn't. She wants to call her father and say, Let's demand Dr. Neckendorf himself, let's drag him in and make him answer all our questions. But do they really want the answers?

Who could want to be doing dangerous drugs in a filthy bathroom? Why should I care about this? If you use the word *gritty* one more time, I will fail you for the semester.

Her mother is with Ottile tonight. It's colder than ever outside. Her father insisted on going back to the burger place and doing the double bacon cheeseburger. She herself had no appetite at all. She can still feel her mother's slightly slack cheek against her own cold face.

Her father had a beer with his burger, but she had nothing herself. Perhaps a glass of wine to help her fall asleep? She won't call her father, or her brother, or her ex-husband, or the night attendant, or a friend, or anyone at all. Won't write nasty remarks on the project plan of Callista from Seattle who dreams of Studio 54 and a high murder rate. She'll suggest some references on the politics of 1970s New York, on city government and the economic crisis, she'll suggest that it might be good to know who was mayor, who was governor, if this

214

is your topic. She'll have a glass of wine, then another, and go to sleep. And when the phone rings in the middle of the night, she will know, before she answers.

My parents insist that I made my own wardrobe decisions.

Caleb Leisure received his MFA in Fiction from New York University. In 2011 he was named a NYC Emerging Writer Fellow at The Center for Fiction, and in 2014 he won the Crazyhorse Fiction Prize. He works for a small winery in Sonoma County and is at work on his first novel. He lives in Oakland.

ATLANTIC ON SUNDAY

Caleb Leisure

1. A Bomb

Sally Downing was fifty-nine years old and all her life she had known: the Atlantic had it out for her. First, it was the family beagle, snatched by a wicked February undertow on her sixth birthday. Then her father, Reginald, miniatured on the deck of a great black ship, his military wave lost in a thousand golden cuffs. Gone for five years to Oman. There was the wave that had split her forehead open against the rotten wood of the pier. All those stitches. That frown of a scar. And the Georgie Peacock episode, in which she was lured nude into the choppy midnight sea, that had to be counted. It was the Atlantic, as much as the boy, who had claimed her virginity. Later, the shipping container. Five illegal Polish immigrants found dead in a false wall. Her brother Philip, a worker at the Docks, had conducted the operation, and a week later he swam out into the same waters and let the waves consume him. That was almost a year ago now. And just last week she had lost a glove. A really very nice, hardly sensible glove from Hobbs of London. Another compensatory birthday gift from her daughter. Torn from her grip by a rough sea wind, such that for a moment, watching the thing take flight over the muscled water, Sally thought her hand dismembered.

It was Sunday, late May, a few minutes before six in the morning.

The seafront was calm and hushed with fog. The seafront was hers. Long, low clouds blocked the sunrise. The water and the sky were the same purple-gray, and the horizon was a hairline porcelain crack. Sally walked barefoot along the surf, as she did each Sunday, the cuffs of her salt-hard jeans rolled above her calves. Giving the Atlantic a little taste of flesh. In front of her she waved a metal detector in long slow arcs, an extension of her body, an insect tendril. The bulky red headphones spoke to her in their private language of clicks.

Sunday morning, and Sunday mornings were sacrosanct: Emer had St. Mary's Church, Reginald had his garden, and Sally, she had the seafront. For a few precious hours each week her universe contracted into the tight orbit of the detector's head, and she felt herself squarely at its center. She felt herself unobligated: from her students at Ravenswood Junior School, from her duties as Councilor of the Libraries and Heritage Advisory Committee, from the ever-more demanding biologies of her progenitors.

The pulse of the clicking developed a little flourish of arrhythmia. Adrenaline seized her. She dropped to one knee and drove a gardening spade into the pebbled beach. How good that felt. Soon there was a flash of silver amidst the sand and the small sea-smoothed stones. She dislodged the object, a teaspoon, and held it to her eye. Classic kings pattern design, tarnished Sheffield silver plate, trumpet and banner trademark, not less than a century old. What luck! Unlikely it was suitable for the Felixstowe Museum, where her friend Tilly was the curator, and it wasn't right for her own collection, but she should be able to sell it. Sally thumbed the spoon clear of sand and burrowed it into her father's old army rucksack, a stiff canvas bag emblazoned with the name Downing in large white letters.

She walked south toward the Docks. The promenade rose up on Sally's right, lofted on a stone retaining wall. A vendor pulled up metal shutters with a loop of chain. In a few hours the tourists would invade with their sunstarved torsos. Terrible creatures. Shivering children would queue for Peter's Ice Cream, dripping saltwater onto the sun-hot pavement. The arcades would grow bright and loud. The tired go-carts would belch gasoline into the salty air. Teenagers would sneak into the back of the Family Fun Center and climb the towering clown face facade and swig candied alcohol. Felixstowe was a resort town, and had been since Victorian times, but its prewar luster had long ago faded. It seemed to Sally that the promenade was no longer a celebration of the ocean, but a defamation of it. Too right.

She glimpsed the purple storefront of Mrs. Simpson's Tea Room, the chipped, hand-painted letters in the dark window. Emer's preferred arena of gossip before her recent troubles. The café was named after the promiscuous commoner for whom Edward VIII had abdicated. In the midst of the great royal scandal, Mrs. Simpson had fled here of all places. That the town took such inordinate pride in this struck Sally as distasteful, although she had to admit that their scones were excellent, and that her enjoyment of them was not uninfluenced by the sugar of a little royal ignominy. Maybe that would awaken her mother's appetite, maybe they would go this week.

Sally passed the old pier, which lay on the water like a dead vein. Her feet crunched through wet pebbles, through glass and wood and bone made smooth and anonymous by the stomach of the sea. A steady rhythm from the detector. The surf lapping over her ankles. Not that she didn't enjoy a Peter's Ice Cream, from time to time, in the appropriate circumstance.

She walked and the air went cool. The early, abstract shadows of ships and cranes and cables latticed the beach. Even through the headphones, the sound of machines. Of straining metal. The air redolent with grease, nearly viscous. Sally looked up. These were the Docks. To the east, rows of massive gantry cranes were silhouetted on offshore platforms, like skeletons of impossible, prehistoric creatures. They moved slowly, lofting colored shipping containers into the dull sky. She had seen these movements most every day of her life, but they still registered as profound, they swept through her. Generations of men with Sally's name had worked under these dockland shapes. Her granddad, her father, her brother, her husband before he left. If you were born in Felixstowe, you were born of the Docks. There was a technical name for the self-pollinating flowers, with both stamen and pistil, for the life of her she couldn't remember. Her father would.

The detector's pulse erupted, a cardiac arrest of the shoreline. The old clunker had blown another fuse. She deserved a new model but couldn't bear to part with this one, what a bloody sap she was. Sally whipped the headphones off. The morning rushed into her head. The Atlantic erased her feet.

Not twenty meters ahead was a dark still shape, its edges softened by the mist. A beached seal or sea something—it had the particular stillness of the once-living—but now it seemed too perfectly geometric. She paced toward the thing, hugging the detector to her chest. She stopped a few cautious meters away, stretched her neck forward. The large cylinder was cocooned in searoot and algae. Small black bugs swarmed around it and a few of them leaped onto Sally's forearms, her face.

She looked to the ocean as though for explanation. Then to the sky. She looked around her, with a child's fear of being caught, flushed with preemptive guilt. If it was what she thought it could be, she should leave immediately, she should get help, she should not walk toward it, as she found herself doing, and she most certainly should not prod the thing with her bare toe. The cylinder held all the coldness of the ocean. It sent a charge up her leg, half erotic. Sally cleared away a few half-dry leaves of seastuff with the detector's head, revealed a brilliant palette of corrosion. In nearly imperceptible white paint were words and characters, and she stared at them for a long time, understanding nothing, ignoring the bugs in her nostrils and in the back of her throat.

The television reporter sported a famously awful combover. The Atlantic wind had a hold of it now, teasing it up and down such that there was a tandem mouth delivering the news. His was the voice and the face that had taken Suffolk through the Diana accidents, the London bombings, the Prince Harry Nazi scandal. He moved and spoke as though a bit drunk, or as if sheer enthusiasm had liquefied his bones. They knew with whom he had slept, they knew the contour of his bare, beach-blunder abdomen. Now his tongue was learning old wartime words: *Luftwaffe* and *Sprengbombe* and *Evacuate*. Spittle shot from his lips. The reporter reported: it was a 1942 German SC shell, maybe the largest to have ever beached on Britain's coastline, and it was very possibly alive. His hair flapped in the wind.

No cause for alarm, said the mouths.

Reginald Downing valued hard work, community, a properly cooked joint of beef, and, above all, routine. He had earned routine. He liked his world small and precise and already the bomb had mucked up the day. The television again flashed to his daughter. He saw as though for the first time in her face his own features—wide thin lips, crooked Byzantine nose, small watery eyes—and he thought himself cruel to have procreated, even with a beauty such as Emer had been.

He tried to change the channel but the presser wasn't cooperating. Sally was supposed to have changed the batteries today. She was supposed to have helped with the laundry and to have brought the meat from SJ Summers, and there were other things, vital things, that he could not remember just now. He had earned not remembering. He banged the presser against his knee, registered the smear of dried food on his trousers with resigned chagrin, tried the buttons again. The football had already started.

I'm hungry, he said to the television.

Hush now. You're ruining my show, said Emer.

She was sitting on the creaky rocking chair closest to the television, far away from her usual spot beside him on the burgundy sofa, and was canted unnaturally into the picture. Her knotted fingers, bruised purple beneath the nails, combed through her thin, brown-dyed hair again and again. Reginald hadn't seen her so engaged for weeks and he decided he didn't care for it, not one bit. He pointed the presser at his wife and thumbed a button, imagined pausing her, rewinding her. There was a mute button somewhere.

Couldn't she just let her hair go gray?

Sundays had a routine. On this Sunday, here is what did not happen. Sally did not come for Emer, did not walk her to St. Mary's, did not give him his unfettered hours in the garden. Then she did not guide them down the ivy-strangled walls of Pembroke Road to visit the ocean. Emer did not say, Nothing like a little good clean salt air in the lungs, and they did not march arm in arm, in military synch, like they had waltzed off the top of their wedding cake, as their grand-daughter had once said. They did not eat lunch at the Putney Arms, and Reginald did not order the cod and chips, and he did not shake the vinegar bottle sixty-two times in honor of the year Ipswich Town won the English League title. They did not plead for Emer to eat something, and she did not drag a spoon though her mash in simula-crum of consumption, and he did not get to complain about the new high-rises throwing strange shadows over their street and depriving his garden of sun. And the way things were going, they would most certainly not make bingo at four.

The sun was a hardboiled yolk in the afternoon gray when Sally knocked on her parents' door. Yesterday's mail was caught in the brass slot. The chrysanthemums on the left side of the concrete walk had been decapitated by the neighbor's terrier. She had forgotten the meat and the batteries, and the fingers of guilt began to disassemble her morning's exhilaration.

The door opened. Her parents were statued in the threshold. The news blared from the television.

How can you be on telly and here at the same time? said Emer.

They studied her in distrustful silence and she began to feel like an imposter. The door would shut and she would be left here, on the balding welcome mat, spurned for her television facsimile, who would enjoy immortality in fiberoptics and cathode ray tubes and RGB. She had spent the morning with the minted breath of reporters and their scribbling pens. They had split her in two.

In truth it had been thrilling. The discovery of the bomb, the blast of attention, the cameras, and most especially the derailment from pat-tern, the crash into uncertainty. The day had been all about her, the day had been wondrously messy.

Emer looked behind her to the television and, seemingly satisfied that the space-time continuum was intact, clasped her hands together in a motion that meant: tea.

Her mum was behaving oddly. She brought out the Belleek china and blew the years of dust out with weak, saliva-misted puffs. She put

222

the needle down on a Dean Martin record. She sat in a different seat than normal, away from Reginald, who sat frozen save for his busy fingers, pulling at the head of a dried hibiscus flower. And then Emer began to speak, slowly, the beads of her words assembling on a string of unusual fluency. Her first true consecutive sentences in months and Sally was too surprised and delighted to collect their meanings.

Then came his name, and then Sally was listening.

Emer's musings had careened into The Yank. It was rare that she spoke of him, her old beau, and any time conversation so much as grazed the Second World War or Germany or the state of Ohio, Sally could see the tension claim her father, as it did now. She watched his fingers crush petals into pigment. Emer reserved a special accent for The Yank, tightly coiled around her Irish roots, deeper in pitch, fatter in tongue. Sounds pulled from a primitive soil. The bomb had dug him up. She was on a roll, talking to Sally or to herself or to the biscuit in her fingers, dropping silent crumbs onto her lap, a prop to her monologue.

But you ended up with Dad, who's much better, tried Sally.

This talk made her uncomfortable as well. It was an alternate vision of the universe in which she could not have existed.

Shall we go for a walk, then? said Reginald.

He had these tattoos, he did, numbers covering his forearms, Emer continued. He did them himself, you know, with pen ink and a sewing needle. I said always, I said, that must hurt, but he said it's not too bad. They were the birthdays of everyone he loved and he let me put my own into his arm. He smiled as he bled. He bled like a codfish, he did. And when—

Reginald switched off his hearing aid, wishing that more of the body was thusly controlled. The room grew larger. He felt his complexion flare brightly into its space. The television was better without sound anyway. The reporter's combover took flight in the wind. He pushed a third biscuit into his mouth and watched the two women, wife and daughter, in silent pantomime. They seemed like actors.

His Emer would have sat next to him on the burgundy sofa so that she could entwine her stockinged feet with his. This Emer was in the rocking chair, legs working like pistons. She wore white trainers and white socks and her jogging bottoms were hitched up over her calves and he studied the thick tendon behind her right knee.

Those legs. Those bloody legs. They did not match the rest of her: too large and robust for her slight torso, her petite head. Before the war, when they used to race along Felixstowe beach to the oyster beds at Cobbold's Point, she would always win, and he would have to pretend that he had let her. Reginald attributed her recent wanderings—she had gone missing twice in the past three months—to the autonomy of her legs. He had always feared that one day they would decide to walk away on their own, back to The Yank perhaps, and take his wife with them.

The thing on the beach, on the television, it stirred long-nested thoughts, frightened them from the high branches of his subconscious. It was unbearable. He popped another biscuit into his dry mouth, unfolded himself from the couch, and went to the garden out back. He needed to get his hands dirty, to feel the grit beneath his fingernails, the life in the soil. He needed the nourishment of a place he could control.

He stepped onto the terrace and the refracted sun attacked his eyes. He had not been able to do any serious gardening since the previous autumn, when he had been approved for the double cornea transplant. Just until the eyes heal, Colonel, a few short months, the doctor had said. Saluting him, the patronizing bastard. And he had never been a Colonel. Although Sally had helped him till and sow the spring and summer vegetables, the garden was a thicket of negligence, insufferably sloppy and overgrown and begging for his inimitable touch.

The garden was a quarter-century delineation of his personality in color and morphology and landscape. A good wine reflected its maker, and the same was true of a garden. His spanned nearly a quarter acre, with delicate cobblestone paths that branched venously from the circle of pawpaw trees that could be called the heart. On the terrace, which faced west and south, grape and kiwi vines rambled over a pergola. By September clusters of grapes—Swenson Red, Brianna, Lorelei—would dangle overhead, along with the smooth kiwifruits that were never quite sweet enough but that he loved for their taste of pineapple and brandy. Almost everything here was edible. The garden, he repeated as mantra, is the nation's medical chest. He had learned in wartime that the efficacy of a flower needed to run deeper than its beauty. A garden could sustain a life.

Reginald stepped into the eastern vegetable patch, dropped to his knees, and shortened his sleeves in three neat folds.

He had looked up The Yank's name once, ran his fingers through a phone book in a sweaty Hamburg café. He had tried to find him. This is what he knew: The Yank was Emer's fiancé during the war, an American stationed between London and Mannheim. He was from a distinguished Midwest family, old money, and he despised his privilege. He ran away, into the romance of the war. His journey brought him to Emer—then Reginald's girl, Reginald's patient girl, waiting for his return from the POW camp—and The Yank had stolen her affections. Reginald knew nothing of their courtship save for its end. The Yank had suffered some terrific wound, maybe in Exeter, maybe in Berlin. This, he understood, was why Emer had left him. A deformity that burrowed into the darkest places of his imagination.

Before his decades on the docks, Reginald had served in the Royal Air Force. Emer kept his medals in her jewelry box. She used to pin them through her pierced ears and march around for him in the nude. This flushed him with pride and terror. He had been badly injured himself: shrapnel from a blast had lodged just above the shelf of his hip. He had spent twenty weeks in a Berlin infirmary. There were pieces of war still inside him. He kept this a secret from Emer, out of an irrational fear that she might leave him, just as she had left the American. It was a fear that had calloused into habit. When they were intimate he kept her hands away from the hard sliver of flesh. After showering he was always careful to cover the scar with a towel. When he ate the wrong thing, and his side burned like flak ripping through steel, he had learned how not to grimace.

The sun had changed position and his trousers were soaked from the soil and the vegetable patch was half torn apart. His eyes ached. The Yank had been laid to rest in neat piles of carrots and potatoes and rhubarb. Reginald was always finding new ways to kill the man. He had found a picture, once, pressed into the pages of Emer's old bible along with a blue flower that he had been able to identify as *Centaurea cyanus*—cornflower. The flower was familiar. He had seen them in the plains of Germany. He had crushed them with his belly and fired shots from between their blossoms. One springtime, not so long ago, he planted cornflower in the northwest corner of the garden and took bittersweet pleasure in depriving the plant of water and watching it die.

Sally was still enduring Emer's rhapsody when Reginald marched into the living room, his wiry arms bundling wet newspaper and rhubarb, and dumped the vegetables onto her lap. His way of saying: leave. Every Sunday Sally took home vegetables from the garden, but this had been, traditionally, a more cheerful exchange. His fingers and cuticles were darkened with soil and he was trembling. There was a small, shiny beetle on his neck. How could she have let him out of her sight for so long? The newspaper had left sweat-lithographed words on his forearms. Emer turned her attention to the television and took a very delicate bite of her biscuit, as though her jaw and the pastry were equally likely to crumble in the exchange.

A minute later, in the filthy kitchen, Sally had her father by the wrists. The linoleum was warped beneath her shoes. The rhubarb was in the sink, bleeding into a bath of cool water. She felt sand between her toes.

You can't do that, she said, angry with him, angry with herself. The doctor says you can't—

You're letting him into this house, he said.

He was shaking. His small red eyes fluttered, as though against a wind that she couldn't sense. He was in another reality.

You're letting him in, he said.

I know it's awful, what she's saying, but at least she's talking.

You made it happen. You're letting him in.

There's only the three of us here, Dad. She's with you. Listen to me: this is ridiculous.

Reginald turned his back to her and faced the living room. Through the thresholds of two open doors she could see into the living room. A mugshot of the bomb filled the television. The light washed out

Emer's features, revealed the skeletal structure of her face, and Sally wondered what it was that her father saw when he looked at his wife. How did he reconcile this woman she had become with all the women she had been? Or did it not work like that? Did he have access to all her selves at once, nested one inside the other like matryoshka dolls, and could he take out whichever one he pleased? However it worked, she was jealous of it. Her marriage had been short, and her aging felt stripped of meaning.

Funny that you should see one before me, he said.

Funny, said Sally.

It looks harmless, doesn't it now?

They say it's not. They say it's very much alive.

Sally imagined that inside the bomb were all the things she had ever lost.

I'm not leaving this house, he said.

How about a rhubarb crumble? It's been a long time since she's talked like that. All those sentences, she might be hungry.

The winter had seen Emer lose her appetite and her skin draw tight to her bones. The doctors had explored the possibility of dementia, but nothing was certain. She ate mostly baked goods, sometimes boiled potatoes with sugar or golden syrup. Once, half a page of sheet music, "Hang Out the Washing on the Siegfried Line," candied in spilt molasses. Sally couldn't say how her father felt, but she found it nearly impossible to glimpse her mother through the calamities of biology and behavior.

Reginald brushed away mites of dirt that clung to Sally's sweater.

Let me trim the rhubarb for you, he said.

But he didn't move. Their attention sank into the warfare of images on the television. A mass of children jumped to be seen by the camera's eye, the crowns of their heads together undulating like so many buoys in the water. Emer poured more golden tea into the bonewhite cups and gestured for Sally to join her, which she did. Emer brought her cup to her face, the steam fogging the lenses of her glasses.

What's an old rusty thing like that want with us anyhow? she said.

•   •   •

The television said, the Royal Navy was preparing a detonation team, to be dispatched without delay. It said, Experts and historians were being commissioned from London. It said, Evacuation was not required but evacuation was advisable. It said, The Royal Navy!

The reporter gestured behind him at the residents who had filled the promenade with doomsday fascination. He spoke to those residents in front of their screens, who blew into cups of tea and dialed the phone numbers that they knew by heart. He said, All schools have been released, all shops closed. He said, with jokey lust, A bomb has been found, and has released pheromones into the salt-sweet air of this sleepy seaside town.

In the late afternoon, as the Queen took her tea, Sally escorted her mother down to the seafront to see the bomb. Reginald trailed some distance behind, affecting indifference by inspecting the gardens of the houses they passed. Emer hardly blinked or paused for breath. She motored on about The Yank, her accent even thicker now and almost incomprehensible. Sally thought of and could not fathom the impoverished childhood on a farm in County Cork that seemed many generations removed, not just the one. There was so much distance between their lives, much more even than there was between Sally and her own daughter.

Emer talked about how the muscles in his forearms came alive like eels when he played guitar, and how he pulled big silver coins from behind her ear, and how he took a shot of vinegar before eating a steak. How lovely it was to see her mother so animated. She saw it now, the young woman breaking through, the bow of a ship materializing in the fog.

Along the way, neighbors and friends and students stopped Sally in excitement. They grabbed her biceps, touched her shoulder, held her handshake. As though to pilfer celebrity, as though she were a blessed ancient stone to be rubbed for good fortune. It was all terribly sincere, and she noted that not a single person mocked her, as they often did in the streets and the school hallways, miming her metal detector walk. This touching was the most bewildering part of her day. It was the

228

contact itself—unusual and unwelcome—and it was what the contact signified: something big had happened, and it had happened to her. The touching held her back a little from the spin of the world, and had gifted her frightening objectivity.

The air moved and a bicycle bell stung her body back to its place on Pembroke Road. The smell of dirt and grease and something sweet like burned honey. A man was pedaling and a gangly boy sat on the rusted chrome handlebars. The tandem passed and the man looked back at Sally, not quite smiling, his lips pearlescent, his knees pumping high into his chest. The bicycle wobbled. The Atlantic peeked over the crest of the hill.

She was normally so good with names, but the man's wouldn't come to her. He was a forty-something Polish immigrant known around town simply as Spider, but she couldn't very well call him that.

Bomb, bomb, bomb! said the boy. Gabriel. He couldn't be older than ten now. His name she could never forget.

She watched the man's muscles move beneath denim and cotton and she thought of the ocean. He was a swimmer, she knew, and he had been infected by its rhythms. He was another artifact of the Atlantic, like the boy. Likely they had both come to this country packed into a shipping container; likely she shouldn't be thinking that way.

The bicycle skidded to a stop, painted rubber onto the coarse pavement. Gabriel toppled from his perch in an abstraction of limbs. The man spat a viscous juice from his mouth.

You are on the television picture, he said. Very beautiful.

He waited for them to catch up.

Gabriel had been in Sally's class a few years back. She had found his surname name impossible to pronounce and she remembered how the boy had taken deep pleasure in this. More and more, she encountered names beyond the graces of her tongue. First it was the Polish, Solidarity immigrants, mostly. Then the Southern Asians and, more recently, families from China and Senegal. Some legal, some not. It was impossible to know.

Gabriel was connected to Spider through some simpatico of blood. She'd been afraid to ask about the parents. A quiet child, small for his age, bullied, he sat in his desk like a shell in the chamber of a gun. He sometimes retaliated, and would always atone with confectionery apologies on her desk: loaves of plum cake, soft gingerbread biscuits, cheesecake topped with fruits and jelly. Gabriel was the only child she'd ever had to expel. He'd stabbed a boy in the stomach with a freshly sharpened pencil.

She knew that the man, Spider, was a farmhand on the sugar beet fields just outside of town and a part-time driver at the Docks. She sometimes saw him around town on his squawking Raleigh, or running along the beach in the morning. His wave always flushed her with guilt.

So, you are famous now, he said. I should ask for your autographing.

A smile of small, gray teeth. His hair was cropped close to his skull, which peaked steeply. His clothes hugged his body tightly, unflattering in places but altogether appealing in its unapologetic laxity.

I wouldn't say that, said Sally.

Then you are wrong.

Foreign muck! said Emer. This was a phrase usually reserved for cuisine beyond the boundaries of the United Kingdom, and maybe her mind was on the lasagna Sally had microwaved for lunch, and maybe it wasn't.

Mother!

The man laughed.

I am Janusz. This is Gabriel.

His name sounded like a painful sneeze. She forgave herself for not remembering.

And now his left hand demanded Sally's attention. The ring and pinky fingers were half gone. They were scarred and shone like wet rockface. A montage of possible metacarpal catastrophes played in her mind. A vengeful cleaver, a work accident, a grenade that was part of a war she had never heard of, and about which she now felt a hypothetical guilt.

Janusz nudged the boy on the shoulder.

Say hello to Ms. Downing, tell her you saw her on the television looking like beauty itself.

The boy said hello and then they were off. Janusz rang the bell and waved without looking back. Sally watched the tandem crest the hill, the boy's white shoes and undone laces held high over the horizon.

That chap, is he American? said Emer.

He's Polish, Mother. He's from Poland.

Well, isn't that a shame?

And how were they supposed to behave? There was no loudspeaker instruction or police ordinance or Hollywood blueprint to follow. No established etiquette. There was only the ancient instruction of impulse. The seafront was chaos. Bodies moved to get closer to the bomb, fish muscling around live bait. The bomb was ringed by caution tape, then fluorescent-jacketed policemen, and then the civilians. A little girl collided into Emer's legs, fell. On another day she might have stayed on the beach and cried, but she instead sprung up and continued in her frenzied direction. The faces were laughing or smiling, they were giddy and showing their teeth. The closer they were to the bomb, the greater its tidal force, the happier they seemed. The faces were talking, too. The bomb was common language. Unspoken divides between immigrant groups—British, Polish, Somali, Bangladesh—dissolved.

Sally and Emer were on the outskirts of the crowd. They had lost track of Reginald, who sat alone on the wall of the promenade nursing an ice cream cone, his back toward the crowd and the bomb and the sea. The people around Sally all seemed to know her face. They met her with stares and nods and half-smiles. The recognition felt better than she wanted to admit. Of all these people, the bomb had chosen her.

A middle-aged man with a foxhound and a walking stick stopped Sally to ask what all the commotion was about.

The Germans bombed us, whispered Emer. Don't you know?

The foxhound, whining, weaved through its owner's legs.

They dropped them from the airplanes, they did.

And Emer looked to the sky as though expecting a plane to rip through the clouds, and Sally and the man and the dog turned their eyes up as well.

By sundown, the town of Felixstowe knew this: the bomb had been dragged out to sea and, rather ingeniously they all agreed, tethered to a buoy several hundred meters out, where it would remain until the Royal Navy arrived the following morning. The detonation was to take place at noon. The plan was applauded and toasted and much ale was consumed.

Teenage couples went out to the beach at dusk and didn't bother with the usual shadowy spots. They had sex in the foam of low tide, alongside sea-smoothed glass and mollusk shells. Their bodies collected sand. There were many of them and they were loud, as though in horny, apocalyptic competition. The noise traveled into restaurants and pubs, where bodies steamed centuries-old windows and mouths and guts were overindulged. It traveled over the serene night waters, into homes close to the beach, into the yellow kitchen where Sally Downing was up past her bedtime, chopping rhubarb in her underwear because it felt good. The knife made a satisfying percussion against the oak chopping board. Her fingers were stained red.

She traced the short path to her parents' house in her mind, into a room lit with ocean-reflected light, where Emer lay awake in bed, in silent courtship with her memory. She saw Reginald in the garden after dark, his unhealed eyes slicked with blood, planting runner beans under a hot floodlight. There was Janusz now, on a redeye shift at the Docks, sitting in the truck cab, looking out into the ocean, killing the engine so that the night would stop shaking.

Sunday nights had a routine. On this Sunday night, here is what did not happen. Sally did not call her daughter, her brilliant, urbane, workaholic daughter, who had a London area code but was seemingly never in London, who had exceeded Sally's wildest expectations of intergenerational social mobility, who never answered anyway, and who, when she did, filled Sally with unpardonable and haunting melancholy regarding the averageness of her own life. She did not do that.

Sally did not sit in the conservatory, did not overturn her father's rucksack, did not catalogue the sea-things collected from the beach, or place them into the mahogany flat files in the sitting room. She did not comb through the loose change in the old Walker's biscuit tin to find the key she kept buried amongst a thousand faces of the Queen, and she did not unlock the small drawer with the brass lock. She did not unfold Philip's letter on the table, or weigh its corners with small, smooth beach stones, or read the words her brother had left behind. For the first time in nearly a year she did not torture herself in this way.

She did not select from an assorted stack of Australian Outback postcards—the silhouette of a kangaroo or an elephant against a fiery sunset—and she did not write a message to her mother from her dead brother, for whom she and Reginald had invented a false life abroad, and she did not allow herself a moment of deep self-disgust.

Instead, she watched herself on television, and she typed her name into the internet, and the sour-sweet smell of the pie perfumed the air. She thought about the bomb. Its contents were live and full of new beginnings.

2. Spangenberg

His fingers were so bloody *alive*. They had become restless, inquisitive, mischievous. The previous day's gardening had awoken them from the dead. The earth was rich with sorcery. They played over flower heads that had pushed through the wrought iron fences and over the salt-eaten brick walls along Newhaven Lane; they fondled leaves and preened outer petals. They left soft fingerprints of pollen on the lenses of his glasses.

His daughter slapped his left hand away from a sad hyacinth.

Not yours, she said.

Had there been a precise moment, he thought, or had the inversion of the parent-child dynamic been a gradual development? He made a note, one that he would undoubtedly forget, to reassert his authority at the soonest available opportunity.

Sally carried an ancient picnic basket that had the patina of salt and sun. Inside were several cucumber and butter sandwiches and a rhubarb pie. Blooming hell, it was more than a little worrisome if that wasn't stoking his appetite.

Orchids in this soil, he said. These codbrains don't know the first damn thing.

He felt knotted with anticipation. The bomb was going to be detonated and, with it, all this maddening talk of The Yank, all of this ugly backwash of history. He walked several paces ahead of Sally and Emer and kept talking so that his wife would not. He was in embittered tour-guide mode, his most safely loquacious.

This never used to be here, he said, pointing at a Wetherspoons pub. His finger then swiveled in the opposite direction, to the Cantonese restaurant.

Foreign muck, preempted Emer.

I remember when this was a sweet shop. They used to sell Coltsfoot Rock and Sherbet Pips. You and Philip would run me over when I came home with that little white bag.

I wonder if they have Coltsfoot Rock in Australia, said Emer.

He scowled away the knowing look from Sally. Harder than accepting what Philip had done had been accepting the impossibility of mourning with his wife. Telling her would have destroyed them both.

They were three of hundreds funneling to the seafront. Schools had been closed, including Sally's, many businesses, too, and palpable in the crowd was a troubling excitement of truancy. So much for evacuation. Today at least there was order. A time, a place, a sense of how to comport oneself. People streamed from their homes, foodstuffs in bags and baskets, fold-up chairs and quilts hanging from their bodies. They moved along sidewalks and they stopped at traffic lights and they looked both ways. Still, all these bodies made him nervous.

This hideous thing wasn't here, he said.

He jabbed a finger at the Spa Pavilion.

This was where the three of them had sat through a tedious production of *Alice in Wonderland* the night the ocean had taken Philip. Sometimes he conflated the hallucinatory dreamworld of the story with his son's death. It wasn't real, it was part of the show. Reginald had done some of the landscaping around the building some decades ago and now he bemoaned the new palm trees, an abomination, decidedly unpatriotic.

Wasn't here when, Dad?

They turned onto the promenade and merged with the thickening crowd. The sun was small and high and the Atlantic's battleship gray was tinseled with light.

All of this change, he said. Stupefying.

You're stupefying, said Emer.

There were new developments everywhere. In recent years they had sprung up like thick, milky weeds. Invasive, unsightly. A new block of flats was being built along their ancient street, Church Lane, and sometimes, lying in bed, he heard the jackhammers before they started. They made the sounds that guns make when soldiers hold them.

He had experienced embarrassingly little combat, but he heard it everywhere. Post-traumatic wish fulfillment. Maybe something wrong with his hearing aid, too. The uniformed men along the promenade, he wondered what sounds they had heard.

Reginald glimpsed his arthritic hand as he saluted one of the soldiers and it seized him with surprise. The eye surgery had brought unwanted clarity to his aging: spots, veins, strange new morphologies. He conceived of himself always as the young, soap-faced soldier, and this old body seemed like an act of perjury. The men on the promenade, he was like them. Peaked white caps and polished shoes. You took them off for the last time and you were as young and old as you were ever going to be.

The Royal Navy lined the main stretch of the prom like fence posts and the crowd respected the invisible barrier between them. Their uniformity, their posture, their chests plumed with accomplishment—they had a calming, tranquilizing presence, at least to Reginald.

He wanted the bomb rid of. No finer men for the job.

Military boats were anchored in the distance, clustered tightly so that their shapes made a floating cityscape. All along the seafront vendors were working furiously behind counters, delivering blistered sausages and giant clouds of candyfloss and cones of newspaper translucent with cod and chips.

I think I'd like to eat now, said Emer.

They found an empty bench along the prom railing, close to the Old Pier. Away from the bulk of the crowd, at his insistence. At his parental authority. It was 11:34 GMT when Sally unwrapped the sandwiches. Reginald took a small bite, but his stomach wanted nothing. He looked out through the bars of the railing, which were knobby with many cycles of rust, blister, paint. The ocean had erased the previous day's crazed footprints from the sand and pebbles, removed all signs of the bomb. Now it was an idea, and he felt its power multiply.

This pier used to have its own train you know, he said.

Emer packed an entire sandwich triangle into her mouth. She had forgotten the size of a civilized bite.

He continued, They tore it down during the war along with most of the pier; they were afraid the Germans would use it as a landing point. Never did build it back right.

We know, said Sally.

Reginald Downing watched his wife's cumbrous, open-mouthed chewing and it locked him up with apprehension. He fantasized of a great white blast that ate not through flesh or bone but memory and emotion. A bomb had the potential to purify, to cure a land of its history. The bomb of his fantasy could do the same to the mind. He could nearly feel The Yank in his skull, a creature of panic, scrambling for bunker. Good riddance, you little bugger.

What time is it? said Emer. I'd like to know the time.

Sally helped them out of their chairs and they looked out at the Atlantic. For a long while the seafront spectators were quiet. Some stood with their eyes closed and ears plugged, shoulders tensed against the impending blast. They checked their watches. They counted down as the clocks reached noon, a big, hearty chant that Reginald followed with taps of fingers on his thigh. And when the blast did not immediately come, they waited with frozen postures and expressions, in the coupled fear of the bomb detonating and the bomb not detonating.

The hearing aids sometimes offered a discomfiting, superhuman leap onto another plane of sensory reality. They took Reginald places he wasn't supposed to be. He heard Sally's fingernails scratch at the skin beneath her bra strap. The whistle of air through Emer's nostrils, which was not cyclical but almost perfectly steady, a deflation. He was sure he could hear the strain of steel cables a mile away at the Docks. And then he heard a voice above the crowd's growing murmur. He could nearly see the words take shape over the many heads. A skywriter's entrails. A newspaper headline. *How in the name of the Queen do you lose a bomb?* The tips of his fingers had climbed into his mouth and he could taste the rust and acrylic and filth of the railing, and he thought of all the microbes deploying into his bloodstream.

Then Sally was alone on the beach. The sun had advanced. Coarse pebbles studded her calves. When had she come down from the prom? She had only a vague impression of the reporters, the interviews she had given, the chill of the microphones close to her face. She didn't exactly remember Emer hounding the shirtless American boys, tourists drinking from cans of Old Speckled Hen, asking them, Are you from Ohio? Do you know the name Sanders? She didn't remember Reginald storming away. She only knew that these things had happened.

She knew as well that the Royal Navy had made an announcement. As the bomb had broken free of its Royal tethers—the Atlantic had taken it, it was somewhere safe on the seabed, not lost but missing, not lost, not lost, certainly not lost—so did the day break free of its shape. The seafront was still teeming, but the excitement had changed register.

She was alone and she needed to go to her parents, and then he simply materialized, the wheels of his bicycle muddying the blue picnic blanket, his bare feet sliding off the pedals.

Well, I am blaming you, said Janusz.

And then the bicycle lying on the beach, a reflector bright with sun, the restlessness of his limbs on the blanket. Grease marks the shape of shark teeth on his calf.

He fished for something in his pocket, his tongue an avatar of his hand's work, and finally produced a dull piece of brass, a small gear of some kind. He set it down on the blanket with the same false ceremony with which—two years prior, when Gabriel was her student—his uncle Janusz had set the glossy nut cake on her classroom desk. He had asked her out then, and she had rejected him easily, on the supposition that he was trying to bribe away, with sugar and sex, Gabriel's latest infraction. She was just a stiff, undersexed obstacle between the boy and his land of opportunity. What more could he have seen in her?

For your collecting, he said.

I'm sorry? said Sally. She felt a blush consume her face.

Where is your magic wand?

Janusz turned his arm into a detector and made a clicking sound with his tongue. He drifted his rigid palm closer to her, quickening his sounds.

I didn't think it would be sensible today.

What do you think it is? he said, tossing his chin at the brass riddle.

I really should be going. My parents.

I found it in the foam of the waves. It requires your expert.

Her nervousness, was it her parents alone or the man on her blanket? She sighed, picked up the object, considered it seriously.

I watch you sometimes. With your wand, stealing from beach.

A fool's hobby.

Hobby, he said. English is full of words that diminish. It is a language of half-true.

Sally laughed though she couldn't think why. How had she ended up here, talking to this man, wanting to talk to this man? Ravenswood, like all the other schools, had announced its closure, and what she felt wasn't freedom exactly, but the bludgeon of that freedom.

Janusz looked out over the ocean, squinted hard as though to make out some distant something. The surface had grown choppy, and the sunny glimmer that had been there earlier in the day had disappeared. The Atlantic was a moody old boy. She imagined the bomb gliding through its murk.

I am glad it escaped, he said. I like the idea of it out there, dangerous.

Sally Downing could not quite fully agree. She suspected the Atlantic was toying with her. Did it mean to take the bomb away from her, was it confessing a mistake, or was it giving her more time in this dim glow of celebrity?

It feels different. I like different, he said.

I like different, too.

She felt a stone tumble from the wall between her mind and mouth.

It is nice to sit here with you, he said.

Right, then. I really should be off.

As she stood, it occurred to Sally, not without self-reproach, that she had never had a true conversation with one of the many Polish immigrants in Felixstowe—to say nothing of the Chinese or Indian—

outside the confines of the school. She had told herself that it was simply not worth the whispering of neighbors; she had become adept at finding hiding places for her prejudices, at shutting them in drawers like so many beach things.

What were those candies you used to send to my class? The chocolates?

Ah, we say *ptasie mleczko*. To English, *bird's milk*. It also means, it is an old saying, *unobtainable delicacy*. Even though the candy is in Poland everywhere.

And he taught her how to say it, how to unlearn the shapes of her sluggard English tongue. They were quiet for a while, observing the silt of panic collecting on the seafront. A human wall shaped by the surf. A soft-faced soldier yelling. Two boys throwing empty, messageless bottles into the ocean. A collarless Labrador, digging forever into the sand. Sally thought of her parents, and got a scary thrill at the image of them suffering without her.

It might be from an old spice grinder, she said. The kind with the crank on top.

Sally handed the gear down to Janusz.

No. You keep it, he said.

Janusz pounded the meat of his legs, stood. His shorts were pinstriped slacks that had been torn off above the knee, a fashion of sabotaged formalwear. She found herself tense, poised to reject the advance she felt coming on. That old detector still had some juice.

I can't, she said.

A gift.

I can only keep it if I find it.

He laughed and dropped his eyes to the beach and seemed to enjoy a private joke. He was the kind of man skilled in projecting a wisdom he did or perhaps did not have.

Why is this? he said.

His eyes were a slate blue that, for a moment, as what sun there was disappeared behind dense cloud, matched exactly the glimmerless ocean, and gave the effect that his very face was a mask. It was frightening, and maybe this was why she found her tongue, that wanton flap of muscle, betraying her.

She told Janusz about her collection, about the flat files in the living room. She told him about her brother's suicide, about the Australian postcards, about her mother's dementia, if that's what it was, and about her father's deteriorating senses and his poor gardening and his reliance on her for the bloody simplest of tasks.

Now she was out of breath and full of exquisite endorphins, and it was the man they called Spider who seemed frightened. The surf had retreated, as though from her. Low tide soon. Dinner time soon.

If you ever need, not to imply, I don't know if you'd even be interested, but the pay would be good, the pay would be decent, my parents have plenty of money squirreled away, though you'd never know it, I don't know what it is they're saving for, it's a generational thing, postwar frugality, but if you have the time and the inclination, I know you do this kind of work, their garden needs help.

For this you want to hire me?

I don't mean to—

You say much and you mean much, but rarely together.

Sally felt her head do that thing she hated. A frenetic shake that had as its logical antecedent the nervous habit of flicking her hair away from her face. It had made sense when her hair was long, but now it seemed to her a little piece of crazy.

I'd like it if you did, is what I mean. Never mind, I'm sorry, forget I said anything.

And you are so often very sorry.

I'm sorry.

Janusz smiled a wet smile.

When? When do I come?

When you can. They live—

I know where they live, your parents. They wait for you now?

The large beach pebbles had swallowed her feet a little, and she kicked free.

I hadn't forgotten, she said.

Combover's baby blue tie was loosened at the knot. He stood at the end of High Street and the ocean, shoreless and horizonless on television, was his entire backdrop. He might have been floating. The winds were heavy. He was shouting and his grip on the microphone was white-knuckled. He explained: strong currents had snapped the tethers connecting the bomb to the buoy, and had likely escorted the bomb southeast. But not terribly far, he was sure. The Royal Navy divers admitted that it could take several days to find the bomb, but they were optimistic, they were very optimistic. The bomb was not lost. It was within a two-hundred-meter radius of where it had been anchored, and they were scouring the seabed with Royal diligence.

Remain calm, said the reporter. The bomb is not lost.

Reginald waked that night to a cold, mute space in bed. He moved down the stairs in panic, nearly hugging the railing, questioning the stubbornness that had kept them from moving the bedroom to the ground floor. He passed the living room, lit bluely by the television. The rocking chair was empty, its seat back flickering with the pulses of the local news.

Reginald found Emer seated before a meal at the round table in the dining room, her nakedness barely concealed by her nightgown, her strong thighs peeking through the fabric. A schizophrenic candle painted her shape onto the wall. On the white plate he could make out an assortment of ancient foods excavated from the freezer—sausage rolls, potato wedges, fish sticks, pork pies, cheesecake, other shadowy foodshapes—all cooked and sluiced with gravy. Her face was in frightening chiaroscuro, now bending into a smile as she recognized him. She dabbed the corners of her mouth with her nightgown.

How terribly inconsiderate of me, she said. Would you care for some?

There were more calories on that plate than she'd eaten in an entire month. Had he been a more loving husband, or just a better human being, thought Reginald, he would have been elated with this drama: silent and fasting wife suddenly loud and hungry, loud and hungry wife suddenly operating the oven, setting the table, lighting an actual candle. But damn if he wasn't who he was, and damn if he couldn't help but see Emer's behavior as a séance for The Yank, couldn't help but see her through the clouded lens of jealousy, that incurable cataract.

No, he said, sitting down across from her. No thank you.

Worse was that she had become impervious, or else oblivious, to his anger. This afternoon, when he had scolded her for harassing the American boys, and left her on the beach, and interrogated her when she finally came home two hours behind him, Emer remained placid, cheerful even. He was angry and he needed his anger ratified, he needed some reflex from the world, or at least his family, so that he knew his message was being received. He had tried to call Sally earlier, and sat for a long time with an interminable ring.

Hungry, are we? he said.

Quite! said Emer, flakes of pastry caught on the downy hair around her mouth.

Then you must by all means eat.

Reginald stood, kicked the chair out from behind him, walked to the back door, and stuffed his feet into a pair of muddy Wellington boots.

I'm putting on my wellies. I'm going out.

Yes, she said. One mustn't forget one's wellies.

I really shouldn't be going out. Not at this hour, not in the dark.

No, but then you do have your wellies.

Then he was out, into the garden, under a ceiling of stars. Constellations that he could not name. He wondered if he had known them once. He had earned not knowing. A light, cloudless rain against the nightdark leaves and petals and fruits made for comforting percussion. Sally was supposed to have come over this afternoon to help resow the radishes, but you couldn't rely on anyone these days, you had to do things yourself. Reginald switched on the floodlight and the colors of the garden were startled awake. He began to dig, the worms pink and translucent in the light, their blue organs visible. Perhaps here, in mineral and mud, he could bury his anger and his doubt and his hate. An old war trick.

Philip would sit on the rag weave carpet in front of Reginald's rocking chair, tug on his pleated cuff, and beg for stories of the war: bloody trenches, air assaults, the Dambusters, something maybe he could brag about to his friends. The precocious boy seemed to lament the generation into which he was born. He believed that the postwar world was one of comfort and distraction and denial, and he longed for hard times, for the real living of the previous decades, for the romance and the glory—and also the nightmare—of war.

Reginald's stories were not those stories. He would answer with lectures in botany and horticulture: peas, brassicas, carrots, potatoes. This he would say—sunnily, with a passing cloud of shame at the thought of disappointing his son—was the artillery of his war.

He arrived at POW camp Oflag IX-A/H in 1941, just as winter was lifting from the hills. Not two weeks since he was deployed. The German spring had a different palette than the English, more reds and purples, the sensational colors of a deep bruise. Spangenberg Castle, its ancient majesty not at all diminished, was not the war camp Reginald had envisioned, and from the beginning it was difficult to reconcile: crossing over the drawbridge, flanked by polished bayonets in which his image was miniatured, he fell in love with the place. Its absurd moat and its soaring ramparts and its cobbled courtyards. It made you feel important to be a prisoner here. The castle filled you with awe and ego.

Philip knew the juicy stuff, he liked this part: Spangenberg was a staging post for many high-ranking POWs bound for the notorious Colditz Castle, where many of them were executed. It was a critical stage in the war. Paris had fallen to the Nazis and the British Expeditionary Force had just completed its withdrawal from Dunkirk. Men were pining for the battlefield or else for their wives or girlfriends or families, for those faces in photographs kept beneath the mattresses stuffed with woodshavings. Hidden in the lining of Emer's jewelry box, these many decades later, was the photograph of her that Reginald had kept in Spangenberg, its surface fingered to total whiteness.

Philip loathed the mushy bits. He wanted to hear about the escapes, there was potential there. He wanted the stuff of the military pulps.

It was all around Reginald, the desperate ingenuity. There were men who studied medical textbooks in the library and replicated the symptoms of mental illness in order to win a transfer to Britain. There were men who stole uniforms belonging to members of the Hitler Youth and bluffed their way out of camp, only to return months later, shadows of themselves, muscles like straw under the skin. There were men who chipped away at the mortar of ancient stones with tools constructed from metal parts of beds, sinks, toilets, cutlery. A few even got beneath the ground after months of digging carefully mapped tunnels. They would carry the soil to Reginald's burgeoning garden and make furtive deposits from pockets and hats and folded waistbands.

There were men bent on the world outside the stone walls and there were men, like Reginald, who subsisted on the distractions within them. Distraction from war, from worried wives, from hunger and death. To these men distraction meant survival. The Geneva Convention allowed the prisoners certain luxuries, little diversions into which some allowed themselves to be subsumed. Ministers preached freely. Lectures and classes were organized. Bands. There was a small library stocked with books that satisfied literary and intellectual cravings, magazines that teased others. A canteen shop sold art materials and there were men who took to sketching and painting the grounds. Prisoners were permitted to send and receive letters. Food packages arrived from the Red Cross, along with bulbs and seeds. In Reginald's first summer a letter came from Emer, the bottom of the envelope bulked with hydrangea seeds, some of which had begun to germinate.

Reginald was able to recruit a few men who shared his sensibility, or else were too cowardly to act on truer desires. They grew fruits and vegetables to supplement their spartan diet, and flowers to buoy spirits. So when Reginald told stories of the war he would detail how they constructed a pit glasshouse from tobacco boxes, or a potting shed from packing cases, or how they raised bulbs in frames made in the camp joinery. He would talk about the German soil. The sandy surface they dug through to get to the fertile peat beneath, the pig dung used for enrichment. He would talk about the flowerbeds planted around the barracks, and the biscuit tins filled with pansies, violets, and bluebell. He would recount the flower show in April of 1942, remembering exactly the songs played by the camp's orchestra as he took in the perfume of those spectacular rhododendron.

Philip would roll his eyes white. Where's the action, he would say. Where's the blood?

On the day he and Emer were to be married, a June day that sat heavy and humid on the Palatine, Reginald planted a row of summer squash, whispering his vows to each seed before thumbing it into the earth. The same earth that welcomed the blood of his countrymen outside the castle walls, that would just as readily welcome his. But in Spangenberg, the war fell away. They were in a castle on a hill, and beyond that: abstraction.

There were men who spent hours perched along the narrow walkway of the ramparts, staring into the waters of the moat, which were alive with the wet backs of wild boar. These were the boundaries of the known world. For Reginald there was only the garden, and the ache for Emer that growth helped soothe. If it was in the ground, he could control it. Even when the letters stopped coming in the winter of 1943, he nursed hope through the garden. And when this hope did eventually die, the garden was where he buried his jealousy and malice.

There were stories that he didn't tell his son: that Emer had found another man, an American solider stationed in Suffolk, that she couldn't wait forever.

1945. The war stayed outside the walls of Spangenberg until the moment it crashed through them. The fire bombs came from the Allies, like giant embers crashing from an incinerated sky, and all Reginald remembered, to his son's great dismay, was the collapse of senses, of all the patterns he recognized in the world. He sometimes thought that maybe he was still in that moment, an insect in amber, bent over a row of radishes. That everything since then had been adrenal illusion, the slipstream before death. The destruction of the garden—the depthless grayout spattered with organic color—uprooted the pain of Emer's betrayal, a pain that entered his body along with the shrapnel and the stone.

Decades later, in Germany on business, Reginald returned to Spangenberg. The castle had been rebuilt and converted into a luxury hotel and restaurant. All rooms equipped with bath, shower, WC, radio, TV, telephone. Checkout at noon. Leave the towels on the floor. He stayed in a room high in the northwest tower, where a German officer would have slept and dreamt. The window looked down onto a section of the gardens, and Reginald wondered if any of the bulbs he had planted were still alive, if any of the lovely flowers were descendants of his work. From the opposite window he could see the moat, now calm with algae, and the green country beyond it. Before checking out he slipped five or six soap bars into his suitcase, enamored with the image of the castle etched into the lavender-scented soap, and on the plane home he felt panicky with guilt for his pilfering ways.

Philip would sometimes say, There's no war in your war stories, Dad. Can't you remember more? Can't you make something up?

But for years the boy kept on asking for the same boring story.

3. Remus

By Tuesday morning over four hundred residents had evacuated, and already the town felt bombed out. On High Street, only the bank and the post office and the Treasure Chest bookshop—the owner of which was or wanted to be oblivious to the drama sweeping his town—remained open. Along the seafront, the amusement rides and the arcades were still and hushed.

Felixstowe was in an elegiac mood, but its favorite reporter was not. He stood on the ledge of the dry fountain in front of the quieted circus pageantry of the Family Fun Center, hyped on caffeine and new intelligence. This was the development: an imaging technology called REMUS (Remote Environmental Monitoring UnitS), an advanced AUV (Autonomous Underwater Vehicle), was being driven down to Felixstowe from Scotland. The Royal Navy Divers, a team thirteen strong, would use this unmanned, computer-operated submarine to picture the seabed. What technology! said the reporter. In the image that popped up next to his face, the submarine was bright yellow, and he could not resist a quick refrain from the famous song.

The diminutive Williams Family Butcher shop on Maidstone Road remained open for business and it was packed with bodies and their heat and their primal cravings. Disaster played to the baser appetites, thought Sally, joining a queue abuzz with laughless gossip. What cataclysm might be potent enough to topple the British instinct to queue? She was sure it would be the last pillar of civility standing. She imagined an orderly file of survivors standing in a post-apocalyptic wasteland. And was it a singularly British phenomenon? Were there lands without queues? Maybe the hunger here was not for meat, but for the queue. Yes, maybe the queuing was the thing. Sally folded her hands behind her and felt at once a swell of patriotism and a prick of regret for having not travelled more.

The windows were sweating and the air was stale with blood. The red-meat availability was low. A tuft of curly parsley sat lonesome on a pink-juiced tray. Though Sally felt a curious empathy with the neglected garnish, she managed to stop her brain just short of formulating a complete life metaphor. The important thing was: no mince. Her father would not be impressed. She was panicky with thoughts of merguez sausage and daughterly failure when Mr. Wood, the name-doomed woodwork instructor at the high school Sally's daughter had attended, grabbed her arm with tough, scar-cobwebbed hands that shot her mind to Janusz, his fingers. No, a woodworking accident was too prosaic for a man like him.

Then the small space was host to an impromptu press conference. Save the bitterness of the ancient Ms. Cakebread, who blamed her for delivering them all to the brink of the apocalypse and the gates of hell, etc., the celebrity, however minor, tasted so good still. Sally wanted to cut her teeth through it, she wanted the fat and the blood of it. Whatever semiotic doubts she harbored about the bomb and the intentions of the Atlantic now vanished in the delirium of this silly but not disagreeable notoriety.

Sally finally got her order in: four Cumberland sausages, a half-pound of diced chicken, and they didn't happen to have any mince in the back, did they? The others cleared a path to the counter for her, their feet scurrying along the sawdusted planks like spooked mice. The butcher with the cherub face shook his head no but slipped her a couple of choice bangers with a wink.

You tell your parents hello, won't you? he said, and Sally left to a smattering of dumb, reactionary applause.

She bought a TV guide and a sack of russets at the greengrocers and strode to her parents' front door thinking that she had momentum and that she was really going to do it, she was going to tell her mother about Philip—he drowned himself, he's dead—just like that, as plainly and assuredly as she would unpack the fresh meat into the refrigerator. The previous day's conversation with Janusz had loosened her. He was grease in her brain, in her joints. He had suggested she do it.

Emer answered the door. Her legs were bare and bright and strangled with thick and knuckled veins in which her quick pulse was visible.

Mother! What if I'd been the minister?

I don't like any of my trousers. They don't fit.

Nonsense.

He didn't seem to mind. Is that our meat? I'm starving, you know. Your father doesn't feed me.

Who didn't mind? And he does, Mother. Stop it.

Come on then, out of the heat.

I can't stay though, said Sally.

She wanted to find Janusz. That morning Gabriel had knocked on her door and silently handed her a box of ptasie mleczko. His face was streaked with dirt and his smile was an unnatural twist of polite-ness. He was on his bicycle before she could say thank you, his thin legs pumping, a plastic bag full of seashells swinging from the handle-bars. She had managed to cry out, Put on a helmet! It was her habit to defuse emotion with cool authority, with the Killing of Fun, but there was little that could be done against the resurfacing guilt she felt about the boy's expulsion, and even less against this schoolgirl giddiness tearing through her body. Unobtainable delicacy, he had said, and the phrase kept on harassing her. She had already spoiled her lunch with a regrettable, but not regretted, binge of the chocolates.

I just wanted to make sure you were—

Alive was probably the word, but she didn't say it.

She walked past her mother and down the hallway, running her fin-gertips over the maroon wallpaper, admiring her handiwork. *He drowned himself, he's dead.* She passed the living room, where the small televi-sion was playing to an audience of biscuit tins, and into the kitchen. She set the potatoes on the counter and unpacked the meat into the refrigerator and knew that she wasn't going to do it.

Where's Dad? she called out.

Her voice was high and sharp, a piano string over-torqued.

Sally saw her father through the small pollen-fogged window above the sink, his torso framed in a warped pane of glass. He was on his knees in the garden, his back turned to her, stabbing at the earth with a small spade. In the shape and motion of his lanky, thick-elbowed arms, she saw herself. It struck her occasionally, and always with great profundity: this man created me. What a terrible kind of debt.

She marveled at how fluid and steady his hands were in the garden, at how a deeply practiced movement could retain so much youth and vitality even as the rest of the body crumbled around it. Reginald looked up, squinting against the sun. He saw her and his mouth traced the shape of her name, and now she saw Janusz. He stood to the side of Reginald, his hands on his hips, the neck of his white T-shirt grasped in his mouth. He had been watching her father intently, but now he looked up, too. His shirt fell from his mouth. He waved and she turned away.

She hadn't even discussed hiring Janusz with her parents. Surely it was wrong that he was here, how confusing it must have been for them when he showed up at their door. But what bothered her most, what was the greater wrong, was the calm of the household. She had expected, and dreaded, the inexorable domestic chaos, the bickering and the resentment waiting for her on Church Lane, but now that she was here, and the chaos wasn't, Sally felt hard done by.

She found her mother in the living room, frozen in the light of the television. Emer turned her head. Sally now saw that she was wearing lipstick, a blotchy coat of red that undersold her full lips. She saw herself here, too. And now, less subtly, on the television again. Her existence felt enlarged, she couldn't make out its edges.

Are you famous now? said Emer.

Sally laughed but didn't mean it. The bomb is perhaps, she said.

That man is here. He's not a real looker, is he? Where did you say he was from?

Sally blushed. Her mother's obliviousness sometimes circled into an illusion of knowing.

Poland. He's from Poland.

An ally!

Sally rubbed the lipstick on her mother's lips into an even shade, wiped a smear of red from her front tooth. *He drowned himself, he's dead.* Was it more selfish to tell her or more selfish to keep it?

Please, you have so many pairs of trousers, she said.

Can I tell you a secret? whispered Emer. She pressed her lips together, attuning herself to their new stickiness. I hope they don't find the bloody thing.

Flying Officer Reginald Downing had forgotten the tremendous satisfaction of giving orders, and the impossible frustration of watching someone that was not himself execute them. The Pole couldn't sow a damn turnip seed to save his life. Weren't the Slavs root-vegetable people? He grabbed the spade from the man, dropped to his knees, and showed him how it was done. A half-inch furrow, an inch apart, wide rows, loosely packed, not difficult.

He had been more offended than confused when the Pole turned up at his door. A face and an accent of sharp angles. He recognized the man from town, seemed to remember his name was Cricket or some such preposterousness, but they had never exchanged a word that he could remember. He wasn't one to socialize with foreigners; it was easier to keep hostility intact if they were a people rather than persons. His garden was in fine shape, thank you ever so much, and where did he get the nerve? The man had shrugged with devastating nonchalance, said Sally would be disappointed, and turned away. Reginald could see already that the man was full of tricks, but sure enough he called him back. The truth was his garden was a state, and so was his wife, and he could use the help, and he could use the distraction, and the thought of reclaiming some order, if only a botanical sort, sounded immeasurably good.

Reginald was overstating the impossible-to-overstate importance of record keeping when Sally's face appeared behind the filthy kitchen window. His hands stopped and he called her name and she disappeared. Reginald feared his eyes or his brain had fooled him, and quickly he tried to find the broken end of his lecture, but the Pole interrupted.

Your daughter was teacher to my nephew, you know. He liked her very much.

Reginald twisted, looked up at him. The Pole stood with his arms crossed, rocking side to side probably to the silent beat of europop rubbish.

Her kindness is rare, said the Pole.

The last few days it's been rare indeed, said Reginald.

He turned back and stabbed the spade into the soil. He felt like talking.

She's always been cursed with empathy, he said. She's always felt sorry for people. She used to give all her allowance to a homeless lady who'd sit outside Woolworth's with her starving sheepdog.

And you think she has reason to feel sorry for me, for Gabriel.

Reginald felt the man squat behind him, heard the air push through his nostrils, angry air. You couldn't talk to these people, they were so quick to take offense.

I joke, I joke, said the Pole, slapping and squeezing Reginald's shoulder, now laughing, delighting in his deception. I take the piss, you understand? I am sorry, it is too easy to make people nervous. People think I am illegal, and they hate me, and they hate more *that* they hate me. To me this is very funny.

Are you? Illegal?

The man came to Reginald's side, planting his knees squarely onto a row of just-sown runner beans in a way that was neither malicious nor entirely unmindful. Either way, Reginald said nothing. He could sense the man looking at him but he kept his eyes on the grimy kitchen window.

Gabriel is a good boy, except when he is not. He has suffers. His parents are dead. He came here on a shipping container. During the journey there was an accident, terrible pressure, and his ears went pop, and now he is almost without able to hear. Learning is difficult and sometimes he has bad frustration. He was taken from school for stabbing another boy with a pencil. It is difficult to find another school because no papers, because behavior. For a long time he has been without education. Your daughter tried to help, she tried to keep him at the school, and I am still grateful, I am happy to give back kindness.

You're sitting on my runner beans, said Reginald.

The Pole shot to his feet, his hands flailing in histrionic apology. You are an expert of the garden, he said. Sally thinks you need more help than you do. Tell me what I can do.

Reginald struggled to his feet, refusing the Pole's hand, refusing the old pain in his abdomen and the myriad of new ones. He felt like talking and what the man could do was listen and not be his wife or his daughter. There was something also about him being an illegal that would make it easy to talk. Reginald pushed the spade into the Pole's hand.

A half-inch furrow, an inch apart, wide rows, loosely packed, he said. Not difficult.

The contents of the flat files were so embedded in her internal self, in the ephemera of her thoughts, that it quite surprised Sally Downing that another human being could access them here in the physical world. It was Wednesday afternoon and Janusz Crzenski sat on the sun-bleached couch in her conservatory, watching her paw through the slim mahogany drawers. Gabriel was there as well, two rooms away but visible through, and framed by, two open walls. The boy was sitting on the floor in front of the television, robotically eating oven chips and mayonnaise. His presence irked her. His calm. She had thought the boy would relax her—he at least lessened the risk that Janusz might try something untoward—but Sally only felt more on edge. There was a peeling seam in the floral wallpaper that was eating at her. And perhaps she wanted a little untoward.

She opened the slim drawers for Janusz and she could feel him enter the private spaces of her mind. She thought, What do you have to gain from this, Sally Downing? and then understood that whatever it was could not take the shape of thought. She would remove an object and read the affixed tag. Where and when it was found, estimated date and origin. Then, with much less certainty, and not without embarrassment, she would disclose the history that she had invented for the artifact. It was this that Janusz wanted to hear. The process was painful and awkward at first, but then she relaxed, and began to enjoy it even.

She allowed him to join her at the flat files, allowed him to touch. His fingernails were blackened with dirt from her father's garden, where he'd now worked two consecutive days. The truncated pinky and ring fingers of his left hand had no nails, and this struck Sally as having certain hygienic advantages. Tell me about this one, he would say. As she spoke Janusz would hold the object up to the late afternoon light, like a precious stone, or consider its weight in his palm. And this one, and this one, and this one. He would read the neat calligraphy of her handwriting, her piffling little narratives, and he would say, To me, it is only a spoon, a coin, the needle of a compass.

The phone rang incessantly: her father. She disconnected the thing.

I have had to learn how to detach myself from objects, said Janusz. I came here with nothing.

They drank whiskey on ice and ate slices of rhubarb pie and hunks of old vanilla ice cream furred with ice crystals. She wondered what the machine called REMUS might find on the ocean bed. She could see the cone of its headlight in the murk.

I've always found comfort in invention, she said, registering in her periphery that the boy had crashed from a ferocious sugar high into a twitchy sleep.

Sally told him about her childhood in Felixstowe, the perpetual summer days spent with her brother, the two of them sitting on the massive sewage pipe that had been ripped from the old water system and left to corrode in the ocean. It offered a good view of the Docks, close enough to smell the fuel, and the scorching metal felt good on her thighs. They picked at barnacles with their toes and let ice-lollies melt over their hands, and they lay on their backs and watched the sleepy cranes unload containers from the ships, and they guessed what was inside. Customs were seizing all manner of exotic and imagination-churning imports: elephant tusks and skulls of endangered buffalo, eleven million counterfeit cigarettes, eighty kilos of cocaine. When an airplane flew overhead, and made a shadow that the dogs chased across the beach, Philip would turn to her and say, That's going to be me someday, in the cockpit. The world felt so much larger sitting on that pipe.

As Sally told him this, she wanted Janusz to interrupt her and tell her his own story, the story of his boyhood, the story of his arrival, the story of his mangled fingers, but the man sat quietly, his body mute except for his feet, tapping, and his jaw, making percussion of ice.

Sometimes, she explained, Philip would take her up the smooth stone steps of Jacob's Ladder and through the overgrown path to a place called Cobbold's Point, where they would sit on the edge of the cliff and stare into the dark spot in the sea that marked the ruins of an ancient Roman fort. Low tide would come, and although they never did spot the ruins, Philip always leaped to his feet and pointed out at the Atlantic, and she always played along, saying, I see it, I see it! Because the promise of seeing, not the seeing itself, was what mattered. And then in the evenings, when the iron had scorched their legs and their games had tired, they would walk the beach home, scouring the sand for artifacts the ocean might have left jeweled in the sand.

Sally was opening another drawer when she felt his breath warm the back of her neck.

You need to tell your mother. It is cruel to keep this. Cruel to yourself, he said, and then his hands were tracing her hips.

I am alone like you, alone worse than you, he said.

Sally turned, pushed him away. She felt the twitch and tremble of her face, felt unformed words play out in its musculature. It was suddenly very late, dark outside.

This is why you let me in, he said. He was loose with alcohol, drifting toward anger. He clasped his arms behind his back as though to keep them from misbehaving. His lips were oyster-slick.

The bomb has brought us together, he said.

I don't believe in that sort of thing, she said, although she only believed that she shouldn't believe in that sort of thing.

This is not what I want. It is not, she said.

She was hoping her raised voice might wake the boy, relieved that it didn't.

You invent lives for these objects because you have forgotten your own. You have forgotten how to live. You have forgotten how to kiss.

Sally pushed past the whiskied bulk of Janusz and walked toward the living room, glaring at the peeling wallpaper as she passed, and woke the boy as kindly as she could. He flailed awake, screaming, and then quieted. Adrenaline cut through her buzz. As she led them to the front door, as she swatted away Janusz's apologies, she felt the truth in what he had said.

She sometimes dreamed of dumping the contents of the drawers into the old military duffel, marching down to the seafront, and, object by object, throwing her collection back into the indifferent water, back into the wild, where human stories had no weight. Showing Janusz Crzenski her collection was a little like feeding it to the tide. She felt exhilarated. Through the thick, rippled glass of the door she watched the shapes of him disappear.

4. The Fiancée's Legs

It was Friday afternoon when Reginald called the police to report a missing person. At 0700 Emer had been out of the house, by noon she was something like astray, but now she was unquestionably missing. He had been on the phone all morning, placing calls to the Community Center and the Bowls Club and the Historical Society and the Ferry Boat Inn and neighbors in good standing. And finally, resignedly, after he'd dialed Sally's number for the umpteenth time without success, and he could feel his pulse in his eyeballs, and his fingers were trembling so much that his dialing success rate was dangerously low, the police. It took him four tries to dial 999.

The anger he felt toward his wife and his daughter and even the ineradicable, pitiless bomb—that undead thing—now dissolved in the drug of worry and guilt, as did the stiffness in his joints, as he loped down the treacherous cobbles of Church Lane. He reckoned that in all the hundreds of years of these stones, nobody could have walked over them, could have worn and polished them, more than him. Except maybe Emer. He couldn't remember the last time he'd walked without her.

Three or four days ago, he recalled. Those American gits on the beach. But when before that?

Reginald had almost given up on Sally when she finally opened her front door. His hand was numb from knocking. She looked physically different, as though she had aged or unaged some months, but he could not place what it was exactly. His eyes were wrong, the surgery was coming undone, he'd had premonitions of this, his cornea deflating like a weathered football. He saw himself as though from his daughter's clear eyes: old, shrunken, senile.

She's gone, he said.

He was unsure of what to do with his hands, he fixed them to his sides with military resoluteness. The military was good for that, for weeding out natural awkwardness.

Your phone, he said. Your goddamn phone.

What? Sally glanced behind her and then stepped outside and closed the door.

Who's gone? Who's gone, Dad?

He told her what he knew, which was nothing, which was all speculation and dread. He wasn't sure the syllables coming out of him made any sense but Sally seemed to understand. In his mind he saw Emer's bare legs, meaty and blue veined, pounding the floors and walls and ceilings of his thoughts.

She left, he said, trying out the phrase. And then he said it again.

She hasn't *left*, said Sally. She's just, I suppose, confused.

Sally grabbed hold of his wrists in a way that he supposed was meant to be comforting, and then told him to wait, and vanished inside with such sorcerous grace that he couldn't be sure she hadn't walked right through the lacquered door.

Sally thudded up the carpeted stairs to her bedroom where she had, after hearing the knock on the front door, banished Janusz. He was sitting on her bed, bareskinned except for a pair of jeans rolled up above his calves, utterly calm, fingering through the pages of an old knitting magazine. He had come over that morning, after a night shift at the Docks, and his skin, when she had tasted it, was metal and grease and salt.

Who was it? he asked, meeting her eyes. He continued to flip the pages.

You need to leave.

Sally's voice was small: if she spoke softly enough she might hide her words from herself.

I don't need to anything. Who was it?

My mother is missing and you need to leave. I would like you to leave.

What does this mean? Your mother is missing what?

It means we don't know where she is, it means we lost her.

Her voice cracked; the sound surprised her. She understood now the direct causality of her having slept with this man and her mother's disappearance. Her selfishness was a vista emerging around a bend. There were places on and in her body where she could still feel him—his foreplay had been a lapping surf to the undertow of his lovemaking—and now she felt that she had been ravaged by Guilt itself.

She missed her students, her routine, her poor mother.

Janusz's face wore that look of sagacious empathy, of having-been-through-it-all. It wasn't so convincing now. She had read that women in Korea had plastic surgery to put their mouths in perpetual smile. An affectation, an invention. Janusz closed the magazine and furled it into a telescope and peered through at Sally.

I can help you, he said.

I just shut the door on my father and I need you to leave.

He stood from the bed with the rolled magazine still over his eye. He surveyed the length of her.

You are embarrassed by me, he said.

It was quiet. The water heater groaned.

I don't know, she said.

You don't want to be seen with me.

I don't know.

He lowered the magazine. She wished he would put on a shirt.

Let me help.

There's a sliding door out the conservatory. You can leave through the gate.

Sally hated how right he was: she was embarrassed to be seen with him, and more embarrassed to feel embarrassed. Even as she demanded and then pleaded that he go, her voice was laced with apology.

Walking down the stairs, pulling a black T-shirt over his head, he said, I feel sorry for you. Is this what it is like to be English, so big with embarrassment?

Janusz heaved the sliding glass door shut, his face on the other side stoic and hurt, and a ring of hairline cracks spidered through the glass around the handle. She thought of the bomb and its blast radius. Hot-eyed with shame and terror and relief, Sally composed herself and her posture and went to see about the old man at her door.

While the machine called REMUS trawled the ocean bedrock, another search was underway: word of Emer's disappearance had fired through the town with synaptic efficiency and many came out to help. A town was a living thing, thought Reginald. Its parts were connected, a town could think and a town could feel.

The group, led by Sally, moved through Felixstowe like blood through a body, confident and purposeful. The residents were grateful for the distraction, for the opportunity to reclaim a little autonomy, and the support filled Reginald with an almost unbearable gratefulness for the simple pleasures of a simple life lived in a simple town. But the afternoon vanished, as afternoons do, and the group lost its pulse, and finally disbanded, and they offered each other hopeful words that were heavy with falsehood.

A missing bomb, a missing wife. Those legs.

Sally continued searching long after dusk. She was hurt that she had allowed this to happen, hurt by what she had said to Janusz, by her capacity to be cruel, hurt that her daughter had not returned her many calls. But the searching felt good, the searching felt purposeful. As though by somnambulant drift, she found herself staring out into the cold infinitude of the Atlantic. The surf crashed into the rocks, invisible and loud. At this hour the ocean always gave her the sense of eons, of landmasses breaking and drifting, of plate tectonics and ocean ridges and the fiery mantle beneath it all. It gave her the sense of great work being done in the cover of night. At this hour she felt something like pride that the ocean had singled her out.

258

Sally climbed down off the promenade and onto the beach. She walked toward the old pier, her stride awkward and her footfall shockingly loud in the rocks. Perhaps her mother had gone missing into these waters, she thought. That would be fitting. Part of her believed that the Atlantic was where all missing things went. Sally realized that it was very possible she'd lost the chance to tell her mother about Philip, and the permanence of this, here before the earth-eating tides, was unbearable. It started to rain and the ocean disappeared and a hunger erupted in her stomach. She trekked up the slope of Bent Hill to the fish and chip shop, the presence of which felt nearly as essential and primeval as the ocean, and whose limpid blue light shone through the spitting rain. She ordered two cod, two chips, and carried the soggy bag against her chest, the warmth and the smell of grease and newspaper enlivening her.

Sally found her father on the burgundy sofa in his sitting room, frozen and trembling as though in hypothermic shock. He was blanketed in soil and leaves and bits of iridescent petal. His face was tight on his skull, his stare mummified. The carpet was streaked with mud. His fingernails were torn and bleeding and for a moment Sally imagined the damage as a physical separation from Emer. They had made a habit of linking or twisting or touching their bodies together, and it struck her that she conceived of them largely as a single entity. It was enviable. Her marriage had been nothing like that. She set the greasy bag of food down on the coffee table.

It's gone, said Reginald.

He told her that he had destroyed the garden, that it was just black soil and white roots and broken vegetables.

Why? she said.

My eyes hurt, he said. Do they look okay?

They look okay, she said. Let's clean you up, shall we?

Although she despised baths herself—not trusting any contained body of water and tolerating showers only because of the open drain—Sally ran one for her father. She sat on the lip of the tub and stared at the water rushing from the faucet. She knew there must be some combination of words that would bring him comfort but she could not assemble them. Steam filled the room. She felt his eyes on her from the doorway. Then she turned off the faucet and let him shuffle past her and left the bathroom and shut the door. She stood with her forehead against the doorjamb, its old and sticky lead paint.

Are you still there? he said.

I'm here, she said.

It was quiet.

I can't do this, he said.

Do what?

These bloody hands, he yelled.

Sally pushed the door open to accommodate her eye, then her head, then her body. Reginald stopped clawing at the top buttons of his polo shirt. He threw his long, heavy arms to his side and into an exasperated pendulum. She thought of orangutans. He looked at his fingers and cursed them. She had never seen him tremble like this and it occurred to her, as she helped him undress, that she was very fortunate to have never done this before. He was a robust ninety. More independent than she liked to think, Janusz was right.

The bathroom walls had vanished in the steam and the dimensions of the room seemed to enlarge. Sally pulled her father's shirt over his head. She folded it and placed it on the edge of the sink. Then his trousers. She didn't mind doing this but she could tell he did.

Don't look, he said, covering the scars on his side, smooth white buttons of flesh that seemed impervious to aging, that reminded Sally that her father had been a young man once.

When she was a girl she would write her name in the fine pebbles of the surf and watch the sea devour it. She liked to believe that her name was still there, in the scar tissue and muscle memory of the beach. She liked to believe that the earth could hold history as surely as the flesh.

You look like something pulled out from Matley Bog, she said, helping him into the bath.

You're looking!

I'm not looking, Dad.

The dirt from his body jumped to the surface of the water as though by magnetic force and the heat brought life into his face. He dunked his head and emerged, the contours of his skull even more apparent.

260

They were quiet for a long while. Then he started talking.

When I was a foreman at the docks they sometimes sent me to Hamburg, said Reginald. That's where the big port was, still is. We ate and drank in beer halls and restaurants. The waiters brought servings of pork knuckle and schnitzel as big as your head and they smiled and they had no guns. I had spent thirty-two months in Germany and I had to ask the bloke next to me what schnitzel was.

Sally sat on the lid of the toilet rubbing the mud and debris from her hands. She told him to stop talking, to just relax. Reginald began to draw shapes in the skin of dirt on the water. He talked to his toes, surfaced on the other end of the tub, disembodied.

I had heard about these kind of colonies on the outskirts of the city, where veterans from the States and England were living. Wounded, maimed men, mostly. They worked there, you see, on the port, they lived in small houseboats. Your mother's—well, I had reason to believe he was there, I would know him by the tattoos, or I would be able to sense him somehow. I had this gun, an old Webley Break-Top, heavy as sin.

Dad, said Sally. You don't have to tell me this.

She stood and turned on the sink and darted her hands beneath the water, something to do. Reginald went on talking and she kept her back to him, her eyes on the dripping faucet. He explained that he had paid a German contact to take him down the canal that led to the port. To the men that aren't men, as the German said. The waters were high against the stately red brick buildings that lined the passage and it seemed that they were gliding through the top of a flooded city, the proud tips of its greatest buildings. Below them he imagined a magnificent city collecting algae and kelp. The buildings gave way to a vertical stretch of metal cranes and hulking containers and that particular alchemic smell of ocean and iron. This is where, said the German, dropping him dockside, next to a small cove of houseboats stagnant and putrid in the water.

Understand I was very angry. Understand that my head was not right, he said.

Reginald skimmed his hand over the bathtub water as though to quiet its undulation.

The Hamburg Port was a place barely alive, he explained. The war and the division of Germany had depleted business and the men in charge were desperate. The place was a meeting of desperations. Everywhere along the pier there were men walking, limping, moving with a slow, lobotomized obedience. Some dragged large platforms on wheels. There was a man with no limbs strapped to the back of another man, infant-like. This man took Reginald in with helpless and quiet panic, eyes skittish in his skull.

He found the courage to knock on several doors, a photograph of The Yank sweated onto his fingers. A few times a door opened. One man, his face badly scarred, angled into the daylight like a sunflower, to show Reginald the total ruin of his skin. At each door Reginald would salute and at each door the salute was not returned. No one had anything to say to him. The gentle motion of the docks in the water made him nauseous and every few minutes he vomited over the edge until there was nothing left in him but bile.

This was in the early fifties now, said Reginald. I thought the war had passed, my eyes and my ears and my mind told me it had passed. But some part of me always suspected it was an act. War doesn't pass. It just hides most of the time.

There'd been a man on the dock, an American, who nodded at the photograph. His fingers and palms were stained with iron, were dark and lustrous as though stricken with a metallic gangrene, and he whispered hey-ba-ba-re-bop in the space between his words. Sure, he knew the guy, sure he knew him, hey-ba-ba-re-bop, who wants to know? Reginald held out a folded bill and the iron-fingered man took it and walked Reginald a few hundred yards along the dockside and pointed at a large houseboat further ahead, its hull septic with the colors of oxidation. He said, Give the church a try.

Now I'd never heard of a floating church in all my days, said Reginald, and I haven't since, but there it was, chained to the quayside like an old dog. I went in. There were candles everywhere, but only a few of them lit. I remember the flames swaying with the boat. I remember incense burning. I can't say what kind of religion belonged there. All religions, no religions, I don't know. The place looked like a junkyard of religious tack, it looked booby-trapped. I remember the prayer beads hanging from the ceiling and I remember the sound they made, swaying, moving over themselves without hands. There were three men sitting on oil drums that had been sawed in half and upturned, and either they didn't hear me or they didn't care. I held the gun like this, you see, like they taught us in Kent.

Sally ran a finger beneath the wet mouth of the faucet and made a sound as though to dam her father's words. She thought now of the day after he had returned from the campaign in Oman. The four of them—father, mother, daughter, son—sitting on striped towels around a picnic basket, eating vegetables from the garden spritzed with lemon juice. She thought of her father's refusal to remove his starched uniform, even as the sun beat down on them and his trousers grew stiff with salt and sand, and a rash took hold of his skin. At the time, his resolve pressed into Sally great shapes of pride and honor and even nobility. It was years before she understood that his obstinacy more likely followed the contours of shame and self-pity and deep insecurity: he didn't want to show his scarred body. Emer took her into the water that day, past the first breaker, where they turned and waved at the dark blue uniform set into the shore. For a long time this was the image that would define her father for her: handsome and distant and stock-still as gorse blossom. Knightly. But this childhood impression had been violated many times over, and listening to him now Sally was reminded that people were ideas and that no idea was constant.

One of the men was rocking back and forth, whispering or maybe humming, said Reginald. It was dark. I couldn't say his age or his height or the color of his skin, but I made it in my mind so that it was him. I thought, This is the back that I want, these are the shoulder blades, this is the neck. I cocked the gun and I imagined blood moving through the cotton of his T-shirt, a flower on his back. I don't know what I regret more: what I almost did or what I did do. Part of me wishes I had shot the bastard, even if it wasn't him. Things would be different. I don't know.

She could not stop the faucet from dripping.

Well, said Sally. Never mind. We'll find her, you know.

Reginald slouched into the curve of the bathtub until his mouth was level with the water. His eyes looked small and sticky, a newborn's eyes. He opened his lips and swallowed a little.

Sally didn't remember leaving her lights on. She found Janusz sitting on the small couch in the conservatory, a storm in his knees, her metal detector across his lap. Its head was loose, limp as a dead pheasant's, its electronic entrails exposed. He looked up at her like I-don't-know-how-to-tell-you-this. She saw the child in him. The theme of the night seemed to be destruction and male pensiveness. She was too exhausted and emotional and disquieted to be angry.

You heard the big news? said Janusz.

How did you get inside?

The bomb. They found your bomb.

Sally grew cold. Her body prickled and her blood shifted, a fleshly cryptogram that she couldn't read.

How did you get inside? she said.

I think you did not find her though, he said. Your mother.

No, we didn't. I need to sleep. You need to leave.

First, I must apologize.

He lifted the detector, cradling the broken head in his right hand. His shame was genuine, and his submissiveness seemed almost physiological. The hard angles with which she had built her conception of him softened.

I was very angry, he said.

He pointed his eyes at the wall behind her and she turned. There was a goodly hole in the wallpapered sheetrock. It surprised her that the walls were hollow, though of course they were. Now she saw the ransacked flat files in the sitting room. Some of her beach artifacts stared at her from the carpet. One of the dark wood drawers had been smashed and its splinters showed bright unstained flesh. Pine. All this time she had thought the piece was mahogany.

Sally turned to him and rubbed her hands over her face. She was frustrated that he hadn't destroyed everything, that he hadn't torched the house, that his temper had a low threshold against the softer emotions.

You should be angry, she said. Tomorrow, I hope you'll help.

Without thought Sally grabbed his left hand. The handle of the detector hit the white tiles and a chip of the orange plastic shot across the floor. She inspected the stumps of his ring and pinky fingers, which were oddly wide at the ends, small fleshy anvils.

What happened to your hand? she said.

Nobody ever asks me that.

They're frightened.

Of what?

Of asking.

But you're not.

I'm frightened to know.

Janusz started to pull his hand away but Sally tightened her grip.

It is not a good story, he said. It is a childhood accident. It is not what maybe people think.

What do people think?

It does not matter what they think. It is that they do think.

What happened?

Now I am embarrassed to say.

Tell me.

A cabinet fell over. A party of adults, drunk. I don't remember the pain.

Sally moved his hand between her legs and pushed his fingers hard up into the denim of her jeans. She looked him in the eyes as she directed his motion. Then she had his pants bunched at his ankles and she stood looking at his nakedness. The pale thighs, the raised tendons and hollows of his groins, the perhaps unwanted excitement. She stood looking until she felt his shyness. She waggled out of her jeans and knickers, thinking that she was quite all right with the bomb having been found.

After Janusz left, Sally lay on the floor a long while, listening. The tiles were warm under her bare buttocks and she felt the mess of their sex dry and tighten on her skin. Outside, the late-night carousing pulsed against the windows: laughter, drunken shrieks, football chants. Celebrations. She imagined metal rubbish bins on the beach chortling with fire, painting the sea foam red. She imagined nightswimmers, bellies rounded with ale and ashen with moonlight. And she imagined the bomb, tethered far from the shore, alone with the waves and the stars and the screaming, shitting gulls. Funny, she thought, how much change the bomb had brought and how little it seemed likely to take back once it was gone.

The conservatory at night was a black prism. The glass panels repeated her image crazily, made her slightly claustrophobic. So much me, she thought.

On television early the next morning, the weary reporter looked to the sky, his jowls inflated like the throat of a warbling bird, and cried, Redeem us, REMUS! Six days after the sea had delivered the bomb to the seafront, four since it had reclaimed it, the bomb had been found. The people of Felixstowe saw this small triumph resonate into larger ones—they saw Trafalgar and they saw Roger Bannister and they saw the Glory of her Majesty the Queen. Under the stiff polyester of the Royal Navy uniforms, Royal postures wilted in relief. News broke like a fever. Phones rang, volume knobs were turned, mouths chattered, full with the regurgitated words of scientists and seafarers. Sunday at four o'clock, said the Mayor into the reporter's microphone, his arms outspread like a preacher or a flightless bird.

Sally rather loved a good train journey: the speed and decisiveness of it, the industrial genius of it, the A to B with connections to C of it. She loved the assigned seats and how the tickets were punched and the predictability of the dining car snacks (she could make a bag of Walker's crisps last the entire two-and-a-half hour trip to London) and most of all she loved the excuse to do absolutely nothing but stare out the panoramic windows and let her mind spill over the rushing landscape. There was on this afternoon the illusory sensation that she was moving not through space but through time. She had lived in London very briefly, had always wanted to return, but circumstance had made it impossible, and who could afford it? London was not for Londoners anymore, so the papers said. The train cut through the suburban spillage of the capital. She guessed it would be a long while before the gays and artists began trickling into Felixstowe.

The phone call had come that morning, while Felixstowe was pulsing with the previous night's news. The police had found Emer at Liverpool Street Station, waiting on a dark and sooty bench on Platform Four, a sunhat planted on her head. Sally had insisted that Reginald stay put. She sat him down in front of the football and kissed him on his glistening forehead.

Then again, maybe it was the Atlantic that had kept her in Felixstowe. Sally stood in the middle of the station, disoriented, an obstacle to the angry human vectors shooting past her. A few people seemed to recognize her, held their eyes on her for a beat too long, but she thought maybe she was imagining this. The whole of London seemed to her, now as always, a simulacrum of her desires and hopes and self-secret perversities. The homeless man peddling the Big Issue, the woman with the impeccably tailored Hobbs suit and the power walk, the little boy throwing a whole-body tantrum on the floor of Marks and Spencer: all her. Above Sally the destination board clacked through its manic updates.

There was her exit. Outside the station, she followed the directions she'd written on the back of a prescription for Reginald's something or other and, after a maddening search, arrived at the small police station where Emer was being held. The sweltering office hummed with metal fans and the papers on the desks and the walls quivered. The officer who greeted her, a middle-aged man with a gaunt face and a wild blink that suggested suppressed trauma, truly did recognize her, and said so. He removed his hat to show his civilian self, his civilian balding. Emer trailed him, pinning her white sun hat to her head to protect against the strange office winds. It was streaked black with city grime. She seemed forlorn, and Sally wondered if perhaps her mother thought she had been stood up.

Where has she been? said Sally. Mother, where have you been?

Did you touch it? the officer said.

He handed her a clipboard saddled with papers and pointed to where she needed to sign.

The bomb, I mean, did you touch the bomb? It's good luck they say.

I haven't heard that, said Sally.

Oh yes indeed. Although maybe not in your case, said the officer, flicking his chin at Emer. A missing mum. Found at Liverpool Street Station, that's all we know. She's a chatty old bird, she is.

I'm dreadfully hungry, you know, said Emer.

We did feed her, he said. We did feed you.

I did touch it as a matter of fact, said Sally, a little pride sneaking into her afternoon. She tugged the white hat from Emer's head and flattened the stalagmites of her hair.

The officer took the clipboard.

Well. Then I reckon you've got good things yet to come.

The train to Ipswich was packed with bodies and their heat and smells. The windows were fogged and there was no good place to put her eyes. A young man had given up his seat for Emer (Where are you from? she had asked) but Sally had to stand. The crowded carriage made her think of Gabriel stuffed in a false wall, in disorienting blackness. She knew that the connecting train to Felixstowe—a single squawking carriage that ran back and forth on the rusted tracks like a tired thought—would be nearly empty and that she'd be able to interrogate her mother then, maybe even gussy up the courage to talk about Philip, but the second train was packed even tighter than the first. Sour with body odor. It occurred to her then, as she studied the passengers (attire, accent, dental work) that these were outsiders flocking to Felixstowe for the next day's detonation.

Through limbs and luggage celebrity found her and soon the carriage was raucous with question and quip. Her face answered with perfunctory spasms of communication. She was done with this. Sally felt the sweat collect under her arms and then break this way or that, a vital leaking.

They took the back roads home, avoiding the masses. Sally considered taking her mother to Mrs. Simpson's, where a scone and good dose of clotted cream might give her the courage to have a real talk, but the seafront on a Saturday, all those bodies and their mouths and their words: impossible. There was no real evidence even that Mrs. Simpson had come to Felixstowe, it was just a story.

The cobblestones were burnished with sunlight, looked almost golden. Their ankles buckled, their hips rammed. The evening felt raw, the visitors had brought an astringency of anticipation, anxiety, disorientation.

I like a good knees-up, said Emer. Are we invited?

You heard they found the bomb, Mother.

Emer took Sally's elbow.

Yes, she said. Pity.

Sally knew it was useless to ask about her mother's journey. She instead found herself talking about what Emer had missed, Reginald and his garden, the bathtub, The Yank, the houseboats on the Elbe. A few days ago such talk would have been taboo, and she feared that maybe it would be again by tomorrow, once the bomb was taken care of.

Oh, I know all about that, she said.

The cobblestones grew smaller, crueler.

Your father leaves his secrets like loose coins on the table, he does.

Emer's voice lifted, shed decades.

Did you know he keeps fruit pastilles in his vitamin bottle?

He does not.

He does so, the mollusk. But what can one do? A man needs his secrets.

As Emer spoke, her words bright and heavy as the evening sun, Sally sunk into old childhood adoration, in which the mother is the well of all forbidden and impossible knowledge. Here was her mother, burning through the fog of years. Sally was a little girl again, feet stamping the pebble beach, her mother's sundress balled in her small fist.

They were close to the house now. They crossed a road that had been newly paved, still exhaling chemical fumes.

We haven't heard from Philip this week, said Emer.

No? Sally's head did that thing she hated. Well, I'm sure he's fine.

Of course you have been very busy, said Emer.

Sally felt the blood leave her face and chest and palms, her body knowing before her mind. And then she understood that her mother knew.

I do hope he visits soon, said Emer.

They turned onto Church Lane and there was Reginald, waiting on the front step with a statue's patience and pose, handsome and distant and still.

5. Cobbold's Point

The Atlantic on Sunday was still and brooding. The sky sat gray and bright and low and the horizon was lost. It felt to Reginald Downing that there was much more of the universe beneath the ocean's surface than above it. A crowd of thousands had convened beneath the ceiling of sky, the kind of numbers that would have the town feeling nostalgic for its Victorian peak. Good for the old girl that was Felixstowe, but bad for him. He distrusted any crowd that wasn't for Ipswich Town FC, because he distrusted popularity, because several thousand people couldn't be right. His hands were clammy. The world was very small and fragile. He would usually seek comfort in the sport of judging of others but it seemed there were no important distinctions left between the gathered. A man in front of him took his sunglasses from his face, put them back on, unable to decide. A woman whitened her squirming child with sunblock, saying, Just because you can't see the sun…

Reginald watched veins of chocolate ice cream spill over Emer's swollen knuckles. He pulled her close to his body, now closer, cycling through hip and shoulder angulations as though hoping to chance upon a mechanism of attachment. Marvelous to feel her hip fit below his. Her legs, though, were not totally quiet. The bomb would blow and things would go back to how they were. She'd said to him long ago, after he'd awoken from a night terror, It's a simple geological fact that we're meant to be. Our bodies fit too perfectly, like the continents before the oceans broke them apart.

Now she said, Where did our Sally run off to? Where's our girl?

How clearly he could still see this little daughter of his, her tiny body shivering in the ocean water, waving to him with both arms.

Oh, I'm melting! said Emer. She licked her fist.

They pump all kinds of rubbish into ice cream these days, said Reginald. I'm sure it never used to drip like that.

They stared out into the Atlantic. They were part of a crowd. Reginald thought about the bomb, he thought about its awesome power, he thought about Trinitrotoluene and entropy and the obsolescence of the senses, and he thought about The Yank, and about The Yank's power, which was greater, and maybe ineradicable.

He pressed Emer to his side. There was a name for the continents before they diverged but he could not remember what it was.

At the entrance to the Fun Center, in the heinous, cavernous grin of the clown face, Janusz Crzenski performed strange calisthenics such that his whole person looked to Sally like a pallid, flexing tongue. He saw her, stopped. He was not a natural smiler. His expressions seemed to her affectations, they seemed learned. She reckoned that maybe most expressions were. The boy was with him, wading in the desiccated fountain collecting oxidized coins.

I found a man. A fixer of things, he will fix your wand, said Janusz.

He had left a message on her machine the night before, asking Sally to meet to watch the bomb. It seemed a kinkier proposition than anything they could do with their bodies. A fifth base of sexual relations. But what it really was, she saw now, was an apology, and in this moment there was nothing unsexier. He walked up to her and kissed her on the cheek very formally. His pulse beat hard at his neck, swelled into actual protrusions of the flesh that suggested some vestigial gill apparatus.

I thought it would just be us, she said.

Gabriel was throwing coins at her by way of greeting. Janusz shrugged, helpless.

He is very difficult to get rid of. I have tried everything, he said, this smile more persuasive. How was London? You will be moving there? To the big smokey? To your fantasy?

Maybe next year, said Sally. Let's walk. Let's move.

She handcuffed his wrist and towed him behind her. They walked through the crowd without discretion and she could sense that this pleased him. This was not precisely a public display of affection, but it was public and it was the best that Sally could do. Her parents were here somewhere, alone in the thousands. That she had only the merest tickle of concern was not negligence but a new confidence. She tugged harder. She needed to get away from this anthropoid mass, whose limbs and voices reached for her. The boy skipped behind them, his pockets chiming with coins.

How much longer? he said, in off-pitch singsong. Bomb, bomb, bomb, bomb!

The ocean is calm today, said Janusz, the vista of the Atlantic tranquilizing his gait.

Keep moving. If you stop you become like them. Let's move, let's march. She exaggerated her walk and got the laugh she wanted from Gabriel.

The ocean was not calm, she knew. It was angry, in a wrathful sulk. She was disappointed that he couldn't detect this.

Where are you taking us, television woman? said Janusz.

He checked his watch.

Twenty-seven minutes! he said.

You like an adventure, don't you, Gabriel? she said.

They walked north along the seafront, away from the hubbub of Pier Bight, away from the rows of pastel beach huts and the Docks. The crowd thinned. The boy darted in front of them, dragging a sticky length of kelp through the wet pebbles. Their footfall on the beach was loud and intimate. A seagull floated above them, unmoving, as though calcified into the haze, a premonition of the fossil it might become.

He said, You found your mother. I'm very glad.

The police found my mother.

And did you give her your secret? You can stop writing those terrible postcards with strange animals?

I think now that the postcards were never for her.

Janusz looked at his watch.

I don't understand, he said.

Maybe tomorrow or the next day or whenever it's possible, if you want, you can pop by my parents' and help my father with the garden. It's quite a state.

What happened?

An accident.

Eighteen minutes, he said.

The crowd was now far away, a single organism. They passed the deteriorating Cliff Gardens of Town Hall, where great tiers of flora had been carved into the rockface, an offering to the Atlantic. The gardens were overgrown now but still a tremendous show of color.

Reginald had planted many of the rare species himself and, improbably, year after year they had returned.

Where are you taking us? said Janusz. Don't you want to say goodbye to your bomb?

Bomb, bomb, bomb! sang Gabriel. Why are we walking away from everyone, how much longer?

It's a secret, said Sally.

A quarter-mile further, the beach was blocked by a jut of rock and a concrete wall stained with the weeping rust of exposed rebar. Sally turned onto a sandy path that led up into the cliffside. This, she explained, was Jacob's Ladder. The stone steps were carved into the rock, saltworn, weatherworn, victim to nature's casual undoing of the work of man. One hundred and seventy-seven steps, she said. Gabriel dashed ahead of them and in his sprightly body she saw Philip, bounding the steps two at a time, socks pulled high, model airplane held high above his head.

Who is this Jacob? said Janusz, angry at this man and his precipitous ladder.

At the summit was a great wall of birch and the unmanicured edge of a golf course, where hundreds of white golf balls languished in the white curls of bark. The three climbers sucked at the air.

Nothing like a little good clean salt air in the lungs! said Sally, her words breath-broken.

She took the boy by the hand and found the trail that descended down to the beach, on the other side of the rock and wall that had blocked them. A dark, foliaged path made by animals. They climbed fences, ignored signs. Marram grass whipped their faces.

I used to come here as a kid, said Sally. We're close.

It should have gone off by now, said Janusz. Your bomb. We should have felt something.

A long, damp quarter mile. The Atlantic revealed itself through the trees in a rush of steely blue. The ocean had such responsibilities: of beauty and terror and inspiration, and Sally did not envy it that. They stopped at a large clearing ten meters above the water. The panorama was too vast to take in without swiveling the head and this reminded Sally of the limitations of biology. She tried to locate the precise point in her periphery where sight ended but could not. Her legs burned with acid. The rocks below were black and wet, like the gums of a large dog. The ocean had licked away a nearly perfect semicircle. A few stone footpaths wound down to a slender beach of sand. Mist hung around their bodies, prismed the air.

The beach below is Cobbold's Point, said Sally. There it is. My brother and I, we would come here in the summer, before it was blocked off. At low tide sometimes you could catch a glimpse of the ruins. Feel that air!

Sally couldn't be sure she had ever seen the ruins, not with waking eyes. Philip had pointed them out to her many times, his stiffened arm over her shoulder.

She found herself channeling her brother's words: It's called Walton Castle. A Roman shore fort, maybe a thousand years old. Sometimes hundreds of oyster shells will wash ashore here. Story goes that Roman soldiers feasted on the shellfish in the oyster beds and buried the shells in the middens, now under the sea. Every now and then the sand will shift and the middens will reopen.

In the many years since she had looked upon it, the beach had become in her mind a lost and found of the Suffolk coast, a warren for the Atlantic's incomparable collection. She stared down at it now, her body swaying and her feet shuffling in effort for vantage, hoping to catch sight of something she recognized. Maybe that really very nice, hardly sensible glove from Hobbs of London.

I don't see any ruins, Sally Downing.

I think I do, said Gabriel. I think so.

Sally suggested they wait a bit longer, until the tide began to roll back. She and Janusz sat so that their feet hung over the cliff and floated above the ocean. They sat for a long time in silence, bodies waiting for the inevitable detonation. The boy slung rocks out into the water. She rested her head against Janusz's shoulder, an uncomfortable position but one that she held. He tapped the face of his watch.

We should have felt something, he said.

The boy sang for the bomb.

I shouldn't have left my parents alone, said Sally.

You are so full of regret, said Janusz. This is maybe what it is to be English.

Perhaps, she said.

Below them the Atlantic punished the rocks. It sprayed the soles of her bare feet and the inside of her thighs, a lover teasing a known body.

On Pier Bight the crowd stared out at the Atlantic. They were quiet with thought and memory and anticipation. It was as though the bomb had already been detonated and its power had been grossly underestimated. It was as though they were caught in the moments of annihilation, those incendiary seconds.

Flying Officer Reginald Downing forgot his mouth and his tongue and his teeth, he forgot his limbs and his vital organs, his injuries and his deteriorations. What remained were synapses, electrical patterns that experience and emotion had imprinted, and that might remain a beat longer than biology. Only the carping of his bladder pulled him back into the mess of corporeality.

Emer's arm was hooked around his waist, to the shelf of his hip and his old scar, and he made no effort to guide her hand away. He had earned that.

From where they were on Cobbold's Point they did not see the blast. They did not see the column of ocean water rise, and they did not see it hold its shape for an instant, a monument to potential unfulfilled. They did not see it fall, or how quickly it was forgotten by the seascape. They did not hear the cheering on Pier Bight. But Sally did feel something—a slight displacement of air or emotion—that quickened her limbs. She shot to her feet and pointed out at the ocean, northeast.

There! Fifty meters out. The ruins, she said.

I don't see it! I see only water, said Janusz, standing.

Right there!

I see it, I see it! said Gabriel.

Where? I see water. I only see water.

It's there, she said. Right in front of us. Right there.

Sally stabbed the air with her finger, again and again, like the wing beat of a gull against ocean winds.

Right there, right there, right there.

The Last Pages

Ferdinand Burmeister (R), died in a trolley-car wreck in Hamburg in 1929, at the age of fifty.

We found it very moving to re-read the ending lines of each story in one go.

Susan ! Lind

During the summers of my childhood, I visited my maternal grandmother's Michigan farm. Many things delighted me about those visits: the lane that extended into the horizon; the ghostly silos; the birdbath shaped like a seahorse. A rotary phone was in the living room where my grandmother and I escaped the harshest hours of the heat. The phone in "We Thank You for Your Cleanliness" is that phone. When my grandmother died I was old enough to experience the grief that comes with the loss of someone deeply loved. I can understand why Amy DeFacto in my story keeps answering Stasia's calls. Objects connected to those we love assume a heightened presence—they ring with the power of the past.

—*Theodora Ziolkowski*

This is an image of the actual bomb that inspired "Atlantic on Sunday." It did indeed wash up in a town called Felixstowe, in 2008, and it did indeed go missing for a week. Felixstowe is my wife's hometown, and I have spent a great deal of time there. It is a historical town, which is to say an English town, and, at least to this American, it is an inexhaustible town. Its historical layers peel and pucker and surface like so many coats of paint on the seafront railings. Repurposed Victorian mansions look out over rundown arcades and amusement rides. There is Landguard Fort, whose first fortifications were built in 1540, and there are the eight Martello Towers built to repel Napoleonic invasion. There is Britain's largest seaport and there is, seven miles off the coast, the world's (unofficially) smallest nation, a six-thousand-square-foot country called the Independent Principality of Sealand, formerly a WWII sea fort. It has a Royal Family. With a small donation you can become a Lord or Lady, a Baron or Baroness.

And there is of course the Atlantic, and the things at its bottom.

—*Caleb Leisure*

There's nothing like looking at home from the outside through a clean window—because there's no dirt where you now stand. On the inside there's something you love, something that is now disintegrating, dying, slowly. On the outside you stand, scratching your chin, trying to learn lessons, figuring out how to explain this to people in other houses. The problem is making others feel what you yourself do not feel, because you've seen it all before. For you it's normal, everyday, mundane. For everyone else it's the end of the world.

Cities like Karachi can do that to you.

This is me the last time I was home. By eleven p.m. that day, seven people had been killed for various reasons in the city. This is proof that we humans can get used to everything.

—Zain Saeed

My parents bought a lake house in the late eighties. The A-frame on a South Carolina reservoir was a time capsule of the previous decade: shag of carpet, greasy of naugahyde, unconvincing in its dark pine paneling. The rumor from the real estate agent was that the sellers had been amateur porn auteurs. Plausible, because the downstairs playroom had all the hedonistic burnt orange touches of a seventies stag film. The shower was built for multiple sponging. The textiles seemed woven from body hair.

My parents promptly replaced the bubbled-plastic fixtures with track lighting. They faux-painted the bar. My dad and I spent two sweaty days ripping out the carpet and scraping up tiles until we'd reached the subflooring. Yet they could never sanitize the old swingers' den completely. Well-hung phantoms, ladies in spectral negligees—they roamed by night, looking for one last money shot from beyond the grave. Houses trap their secrets; those secrets bind the inhabitants. Sometimes the only remedy is to knock down the walls.

—*Jeffrey Rotter*

The first fiction I wrote was relentlessly sequential. I tried to get a character from here to there, not realizing I could simply put her there. As you can see from "Your Swim," I figured out that as a writer, you drive the ship, which can be a time machine. The story grew out of a moment on a beach when I found myself wanting the day to pass instead of appreciating, or trying to appreciate, the present. I was, after all, on a beach with my family and friends! Then the usual thoughts, no less crushing for their banality: Life is short, live, goddamn it, etc. My children didn't inspire the children in the story, but being a father did—the hope that your children will be okay, the fear that they won't be.

—*David Mizner*

Here I am, on a beach with my wife Miri and our three sons, Milo, Gideon, and Izzy.

California, a geographically vivid state, is my current home, far from my birthplace of Milwaukee, Wisconsin, a meteorologically intense place. Often, I feel as if I'm biologically attached to two worlds: residing where the views and terrain are astonishing but the omni-season is as sensational as flavorless pudding, but *from* the Great Lakes area, where land may be predictable and extensive, but the storms, the seasons, the lakes, snow! Restlessly, I've spent a lifetime of yearning to find that right place that combines dramatic climate and dramatic topography. Puget Sound, Alaska, and Tahoe call to me. Need to be closer to water. For a few years I attended (or mostly missed) class at the University of Wisconsin Oshkosh, where the Fox River enters Lake Winnebago. Just like Milwaukee, Oshkosh was rich with clouds, fog, water, seasons. So, how did I end up somewhere so brightly dry you cannot leave home without sunglasses and a drink? And why can't I calm the restlessness? There is a Welsh word for this disquiet: hiraeth, *homesickness for a home you cannot return to, or never was.*

—*Stefanie Freele*

Glimmer Train Stories

When 9/11 happened, I was twenty-one years old and freshly home from college. My cousin Sana was six. For days she carried around the *Time* magazine issue that covered the attacks. She asked her parents, her grandfather, me to talk to her about what was happening. I don't think we did a very good job of explaining things to her. We were probably too confused ourselves. But the media coverage of the attacks was constant, and it seemed to deeply disturb her. Like the budding artist she was, Sana took her curiosity and her confusion to her art. She drew image after image of the planes crashing into the Twin Towers. I saved those drawings, but in the many moves I've made since then, I've misplaced them. I asked Sana to revisit what I call her "Twin Towers Period." And she humored me. This image was drawn by a twenty-one-year-old in twenty-first century fashion: on an iPhone.

—*Taiyaba Husain*

—Ezekiel N. Finkelstein

Here's a metaphor: a mountain called Language exists in the mind from which are mined bits of ore or minerals called words. To write, one must have two teams working. Team one consists of miners: the people you send down into the dark. They churn up stone that might contain some gems. But these are low-paid workers without benefits fumbling around in the sulci of the subconscious. Miners without much experience can't tell opal from guano. So the mined materials get sent to team two—geologists, mineral scientists, and jewelers. You can't send them into the mine: they went to college, they wear cardigan sweaters, they don't like dirt under their nails. Team two inspects each stone, cutting and polishing them before arranging them into accessories we'll call "stories" and "poems." But what if there's only stone and no gems? Or what if nobody's buying your jewelry? Simple. Give the miners more experience. Send your geologists to get a PhD. Certify your jewelers in faceting machines so they aren't churning out cabochons every time.

No matter what you do, though, it all begins in the same place: You sit down. You open the mine.

—*S. P. MacIntyre*

Photo: Anthony DeLorenzo

Every writer needs unconditional love and support. My writing would still be locked in hard drives and notebooks if it wasn't for my significant other. Thank you, Cass, for reading draft after draft, and for pushing me to be the best version of myself."

—*Anthony DeCasper*

Glimmer Train Stories

Afer finding the photo I wanted to use with my story, I was curious to see if that tree was still growing in my childhood backyard. It's a six hour drive from my house now, which seemed a long way to go to find out about a tree. (I arrived moments later driving Google Street View.) It's still there, unmistakable because of its conjoined trunks, both about forty feet tall. I wondered why my grandfather would have picked such a tree for transplantation. He had a vast supply to choose from on his place in northern Idaho. And he was a guy that had a reason for everything he did, and usually a single way to do it once he'd decided it should be done. I thought maybe it was a joke, so that in ten years he could ask my father why he hadn't pruned back one of the trunks as a sapling when the work would have been easy. That would have been a hilarious joke to Swede. That's just how he was. But such trees sometimes grow back together, and are known as "husband and wife" trees, or "marriage" trees. And that would have been like him too.

—*Gabe Herron*

I have always had small handwriting, and in medical school and then in residency, my writing got smaller and smaller—my colleagues would regularly diagnose me with "micrographia," a sign of neurological disorders in which handwriting shrinks and becomes more and more cramped. I used to argue back that at least my handwriting was legible—unlike the proverbial doctor's scrawl—as long as you magnified it sufficiently. But the truth is, for my own personal notes, at least, I wanted to boil down the most complicated patient stories, the most convoluted sagas of symptoms and lab tests and changing medical opinion, organize each story onto a single page, as if that would somehow help me see what was really there. And of course, we've now left the days of the handwritten medical chart far behind, and my micrographia—which persists to the point that I insist on reducing my computer font till I can no longer read it without peering over my trifocals—is now reserved for my own notebooks, where I keep trying to organize signs and symptoms, histories and test results, opinions and observations.

—*Perri Klass*

Hoi An at night.

—*Lara Markstein*

PAST CONTRIBUTING AUTHORS AND ARTISTS

Robert A. Abel • David Abrams • Linsey Abrams • Steve Adams • Hubert Ahn • Lynn Ahrens • Diane King Akers • William Akin • Daniel Alarcón • Susan Alenick • Xhenet Aliu • Ed Allen • Will Allison • Rosemary Altea • Julia Alvarez • Kyoko Amano • Brian Ames • Scott Alan Anderson • Selena Anderson • A. Manette Ansay • Graham Arnold • Joanna Arnow • Raymond Philip Asaph • Margaret Atwood • Dalia Azim • Kevin Bacon • Michael Bahler • Doreen Baingana • Aida Baker • Sybil Baker • Kerry Neville Bakken • Carmiel Banasky • Olufunke Grace Bankole • Russell Banks • Brad Barkley • Andrea Barrett • Victoria Barrett • Ken Barris • Marc Basch • Kyle Ann Bates • Richard Bausch • Robert Bausch • Charles Baxter • Ann Beattie • Sean Beaudoin • Brad Beauregard • Barbara Bechtold • Cathie Beck • Jeff Becker • Janet Belding • Matt Bell • Pinckney Benedict • Janet Benton • Marni Berger • Sean Bernard • Sallie Bingham • Kristen Birchett • Melanie Bishop • James Carlos Blake • Victoria Blake • Corinne Demas Bliss • Valerie Block • Carol Bly • Will Boast • Dennis Bock • Belle Boggs • Joan Bohorfoush • Christopher Bollen • Matt Bondurant • David Borofka • Aurora Brackett • Robin Bradford • Harold Brodkey • Barbara Brooks • Karen Brooks • Kim Brooks • Oliver Broudy • Carrie Brown • Danit Brown • Karen Brown • Kurt McGinnis Brown • Nic Brown • Paul Brownfield • Gabriel Brownstein • Ayşe Papatya Bucak • Judy Budnitz • Susanna Bullock • Christopher Bundy • Kimberly Bunker • Hugh Burkhart • Jenny A. Burkholder • Gillian Burnes • Evan Christopher Burton • Robert Olen Butler • Michael Byers • Christine Byl • Sarah Shun-lien Bynum • Gerard Byrne • Jack Cady • Annie Callan • A. Campbell • Joshua Canipe • Kevin Canty • Peter Carey • Ioanna Carlsen • Ron Carlson • Aaron Carmichael • H.G. Carroll • Paul Carroll • Nona Caspers • David Allan Cates • Marjorie Celona • Jeremiah Chamberlin • Brian Champeau • Vikram Chandra • Diane Chang • Mike Chasar • Joseph Chavez • Xiaofei Chen • Yunny Chen • Terrence Cheng • Robert Chibka • Chieh Chieng • Jon Chopan • Carolyn Chute • Christi Clancy • Caro Beth Clark • George Makana Clark • Rikki Clark • Dennis Clemmens • Christopher Coake • Aaron Cohen • Andrea Cohen • Robert Cohen • Lee Conell • Evan S. Connell • Michael Conforti • Joan Connor • K.L. Cook • Ellen Cooney • Rand Richards Cooper • Lydia E. Copeland • Michelle Coppedge • Rita D. Costello • Wendy Counsil • Frances Ya-Chu Cowhig • Doug Crandell • Paul Crenshaw • Mojie Crigler • Lindsey Crittenden • Eugene Cross • M. Allen Cunningham • Colleen Curran • Ronald F. Currie Jr. • William J. Cyr • Quinn Dalton • Edwidge Danticat • Bilal Dardai • Peter Ho Davies • Tristan Davies • Bill Davis • C.V. Davis • Annie Dawid • Michael Deagler • Erica Johnson Debeljak • Francisco Delgado • Laurence de Looze • Jane Delury • Anne de Marcken • Toi Derricotte • Janet Desaulniers • Tiziana di Marina • Junot Díaz • Tom Dibblee • Stephanie Dickinson • Stephen Dixon • Judy Doenges • Matthew Doherty • Leslie Dormen • Michael Dorris • Siobhan Dowd • Greg Downs • Eugenie Doyle • Tiffany Drever • Alan Arthur Drew • Andre Dubus • Andre Dubus III • Matthew Ducker • E.A. Durden • Stuart Dybek • Wayne Dyer • David Ebenbach • June R. Edelstein • Melodie S. Edwards • Jennifer Egan • Ron Egatz • Barbara Eiswerth • Mary Relindes Ellis • Sherry Ellis • Susan Engberg • Lin Enger • James English • Tony Eprile • Louise Erdrich • Zoë Evamy • Eli S. Evans • Nomi Eve • George Fahey • Edward Falco • Omid Fallahazad • Anthony Farrington • Merrill Feitell • Beth Ann Fennelly • J.M. Ferguson Jr. • Lisa Fetchko • Gil Filar • Lydia Fitzpatrick • Joseph Flanagan • Charlotte Forbes • Alyson Foster • Patricia Foster • Ben Fowlkes • Susan Fox • Michael Frank • Tom Franklin • Soma Mei Sheng Frazier • Stefanie Freele • Jonathan Freiberger • Pete Fromm • Abby Frucht • Aja Gabel • Daniel Gabriel • Avital Gad-Cykman • Ernest Gaines • Mary Gaitskill • Riva Galchen • Tess Gallagher • Louis Gallo • Elizabeth Gallu • Barbara Ganley • Kent Gardien • Abe Gaustad • Amina Gautier • William Gay • Abby Geni • Aaron Gilbreath • Ellen Gilchrist • David Goguen • Myla Goldberg • Allyson Goldin • D M Gordon • Mary Gordon • Peter Gordon • Trevor Gore • Amy S. Gottfried • Jean Colgan Gould • Joshua D. Graber • Elizabeth Graver • Lisa Graley • Jo-Ann Graziano • Lauren Green • Lauren Green • Andrew Sean Greer • Cynthia Gregory • Marko Gregur • Gail Greiner • Brian Gresko • John Griesemer • Zoë Griffith-Jones • Paul Griner • Lauren Groff • Cary Groner • Michael L. Guerra • Lucrecia Guerrero • Aaron Guest • Tracy Guzeman • Aaron Gwyn • L.B. Haas • Rawi Hage • Syed Ali Haider • Garth Risk Hallberg • Patricia Hampl • Christian Hansen • Edward Hardy • Ann Harleman • Baird Harper • Elizabeth Logan Harris • Marina Harris • Erin Hart • Kent Haruf • Ethan Hauser • Jake Hawkes • Daniel Hayes • David Haynes • Daniel Hecht • Ursula Hegi • Katherine Heiny • Amy Hempel • Joshua Henkin • Patricia Henley • Cristina Henríquez • Nellie Hermann • David Hicks • Patrick Hicks • Julie Hirsch • Mark Hitz • Andee Hochman • Rolaine Hochstein • Alice Hoffman • Ming Holden • Cary Holladay • Jack Holland • Noy Holland • Travis Holland • Lucy Honig • Ann Hood • Linda Hornbuckle • Caitlin Horrocks • D. Seth Horton • Michael Horton • Kuangyan Huang • Janis Hubschman • David Huddle • Sandra Hunter • Tim Hurd • Siri Hustvedt • Quang Huynh • Frances Hwang • Leo Hwang • Catherine Ryan Hyde • Spencer Hyde • Stewart David Ikeda • Lawson Fusao Inada • Elizabeth Inness-Brown • Debra Innocenti • Matthew Iribarne • Tamar Jacobs • Bruce Jacobson • Sanja Jagesic • Perry Janes • Andrea Jeyaveeran • Ha Jin • Joseph Johns • Charles Johnson • Cheri Johnson • E.B. Johnson • Leslie Johnson • Sarah Anne Johnson • Wayne Johnson • Bret Anthony Johnston • Allen Morris Jones • Nalini Jones • Thom Jones • Cyril Jones-Kellet • Elizabeth Judd • Tom Miller Juvik • Elizabeth Kadetsky • Jiri Kajanë • Anita Shah Kapadia • Hester Kaplan • Wayne Karlin • Amy Karr • Ariana-Sophia Kartsonis • Andrew Kass • Kate Kasten • Ken Kaye • Tom Kealey • David Kear • John M. Keller • Andrea King Kelly • Jenny Kennedy • Thomas E. Kennedy • Tim Keppel • Jamaica Kincaid • Lily King • Dana Kinstler • Maina wa Kinyatti • Carolyn Kizer • Perri Klass • Rachel Klein • Samsun Knight • Carrie Knowles • Clark E. Knowles • Elizabeth Koch • N.S. Köenings • Jonathan Kooker • David Koon • Karen Kovacik • Justin Kramon • Jake Kreilkamp • Nita Krevans • Anasuya Krishnaswamy • Dana Kroos • Erika Krouse • Marilyn Krysl • Frances Kuffel • Evan Kuhlman • Mandy Dawn Kuntz • Anatoly Kurchatkin • Vera Kurian •

290

W. Tsung-yan Kwong • J.P. Lacrampe • Victoria Lancelotta • Christiana Langenberg • Stepyen Langlois • Rattawut Lapcharoensap • Matt Lapata • Jenni Lapidus • Peter LaSalle • Danielle Lavaque-Manty • Doug Lawson • Danielle Lazarin • David Leavitt • Don Lee • Frances Lefkowitz • Melanie Lefkowitz • Peter Lefcourt • Linda Legters • Jon Leon • Doris Lessing • Jonathan Lethem • Jennifer Levasseur • Adva Levin • Debra Levy • Janice Levy • Lillian Li • Yiyun Li • Jennie Lin • Christine Liotta • Rosina Lippi-Green • Jo Lloyd • Eva Lomski • David Long • Nathan Long • Salvatore Diego Lopez • Melissa Lowver • Meredith Luby • Claire Luchette • Alexander Lumans • William Luvaas • Clayton Luz • Barry Lyga • David H. Lynn • Richard Lyons • Rowena Macdonald • Bruce Machart • Jeff MacNelly • R. Kevin Maler • Karen Malley • Kelly Malone • Paul Mandelbaum • George Manner • Ben Marcus • Christopher Marnach • Jana Martin • Lee Martin • Valerie Martin • Juan Martinez • Daniel Mason • Brendan Mathews • Alice Mattison • Bruce McAllister • Natalie Teal McAllister • Jane McCafferty • Colum McCann • Sean Padraic McCarthy • Judith McClain • McFadyen-Ketchum • Cammie McGovern • Cate McGowan • Eileen McGuire • Jay McInerney • Susan McInnis • Emily McKay • Gregory McNamee • Jenny Drake McPhee • Amalia Melis • Askold Melnyczuk • Matthew Mercier • Susan Messer • Frank Michel • Paul Michel • Nancy Middleton • Alyce Miller • Anne Walsh Miller • Greg Miller • Douglas W. Milliken Katherine Min • Lee Montgomery • Mary McGarry Morris • Ted Morrissey • Mary Morrissy • Jennifer Moses • Bernard Mulligan • Abdelrahman Munif • Manuel Muñoz • Karen Munro • Devin Murphy • Scott Nadelson • David Naimon • Paula Nangle • Vi Khi Nao • Jim Nashold • Micah Nathan • Stefani Nellen • Antonya Nelson • Kent Nelson • Randy F. Nelson • Lucia Nevai • Thisbe Nissen • Katherin Nolte • Anna North • Miriam Novogrodsky • Sigrid Nunez • N. Nye • Ron Nyren • Joyce Carol Oates • Tim O'Brien • Vana O'Brien • Gina Ochsner • Mary O'Dell • Chris Offutt • Jennifer Oh • Mehdi Tavana Okasi • Laura Oliver • Felicia Olivera • Jimmy Olsen • Joseph O'Malley • Thomas O'Malley • Stewart O'Nan • Shannon F. O'Neill • Elizabeth Oness • Karen Outen • Mary Overton • Zeynep Ozakat • Ruth Ozeki • Patricia Page • Ashley Paige • Ann Pancake • Michael Parker • Alexander Parsons • Peter Parsons • Roy Parvin • Karenmary Penn • Susan Perabo • Benjamin Percy • Marissa Perry • Susan Petrone • Dawn Karima Pettigrew • Jessi Phillips • Constance Pierce • William Pierce • D.B.C. Pierre • Angela Pneuman • Rebecca Podos • David James Poissant • Steven Polansky • Michael Poore • Robert Powers • John Prendergast • Adam O'Fallon Price • Jessica Printz • Melissa Pritchard • Annie Proulx • Eric Puchner • Lindsay Purves • Kevin Rabalais • Jonathan Raban • George Rabasa • Margo Rabb • Mark Rader • Wendy Rasmussen • Paul Rawlins • Analisa Raya-Flores • Yosefa Raz • Karen Regen-Tuero • Frederick Reiken • Nancy Reisman • Yelizaveta P. Renfro • Adam Theron-Lee Rensch • Linda Reynolds • Kurt Rheinheimer • Anne Rice • Michelle Richmond • Alberto Ríos • S.A. Rivkin • Andrew Robinson • Roxana Robinson • Anya Robyak • Susan Jackson Rodgers • Andrew Roe • Paulette Roeske • Stan Rogal • Carol Roh-Spaulding • Josh Rolnick • Christa Romanosky • Frank Ronan • Emma Roper-Evans • Maxine Rosaler • Julie Rose • Sari Rose • Elizabeth Rosen • Janice Rosenberg • M. Sean Rosenberg • Jane Rosenzweig • David Rothman • Edwin Rozic • Sam Ruddick • Karen Russell • Elissa Minor Rust • Erin Kate Ryan • Karen Sagstetter • Kiran Kaur Saini • Mark Salzman • Mark Sanders • George Saunders • Ron Savage • Sommer Schafer • Carl Schaffer • R. K. Scher • Michael Schiavone • Ian Schimmel • Robert Schirmer • Libby Schmais • Samantha Schoech • Natalie Schoen • Scott Schrader • Greg Schreur • Adam Schuitema • Jim Schumock • Chad Schuster • Lynn Sharon Schwartz • Barbara Scot • Andrew Scott • Andrew Thomas Scott • Peter Selgin • Amy Selwyn • Courtney Sender • James Sepsey • Catherine Seto • Bob Shacochis • Evelyn Sharenov • Hugh Sheehy • Cathal Sheerin • Karen Shepard • Maggie Shipstead • Sally Shivnan • Evan Shopper • J. Kevin Shushtari • James F. Sidel • Daryl Siegel • Ami Silber • Al Sim • Mark Sindecuse • George Singleton • Peter Sipe • Melissa R. Sipin • Hasanthika Sirisena • Johanna Skibsrud • Floyd Skloot • Brian Slattery • Aria Beth Sloss • James Smart • Austin Smith • Louise Farmer Smith • Janice D. Soderling • Roland Sodowsky • Stephanie Soileau • Adam Soto • Scott Southwick • R. Clifton Spargo • Gregory Spatz • Diana Spechler • Brent Spencer • L.M. Spencer • Lindsay Sproul • Lara Stapleton • John Stazinski • Lori Ann Stephens • Barbara Stevens • John Stinson • George Stolz • Julia Strayer • Robyn L. Strong • William Styron • Virgil Suárez • D.S. Sulaitis • Karen Swenson • Josh Swiller • Natalie Sypolt • Liz Szabla • Shimon Tanaka • Mika Tanner • Deborah Tarnoff • Philip Tate • Lois Taylor • Paul Theroux • Abigail Thomas • Randolph Thomas • Jackie Thomas-Kennedy • Eric Thompson • Joyce Thompson • Clare Thompson-Ostrander • Patrick Tierney • Aaron Tillman • Tamara B. Titus • Jennifer Tomscha • Andrew Toos • Daniel Torday • Justin Torres • Pauls Toutonghi • Johnny Townsend • Vu Tran • Patricia Traxler • Jessica Treadway • Eric Trethewey • Doug Trevor • William Trevor • Rob Trucks • Kathryn Trueblood • Eric Scot Tryon • Jennifer Tseng • Carol Turner • Christine Turner • Kathleen Tyau • Michael Upchurch • Lee Upton • Laura Valeri • Laura van den Berg • Vauhini Vara • Michael Varga • Gerard Varni • Joseph Vastano • Katherine Vaz • A.J. Verdelle • Daniel Villasenor • Robert Vivian • Matthew Vollmer • Siamak Vossoughi • Sergio Gabriel Waisman • John S. Walker • Daniel Wallace • Ren Wanding • Weike Wang • Eric Wasserman • Mary Yukari Waters • Claire Vaye Watkins • Jonathan Wei • Josh Weil • Eric Weinberger • Jamie Weisman • Natasha Tamate Weiss • Lance Weller • Ed Weyhing • J. Patrice Whetsell • Sara Whyatt • Andrew Wickenden • Joan Wickersham • Vinnie Wilhelm • John Thornton Williams • Margo Williams • Lex Williford • Gary Wilson • Robin Winick • Mark Wisniewski • Terry Wolverton • Joy Wood • Monica Wood • Christopher Woods • Leslie A. Wootten • wormser • Celia Wren • Callie Wright • Calvin Wright • Brennen Wysong • Geoff Wyss • Melissa Yancy • June Unjoo Yang • Kathryne Young • Rolf Yngve • Ella MeiYon • Paul Yoon • Nick Yribar • Julian Zabalbeascoa • Nancy Zafris • Yuvi Zalkow • Alexi Zentner • Jenny Zhang • Silas Dent Zobal • Jane Zwinger

Right to left: Heinrich, his wife Elisabeth, and his sister Lina.

COMING SOON

"You don't remember me?"
"I don't think so," he said. "Maybe I do."
"Or Howard?" she said.
"Are you Howard and Vicki?"
"Yes we are," she said, delighted.
from "Obsequies" by Steven Polansky

I've figured out that if you don't ask permission, if you just go ahead and do, there's a moment of confusion to capitalize on.
from "Supernova" by Mary Kate Varnau

Theo tried to let the hurt feelings go and played chase with the satellite channels, finding upcoming biographies on twentieth century world leaders: FDR, Churchill, Stalin.
from "80,000,000" by Christopher Bundy

My brother is a lonely man, but he isn't much of a phone-talker. Our routine is to miss each other, leave messages, and then listen to them on speakerphone while brushing our teeth or pulling whiskers or sorting the week's vitamins into pill holders.
from "You or a Loved One" by Gabriel Houck

At the top of the stairs, I locked the baby gate behind me. A last defense. Like the children of 1945 Dresden pulling the blankets over their heads.
from "Summerwalk Circle" by Ariel Djanikian